ANGEL OF DEATH

ROB SINCLAIR

Boldwood

First published in Great Britain in 2024 by Boldwood Books Ltd.

Copyright © Rob Sinclair, 2024

Cover Design by Head Design Ltd.

Cover Images: Adobe Stock and Head Design Ltd.

The moral right of Rob Sinclair to be identified as the author of this work has been asserted in accordance with the Copyright, Designs and Patents Act 1988.

Every effort has been made to obtain the necessary permissions with reference to copyright material, both illustrative and quoted. We apologise for any omissions in this respect and will be pleased to make the appropriate acknowledgements in any future edition.

A CIP catalogue record for this book is available from the British Library.

Paperback ISBN 978-1-83561-824-0

Large Print ISBN 978-1-83561-823-3

Hardback ISBN 978-1-83561-822-6

Ebook ISBN 978-1-83561-825-7

Kindle ISBN 978-1-83561-826-4

Audio CD ISBN 978-1-83561-817-2

MP3 CD ISBN 978-1-83561-818-9

Digital audio download ISBN 978-1-83561-820-2

This book is printed on certified sustainable paper. Boldwood Books is dedicated to putting sustainability at the heart of our business. For more information please visit https://www.boldwoodbooks.com/about-us/sustainability/

Boldwood Books Ltd, 23 Bowerdean Street, London, SW6 3TN

www.boldwoodbooks.com

PROLOGUE

'They call you the Kingmaker. Tell me about that.'

Davis Bracey, his face twisted in agony, didn't answer. Sweat beaded off every inch of his bare upper torso. Not because of the heat of the room, but because of his body's physiological response to stress. To pain. He clutched his right hand – the mangled fingers on it – to his chest, his body crumpled into a heap in the corner of the tastefully decorated room. Tastefully decorated like all of his plush townhouses. Bracey's home. A sanctuary, usually.

Not tonight.

'They call you the Kingmaker,' James Ryker repeated from the chair in the middle of the room. A chair Bracey had originally been sitting on for this... *conversation*. Until he'd slipped off the seat as he writhed about in terror and pain after he'd suffered the third of several breakages to his digits. So Ryker had decided to use the chair instead. Relax a little until he was finished here. 'Tell me about the name.'

'I... didn't choose it.'

'No?'

'No. And it nearly got me killed! The... They...'

'The Syndicate?'

A pause before Bracey responded, as though weighing up whether to acknowledge the reference. 'They hated that the press were... talking about me like that.'

'Like you were more important, more influential than you really are?'

Bracey found an inner strength to send a fighting glare back at Ryker. Which only told Ryker this man could still take more suffering if that was the path he chose.

'You're called the Kingmaker because according to many people, you pulled the strings to get the last three UK prime ministers into office.'

Bracey humphed, defiant now.

'You're saying that's not true?'

He didn't answer.

'But I know the real story,' Ryker said. 'It wasn't you at all. Look at you. You're nothing. You only ever did what you were told.'

Still no response. So Ryker rose from the chair, towering over the man on the floor. The intimidation worked and Bracey cowered.

'Tell me about the Syndicate,' Ryker asked.

'I don't know anything!'

'Who's in charge?'

Ryker crouched down and reached forward and Bracey initially tried to fight him off but his resistance didn't last long. Ryker took hold of the injured hand, held it gently like it was a bird with a damaged wing.

'You know what comes next,' Ryker said.

'Please!' Bracey screamed. 'Please, don't.'

'Then tell me what you know.'

'I do what I'm told! That's all. I'm not one of them. I have to do what they say to keep me and my family safe!'

'Who's in charge? Give me names. Then I'll be gone.'

'I don't know who's in charge!' Bracey yelled, defiance winning out again in a momentary burst of strength. Until Ryker slapped him hard in the face and then crushed the stricken hand in his grip. Bracey's eyes popped wide open and he gasped and silently screamed as though the pain was too much to even make a noise.

'Last chance,' Ryker said, taking hold of an intact finger.

'Please! Don't...'

'Then tell me.'

'Okay! I'll give you a name.' Tears fell as he sobbed. 'But please... Promise me... Promise you won't kill me.'

'Just tell me the name.'

'Okay.'

1

SIX YEARS AGO

Beirut, Lebanon

The sun in the ocean-blue sky did little to lift the chill of a cold winter's morning. The tall buildings of the inner city dragged icy air through the streets at breakneck speed. She huddled down in her sweater as she walked. She hadn't put on a coat. She hadn't even brought a coat here as she wasn't expecting the unusually chilly weather. Regardless, a bulky coat would have been far too cumbersome anyway. If she needed to move quickly, she was better off without it. She turned the corner and a man carrying a coffee in one hand and his phone in the other – his eyes glued to the device – nearly slammed straight into her.

'*Ana asif,*' she said to him in apology, dodging out of his way just in time. He barely made eye contact, grunted, and carried on walking. She grumbled under her breath and jostled the backpack on her back as though she needed to reaffirm it was still there.

'*Making friends with the locals?*' came a gritty voice in her ear, the sound pulsing out of the tiny earbud device, only visible if someone were to focus on and stare inside her ear. Which would be pretty weird.

'*I'm freezing my balls off out here.*' A different voice this time, accompanied by labored breaths. He was on the move too.

'*Thought you Northern boys were used to the cold.*' A third voice. Noticeably different for the lack of background noise. C. C for control. He had the best job today, sat in a windowless office in Central London. At least it was heated.

'*I've spent most of the last three years in the desert.*'

'It doesn't get cold in the desert at night?' she asked.

'*Not with you pressed up by my side, Angel.*'

'*More like you prodding your little woody into her side every night, begging for a bit of action. Isn't that right, Ang—*'

'*Guys, remember the damn rules,*' said C, sounding agitated. '*None of you is new to this.*'

'*You got it, C.*'

'*Understood.*'

'Sorry,' Angel said, even though she hadn't strayed.

No names was C's point. Perhaps Red's first mention of her name could have been misconstrued as a term of endearment to anyone listening in. Today, as long as they were here in this country, she was Pink. Which was quite clearly pathetic given she was the only female on the team of four, but C was calling the shots and that was the name he'd given her.

Anyway, Angel wasn't even her real name, not really. A nickname. At least, that's how it'd started, although it'd taken hold among everyone she knew, except her parents who still insisted on calling her Angela.

Paul had started it. Angela, Angel, she still didn't know if he'd simply tried to find some shortened version of her name or if he'd meant the direct angelic connotation, but she still remembered how it'd made her feel to hear him say it that first time. The name had stuck. She really didn't know how it'd spread to every corner of her life, but it had. When she heard it coming from the mouths of her colleagues it didn't bring with it that same fuzzy warmth in her gut as it had all those years ago with Paul, but if she ever stopped to think about it, Angel just made her feel more... normal. Made her feel better about the things she'd done. Some sort of atonement.

'*Pink, are you still there?*' C said, sounding even more agitated now.

'Yeah.'

'*Then answer me when I'm talking. Are you on time?*'

'I'm right around the corner. I'll be there in less than sixty seconds.'

'*I'm already in place,*' Blue said and Angel could imagine the smug look on his face as he said it. Blue saw himself as the most able of the team. He was simply one of those guys who believed himself to be way more gifted than he really was. A lot of guys were like that, actually. Today he had the second most cushy job after C. Blue was here as an extra pair of eyes. The real work would be down to Red and her.

'*I'm approaching the convenience store now,*' Red said. By convenience store, he meant Location A. His final destination.

Angel slowed this time as she rounded the next corner. Not just in case another passerby knocked into her, but because of her increased vigilance now the op was heating up.

'I'm closing in too,' she said, eyes resting on the sign for the hotel a few yards in front. A hotel that was noted on the op files as Location B. She carried on past the main entrance, keeping her head low. Too many eyes for her to go inside that way, both in terms of the real world and the virtual eyes of so many cameras. She took another corner into a quieter side alley and came to a stop by a metal service door. She looked left and right, all the while keeping her head low, the peak of her cap enough to shield her face from the single camera above her.

No one in sight.

She pulled the key card from her pocket then pressed it up against the pad by the door.

Green light.

She opened the door, her free hand resting by her hip in case she needed to quickly pull out her concealed sidearm.

No. She didn't.

'I'm in,' she said, her voice lower now, even though there was no one around to overhear.

'*Same,*' Red said.

'*Nice synchro,*' Blue said with a chuckle. '*I'll just order myself a cappuccino and a croissant while you two get yourselves ready.*'

Slowly, quietly, Angel pulled the door closed then stood in place a moment, composing herself. She took a deep breath then set off along the carpeted corridor where food smells drifted from the hotel restaurant's kitchen somewhere nearby.

She headed for the service elevator. Further afield a door opened and banged closed. She heard a male voice. Arabic. The guy spoke loudly into a radio or phone. Footsteps coming her way. She didn't look from the elevator doors, willing them to open.

They did. She jumped inside and used the key card to activate the panel then pressed for the thirty-sixth floor. One floor higher than the penthouse guest rooms.

'Come on,' she said under her breath as though doing so would speed up the closing doors.

Too late – the chatty man came into view. Cocked his head her way. She tried to act as confident and natural as she could.

She smiled and nodded as the doors finally started to close. Her hand hovered by her concealed handgun once more. The guy held her eye, paused in his conversation a second before responding and carrying on past. His conversation started up again as the doors closed with a soft *thunk.*

Angel silently sighed in relief.

The elevator glided up at speed, no stops until she'd reached the very top. She stepped out into a concrete-lined corridor. Nothing luxury or fancy up here and the cold look came with a colder temperature that caused her skin to prickle and the hairs on the back of her neck to dance.

'I'm heading outside now,' she said before pushing open the door for the rooftop. A blast of icy air hit her as she stepped out, but at least the space was in the sunshine, making it feel far more inviting than the gray corridor behind her.

'Anything happening at your end, Blue?' C asked.

'Just enjoying some breakfast,' came Blue's reply, and it actually did sound like he was chewing as he spoke. Bastard.

'I'll take that as an A-OK,' C said.

'You got it.'

'Confirmation that Alpha has entered the central district,' C added. *'Red, Pink, I need you set up within the next two minutes.'*

Confirmation? Certainly she nor Red nor Blue had given any such confirmation. This op, officially, was the four of them. Officially? No, that didn't really work for an op like this. But their team was four. Of course, Angel knew C had intel coming from elsewhere but neither she nor the others asked anything about that because they knew damn well they'd get no truths in return. But the op was simple enough. One target, three of them on the ground to get the job done. Blue was all of fifty yards from the expected location of Alpha, hiding in plain sight, but he knew how to blend in. He was there to provide up-close visual contact. Pink and Red were located at two different locations, both high up, and between four hundred and five hundred yards away. Pink to the south, Red to the east to give them a wide view of the target location which sat just a couple of streets away from the glistening Mediterranean to their north and west.

'*He's ahead of schedule, isn't he?*' Red said.

'*So are we. Right?*' C responded.

'Yeah,' Angel confirmed. 'I'll be ready.'

'*Give me the affirmative when you are.*'

She got onto her knees at the far corner of the rooftop where the murmur of traffic drifted up to her position from far below. She slid the backpack from her shoulders and opened it. Carefully, she took out the pieces for the Remington sniper rifle – a concealable version of the MSR model that broke down into its constituent parts for easy transport. Most sniper rifles were big, heavy, cumbersome, but she'd carried this thing around the city for more than a mile no problem, and with not one person suspecting what she had on her back.

She twisted the AAC SR7 suppressor in place then loaded the ten-cartridge magazine, did her final checks before laying the rifle down. Then she lay down too, chest to the cold floor, eye to the scope which she spent a few seconds adjusting.

'What a view,' she said, looking around. 'OK,' she said a few moments later, as much to herself as to the rest of the team. 'I have the target location in sight.'

'*Good,*' C said. '*And you, Red?*'

'*Nearly.*'

Angel moved the barrel a few inches left, right, up, down, familiarizing herself with everything around the front of the hotel in the distance.

'*OK,*' Red said. '*I'm good to go.*'

'Anyone got a visual yet?' C asked.

He got three nos in response.

'*What are you two doing after this?*' Blue asked as though they had the time to chat. But she'd play along. Better to fill the time with banality than allowing doubts and nerves to creep in.

'*I move out before nightfall,*' Red said, sounding a little unhappy about that fact – as though he'd wanted to stay to see some sights.

'*Pink?*'

'I brought my favorite black dress with me. Tonight I'm going to the cocktail bar at the top of the Grand Hotel and I'm staying there until I've run out of suckers to buy me free drinks.'

Blue and Red both laughed. '*If I had your assets, I'd probably do exactly the same,*' Red said.

'*And what does Mr Pink think about that?*' Blue asked. '*You hooking up with random horny Arab guys?*'

'*I didn't say anything about hooking up.*'

'*Still, it's not how I'd want my wife behaving.*'

'*I'm not your wife.*'

'*You don't have a wife, or a girlfriend, or even a friend with benefits,*' Red added. '*With a face like yours, it's hardly a surprise.*'

Angel held back a laugh; actually, Blue's face wasn't that bad – it was his misogynistic attitude that put most sane women off him.

'*Funny,*' Blue said and Angel allowed herself a smile at his more sulky tone. Typical of him. Happy to dish it out, but he hated getting it back. '*Anyway, Pink, I'm here all night too. If you want to—*'

'I think they're here,' Angel said. 'Black Range Rover, one hundred yards.'

'*OK, all of you, no more chatter,*' C said, as if any of them really needed to be told that. '*Blue, Red, you see it too?*'

'*Got it.*'

'*Yeah.*'

There was a few moments' silence. Angel slowly pulled the barrel of the rifle to the right, keeping the Range Rover in her crosshairs as it approached the entrance to the hotel. Her heart rate remained steady, she felt no nerves, but now that the crucial time approached her mind began to flicker more erratically. Her sight wholly focused on the car now, she awaited the moment of seeing their target. His face. She had to keep her cool and she was sure she would, but still... Knowing who this man was, what he'd done, would make it a harder task.

'*Do any of you have visual confirmation on Alpha?*' C said. He spoke quickly now, sounding nervous.

'*Tinted windows, obviously,*' Red said.

'*Vehicle coming to a stop now,*' Blue added.

'Driver's side rear passenger door opening,' Angel said.

A man stepped out.

'*Shit,*' she said and for a moment she couldn't quite catch her breath and her heart skipped two beats before gently thudding away again. '*That's Alpha.*'

'*It's really him?*' Red asked. Or was he confirming what she'd said? Angel wasn't sure.

'*You see him?*' C asked. '*Please confirm.*'

'Yeah,' Angel said. 'It's really him.' And she noted the surprise in her own voice, but then their target being here had been anything but a dead cert given his reclusive nature. They'd debated more than once whether the intel they were working off was too good to be true. Apparently not.

'*He doesn't look half as bad in the flesh,*' Red said. '*Just a normal guy.*'

'*What were you expecting?*' Blue said. '*The boogeyman?*'

'*No, I—*'

'He's not a boogeyman. He's a real-life monster.'

She noted the harsh tone to her words, but then she knew what this man had done. What he'd do again. She'd seen the grotesque videos. Not back in the day when they'd first been released in order to terrorize. Back then she'd been a teenager still and had no interest in seeking out something so macabre, even if she recalled the stories in the news. But before this job... She'd forced herself to watch the grim content in preparation for the task at hand.

She really wished she hadn't. The sick images would haunt her forever.

'*OK, that's enough chatter,*' C said. '*You don't have—*'

'I've got him in sight,' Angel interrupted. 'I'm good to go on your word.'

'*No, wait,*' Blue said, and Angel's finger twitched on the trigger. '*His wife's out the other side, but—*'

'*Kids,*' Red said. '*Two kids. A boy, a girl.*'

'I thought the kids weren't here,' Angel said.

'*And who's this other woman?*' Red added.

A second woman had stepped out of the car, but Angel didn't recognize her either.

'*Guys, stay on track,*' C said. '*Do you still have Alpha?*'

'Shit,' Angel said. 'No, I don't have him.' Alpha had moved around the other side of the vehicle.

'*We weren't expecting all this company,*' Red said. '*Who are they?*'

'*Sending you images now, C, for confirmation,*' Blue said. '*We need the go-ahead asap. We only have seconds.*'

'*OK, OK,*' C said. '*Confirmed, it's Alpha's kids. The second woman is the wife's sister.*'

'Quick work, C,' Angel said. Had he got someone else to confirm about the kids or did he already know them? She'd imagined him sitting alone in that room back in London but perhaps he actually had a whole team with him. For some reason, she didn't like that idea.

'*But we need to be quicker,*' Blue said. '*They're moving away from the car now, toward the hotel.*'

'*Yep, and my moment's gone,*' Red said, and he sounded disappointed by that.

'*Pink?*' Blue prompted.

Alpha took the girl's hand as he moved up the steps to the hotel, the boy at his sister's side, Alpha's wife and her sister two steps behind and intermittently stepping between Alpha and Angel's crosshairs. They all looked so... normal. A happy little family. Did the others even know him, really?

'I've... got him again,' she said. 'But not for long. Am I good?'

No response.

'C, *what the hell is the holdup?*' Blue asked.

'*I'm waiting on confirmation.*'

'Confirmation for what?' Angel shouted out. 'I've got about four seconds here before he's inside.'

'*He can't stay in there forever,*' Red said.

'C, do I do this or not?'

'*Pink, do it,*' C answered. '*You're good to go. Go, go, go.*'

The wife took a step that moved her out of Angel's crosshairs and she was left with an unobstructed view of Alpha's back. She ever so slowly exhaled, pushed her finger onto the trigger, pushed a little more, feeling the resistance. She held the crosshairs in place as Alpha moved. She focused on the spot right behind his heart. The bullet could pass between his ribs, slowing the bullet down less than the bone would on its route. But it wouldn't matter if it didn't. At only five hundred yards the high caliber and high velocity of the .338 Lapua Magnum round was capable of piercing military-grade body armor. The projectile would punch straight through the bone. It'd tear through Alpha's flesh, destroy the heart muscle, punch through the bones on the other side before erupting through his chest to leave an orange-sized exit wound and a hell of a lot of his insides on the floor.

Alpha would be dead before he hit the stone steps.

'*Pink!*' Blue shouted out.

Angel pulled the trigger. Or, at least, her finger was moving back, beyond the resistance, initiating the shot. But in the split-second motion, she felt air moving against her cheek. Cold air. Not from the breeze. Something else.

The round fired with a jolt, Angel rolled away, looking up, behind her position as she moved.

She saw a man. Black clothes. He held a gun in his hand which he fired as she reached down to her side.

The bullet cracked into the concrete next to her, so close she felt it whizzing past. Concrete fragments stung her cheek, dust caught in her nose and mouth. Angel pulled out her handgun as voices rattled in her ear. She took a rushed aim before firing. She hit the man's hand, or maybe just the gun, which flew from his grasp as he growled in pain or anger. She'd not aimed there but for his head. A kill shot. One of the few places she'd get one as she could see from the bulk beneath his sweater that he had a tactical vest on.

She fired again but the man stooped down at the same moment and the bullet missed. Before she could fire another shot his foot swung out and kicked the gun from her grip. He dove for her, knife swinging down to her chest. She flung her hands up, wrists criss-crossed to catch his flying arm.

Angel winced, strained with effort as the knife came to within an inch of her chest.

The attacker pushed down, the knife edging closer. He was too strong for her. He doubled his grip on the knife and it felt like her arms would snap from the force as he pushed down harder, harder.

Angel gave up, pulled her arms down, pulled to the side as much as she could at the same time and the knife plummeted down, the man unable to adjust his aim in time with her move-ment. The blade sliced across her shoulder. Better for her than what he'd intended. She ignored the rush of pain and hauled a knee up which smacked into the man's lower back. Not enough to hurt him or to get him off but at least enough to unbalance him a little before he unleashed a killer blow.

But she had a knife too. She pulled it from the strap on her ankle. Lifted her left arm to block his second attempt then thrust her knife up, under his chin. She roared with effort as she did so and the blade slid into his head with a suck and a squelch, leaving nothing but the handle protruding. His eyes bulged, he gargled, the blade of the knife through his throat making the noise sound surreal, alien. She lifted her knee again and roared once more as she turned over, tossing him off her in the process. The knife came free and a spray of blood spattered her face and chest causing her to flinch. She wiped at the blood as she heaved heavy breaths.

'*Pink, damn it, what's going on?*' C shouted. Not for the first time. The voices in her ear had continued through the fight but she'd had no chance to respond.

'*I'm outta here,*' Blue said before a click to show he'd disconnected.

'*Packing up. See you on the other side,*' Red said. Another click.

'*Pink, what is happening?*'

'I... I...'

The man next to her twitched as blood gushed. She rolled further away from him, to the rifle. Put her eye to the scope.

'No!' she cried out in shock as she stared at the group of people outside the hotel. To the man – Alpha – cradling a small, limp, bloody bundle like a rag doll.

'*Pink? What the hell have you done?*'

She didn't answer. Instead, she focused on the sound of the sirens, right below her.

'*Pink, you need to—*'

She didn't hear the rest of the sentence before she pulled the earbud out and stuffed it in her pocket. She tried her best to bury the image of the bloody scene from the hotel front. She wasn't sure she could.

With the sirens multiplying, closing in, she left the rifle and the dead man in place, jumped to her feet, and rushed for the door.

2

PRESENT DAY

London, England

The hundreds of thousands of twinkling lights of the city stretched far into the distance, morphing into an indistinct orange glow at the horizon. James Ryker sucked in cool, cold air as he took in the cityscape. With no clouds in the sky, the temperature had dropped close to zero since nightfall. He exhaled and watched his breath swirl into the darkness above him.

Then he grasped the railing and jumped over it to perch on the very edge of the balcony.

Teetering, fourteen stories up, the world down below looked dizzyingly distant. He turned to face the building and shuffled along, only the tips of his toes touching the concrete, his gloved hands on the metal railing stopping him from toppling. The balcony of the neighboring apartment sat five feet away, a sheer drop in between. He moved as far over as he could, the toes of his left foot still touching down, his left hand grasping the railing, but his body suspended over nothing. He reached out with his right hand, his fingers several inches from touching anything but air. He reached out with his right foot. Still not close enough.

So he pulled his body back to the left, bent down a little then sprang up and across. Mid-air for a couple of beats, gravity yet to fully take over before his right foot hit something solid. But the ice-cold concrete was slippery and his foot slid from the surface and Ryker grabbed at the railing but for a moment, with his body falling, he doubted he'd be able to hold on to that either. Until he whipped his left hand over, just in time. His feet scrambled beneath him. He won the battle and soon had two feet touching down. Two hands holding him in place.

Ryker took a couple of deep breaths, steadying himself, allowing the surge of adrenaline to pass and his heart rate to climb down. He stared at the windows of the apartment beyond the balcony railing. The curtains were closed but the lights were on. He could tell from the flicker that whoever was home beyond was watching TV. He didn't think he'd made too much noise in the jump but he stayed in position a few moments longer, waiting to see if there'd be any response.

No. Nothing.

He looked to his right again. One jump made, but he wasn't where he needed to be yet. His destination was another apartment to the right. One floor up. A small part of him regretted the conclusion that this was the best means of access, but the simple fact was that it'd be easier to break through the balcony door than the front door of his target's home. The apartment he'd started at was the closest unoccupied lot. He'd viewed it earlier in the day with the agent selling the property. Then 'acquired' the code for the key lockbox attached to the front door. So yeah, he'd broken in, but he hadn't actually had to break anything to do so.

Now he was hanging on to the edge of a balcony fourteen stories up on a cold midwinter's night.

Time to get moving. He shuffled to the right, same as before. Made the jump more easily this time. This apartment sat in darkness. He crept to the window and put his ear close to the glass. No sounds beyond. He pulled the balcony's small round bistro table right up against the railing. He climbed onto the table and crouched down, before he slowly straightened up and moved to the edge – one foot still on the table for better, full-contact traction, one foot straddling the metal railing.

Ryker looked up. The concrete platform above was too far out of reach and he wasn't stupid enough to simply jump up and try to grab it. He took the rope from his backpack and tossed the end upward and the attached carabiner clanked on the metal railing. A little louder than he'd hoped but the throw was good and the carabiner landed on the other side of the railing, and with a bit of teasing, he managed to slip it off the balcony and eased it back down toward him. He attached the rope to his belt then, ignoring any remaining doubts, he pushed off and was left swinging.

He grasped the rope above him and strained as he reached higher, higher, one hand at a time, hauling himself up. He took hold of the concrete edge and pulled himself up, and with one final burst of effort, he vaulted the railing and found himself crouched on the balcony.

He unclasped the rope and put it back into his backpack. Stayed low. No lights on. No one was home. The man of the house was working late at a function. His wife was working abroad. Their young daughter was staying with family.

At least, he hoped he was right about all that.

Ryker moved to the balcony doors. He tried the handle. Worth a shot, but no luck. It didn't matter. This building was two years old and as high-end as the apartments up at this level were, every single balcony door was the same, all with the same standard locks. Ryker had already paid great attention to such things on his thorough look around the apartment on the floor below.

There was no keyhole on the outside, just a panel beneath the handle to hide the back of the inside lock. The door had a multi-point locking system – supposedly highly secure – but that system was connected to the handle. If he dealt with the main lock, which kept the handle in position, he'd be in.

Ryker took out his flathead screwdriver and a small hammer. He pushed the tip of the screwdriver up under the edge of the panel then smacked the end of the screwdriver's handle with the hammer. Not a hard shot to start with but enough to wedge the screwdriver's tip under the panel casing. He hit the handle again, harder this time, then a third time and the screwdriver dug deep, and Ryker heard and felt the crack as the backside of the lock snapped. The panel dropped away. Ryker took the screwdriver and jabbed the end into the hole and the remainder of the lock dropped free on the other side and clanked to the floor.

He pushed down on the handle.

Bingo.

He took out his radio jammer. A little bit of phishing online had confirmed that the occupants had a subscription to a well-known wireless alarm company. Like most wireless alarms, the system utilized good old radio signals to allow the components to talk to one another. If a magnetic contact on the door was broken it'd send a signal to the base unit which would in turn trigger the alarm. Block that signal, no alarm.

Ryker took a couple of minutes to set the frequency then pushed the door open. He waited a moment, making sure.

Success.

He carried on inside into a large open-plan, modern space. He'd seen the layout for the apartment in blueprints. Together with the large living area, the apartment had four bedrooms. No sign of a desk or computer in here so Ryker quickly made his way to the main internal corridor, off which sat each of the bedrooms. With only one child that meant at least one spare bedroom, possibly an office.

Yes. An office. Not particularly well decked out. The occupants hadn't been here long. The room had only a simple, functional desk, a filing cabinet, a single swivel chair. Ryker headed over to the snazzy-looking iMac on the desktop and took out his thumb drive and plugged it into the Thunderbolt port at the back of the large screen to begin the process of copying the hard drive contents. No login needed for this. His software would take a direct copy of every bit of data from the hard drive. He'd later be able to break through any passwords or encryption as needed.

Half an hour later he was done.

With the data-packed thumb drive tucked away, he moved back out to the open-plan living area. He looked over to the balcony door. Nothing he could do about the obliterated lock. The owners would know their home had been broken into. Would probably figure, given the lack of missing items, what had been targeted. Ryker didn't care so much about that. He could trash the place, take some of the expensive jewelry he'd noticed in the walk-in closet of the main bedroom to try and suggest a simple burglary. But what would be the point in trying to hide the real motive for the break-in? Actually, he wanted them to know *why* they'd been hit tonight. Let them sweat about which of their secrets could now be exposed.

Ryker walked toward the front door – no need for him to take the hard route out. He paused a moment as he looked through the peephole. No one out there.

He opened the door, looking left and right. The corridor was empty. The door closed softly behind him. He turned off the jammer. Still no alarm, with the magnetic contacts on the front and back doors both in place.

Ryker strode along the corridor toward the bank of three elevators. He heard the ting as one of them arrived. He didn't let up as a man emerged. Long overcoat. Shiny, polished black shoes. Neatly slicked-back hair. Designer glasses over his nose. Despite his high-end, well-groomed look, he moved unsteadily, his eyes a little glazed. Too much of the free champagne.

Ryker hadn't expected to run into the guy. The function officially went on until eleven and it was only nine thirty.

He'd had only seconds to spare inside the apartment.

Not to worry. Ryker had made it in and out in time nonetheless.

The man locked eyes with Ryker as he approached. He had no clue. Ryker knew so much about him and his wife, but this guy had never seen or probably even heard of Ryker.

'Good evening,' Ryker said with a nod and a smile.

The guy slurred in response. He looked a little surprised at Ryker's cheery greeting but carried on toward his apartment regardless.

Ryker pressed the button for the elevator. It hadn't yet moved and the doors opened straight away and he stepped inside, taking one last glance at the drunk and entirely oblivious man before he stepped inside.

In his state, maybe he wouldn't even notice the broken lock on the balcony door until the morning. Most likely within a few minutes, he'd be snoring like thunder.

Ryker, on the other hand, had a long night ahead of him, searching for the evidence of the dirty secrets he hoped now lay within his reach.

3

Feet crowded around him. He struggled to keep his head up, his eyes open now. He grimaced as he swallowed a mouthful of blood. The smell caught in his smashed nose, which whistled as he tried to breathe.

The men wrestled him from the chair and to the ground. It didn't take much effort, he had so little strength left. His face smacked against the cold concrete with a thud.

He couldn't move, not just because of the torture he'd suffered, but because each of his limbs was pinned down, a knee in his back too. He noticed the glint of metal above him, tried not to look at the face of the man holding the sword.

'This is it for you, my friend.'

Cold steel against his neck.

The next moment he felt warmth as blood flowed free and over his skin.

Then came the pain. And the sound. The sound of flesh tearing.

His flesh, as the sword was pulled back and forth, the blade sinking deeper, deeper...

* * *

Ryker pulled his fingers from the lumpy scar on his neck and tried his best to shake the images, the memory away. A memory he'd long ago thought buried. He never imagined it'd be dredged up now, after all this time, after everything that had come since.

Yet it had been. Because of a single name given to him in a man's moment of weakness and desperation.

He took a left turn as he walked. Thick gray clouds sat above him and the biting wind made the barely above freezing temperature feel even worse, but he didn't mind the weather. He didn't dislike the cold. He disliked London. He'd never liked it. Too much traffic, too much concrete. Smoggy air. Too many people. He tried to stay here as little as possible but the city drew him back in so often, in the same way that his old life did.

Old life. Except he was still living it now, wasn't he? Yet he liked to think that he was a different person from when he'd first started out working in the intelligence services more than two decades ago, but the fact he was still in this city, still doing *this*, perhaps told a different story.

Especially with those old memories resurfacing now too.

He had time to spare so he headed to a café and sat in the corner, checking his phone again and again as he ate his sandwich and drank his coffee. Still no response. He turned the phone over and watched the others in the café for a few minutes. Tried to think about their stories. He saw couples in casual clothes, perhaps tourists, enjoying an early morning treat. More smartly dressed men and women grabbing something on the go on the way to the office. Friends, a couple of larger groups, a few people on their own, just like Ryker. Except most likely not like Ryker at all.

He'd tried it once. Normality. He'd really tried to make it work. House, partner, normal things like paying bills and shopping and... He *could* have made it work. He'd wanted it to work, so, so badly. For her, as much as for him. Except it – *she* – had been ripped away from him so painfully. So finally.

The hurt he still felt would never leave him. It was why he'd never tried to find that normality again. Since that time, a few years ago now, he'd tried different tactics. Roaming around, country to country, city to city, exploring. It'd been fine but he still had a habit of coming across trouble. Or of trouble finding him. So he'd stayed put a while, a few different places. Trouble. Usually from his past, but not always.

So over more recent times, he'd decided just to admit who he really was, who he would always be, rather than try to fight it or run from it. Because he had something to offer to the world still, and it wasn't a warm, loving environment for a wife, it wasn't as a father to children, it wasn't as an educator or anything like that. He was the guy willing to work in the darkness, beyond what most people saw in their everyday, safe lives. The guy who not only knew of the terrible people who existed in the world, but who was prepared to put himself on the line to bring them down, whatever it took.

Twenty years ago he'd started out doing that because it was his job, because he was given orders to do so, because he got paid. For survival.

Now he did it because it had come to the point in his life where he really didn't know what else he could or should be doing because he hated the idea that those monsters existed out there and would get away with their deeds if he didn't stop them.

Honestly, he thought he was pretty damn good at it too.

Although this time... This time it'd become personal too.

He felt his neck twinge but didn't let the memory take hold.

He finished his food and drink and stood up from his chair, and noted the flirtatious smile from the server behind the counter. He'd been here a few times over the last couple of months and she was always there. Always gave him – and not the other guys –

the same look. He'd never said more than the obligatory pleases and thank yous to her, but maybe next time he'd speak to her a little.

He would never settle down again now, never again try for that life he'd once had within his grasp for such a short time.

But that also didn't mean he didn't enjoy the company of others.

He smiled back and waved a goodbye, and she blushed and went back to making the coffee as he headed on out.

He checked his phone a few more times as he walked a couple of streets, stopping by a railing overlooking the choppy, murky waters of the Thames. He waited there. Waited. Still no response. He looked up at the dull-looking building across the street. Ten stories of nothing much. He checked his watch. Already twenty minutes late.

He put the phone to his ear as he headed for the traffic lights. The call rang out, went to voicemail, just like it had the other times.

'Winter, what the hell? You'd better be upside down in your car somewhere, because if you're ignoring me...'

He ended the call. OK, so perhaps that was a bit harsh. He wasn't actually wishing harm on the guy, although with his bad mood rising...

The green walk signal flashed on and Ryker began to stride across the four lanes of traffic, along with the several other people who'd waited at the lights. A man in a suit, no coat, old-school leather briefcase in one hand marched ahead. Too focused on where he was going rather than the world around him, he didn't see the cyclist on the far side blast through the red light at fifteen, twenty miles an hour. The cyclist shouted out at the man as though it was his fault. The pedestrian dodged but the cyclist still had to swerve hard to avoid a collision and after a half second trying to keep control the bike flipped and he went flying through the air right past Ryker. The cyclist rolled to a stop and a couple of helpful bystanders rushed to his aid. The suited man brushed himself down, looking shocked.

'Lucky you,' Ryker said to him with a wink as he strode on past. 'Same old London,' he said more quietly to himself.

He reached the building. No signage, no big open entrance or revolving doors. Just a single, security-locked glass-paneled entrance. He pressed the intercom and looked around. Back by the roadside, an argument had started between the cyclist – blood oozing from a graze to his cheek – and a taxi driver. Ryker had no idea how that'd come about. No sign now of the man who'd nearly been smashed.

'*Can I help you?*' came a tinny voice from the intercom.

'It's James Ryker.'

'*You're late.*'

'Traffic was bad.'

A kind of *humph* in acknowledgment. At least, that's how Ryker interpreted the noise before the door clicked open.

Ryker moved inside. The small atrium was as bland as the outside of the building, the gray space containing a staircase, a door to a stairwell, no people, and still no indication of who occupied the building. Which was kind of the point, but it also felt so down-trodden and depressing. Nothing like the big, glitzy SIS building at Vauxhall Cross that everyone knew as the home of MI6.

Ryker stepped into the elevator and pressed for the eighth floor. A suited man stood on the outside when he arrived there. Late forties, early fifties, he had thinning gray hair and a lightness to his face, in his eyes, that suggested he had a pretty cushy life.

'James Ryker, I'm Kevin Goldman. Pleasure to meet you.'

Ryker shook his hand. Goldman. Winter had warned Ryker about him. A go-between who bridged the divide between the government and SIS. Not a politician as such but someone whose job it was to make sure the Secret Intelligence Service remained politicized and dancing to the tune of the government. Which, as Ryker knew, didn't always happen.

'Please, follow me. The others are waiting for you.'

Goldman took Ryker through to a meeting room that sat at the front of the building overlooking the Thames. Two other people were already in there. A woman, in her thirties, who wore a head-scarf and another suited man, older and plumper than Goldman. A little harder in his demeanor too, although with the same stuffy suit.

'James Ryker, I'd like you to meet Fatma Yaman and Frank Podence.'

More handshakes.

'Fatma is one of our political experts. Frank oversees a number of field operations.'

These were descriptions rather than any kind of job title. Even though no one had confirmed it, Ryker knew both Yaman and Podence were MI6 desk pushers, and actually, he knew a lot more about each of them than they realized.

'Nice to meet you all,' Ryker said with a forced but genuine enough smile. 'And sorry I'm late.'

'You were enjoying the view,' Podence said, nodding to the window with a chuckle. So they'd spotted him standing outside? Didn't bother him.

'I was... Yeah, something like that. Shall we get started?'

Whoever had set the room up – there was no sign of a receptionist or anything like that – had put out coffee and tea and water and Ryker helped himself to a black coffee and quickly checked his phone one last time as he settled into his seat. Still nothing from Winter. Not that he'd been officially invited to this meeting, but he'd brokered it and Ryker had insisted to his long-time ally that he be involved. Mainly because this sort of thing wasn't and never had been Ryker's bag. He hated offices. He hated bureaucracy and office politics. And in an office like this, politics were often the be-all and end-all.

'Why don't we get things moving,' Goldman said. 'None of us has met you before, but we've each been privy to your background. At least the elements of your background which are openly available to us. Which isn't much for someone with such a long-standing career.'

He laughed at that. The other two smiled a little insincerely. Ryker said nothing, though it was interesting that Goldman hadn't been provided with – perhaps wasn't senior enough to have been provided with – full access to details of Ryker's past operations.

'As we understand it, your previous role was as an operative in the Joint Intelligence Agency, the JIA?'

'For many years.'

'A field agent?'

'Is that an official title? I don't know. I never had a business card to hand out to people, or even a contract of employment. The JIA was several further steps removed from a normal employer than SIS even. I did what I was told and I got paid. Basically.'

'Your commander was originally Charles McCabe.'

'Until he got a bullet in the head in Russia.' Ryker said that with little feeling, which betrayed the fact that the memory of that moment still hugely stung.

'And subsequent to that, Peter Winter?'

'Winter took over from Mackie. He never officially took over as my commander. I'd left the JIA by that point.'

In something of a shitstorm, which had hung around him ever since, one way or another.

'But you've maintained a close working relationship with Peter Winter since your departure from the JIA.'

'Working relationship? It's not as formal as that. Our paths have crossed numerous times over recent years.'

He could tell they didn't believe it was as coincidental as that at all.

'Even though you long ago left the JIA. Officially.'

'Yeah. If anything could be said to be official about the JIA.'

He got a series of chuckles and nods for that apparent quip.

'What I'm saying is, it's been years since I worked for the JIA.' Which didn't even exist anymore. 'And I've not had any formal employment from SIS or any other similar organization since then.'

'It's OK,' Goldman said. 'You can be candid with us if you like. We know far more than most people about how shadow organizations like the JIA operate, and we're not here to put pressure on you to reveal what you've had to do in the past.'

'Except for your most recent past, that is,' Podence added, glaring at Ryker for a few seconds afterward as though he disapproved of something.

'So let's move on to that,' Goldman said. 'You're here because you've been privy, one way or another, to very sensitive information. And I mean, incredibly sensitive information. And we need to know exactly what you know, and how you came across it.'

'Sounds a bit like I'm on trial here.'

'This isn't a court. Perhaps you can start by telling us about Davis Bracey.'

'What do you want to know?'

'Pretend we're ignorant. Tell us what you know about him. How you met him. What he told you that's led to... Well, that's led to you being here with us today.'

Ryker kept his mouth shut as he looked over the three people on the other side of the table. Of course, they knew the answer to what they were asking. They wouldn't be in this room otherwise. So what game were they playing here, asking for him to regurgitate like this?

Damn, he really wished Winter was here. This bureaucratic

crap was the exact reason Ryker had wanted the guy by his side. When he caught up with him...

'Davis Bracey, I believed, was under the control of a group of people acting with nefarious purposes. Rich, powerful people with a lot of influence, financial and political. Bracey was a lifelong civil servant known as the Kingmaker in the UK press because he'd had a big hand in promoting the winning candidate in three successive general elections.'

'Democratic elections that were run fairly and lawfully, unless you're suggesting otherwise?' Podence said.

'I'm not. And I didn't give him the moniker Kingmaker. The UK press did, as they had already concluded Bracey was a puppet for those behind the scenes wielding power long before I came along.'

'And why did you come along? To... this?' Goldman asked.

'Not of my own free will, but I don't think we need to get into that. The fact is, Bracey was someone who I believed knew about this group of people. I've heard it being referred to as the Syndicate.' He studied their reactions to that for a couple of seconds but none of them gave away a thing. 'Bracey worked for the Syndicate, and was playing to their tune, doing whatever they told him for years, just one of many ways they've been able to control UK politics.'

'And you know this how?' Podence said.

'Because I asked Bracey about it. And he told me.'

'You tortured him.'

Was that a statement or a question?

'I asked him quite persuasively.'

'You broke several of his bones.'

'Did I?'

'Did you kill him too?' Goldman asked.

'No, I didn't. The papers said he died of a heart attack.'

'They did. A heart attack. Although this was several days after he'd been released from hospital with six broken fingers and five broken ribs, among other injuries.'

'From a fall down the stairs, I read online.'

'He didn't fall,' Podence said, shaking his head, looking disgruntled with Ryker's casualness.

Ryker shrugged as nonchalantly as he could.

'And you *didn't* kill him?' Podence asked.

'No, I didn't. But I don't think he had a heart attack either, do you? Not one brought about by natural causes, anyway.'

'Then who are you suggesting did kill him?' Podence asked.

'You, perhaps.'

Podence scoffed and shuffled nervously in his seat.

'But most likely the people paying him to pull political strings in the UK,' Ryker added. 'My guess as to how he really died? Nerve agent, or something like that. The death was recorded as a heart attack and signed off by a pathologist as natural causes, but the body was cremated without an autopsy. So I guess now we'll never know.'

Silence as the three stared at Ryker. Had he told them anything they didn't already know? He didn't think so, yet the mood in the room had definitely shifted since he'd first arrived.

'Let's move on,' Goldman said. 'Andrew Lebedev.'

Obviously, they'd bring him up next.

'What about him?' Ryker asked.

'Did you know him?'

'I never met him.'

'You knew of him?'

'You know I did.'

'Then tell me what you knew. Do you believe *he* belonged to this mysterious Syndicate?'

Goldman twirled his hand around as he asked that, as though indicating the whole thing was some hocus-pocus fairy tale.

'You know what?' Ryker said. 'I think he probably did.'

'Because Davis Bracey told you so when you were torturing him?'

'Yes.'

They all looked a little taken aback by that, as though they hadn't expected such a direct response.

'Lebedev was the anglicized son of an oligarch,' Ryker continued. 'That itself, to me, tells a story about cross-border billionaire corruption. Using his family's wealth and political clout Lebedev junior had his dirty fingers in business dealings across Europe, the Middle East, Asia, not to mention he was in cahoots with Bracey as a gateway into the British government. If you've read anything at all about what's been uncovered about Lebedev you'll know there's enough evidence of his misdeeds that should have seen him imprisoned for the rest of his life. Instead, the UK government decided to keep relations with Russia on an even keel and sent him packing to Moscow in exchange for four of our alleged spies who'd been languishing in a Siberian gulag for several years. By the way, do you know any of them?'

No answer to that. Podence looked annoyed now. Ryker had hit on a nerve. But his focus rested on Yaman. She hadn't said a word throughout the meeting.

'For years Lebedev got away with living above the law, all because he's dirty stinking rich, and because his family has connections all over the place.'

'Connections to your so-called Syndicate, you mean?' Goldman asked.

'I believe so, yes. Lebedev would have spent the rest of his life in prison in England if it wasn't for his powerful friends.'

'Actually,' Podence said, 'I think the main reason Lebedev *got away with it* was because a lot of the *evidence* so far uncovered was based on information leaked to the press. Information that came from you, I believe.'

Ryker shrugged once more.

'And I'm sensing you have no particular regard for the laws of this country—'

'I'm offended you think so.'

'I think you're not at all. But the point is, any evidence uncovered on Lebedev was tainted by your actions.'

'Maybe. But not the vast reams of additional evidence that could have been uncovered if anyone actually cared to carry out a real investigation. I only scratched the surface.'

'The prisoner swap was a better deal, politically speaking,' Goldman said. Of course. Politics above morality, always.

'Maybe it was a better deal for you guys,' Ryker said. 'Probably not for Lebedev after that nasty car accident he had in Moscow though.'

'And do you know anything about that?' Goldman asked.

'I know it killed him and his wife and his two children. Three unnecessary deaths. I don't mind a bit of fatal karma, but they were three innocents. Definitely not my style. How about you three?'

'I can assure you we had nothing to do with his death,' Goldman said, a little too defensively. 'The most obvious culprits are the Russian government themselves. Lebedev was a danger to those—'

'Why don't we get to the point,' Ryker said. 'We're talking about events from months ago now. Why am I here?'

'Isn't it clear from our discussion so far?' Goldman said. 'We want to—'

'Actually, it's not clear to me at all. Everything we've talked about so far is information you already had from me through Peter Winter. So what's the point of any of this? Are you asking for my help here to take what I found further forward? If you're putting together a team to investigate—'

Podence held up a hand to halt Ryker. He stopped talking and balled his fist under the table.

'We do not want you to perform any further investigation of any kind into these matters. The damage you have done is already greater than you can imagine.'

Ryker sighed even though this turn wasn't really a surprise. 'So you're burying it. Everything I've found.'

'That's not what I said.'

'But your point is that no one is going to be investigating these people any further.'

'My point is that *you're* not, and you don't need to know anything more than that. And, quite frankly, rather than sitting there and talking to me like a spoiled schoolboy you should be thanking me, all of us, for allowing this conversation to take place like this at all. Were it not for your track record at the JIA, and the good word of Peter Winter, my preferred response would have been to see *you* behind bars. Have you any idea the number of crimes you've actually committed in obtaining the information you have?'

Ryker decided not to answer that. He didn't know the number, but he knew it wasn't small.

'We're done here, then,' Ryker said, pushing back on his chair.

'Actually, we're not,' Goldman said. 'One last question for you. And, Ryker, please do yourself the favor of answering honestly, because if you don't it will only come back to bite you. And trust me, none of us will be so accommodating to you in the future if that is the case.'

'And the question is?'

'Is there anything else at all that you've uncovered about Davis Bracey, Andrew Lebedev, their associates, this so-called Syndicate? Its operations, its members? Any evidence of links to our government, to SIS? Anything that you haven't already disclosed to us in the information we were provided from Peter Winter?'

Goldman waved the manila folder in front of him at Ryker as though all of the evidence of the misdeeds of the people he'd just mentioned could possibly be contained in the few sheets of paper in between.

'No.'

'Just take a moment,' Podence said. 'Think very carefully because after you leave this room, you don't get a second chance to come back with *sorry, sir, I forgot*. You'll be put on trial for your crimes, treason the biggest of them, and you'll spend the rest of your days behind bars. So is there anything else we need to know?'

'Punish the whistleblower. Classy.'

'Ryker, answer the damn question,' Goldman said.

'I've told you everything you need to know.'

Podence sighed. Goldman looked disappointed. Yaman looked... devoid of any emotion. Like she had the entire time Ryker had been there.

'Then I think we're done here,' Goldman said.

'I think you're right,' Ryker concluded, getting to his feet.

4

Ryker exited the building and pushed his phone to his ear. The call was answered on the third ring. Ryker found himself caught out; he'd fully expected it to go to voicemail again.

'You're finished already?' Winter asked, sounding a little too happy. Ryker could well imagine the smug face on the guy as well.

'What the hell, Winter? And how did you—'

'Know that you're finished? Look to your right.'

'You piece of shit.' Ryker stopped and stared along the street to where Winter stood fifty yards away by the trunk of a looming oak tree in a small park area overlooked by towering gray office blocks. He even had the audacity to give a cheery wave. 'You've got some explaining to do.'

'Let's get out of the cold,' Winter said before ending the call.

Ryker managed to mostly keep his dissatisfaction under wraps while they walked a short distance to a quiet coffee shop on a back street, away from the bustle of the river. Not the same place he'd been to earlier; he didn't want the cute server there to see him so annoyed.

They sat in a corner, coffee each, Ryker with his back to the wall so he could look out across the small and nearly empty space, a glimpse of the street outside too. Not that he saw any threats here. Not yet.

'So you were simply ignoring me,' Ryker said. 'You were outside the whole time.'

'You didn't need me in there.'

'I *wanted* you in there. And you know exactly why.'

Winter said nothing.

'You set me up.'

'Not really. I just knew... I needed you to do that meeting alone. I needed you to see the roadblocks for yourself, not have me use my influence to try to get a different outcome.'

Ryker said nothing as he sipped his coffee.

'Are you going to tell me what they said?' Winter asked.

Ryker thought about the question before he answered, took in the man sitting across from him as his mind churned. As ever, Winter was well-presented in a nice shirt, pressed suit trousers, coifed hair. A true desk jockey, the same as those three in the meeting. What Ryker hadn't really noticed about Winter before was the amount of gray hair he now had compared to when they'd met years ago, or the lines multiplying across his face. It'd been nearly ten years since Winter had taken over the role of commander at the JIA following Mackie's death. Ten tumultuous years for them both.

Those ten years had taken a toll. Winter had nearly lost his life in a bomb blast in London a few years ago. Having overcome that, physically and mentally, the JIA had ultimately imploded when details of corruption within the clandestine unit were brought to the fore by Ryker. Winter had remained in the intelligence community after, and as Ryker initially sought a quieter life, their lives had drifted apart, more and more.

But never fully apart.

Most recently Winter had been operating for an offshoot of MI6 in the Middle East. A role which had brought the two of them back together, unexpectedly, when Ryker became embroiled in a geopolitical conspiracy – involving the now-dead Davis Bracey – which had ultimately led him to the fringes of something much larger. A conspiracy involving some of the most powerful – but not necessarily most prominent – people on the planet. A shadowy group who he'd heard referred to as the Syndicate.

Once more he and Winter were unofficial allies. Winter was still tied to the big machine. He always would be. Ryker was still tied to his past and to his inability to walk away from trouble when he saw it. His inability to stop looking for it, really.

Analyzing his ally's appearance now, Ryker had no doubt the years hadn't been kind to Winter. He wondered whether Winter thought the same about him?

'Ryker?'

Back to reality. 'What?'

'What did they say to you?'

'That they couldn't give a crap about anything I've found, or the fact that I think it's only the tip of something much bigger.'

'They actually said that?'

'Not in those words, but it's clear there's no appetite for investigation from any of those three. Whether that's because they don't believe the Syndicate really exists, or because they're already under their influence, either directly or from somewhere higher up, I'm not sure.'

Winter didn't say anything to that. Did he know more?

'I can see it's eating away at you,' Winter said.

'What is?'

'Your never-ending quest to right the world's wrongs.'

Ryker humphed. He didn't like the way Winter said that, as though Ryker's work over the years was just some stupid hobby.

'You know, you could ride off into the sunset and forget all about Bracey, Lebedev, the Syndicate, which you don't even know for sure exists.'

Ryker said nothing.

'Tell me why you're here,' Winter said.

'In London?'

'Yes. And with me, in this café. What do you want from this?'

'Whether the Syndicate exists or not, what we already know is there are people out there, powerful people, billionaires and politicians who follow their own set of rules. For their own gain. They break laws, they rig our politics for their own gain, they have people silenced, ruined, hurt and killed, they do all sorts of other terrible things. Because they can. Because it's the only way for them to keep a stranglehold on the two things they love the most. Money and power.'

'I don't doubt those people exist. But—'

'What's my endgame?'

'That wasn't my question. But... What *is* your endgame?'

'Expose them all, and anyone who's been helping them. I don't care if the Syndicate, as an actual entity, even exists. It's the people who live like that I'm after. And I don't care if it takes me the rest of my life. I'll go from one to the next, doing whatever I can. This is what I'm good at, and it's already been made clear to me that the authorities, SIS, only care when it suits. We can't trust them to do the right thing here. But to me, it always suits. Scum is always scum.'

Winter didn't say anything to that. Ryker wished he had. Some sort of reassurance or even just a nod to say he agreed that Ryker *was* good at what he did.

'Have you met Fatma Yaman before?' Ryker asked.

'I know of her. We've never met.'

'She sat through that whole meeting without saying a word.'

'Out of her depth?'

'Something else. The fact is, I know these people already understand more about Bracey, Lebedev, the Syndicate than the information I've given them.'

'And you know that how?' Winter asked, sounding suspicious like he had a bad feeling as to where Ryker was going next.

'Do you remember Yousef Selim?' Ryker asked.

He knew the answer of course, but Winter's look of disquiet suggested hearing the name now was completely out of the blue. Which was a good thing, really.

'Yes, I remember Selim. And I remember what he did to you.'

Winter's gaze ever so quickly fell to the scar on Ryker's neck. The skin there prickled.

'And I remember that you already got your revenge on Selim, many years ago. He's dead. You killed him.'

'Yeah. But Selim was just one of many high-profile terror operators back then. High profile, and often very, very rich. Rich enough to start civil wars, to take down governments.'

'Where are you going with this?'

'The world's moved on since the war on terror; to many people, it's the distant past. And many of the most prominent adversaries of the West from back then are long dead. But not all of them. Some slipped through the net.'

'I'm sure they did. But you can't possibly be telling me that you think Selim was part of the Syndicate too?'

'I have no evidence of that,' Ryker said. 'But... Tell me what you know about Ismail Karaman.' Time to move this story on, because Bracey and Lebedev were already dead. But the crooks who sat alongside and above them weren't. And Ismail Karaman was one of those crooks. A real nasty one at that. The fact Ryker knew the man – the name, at least – as being a one-time close associate of Yousef Selim only made his being here now all the more personal.

He held Winter's eye as his old ally searched for a response. No doubt Winter knew Karaman's name, but was he simply racking his brain as to how, or was he thinking of which parts of what he knew he'd be prepared to divulge? As much as Ryker liked and trusted Winter, there was no getting away from the fact that he was still a government man.

'Why are you asking about him?' Winter eventually said. A cop-out.

'You know Selim and Karaman were—'

'Selim is dead, Ryker,' Winter said, sounding exasperated. 'He's been dead a long time.'

'I know. We've been through that already. But I know for a fact that Selim was an ally of Karaman. So what do you know about him?'

Winter sighed. 'I've not heard his name for years. But Karaman officially is, I believe, still on the UK's most wanted list. The most wanted list of some other countries as well.'

'Because?'

Winter looked around him as though suddenly nervous that someone might overhear the conversation. He needn't be. There was now no one else inside the café except the young man behind the counter who was nodding his head to whatever music was coming out of his earbuds.

'Karaman was a very successful businessman, originally from Türkiye but he lived in London for a long time,' Winter said. 'Despite residing here, he had friends in high places in a lot of countries that we, historically, haven't gotten on with very well. Syria, Libya, Iran, Russia, to name a few. Those connections eventually saw him leave here for his native Türkiye where he only became richer and more powerful. Although he started out in property and made a fortune in the property boom across the Gulf, his notoriety came from arms dealing.'

'Notoriety? He wasn't just an arms dealer, he directly funded terror cells and rebel groups, alongside the likes of Selim, Bin Laden.'

'*Apparently*,' Winter said.

'Apparently? OK, so you haven't seen the videos of the captured US journalists who his group beheaded?'

'His *group*. Not him personally, as far as we know.'

'Although the assailants were always masked, so how do you know?'

'We don't know. For sure.'

'Plus he was widely believed to be *directly* responsible for the attack on the UK embassy in Syria. Fifty-four people were killed in one night. He applauded the attack online afterward and blamed the British government for the deaths.'

Winter's face hardened and his cheeks pulsed as he clenched his jaw. 'I know that, Ryker. I had good friends in that building who died. And it wasn't pretty. A mini army stormed the place. My colleagues were rounded up, brutalized, murdered.'

Winter spoke with true bitterness, hatred. Unusual for him.

'Hence why Karaman found himself at the top of the UK's most wanted list,' Ryker said.

'He did. But I also heard rumors that he'd been set up. That he had nothing to do with organizing either of the incidents you mentioned. He was just a mouthpiece congratulating the carnage.'

'And encouraging more of it.'

'Maybe. But still, you should know better than anyone not to believe everything you read in the press.'

'And what do you believe?' Ryker asked.

'I'll tell you what I *know*.'

'OK?'

'What I know – and don't ask me for any further details on this – is that Karaman, for all his wealth and connections, was at one point in time targeted for… elimination. Not long after the embassy attack.'

'SIS?'

'I said don't ask for details. But it didn't go to plan. Karaman escaped, and he's hardly been seen since.'

'But he's remained a wanted man,' Ryker said.

'He has.'

'Except it doesn't seem to me like SIS or anyone else has been actively searching for him this whole time, does it? So why not?'

Winter looked pensive for a few moments. 'You're going to tell me Karaman is part of this Syndicate you've been talking about?' Winter asked.

'I think he's connected to it, yes.'

'Based on what?'

'Based on the fact Davis Bracey gave me his name as someone who was involved in business deals with Lebedev.'

'You never told me that before.'

Ryker shrugged. Winter looked annoyed.

'Anyone who's connected to those two warrants further investigation in my eyes. And we already know for sure Karaman isn't a good guy. I want to know where these connections lead.'

'Did you tell—'

'No. I didn't tell your colleagues anything about Karaman.'

'Why?'

'Because I don't trust them.'

'And me? You don't trust me?'

'I just told you what I know, didn't I?'

Winter snorted. 'Where are you going with this?'

'Not only do I believe Karaman knows a lot more about this Syndicate, but I'm confident SIS knows where he is. They've probably always known. Followed his every move, most likely. The question then is why they've done nothing about it.'

'Where are you getting this?'

'Remember I told you about Fatma Yaman? How she didn't say a word?'

'And?'

'And I think I know why. She was scared. Of me.'

'You can be quite intimidating.'

'I'm flattered,' Ryker said with a chuckle. 'But ask me why she was scared?'

Winter sighed as though making a point that he didn't like that Ryker was toying with him. 'Why was she scared?'

'Because a few nights ago I broke into her apartment.'

'Shit, Ryker!' Winter hissed, again looking around him.

'I stole data from her home computer,' Ryker continued. 'I've not finished searching it yet, but I managed to use what I found to hack into her SIS accounts. I found an email trail that proves she knows exactly where Karaman is. Not only are SIS not investigating Karaman anymore, I think at least some people there are protecting him.'

Apparently, Winter had nothing to say to that revelation.

'Maybe this is all unofficial,' Ryker continued. 'Just a few bad apples within SIS, or maybe it's official policy. I don't know. But Yaman knows her place was broken into. I made sure to leave some clues. I think she knows her computer was targeted too. I suspect she knows it was me. Does she know what I've found? Possibly not. But I think she fully expected me to hang her out to dry in that meeting.'

'But you didn't.'

'Because I don't know if Goldman and Podence are with her or not. They're not included in any of the communications I've seen.'

'You know there could be multiple explanations for what you found?'

'Maybe, but the most obvious is also the most likely. Karaman was, maybe is, working with the Syndicate, whatever it really is. But it doesn't even matter to me that much if that's not the answer. Karaman is bad, and for whatever reason I'm certain that people within SIS are helping to protect him.'

Winter brought his hands to his face and rubbed at his eyes for a few moments as though in despair about something.

'Ryker, just tell me what you're planning. What are you asking for?'

Ryker smiled. 'Karaman is still a wanted man. In the UK. The US. Israel. Egypt...'

'I said, what are you asking for? From me?'

'Give me a small team. Another two people are all I need. We'll get to Karaman. We'll extract him to a safe country.'

'You want to kidnap him and... interrogate him?'

'Yes.'

Winter's face had gone pale.

'And if we find nothing more on the Syndicate—' which he really hoped wouldn't be the case '—we hand him over to the authorities and let them deal with him. Let him pay for his past crimes. Finally.'

Winter said nothing. He finished his coffee. Looked off into the distance. Sighed about a hundred times.

'At least you haven't said no already,' Ryker said.

Winter sighed once more. 'If I pull any of my people in, I'm already much closer to this than I want to be. You don't have any old friends who could help you?'

'*You're* the old friend. I'm sure I could get to Karaman on my own. I could put a bullet in his head but in this instance, it doesn't give me the answers I'm looking for.'

Winter cringed. Perhaps at Ryker's matter-of-fact way of saying he'd happily execute someone. Someone who deserved it, but still.

'I need help getting him somewhere safe,' Ryker added. 'Transport. Access to facilities. A word in the right ear of the right people to keep the authorities off our backs. If you can give me two people to help on the ground too, even better.'

Winter scoffed. 'Not sounding so simple right now, is it? You know I can't do any of this officially.'

'I wouldn't want you to. It'd defeat the purpose as we don't know who we can trust. And anyway, most of your career hasn't been official. But this could be the difference. A way to break into the Syndicate. Right now, what else do we have to go on?'

'Where is he?'

Ryker leaned forward. 'Dubai.'

Winter snorted as though that made some sense to him.

'Give me two days,' he said before he stood up and headed for the exit.

5

CUMBRIA, ENGLAND

Down, up, down, up, down, up. The rhythm of her push-ups was constant, steady. A short pause at the bottom before exploding back to the top. A longer pause there before lowering herself back down with the smooth precision of a highly engineered machine.

Down, up, down, up, down, up. Four hundred and ninety-eight... Four hundred and ninety-nine... Five hundred.

Angel held the position, her knuckles – taking most of her weight – on fire, her legs quivering, big globules of sweat dripping from her brow and to the carpet below. After a few seconds, every muscle in her body burned and screamed for mercy. She still held the high plank position longer, as long as she could until her muscles rather than her willpower gave in and she collapsed to the floor. She rolled over, staring up at the ceiling, panting heavy breaths to suck in as much oxygen as she could while endorphins rushed through her blood and through her brain. A natural high? Fuck that. The feeling didn't even come close to the highs brought on by external chemicals. But this type of high... The reward was good, yet the punishment, the atonement, and more than anything the relief that it was over made it all the more powerful.

A knock on the bedroom door. Gentle. Like everything in this place. Light touch.

She really didn't fit in at all.

'Angel, we're going to the woods soon.'

'Got it,' she shouted out.

She rolled forward onto her heels and bounced upright sending a renewed rush of blood to her head. She looked out of the grimy little window. A room with a view? Yeah, it was nice. If she pressed her right cheek up against the right-hand side of the glass she had the smallest glimpse of the edge of Lake Windermere about a mile in the distance. Only visible at this time of year because the trees had now lost all their leaves. So yeah, the view was OK even if in winter it all looked a little barren, and she'd been here for nearly two weeks and still hadn't seen any sunshine. Every day that went by with nothing more than dull gray all around her it took away another small part of her soul.

This place was supposed to be for recovery, but if she was to set up competition she'd put her retreat on a white sand beach in the Caribbean and have everyone sip on frozen margaritas all day long. Virgin margaritas, obviously.

Well, maybe anyway.

At least it had finally stopped raining, although she knew that once again she'd need her Wellington boots for this 'adventure' as the ground all around here had turned to thick mud and likely would stay that way now until some dry and warm weather returned in several months' time.

Angel sighed and tried to push the downtrodden thoughts away, but turning around and looking at the poky room and the poky bed and the tired furniture didn't exactly make her feel any more positive about being here.

Still, it was a lot better than what she'd had to become used to over recent years. She'd spent way too long confined to spaces much smaller and worse than this one. Which was one very big reason why she'd started her grueling routine of push-ups, sit-ups, squats, burpees, anything she could do in a small space and with nothing more than her body as equipment. To keep fit. To fill time. To make her feel something at all other than hate and regret.

Another knock on the door.

'Angel, we're going in five minutes.' A different but no less gratingly gentle and pleasant voice this time.

'I know!' she shouted. 'Give me some fucking peace, will you?'

No response to that.

She headed to the bathroom and stared at her reflection in the mirror for a few seconds. Her face was beetroot red, she was covered in sweat, her hair sodden. She should shower but within half an hour she'd sat by the smoky campfire, stinking anyway.

Screw it.

She washed her face with cold water, stripped off her leggings and sports bra, and used a damp towel to at least absorb some of the sweat from her body. Which kind of worked, until more sweat rippled along her skin.

Whatever.

She put on some jogging bottoms and a big hoodie. She tied her damp, scraggy hair into a tight bun and pulled her hood over her head. Then she put on her boots and went to the door.

She paused. Sniffed. She didn't know whether it was the clothes, or the boots, or just her but... That wasn't a good odor. She rushed back to the bathroom and dug into her toiletry bag and right at the bottom found the perfume bottle. Coco Chanel. Her mom had bought it for her eight years ago this Christmas. A strange gift as Angel had never been much into wearing perfume, and she'd hardly ever used it even before... all that. Yet it remained a regular fixture in her toiletry bag wherever she went. In fact, it usually stayed in the bag, the bag in the cupboard when she was at home.

She sprayed ten squirts all about her and spun around trying to catch every last molecule. She sniffed then coughed when the fragrance caught in her nose. She scrunched her face and rubbed at her nose but the smell, the taste at the back of her throat remained.

'At least you can't smell yourself anymore,' she said, looking at herself in the mirror with a wry smile.

Then she finally headed out, down the creaky stairs of the old and poorly kept building to the shoddy reception area where thirteen people were already waiting, a few chatting quietly, but most standing alone and looking somber.

'Ah, Angel, you're here,' said Lee, a big false smile plastered on his nerdy face as he strode over and patted her on the shoulder. The smile faltered a little. 'You look—'

'Like she's run a marathon through some prickly bushes,' said Deidre – a grumpy sort who'd taken a disliking to Angel immediately. Or was it the other way around? Either way, they weren't compatible.

'Running?' said Jason – a worm of a man who only spoke if he had something snide to say about others. 'Not with all that grunting and moaning I keep on hearing. Something else, I think.'

He smirked and looked around as though expecting others to find him funny. As usual, no one did.

'Anyway,' Lee said, tilting his head forward to look at Angel like a parent would with a child they were trying to convince of something they knew the child wouldn't like to hear. 'I'm glad you decided to come with us. I wasn't sure if you would again. After... You know.'

'After she smacked Clive around the head with a burning stick?' Jason said, still smirking.

'An appropriate response given what he said to me,' Angel countered.

'OK, OK,' Lee said, turning and using his best authoritative tone. Which wasn't really very authoritative. 'I don't think we need to revisit old ground. As everyone here knows, Clive has been sent home because of what happened. What he said was horribly inappropriate and, while we never condone violence, I just hope we can all move on now.'

He turned back to Angel with an imploring look, as though asking her to be on her best behavior. If only he knew how much restraint it had taken to just smack Clive one time with that log. She'd wanted to force the flaming end down his throat.

She rubbed her fingers across her palms, the rawness from the burns still there. A reminder of sorts.

'OK, then,' said Gloria, striding out of the office with purpose, and a similarly giddy smile on her face which she shared with Lee, her underling. Did the two of them practice it together? 'Shall we get going?'

So they all did. A nearly two-mile trek across muddy fields, through muddy woodland trails, until finally, they came to a clearing where soaked-through wooden trunks had been arranged as benches around a small circle of stones that would become the boundaries for their campfire.

'It's a bit... wet,' Jason said while slopping his foot down into one of several pools of standing water around them. 'Is this going to work?'

'Fail to prepare, prepare to fail,' Lee said, undeterred in spirit as he strode across to the small shelter a few yards away. 'Someone come and help me,' he shouted out, head inside, his ass sticking out which Angel found herself laughing at... It reminded her of... something. She couldn't remember what.

'Shall we get this place looking nice?' Gloria said in her loud matronly voice.

She received some murmurs of acknowledgment and roughly half of the party joined her in the fruitless task of mopping down the logs and trying to cover the pools of water with leaves and other mulch.

Angel helped a little, but not exactly enthusiastically. She still had her eye on the new guy. She'd first spotted him in the reception area, talking to Jenn – a young woman who all the guys had shown an interest in at some point. Was she pretty? Maybe not in the middle of the city with lots of competition, but out here she was clearly the pick of the bunch with her sparkling green eyes, blemish-free skin, and her dyed blonde hair. Anyway, the point wasn't about her, but about the man. Angel didn't know him but something about his face, his serious but commanding manner, put her on the back foot. Perhaps because he reminded her so much of—

'I thought this sort of thing would be right up your street,' Jason said, his tone less than friendly as he walked past lugging some wood and making a real meal of it as though it was a huge strain to carry a few logs.

'My street being?' Angel said as he dumped the logs next to the fire pit.

'Girl of adventure. Tomboy. You know.'

She glared at him, waiting to see if he had anything else to add and he shrank a little as though well aware she wasn't impressed with whatever insinuation he'd been trying to make.

'It's just... You're not a... girly girl. Are you?'

'I'm thirty-freaking-one, Jason.' She caught herself just in time from saying the actual f-word. Not allowed here, and she did at least try to follow the rules. 'I'm not any kind of girl. So please stop projecting your own depraved preferences my way.'

He looked like he'd swallowed several wasps and he stuttered and glanced around him as though embarrassed someone else might have heard.

'That's not... That's...'

Angel turned away from him and went and sat down on one of

the logs that Gloria had hastily covered with a blanket, which at least partly helped to keep the moisture away.

While Lee and some of the other wannabe alphas – or maybe just helpful souls – got the fire going, Angel sat and watched the people around her, contemplating where she fit into it all, how being here really had become the sum total of her life. As the fire took hold, the not-quite-dry enough wood spitting and fizzling and sending thick plumes of smoke upward, everyone eventually settled down on the trunks. Nearly everyone. Lee remained by the fire. His fire. The new guy remained talking to and giggling with Jenn. And as the two of them were ushered over Angel was sure they'd find a seat together. Or, at least, the guy would follow Jenn wherever she was going. But instead, Gloria stuck her hand out to guide Jenn toward her – a deliberate attempt to break up the flirting? – and the next moment the guy locked eyes with Angel and she kind of froze.

Damn embarrassing. But the way he looked at her...

He smiled and she didn't move as he came over to her and sat down on her trunk.

'Hi,' he whispered as Lee began his spiel about what he had planned for the night. How it'd make them all feel wonderful and aid their recoveries and provide a safe environment for blah, blah, blah.

'I said hi,' the guy said, leaning in a little. 'Don't I know you?'

'No,' Angel said. 'You don't.'

He kind of laughed. 'Hopefully, I will soon enough.' He leaned further over and nudged her shoulder a little.

Angel didn't react. The guy straightened up and Lee carried on addressing the group, but Angel blocked out his words. Her brain was too busy as she stared at the swirling flames of the fire. She rubbed at the sore spots in her palms again, eyes focused on the red-hot, glowing logs, the smooth and confident voice of the man sitting next to her reverberating uneasily in her mind.

6
_____

'Angel!' Lee shouted, finally snapping her from her thoughts.

'What?' She looked from the fire and up at his critical face.

'Glad you're still with us.'

Jason grumbled something – probably a slur – under his breath while others stifled snide giggles.

'I wouldn't be anywhere else,' she said.

'Good. Good. So?'

'So what?'

'I was saying, tonight we're welcoming our newest member here. The man sitting next to you?'

She glanced over at the guy by her side, a really pleased look on his face.

'And?' she said to Lee.

'Were you listening to anything I said?' Lee was doing his best schoolteacher voice now. Condescending on another level.

'Not really.'

Lee sighed. 'I'll backtrack. Our newest member, Andre, has driven all the way from Devon to be with us today. It's his first time at Heartlands Retreat.'

'First time I've done any kind of rehab,' Andre blurted out as though the qualification was an important one to him.

But Angel knew even before Lee's face soured that the host wouldn't like it. 'We don't use that word here,' he said. 'This isn't *rehab*. This is a wellness retreat. A chance for us all to connect, reconnect with our minds and our souls. To learn and to grow. To—'

'OK, I apologize,' Andre said, holding his hands up, although he didn't exactly sound contrite.

'It's fine,' Lee said. 'The point, Angel, is that I know you've had a hard time opening up to us here about your... past. Your troubles.' A few others around the campfire nodded as though cementing the fact that they saw a problem in Angel not wanting to air her pain. 'And that's your right. We will never force people around this circle to discuss anything that they don't want to discuss. But I do know from my many years of experience that one of the best forms of healing is talking.' Murmurs of agreement. 'And... Of course, I'm privy to both of your backgrounds, and I can only say that the two of you share some striking similarities.'

'We do?' Andre said, looking pleased with himself.

'You've both suffered through... addiction,' Lee said, treading carefully as though trying to recall what Angel had already made public. Not a lot, but she had spoken about how she was now clean. Which wasn't entirely true, but still. 'And both of your home lives have been affected adversely as a result.'

Angel held her eye on Andre now, looking for a flinch or other reaction that would show his pain. A pain she could truly understand and feel sympathy for. If it was real.

'So?' Lee prompted after a few moments of silence.

'What?'

'Is there anything you'd like to share, Angel? Perhaps some words to explain how Heartlands has helped you on your journey.

Why you keep coming back here, even now that you're... You know?'

'Not mandated to come here by the terms of my probation?' Angel suggested. The mention of the p-word led to a few raised eyebrows. And Angel was well aware that some others were here because it was mandated as part of their early release from prison – they'd openly stated that – but she'd never specifically talked about her time behind bars. She did everything she could to not even think about that time.

'Yes, I guess so,' Lee said rather feebly.

'I think the point's already been made,' Angel said. 'I spent a few years behind bars—'

'Figures,' Jason said, just loudly enough for everyone to hear. Angel sent him a death glare but pushed thoughts of violence away.

'And when I got early release it was based on various conditions. One of which was that I continue to see a psychotherapist, to help with my PTSD. I also had to come here.'

'Yes, but you've continued to come here even though it's no longer required of you?' Lee said, in such a way as to suggest he didn't want to dwell too much on the prison aspect of her past even if that, and everything that went with it, was the whole point of how her life had spiraled downward.

Plus, if she was still coming here, didn't that kind of suggest that the wellness methods here weren't really all that successful given she was still messed up in all sorts of ways?

She decided not to make that point.

'I have,' Angel said. 'I just can't get enough of this damn rain.'

She smiled and received a few sniggers in response.

'Anything else?' Lee asked. 'The fact you're such a repeat visitor suggests you've found healing here? Trust, in yourself and others? Can you tell us about that?'

'Trust?' Angel's mood soured as she dwelled on that word.

'Sorry, Lee, but... One thing I've learned through all of my... turmoil, is that I simply can't and never will be able to trust anyone or anything, not anymore. Not in the outside world, *or* here.'

This wasn't going how Lee had wanted it to. He really should have picked someone else if he'd wanted someone singing the praises of this place. Karen, perhaps, who was so up to her eyeballs with anti-depressants she'd have exclaimed how wonderful it was if someone went over to her and hacked her arm off with a blunt dinner knife.

'That's sad to hear,' Lee said. 'We strive to create an open, trusting environment here, where we don't pass judgment because of what our residents have done or have suffered from in the past.'

Nods to that, everyone trying to convince themselves. Lie to themselves, more like.

'Why, Angel, do you feel you can't trust people anymore?'

'Because everyone lies for their own benefit.'

'You've been—'

'So, Andre, you were an addict?' Angel said, turning from Lee and to the newcomer.

'Yeah, I've struggled.'

'Alcohol?'

'Mainly.'

'You're sober now?'

'Three months.'

Angel laughed. Something about the way he said that.

'Liar,' she said and Andre looked annoyed, and a little embarrassed, and a few others groaned in shock as though they couldn't bear where this was going. Another Angel calamity in the making.

'Angel, please—'

But once again she had no interest in whatever bullshit Lee was about to say.

'See what I mean?' she said, addressing the group. 'We're all liars. We do it to convince ourselves, others. We do it to hide from truths. But I can tell just by looking at him that Andre hasn't been sober for three months. If he was finding it that easy he wouldn't be here, for starters. Yeah, it's not rehab. But it's also not for people who have their shit together. Is it, really?'

No one answered that.

'So, Andre, how many drinks have you actually had in the last three months?'

'A few,' he said.

'But you're trying to be sober, right?'

'Right.'

'So, what gives?'

He thought about that for a few moments, never breaking Angel's eye contact. 'Life is shit without it,' he said. 'Alcohol makes me feel... something.'

Angel laughed. 'Yeah, and that's crap too, but at least *you* believe it. But maybe Lee's right. Me and you? We share some similarities. Let me guess – your wife wants you to quit for good?'

She'd noticed the ring on his finger.

'I have to,' Andre said. 'For her. For my kids.'

'How many?'

'Two. Girl and boy. Eleven and nine.'

'They know you're an alcoholic?'

'A recovering alcoholic. And no, they don't.'

'Good for you. So if you stay sober, you stay married?'

'No,' he said. 'She left me already. Divorce is pending. But if I stay sober, the judge pulls the restraining order and I maybe get visits, or something.'

Angel paused there, a little taken aback by his responses – his pain – because she hadn't expected quite the parallel to her own life that she'd just heard. Which annoyed her. As though she was special and suffering more than the other people here.

'But I really am trying,' Andre said. 'I don't want to let them down. I'd do anything for them. I want to quit, and I'm determined that I will. And if I slip up every now and then... It's early days. But I'm in this for the long haul. I'll get there and I hope that coming here will only help me achieve that, in the long run.'

'You're very brave,' Gloria said, clasping her hands together like she'd just heard the most heartwarming story.

'Thank you,' Andre said. 'So what about you, *Angel*? Shall I dissect you now?'

'If you want.'

She had nothing to hide here. She'd only not spoken much before because it was none of anyone else's business, but she wasn't scared of talking about her life.

'Alcohol?'

'Anything I could get my hands on,' she said. 'Opium, to start with. Or some cheap derivative, at least. That was what everyone was given in prison in Beirut.' She'd never mentioned Beirut here before. Too painful. Too complicated. She kept her focus on Jason so she couldn't see the others' reactions but she heard the *oohs* and other murmurs. Shit, the rabble were loving this. Jason would be salivating, most likely. 'But it's not so easy to get that kind of stuff here in England. So when I was finally transferred here, I went on to painkillers.'

'How long were you in prison?'

'Five years of a ten-year sentence. Four of those in Lebanon. And believe me, those four felt like forty. Prison in England was like a holiday camp.'

'What were you in for?'

'Attempted murder.'

'You tried to kill someone?' Andre said.

'Obviously. That's what it means, dickhead.'

Andre smiled. Not the most appropriate response.

'Who'd you try to kill?'

'Someone I didn't know. Accidentally.'

'You were—'

'I was fine before I went to prison. Husband, and the most amazing daughter you could imagine.'

She fought back the emotion now. She thought she did pretty well.

'You want to know how and why I became an addict?' she asked.

Andre nodded.

'Because I never expected for my life to crumble like that. And ten years? I was set to miss most of my daughter's childhood. I wasn't getting out until she was sixteen. The thought alone nearly killed me. And that rotting cesspit in Lebanon could break anyone. So I fell into a hole. Pretty quickly, actually. I honestly didn't think I'd make it out of there alive. But then I got brought back here. Low security. Except the damage was already done and there it was easier to smuggle stuff in. My favorite mix? A bottle of vodka and half a dozen anti-psychotics in an evening. Fuck, the release that gave me. It was like floating out of my own body. I got to be away from *me*. I finally got to see the mess I was to everyone else too and I didn't want to be it. So I wanted that release more and more. I lived for those moments where I didn't have to be Angel at all.'

'You still got early release, even though—'

'I'm an even better liar than most. It's how I'm so good at spotting others. No one knew.'

'You lied to the parole board?' Jason piped up, as disgusted as he was enthused.

'Jason, please, we're not passing judgment here,' Lee said. 'Remember?'

'But you know the worst part of it all?' Angel said to Andre. 'And what really sent me over the edge?'

'What?' Andre asked.

'The whole time I was inside... My husband, Paul... He talked as though we had a future. All I had to do was get through prison. I'd come out, I'd get clean, we'd be together again. Him, me, Sasha.'

'But?'

'But he's a lying piece of shit and a coward,' Angel said. 'I dunno. Maybe he actually thought it'd be ten years and he had more time than he thought to tell me the truth. But he... he jumped on my problems the second I got out. So, Jason, before you go getting all excited about stabbing me in the back, the parole board knows *now*. I came out and I got... worse. A lot worse. Paul kicked me out less than three weeks after my release. It was the morning after I came home from having my stomach pumped in hospital because the bottle of vodka I drank the night before together with a box of painkillers was a lot stronger than the watered-down, fake shit in prison. I begged and pleaded and begged some more for him to take me back, for him to let me see Sasha, but before I knew it he had lawyers involved and then the courts and then...'

Silence. Everyone stared, waiting for her to carry on. Clearly, they all knew what was coming next was the most painful part for her and they couldn't get enough of it.

'Not only did he divorce me, but he got sole custody of Sasha and an order from the courts that I couldn't see my daughter, not at all, until I'd got a clean bill of mental health from a doctor of his choosing, with open access to my medical records, plus evidence of me being sober, drug-free, for at least a six-month period.'

'How long ago was that?' Andre asked.

'That was nearly two years ago. Except, I didn't touch a drink, take any medication whatsoever, not even a damn painkiller for nearly twelve months. I came here several times during that period. I saw every doctor he insisted I see. And what happened? He fought with everything he had to block me from her still. You want to know why?'

'Why?'

'Because he'd long since shacked up with his new thing. Bella the fucking bimbo. Not only was he living with her, with my daughter, but they got married, had their own kid. And the worst of it? He met her while I was inside, languishing in Beirut. He'd done nothing but bullshit me for years. He'd never intended on taking me back, even if I hadn't been a suicidal junkie.'

'Shit,' Andre said and for some dumb reason he reached out and put his hand onto hers and she had a tough call to make. Leave her hand there, smothered by his touch, or go and grab a burning log and pummel his nicely framed face a few times until it wasn't so nicely framed anymore.

'Yeah,' was all she said in the end, not moving. She looked around the group and tried to somehow eke out confidence from their shocked, disgusted glares. 'Which all explains why I'm not the trusting type these days.'

She laughed but no one else followed suit and soon most people were looking away, trying to find a distraction. Andre finally took his hand back.

'Shall we get the sausages out?' Gloria suggested.

Jason sniggered like a small child but at least the mood lightened a bit.

'Yes, Gloria,' Lee said. 'Let's do that.'

* * *

Four hours later Angel finally got to take a much-needed shower, washing away sweat, tears, a lot of campfire smoke, and a decent amount of tension with it all too. She came out of the bathroom – a towel wrapped tightly around her cleansed skin – feeling all kinds of rejuvenated, not just from the warm water but from the whole night, really.

She hated the niggling little voice in her head. Lee's voice. Telling her how proud he was of her for opening up, talking candidly about her troubles finally, but... The truth was, she did feel better for it. Just a tiny burden lifted, even if it didn't actually change reality at all.

More than that though, she'd enjoyed the night. After the shaky start, after her anguish, everyone had steered well clear of tension. They'd laughed, told stupid jokes, stories. They'd bonded. More so than at any other point that Angel had been to this place.

And she knew one reason for that: the person who'd sat next to her through the night.

She flinched at the knock on the door. Waited to see if whoever it was would announce themselves. They didn't, so Angel edged quietly to the door and pushed her face close to the peephole.

She opened the door a few inches and Andre clocked her, and the towel – and she noticed the sparkle in his eyes.

'What do you want?' she asked.

'Just seeing if you were busy. Or... if you wanted some company.'

'You brought anything with you?' she asked.

'Sorry?'

'Wine, whiskey.'

'You serious?' And the questioning look suggested *he* was.

'No, idiot.' She opened the door, keeping herself mostly hidden behind the wood as she beckoned him in. She closed the door softly, standing with her back up against it as Andre looked around the room, as though searching for something, before he turned to face her.

'You... just showered?' he asked.

'You're some detective.'

He shrugged.

'So why don't you tell me what you're really doing here?' she said.

'You invited me in.'

'You didn't expect that?'

He didn't answer.

'You wanna screw me?' she asked and then held his eye as his cheeks blushed a little. Cute. 'You can't if you won't even say it,' she added.

He pulled himself together. It didn't take much. The guy was confident. Sure of himself. She'd figured that from the moment she'd first laid eyes on him.

'Ask me again then,' he said.

'You wanna screw me?'

'Yeah. I do. Why else would I be here?'

She said nothing. Neither did he. It was a standoff of sorts – who'd break first?

'So?' he said. She smiled and he shook his head, knowing he'd crumbled before her. 'Do *you* wanna screw *me*?'

'Why else would I have invited you in here,' she said.

She slipped off the towel and enjoyed the hungry look in his eyes as he moved toward her for the kill.

7

DUBAI, UNITED ARAB EMIRATES

The weather in the Gulf was more than a little warmer than back in England. Ryker certainly wouldn't have enjoyed doing this in the British Channel or the North Sea at this time of year. The waters of the Gulf were calm with little nighttime breeze, although at their hefty speed in the highly powered inflatable dinghy, moist, salty air blasted against Ryker's face and he was glad to have the protection of the tactical wet suit.

'It's a great city,' the guy in the front of the dinghy said, looking out at the vast expanse of lights from the many skyscrapers of Dubai that clung to the shoreline. 'You been before?'

'Yeah,' Ryker said.

His companion turned around, a quizzical look on his face as though he didn't like the answer much. Companion? Not the best word, really. It suggested some sort of friendship and Ryker was already feeling like the two of them were far from compatible.

The man was Brock Van Der Vehn. South African. Six foot six and two hundred and fifty pounds of pure muscle and testosterone with a macho attitude to go with it. He looked like a rugby player or a gladiator. Probably more the latter, really, with the obvious scars on his arms, hands, face, and half an ear missing.

'I love it,' Brock said. 'Dubai is a city where you can get whatever you want, whenever you want it.'

'If you have the money,' Ryker said.

Brock scoffed at that. But Ryker was cynical. Over recent years Dubai had become one of the most prosperous and most developed cities in the world. But to Ryker, it all felt a little fake. The fact was, for all its fancy buildings and luxury beach resorts and high-end shops and whatever else made it attractive to tourists and business people from all over, Dubai, the UAE as a whole, remained a place where rules and laws were heavily entrenched in religious ideals, and public freedoms were severely limited. Unless you were rich, of course. Rules and laws didn't apply then. Which only made Ryker dislike the place all the more.

The city remained a couple of miles in front of them but they were only a few hundred yards from their destination, so Ryker slowed the motor and the boat's front end dipped down as the craft crawled along at a much slower speed.

'You done shit like this before?' Brock asked.

'Of course. You?'

'Buddy, this is what I live for,' he said with a wide grin.

Ryker had no response to that. Three days ago he'd asked Winter for a team of two others for this extraction. Winter had provided half of that. Van Der Vehn. He and Ryker hadn't met until they'd arrived at the shore less than an hour ago. On the journey across the water so far Ryker had gleaned that Brock was ex-special forces but it seemed like he'd spent far longer, and his most recent years, as a mercenary. He went where he got paid to go.

'You don't talk much, do you?' Brock said as Ryker turned the engine off and the boat bobbed along on the not-so-choppy waters.

'We're not here to chat. We're here for a job.'

'A risky, life or death job. I like to know who I'm working with, who's got my back.'

Fair points.

'I used to work in the intelligence services,' Ryker said. 'Most recently I've been freelance. Kind of like you.'

'You think you're like me?' Brock said with a laugh. Ryker didn't bother to ask what he meant by that.

'How do you know Peter Winter?' Ryker asked.

'I don't. All I know is he's paying me.'

Ryker hid his scathing reaction to that. When he caught up with Winter...

'What's your favorite weapon?' Brock asked as the two of them checked through the contents of their waterproof backpacks.

'Weapon for what?'

'What do you think? You like guns?'

'They're functional.'

Brock was looking more and more sullen.

'My favorite weapon? Knives. Hell, I'm the best shot you've ever seen with any type of gun. Pistol, shotgun, rifle, sniper, I'm your guy. But guns are... too easy. Know what I mean?'

No. 'Kind of.'

'You killed before?'

'What kind of a question is that?'

'A simple one. Have you?'

'Yes.'

'How many?'

'It's irrelevant.'

Brock cackled. 'I'm not so sure. It's very relevant to me. And I know exactly how many. Twenty-five. Most of those were up close and personal.'

He said that with a wink and Ryker gave no response. The unfortunate fact was that he'd killed a lot more than twenty-five people, but he took no pride in that. Satisfaction? OK, he'd be lying if he said it hadn't felt satisfying to dispose of some of the most despicable people. But not pride. He certainly never gloated about killing.

Brock finished looking through his bag and huffed as he slapped it down on the bench.

'So we get nothing but a few darts and a fishing knife.'

'Thought you liked knives.'

'Yeah. I do. But I'd feel safer for something like this with at least one gun.'

'We don't need guns. This isn't a kill mission.'

'You don't think the other guys will be armed?'

'They probably will be. So just try not to get shot.'

Try not to get me *shot* was probably more apt.

Brock laughed again. 'Doesn't matter. I'll use whatever I can to get the job done. You wanna know what the weirdest thing is I ever used to protect myself?'

Ryker didn't really, but he also had to at least try and keep this guy on his side until the job was done. 'What?'

'A wooden spoon. You know, like what you use for stirring cake mixture and shit.'

Ryker smiled, but more because of Brock's last few words. Shit stirrer. He definitely was one, Ryker felt. But the smile unfortunately only added to Brock's animation.

'Yeah. The deal was we were targeting this asshole trafficker. He'd been selling teenage girls. Taking them from refugee camps at the start of the Syrian war. Taking money from their parents, pretending he'd get them somewhere safe. Europe, wherever. And a lot of them did end up in Europe, but only so they could be passed around gangs. It's sick. Really fucking sick, and I mean sick in the old sense of the word, not how kids use it.'

'I understand,' Ryker said.

'Yeah, well, this guy... He had a mini army at his compound. Five of us. We stormed it at night. Popped them off, one after the other. Except we couldn't find our guy. We searched high and low. I ended up in the basement where he had this huge industrial-style kitchen, all stainless-steel units, you know?'

'I guess.'

'You know where I found him? In the fucking walk-in freezer. I still don't know if he put himself in there and got trapped or if his friends hid him there, expecting to go back. I could have left him to freeze, but we needed to clear out and I wanted to make sure he was finished. So I opened the door and he comes at me with a meat hook. I let rip with my Glock but he's wired and I hit his Kevlar four times but he just keeps coming for me. The gun's spent, I'm all out because we've already taken out fifteen other guys between us. So I toss the gun and go for the only thing I can reach.'

'A wooden spoon.'

'A wooden fucking spoon. Still in the mixing bowl with some shit or other all over it. Pancake batter, I don't know. I slap him around the head a few times with it as we scuffle.' Brock paused and laughed as though fondly reminiscing on the moment. 'He's got pancake mix all over his face, he's screaming every obscenity at me, still trying to get at me even after I snap his arm in two and pretty much gouge out one of his eyes. We end up on the floor. And that wooden spoon... The handle ends up right through his other eye.'

Brock paused and deflated a little, as though the gravity of the harrowing situation had come back to him, something real above the unnecessarily jovial telling of the story.

'So I'm lying on the floor panting, sweating.' Somber now. 'I've got a meat hook sticking out of my shoulder, blood everywhere. But I'm alive. Him, on the other hand – he's lying next to me.' Brock laughed again and his horribly upbeat manner returned. 'And there's this wooden spoon just sticking up in the air, out of his face, pancake batter still dripping down it.'

'Resourceful,' Ryker said, not really knowing what else he should say.

'Damn right.'

'But like I said, this mission isn't about elimination. Right?'

'Whatever you say, *boss*.'

'We ready?' Ryker asked.

'Yeah.'

They both pulled on their backpacks, tightened the straps, then grabbed their goggles and mini oxygen tanks – the kind small enough to fit right underneath the mouthpiece. Brock tossed the weighted line into the water while Ryker took out his knife and plunged it into the side of the dinghy. He sheathed his knife and they both pushed themselves off the rapidly deflating craft.

They trod water for a few moments, watching their destroyed boat slowly disappear as they readied their diving equipment. Once the boat was fully submerged, Ryker gave Brock the OK signal and the two of them slipped under the water.

8

Ryker and Brock resurfaced a little over fifteen minutes later, both of their oxygen tanks running on empty. The city looked as distant as it had before, but the surroundings had definitely changed following their underwater swim. Most notably, jostling on the water not twenty yards from them was a huge yacht, over a hundred feet long, its sleek bodywork glistening in the moonlight.

Ryker saw no one in sight at the back deck of the craft and hardly any lights on inside. As expected, given Karaman and his main entourage were partying in the city.

Ryker and Brock glided through the water to the back and, as quietly as they could, pulled themselves out of the sea. They both placed their diving equipment into their backpacks as they remained crouched, looking around, alert to any movement on or off the yacht.

'OK, let's get this thing secured and ready,' Ryker whispered.

Which meant incapacitating anyone who remained on board so they could lie in wait for Karaman to return.

He received a nod from Brock before the two of them moved

stealthily toward the closed doors on the lower deck. On the approach, Ryker heard noise above and signaled for Brock to stop. Ryker pointed up. Brock nodded again. Whoever was on the upper deck was coming down the stairs. Ryker and Brock both disappeared into the darkness, Brock closest to the foot of the staircase.

The man's legs came into view. Dark-clothed. When he was halfway down Ryker spotted the barrel of his rifle, pointed to the floor. Brock sent Ryker a look. Ryker shook his head and only hoped the message was understood.

The next moment and the man reached the bottom of the stairs and turned toward them – still unaware of their presence – and Brock burst into action. And for a big guy, he was remarkably spritely. The guard didn't see him coming until the last moment and couldn't even get his hands around the grip of his weapon before Brock prized it away and smacked the guy around the face with the hefty metal butt. It sent him to his knees and Brock lifted the weapon and pummeled the man's face with it.

'Stop!' Ryker hissed and Brock paused midair with the rifle, his teeth bared like a mad dog.

Brock slung the rifle strap over his shoulder and grabbed the man around his neck, choking him.

'How many of you?' Brock barked at the captive as Ryker moved over.

No response so Brock took out his knife and stabbed it through the man's thigh and forced his gloved hand over the guy's mouth to stifle his scream. Ryker stood there dumbfounded when what he really wanted to do was grab Brock and toss him overboard.

'I said, how many?' Brock demanded.

'Three.'

'Where?'

'In... side.'

'Let's get him out of sight,' Ryker said. He took the tranquilizer from his backpack, getting ready to jab it into the guard's neck.

'He's better off awake and talking until we find the others,' Brock said.

'Too risky,' Ryker said. Mainly because he saw no need to allow Brock to torture the guy anymore. He sank the pointed end into the guard's neck and he squirmed for a few moments, perhaps unsure what was happening to him, before his body went limp in Brock's grip.

Brock looked angered.

'Come on,' Ryker said.

Ryker led the way. Brock cable-tied then dragged the guard through to a kitchen and dining area where they found a storage cupboard to hold him.

Then they both stood there, listening.

'I don't hear anyone else,' Brock said.

Nor did Ryker. But it was a damn big boat.

'Maybe he's the only guard,' Ryker said. 'Maybe the other two he mentioned are crew.'

But they were standing in the kitchen and there was no sign of anyone else – a cook or waiter – no sign that anyone had been preparing food in there at all.

There was a clunk from somewhere outside. Toward the front of the yacht.

'Let's go get him,' Brock said.

Ryker nodded.

Brock exited first, Ryker a step behind. Ryker and Brock silently signaled to each other, one to go left, the other to the right.

Having split up, Ryker was on the starboard side of the yacht, facing east toward the city lights.

He'd only moved a few yards when he spotted the object in the water. Coming toward them at speed. And he had no way of alerting Brock.

Ryker sped up, moving toward the front of the yacht. With any luck, he'd get there and out of sight before anyone on the approaching dinghy spotted him.

That was the plan, at least, but he was still a few yards from the end of the cabin when he heard banging and then groaning voices ahead. A scuffle. He flinched and ducked when a barrage of gunfire erupted, and he pulled himself up against the wall of the cabin. He looked to the dinghy, only fifty yards away now. They must have heard because a spotlight turned on and pointed his way. Brock burst into view in front of him, rifle in his hands. No sign of who he'd tackled but blood spatters covered his face.

'I got them both!' Brock shouted. 'Go!' He charged toward Ryker who spun and raced for the back of the yacht.

Shouting came from the approaching boat. Then a cacophony of gunfire. Bullets zinged and clanked all over. Ryker hunkered and then dove for cover on the back deck as Brock opened fire with the rifle.

'Ryker, take this!' Brock shouted, careening around the corner and tossing a handgun toward him.

Ryker caught the gun, checked it over.

Brock continued to exchange fire with the dinghy which was all of ten yards away now. Ryker peeked out, gun at the ready, then pulled back for cover again when a bullet lodged in the metalwork right by him.

Then silence. Except for the lapping water at the side of the yacht, and the whir of the dinghy's engine. Only a whir now, not a roar. Idling.

'Brock,' Ryker said.

'I'm... good.' Brock came around the corner and slumped down next to Ryker, clasping his upper left arm.

'You're hit?' Ryker said.

'I'll be fine. Karaman?'

'Shit,' Ryker said.

He jumped up just as the now driverless dinghy nudged against the side of the yacht. It was carnage on there. Four men. Three were riddled with bullet holes and likely dead. Karaman lay slumped at the back, tuxedo on, breathing heavily as a dark patch widened on his white shirt.

'Told you I was a good shot.'

'You fucking idiot!' Ryker shouted a moment before he jumped over the edge onto the dinghy.

Yep, the three others on the boat were definitely dead. But Karaman...

Ryker rushed over to him, crouching down.

'Let me see.'

He pulled Karaman's limp hands out of the way, lifted his shirt. The bullet had gone into his side more than into his gut. Good news.

'We should just finish him off, the terrorist scumbag,' Brock said. Yeah, Karaman was a terrorist scumbag. But Ryker wondered exactly how much this guy knew of their target because he was sure Winter would have kept things brief, and Ryker certainly hadn't talked to Brock about it.

He turned and glared as Brock stood on the edge of the yacht, rifle at the ready.

'You kill him, I kill you,' Ryker said.

'You haven't got it in you,' Brock said. 'From what I've seen you haven't got anything at all. I've just taken out six men while you sat cowering.'

'Because this wasn't a mission to take *anyone* out! It's an extraction. Simple as that.'

'No. You're just a coward.'

Ryker jumped up and strode over and hopped back onto the yacht and went straight for Brock. The big guy looked undecided, as though he couldn't tell if Ryker really was about to attack him. Until the last moment when Brock brought the rifle barrel up.

Too late. Ryker grabbed the barrel and swiped Brock's left foot from the floor. He took hold of Brock's injured arm and with the man already off balance, twisted the limb around, forcing Brock down as he tried to avoid a broken bone. With Brock's arm pushed to bursting point, Ryker held his gun next to Brock's half-ear and pulled the trigger.

Brock screamed from the deafening sound so close to him. At least until Ryker sank down and dug his knee into his neck, all but cutting off his air.

Ryker twisted on the arm a little more and Brock grimaced and groaned in pain as blood dribbled from the inside of his ear.

'Have I proven myself to you?' Ryker asked.

Brock said nothing. He couldn't, really, with Ryker's weight pressing down on his throat.

'I asked you a question.'

Brock still didn't attempt an answer but bucked a little as though he still thought he could fight Ryker off him.

'An A-OK with your good hand will do,' Ryker said. 'Then I get off you.'

Brock hesitated then reluctantly lifted his hand and gave the signal.

Ryker let go and climbed off him.

'I said no one needed to die,' Ryker said.

'They shot first,' Brock croaked before coughing.

'Whether that's true or not, if you don't follow my orders again, I'll tear your throat out next time. Got it?'

Brock glared. He glanced from Ryker to the rifle on the yacht's deck, as though weighing up if he could get to it and fire at Ryker.

'And if you get the stupid idea to sucker punch me, now or at any point... A whole world of shit will come your way whether you succeed or not. Just do your job, get your money. We won't ever see each other again after tonight. Yeah?'

'Yeah,' Brock said.

'Now help me get Karaman on board. It's time to get out of here.'

9

Ryker and Brock hadn't spoken since they'd departed Karaman's yacht. They'd made a hasty exit, Ryker more concerned than Brock about the gunshots which they had to expect had been heard on shore. No time to even consider what to do with the six dead bodies, their only focus on readying the bowrider attached to the yacht. A decent runabout boat with a powerful engine that propelled them at speed away from Dubai, to the south and east toward their destination.

No flashing lights had chased them out across the Gulf, and now they were in international waters the threat of an immediate response from the authorities in Dubai was highly unlikely. They weren't safe yet, but they'd gotten their man and they'd gotten away, even if the extraction had gone far from how Ryker had intended. Because of Brock Van Der Bloody Vehn.

Ryker captained the small vessel, still stewing over what had just taken place while Brock tended to the wound on his shoulder, stitching the large gash one-handed. A not-so-simple task, and a painful one, but Brock performed the procedure unflinchingly.

Clearly not his first time. Not that Ryker was impressed with the guy's toughness.

Karaman meanwhile remained awake but fatigued and he hadn't said a word. He still clutched at the wound on his side. He wasn't losing too much blood, but they needed to do something about it before long.

'When you're finished you need to take a look at him,' Ryker shouted at Brock who he knew was now having trouble hearing since Ryker's gunshot next to his ear. A burst ear drum? Possibly. 'The bullet's still in there.'

'Oh, don't you worry,' Brock shouted back. 'I'm looking forward to *helping* him.'

Brock snipped the end of the thread from the stitches, stood up, his wet suit hanging around his waist showing off his heavily muscled body, lined with scars, some pretty horrific-looking. Ryker had plenty just like them. Not just battle scars. At some point in time, Brock had suffered badly, inhumanely.

'I know you don't like me,' Brock said. 'But I'm not in this to make friends.'

Brock slipped the wet suit off fully and went to his bag for his change of clothes. Ryker had done the same earlier.

'And I know what you're thinking,' Brock continued. 'I saw the mess on your body earlier. You and me... We're more alike than you want to believe. We've seen shit, been through it. We've come out the other side but no doubt what we've been through... It's changed us. There's nothing *normal* about either of us. We're outcasts. Soulless outcasts. The only difference? You still see yourself as a good guy. But I figured a long, long time ago that there's no such thing as good and bad. Just winners and losers. I don't lose.'

'You're wrong,' Ryker said.

'About which part?' Brock said with his now grating laugh.

'There is good and bad. I'm sure you know that, really. The only difference is you've convinced yourself otherwise to justify the things you've done, the things you still do.'

Brock seemed to consider that, looking off into the distance for a few moments.

'You're telling me you never did anything bad?' he said. 'Anything morally questionable?'

'The problem is, everyone has a different line as to what's morally questionable,' Ryker replied.

'My point exactly. You think I'm bad. But I'm betting a hell of a lot of people would think the same about you, right?'

Ryker had to accept that. 'Right.'

'So how do *you* justify what you've done? The people you've hurt and killed?'

'Whatever I've done has always been... necessary.'

Ryker cringed at his own lack of eloquence and Brock gave an even more hearty laugh than before. 'Yeah, you really are full of shit, aren't you? Like I said, I reckon we're more alike than you want to admit.'

Ryker had nothing more to say about the subject, but Brock had gotten under his skin.

'Now it's time for you,' Brock said with a sneer as he stared down at Karaman who suddenly looked more alert, more fearful, now that Brock's attention was on him. Brock crouched down by him. 'Show me.'

Karaman didn't move.

'You want me to let you bleed out?'

Karaman said nothing but slowly pulled his bloodied hands away from his side. Brock lifted the soaked dress shirt and jostled Karaman back and forth, inspecting him forcibly before he whistled. 'Yep, the bullet's still in there, alright. So why don't we get it out?'

Brock reached forward and dug his fingers into the open wound and Karaman bucked and panted and grimaced but didn't scream.

Ryker didn't respond at all, even as Brock stared over at him as his fingers rummaged inside Karaman, clearly hoping for a reaction.

'Too far in,' Brock shouted at Ryker, pulling his blood-dripping fingers out. 'So let's try this instead.'

He grabbed his knife and Ryker looked away as Karaman's anguish intensified... and then subsided to little more than murmurs as he drifted from the pain.

Ryker flinched when something hit the back of his head and he turned to see the pellet rattle along the deck.

'Got it,' Brock said, wide grin on his face. Karaman was slumped now, eyes glazed. 'Time to close that wound up.'

Brock grabbed a flare and set it alight, and Karaman immediately became more alert. He pleaded and begged and then he screamed – he really screamed – as Brock thrust the red-hot end onto his skin. Blood fizzled, skin bubbled, and Ryker gripped the wheel of the bowrider a little more tightly to try to channel his feelings and not outwardly react. Brock took the flare away then leaned over the side and held the flame under the water until it was extinguished.

'And now it's sealed.'

Karaman murmured under his breath, his words incoherent.

'You don't like me hurting him?' Brock asked Ryker. 'Except I know what you have planned for this guy. Oman? Tell me, what's in Oman?'

Ryker didn't answer.

'I'm not as dumb as you think I am. This guy... I know what he did. And I know he's wanted in nearly every Western country. But you've no intention of sending him back to stand trial in a court-room, have you? Not in England, not anywhere else.'

Ryker still kept his mouth shut.

'So what's in Oman? My guess, a safe house at the least. Most likely, though, you've pulled some favors with your intelligence grunts and we're heading to a black site. Some dungeon off the grid where you can interrogate this guy without anyone seeing, hearing. Tell me I'm wrong.'

Ryker held his tongue.

'Tell me I'm fucking wrong you hypocritical piece of shit!' Brock yelled, so loud Ryker felt the force of the bark on his cheek.

'You're not wrong,' Ryker said. 'This man has information that I need. Information that could help save lives, help bring down some of the most corrupt people in the world.'

Brock whistled again. 'No shit?'

'And I'm prepared to go to lengths to get what I need from him.'

'See what I mean?'

'The difference is, I won't get any enjoyment out of making him talk. I'm not about to torture him for my own pleasure. I never have done that, I never will.'

'You're a liar. I'm betting at least once in your life you made someone suffer just because you could. And it brought you satisfaction.'

'You know what—'

'Wait a fucking minute,' Brock said, grinning widely as he dug his hand into the storage compartment next to Karaman. Ryker was glad for the distraction even if he didn't like the pleased look on Brock's face. 'What have we here?'

He pulled out a small bound book. Ryker noted the twinkle of the gold embossing on the front. He knew what the book was even before Brock had confirmed it.

'Shit, does this freak have one of these everywhere he goes?'

Karaman, previously looking on the edge of unconsciousness, found a renewed focus, hatred in his eyes as he glared at Brock.

'This is what it comes down to,' Brock said. 'All the people that die because of scumbags like this? Religion. Quran. Bible. Whatever. All religions are fucking nuts. They turn normal people into crazed psychopaths. You know the only good use for this thing?' He held the Quran aloft. No one answered his question. 'This.' He swiped the book down, catching Karaman on the side of his face with an almighty *thunk*.

'Leave him,' Ryker said.

'Or what?'

'Or he's too injured to talk to me. Then you don't get paid.'

'I get paid for the extraction.'

'Extracting him in good condition. Not dead or dying.'

Brock scoffed, grabbing Karaman by the chin, checking his cheek. 'I only hit him once.'

'And that's the only time you will.'

Brock's face twisted with distaste. 'Whatever, but this thing is poison. Religion of peace? My stinking ass. What about the heads you chopped off, Ismail?'

No response from Karaman.

'I don't think those guys found that too peaceful, do you?'

He slapped Karaman with the book again.

'Scum like him don't even want peace. Not really. They never have and they never will. Their goal is to wipe out everyone else, and violent means are the only way they can do it.'

'OK, you've made your point,' Ryker said.

'You know what? I don't think I have. The hatred they have for anyone not conforming is other level. Tell me, would you feel safe walking around *any* Muslim country wearing a kippah? Or with a cross around your neck, holding a Bible? They'd burn you in the street.'

'And would you feel safe walking around a South African city wearing a thawb? It works both ways.'

'No. It's not the same. It's—'

'You can shut up now,' Ryker said with enough conviction to cause Brock to pause. 'We're nearly there.'

He nodded to the shore, to the small docking area a few hundred yards away where a single orange lamp lazily lit the area. No real indication of what lay beyond that, just one small rowing boat moored up.

'That's it?' Brock said, sounding surprised.

'Bit different to Dubai.'

'Where'm I supposed to go from here?'

Far, far away would be Ryker's preference.

'Wherever the hell you like. The boat's yours. Muscat's fifty miles or so.'

Ryker slowed the boat, keeping his eyes busy across the shoreline. The area behind the dock was pitch black although Ryker knew there was nothing there, no buildings within a quarter of a mile. What he would find – at least, he hoped Winter had provided – was a car. A car for him and Karaman.

'Help me tie us up,' Ryker said, tossing the rope to Brock.

The big guy stepped off the boat onto the wooden dock. He was crouched down, rope in hand when four big spotlights blared.

Ryker froze, Brock froze. Shouting erupted everywhere and for several seconds Ryker could see nothing but the glare of the lights. As his eyes adjusted the figures came into view. Ten, fifteen, twenty uniformed police, guns held out, crowded by their cars along the edge of the dock.

'I'm guessing this isn't your plan,' Brock said, sounding pretty damn calm as he straightened up, the police to his right, Ryker to his left as if wanting everyone in his sight.

'No, it's not,' Ryker said.

The shouted instructions continued. *Drop your weapons. Hands up. Off the boat.* Two police officers edged forward onto the dock, crouched down with rifles pulled up to their faces.

'You loaded?' Brock said under his breath.

Ryker still had the handgun Brock had thrown to him earlier in his waistband. Plus a rifle lay on the deck a few feet from him. And Brock was armed too. From his position, Ryker could see the butt of the handgun sticking out of the back of the guy's jeans.

'Yeah,' Ryker said.

Brock turned his head to Ryker, as though looking for further confirmation of what to do next.

Ryker really didn't want to fight here. If these people wanted to shoot, they already would have, so he'd rather see how this played out. Ryker's biggest problem was that he knew Brock only knew one way: Fight. To the death, if necessary.

Ryker wasn't dying because of this guy.

'Are we doing this?' Brock whispered.

Ryker's hand barely twitched. Brock took that as confirmation.

'I never lose,' Brock said, grin rising.

The next moment he whipped the gun from his jeans as he spun and stooped down.

Ryker ducked too and made a move for his weapon. But only to toss it overboard. Brock managed to fire off two rounds before the police returned fire. And they didn't hold back. A volley of bullets burst free, flashes of fire lighting up the area as Brock's body jolted, hit after hit. He stumbled back, the gun still in his grip but not enough life left in him to fire it...

Brock collapsed backward into the water, dead.

Ryker stood up, hands aloft as police rushed forward.

'It's OK!' Ryker shouted. 'It's OK. Please, don't shoot.'

And they didn't. Ryker briefly glanced at Brock's body, partially submerged now, no real feeling for the dead man.

A much bigger problem – for him – was still to come, because the police turning up was not part of the plan.

Moments later the police had Ryker in cuffs and they dragged him along the dock to their waiting vehicles.

10

CUMBRIA, ENGLAND

Two hundred forty-eight. Two hundred forty-nine... Two fifty.

Angel dropped her knees to the floor. She sank her head down toward her chest as she got her breathing back under control and allowed her muscles to recover.

'Not bad,' Andre said from the bed.

She hadn't realized he was awake. She'd been trying not to make *too* much noise. Not as much noise as last night, that was for sure.

She rolled over, sitting up on the carpet. Andre was perched on the edge of the bed, head tilted toward his shoulder as he stared down at her looking pleased with himself.

'Just a starter for the day.'

Andre whistled. 'A starter? How many was that? A couple hundred?'

'Two fifty.'

'Shit.'

'I can do a lot more. I'm saving my energy for something else.' She winked at him as she got to her feet and enjoyed his eyes wandering over her body as she stood in nothing but her underwear.

'It definitely explains that body,' he said.

'I don't do it to impress men. Or anyone else.'

He shrugged. 'Still... What's your record?'

She didn't answer straight away. Something about the tone of his voice sounded off. Like he was almost mocking her.

'What's yours?' she asked.

'Me?' He shook his head. 'Not my thing. Fifty, a hundred maybe.'

'You look in good shape to me.'

He returned that compliment with a broad smile. He certainly liked his ego being stroked.

'Maybe it's just good genetics,' he said. 'And a lot of time in the gym when I was younger.'

Not a great explanation really for someone who was as lean and muscular as a professional fighter.

'So?' he said. 'What's your record?'

'In one go? Five hundred and eighty-three. In a day? Two thousand seven hundred and one. The one nearly killed me, no kidding.'

Andre nodded in some sort of appreciation.

'But I couldn't get out of bed for two days after that. And it wasn't because of the drink.'

'See, that's the thing though,' Andre said as Angel mopped at her brow with a hand towel and then went and sat on the bed by Andre's feet.

'What is?'

'This fitness regime. You always had it, or was it... You know?'

'Did I pick it up in prison, you mean? When I was stuck in a cell for way too many hours every day?'

He looked so sheepish about mentioning prison. Embarrassed. But she wasn't at all.

'Yeah,' he said.

'Kind of. I joined the army when I was eighteen. One of the reasons was that I loved the idea of boot camps and the drills I'd seen in movies. But... Yeah, the routine began in prison. In Lebanon. There was no yard there. No anything apart from twenty-four hours a day of hell. Exercise gave me one way to feel something, one thing I could control. I guess it became... an obsession.'

That wasn't the word she'd been searching for, but it probably explained how she couldn't not put herself through physical pain every day. Or was addiction a better description?

'I don't even... How did that...'

'What?' she questioned.

'I'm not trying to offend you, but... If you were drinking... High on meds, whatever, how the hell did you—'

'Exercise was my way of coping. Of convincing myself that even if my mind was messed up, I wasn't entirely destroying my body. If I could get to oblivion on opium, or drink a bottle of vodka and still wake up the next day and push my body to the very limit... It... just made sense. To me. At the time.'

'But...'

'I'm not saying I didn't suffer. But maybe that's why I did it. So yeah, I hated it. I got stomach cramps like you wouldn't believe. Migraines. I'd puke up my guts midway through push-ups and just carry on with the vomit right underneath me. A kind of spur for me to keep on going.'

'OK, now that's too much information,' he said, overly jovially. There was nothing jovial about putting herself back there. He seemed to get that because a moment later his face turned somber and he shuffled closer to her and put his hand on her arm.

'I've never met anyone as... intense as you.'

She said nothing.

'You've been through hell and—'

'I need a shower.' She stood up from the bed. He looked like he wanted to say something else, to keep the conversation going but she was done with it. She took off her bra and pulled her panties down and straightened up, hands on hips. 'You coming?'

Andre couldn't have bounced up from the bed any quicker.

* * *

Angel pulled on some jeans and a thick roll-neck sweater while Andre stood by the window in his boxers, checking his phone.

'What are your plans for the day?' he said, turning to her and looking pensive about something.

She shrugged.

'I've got... a few things I need to sort,' he said. 'But we could meet up later.'

'Maybe.'

'Maybe?'

He moved toward her, took her hands as he looked down on her. He'd said earlier when they'd chatted that he was six foot three but like most men, he'd added at least an inch to that, but still he was several inches taller than her and she reached up on tiptoes to peck his lips.

'It's still early,' she said. 'And I have some questions for you before you go.'

He raised an eyebrow.

'I talked a lot about me last night. This morning. Now it's your turn.'

'I—'

She spun him around and shoved him and he fell back onto the bed, bouncing a little awkwardly as the expression on his face switched from smiley to perplexed and back.

'I'll make us a coffee.'

Which gave him a few minutes to stew at least while she made the drinks from the kettle in the corner and the cheap packets of freeze-dried coffee the retreat provided. They spent the time in silence, him back on his phone again. She took the two steaming mugs over and sat on the edge of the bed with him. He'd at least put on his clothes in the meantime, though once again he had his phone out, typing away.

'Business?' she asked.

'Yeah.'

'What do you do?'

'I'm... a consultant. It's... really boring.' He put his phone and coffee down then turned and looked at her. 'Right. Go on then, fire away.'

'I mean... I didn't actually mean for it to be an interrogation.'

He laughed. 'Sorry. But what do you want to know?'

She could start with something mundane. How he met his wife. The names of his kids. But what was the point?

'Why'd you start drinking?' she asked.

'*Start* drinking. I started drinking when I was fourteen. Like most teenagers. A few cans here and there whenever we could get hold of them.'

'That's not what I meant.'

'When did it get out of control?'

'Yeah.'

'When I lost my job. Then my parents died, close together. It was just... I didn't mean for it to go so far. It kind of just got worse and worse.'

'Until your wife left you.'

'She didn't leave me. She kicked me out.'

'Why? Did you get violent with her?'

He didn't like that question. She could tell by the throbbing vein at the side of his head and the tension spreading through his body. He was doing his best to hide it, but he was working damn hard.

'No,' he said.

'Then why'd she kick you out? You were a functioning alcoholic?'

'That's such a bullshit term.'

'Is it? You're either an alcoholic who drinks from compulsion yet still keeps their job going, their marriage going, even as they're destroying their body through their addiction. A functioning alcoholic. You do get them. Or you're an alcoholic whose entire life is destroyed because of the drink. Because of how they lose control, wreck their careers, wreck relationships because the booze makes them crazy, angry, violent.'

He reached forward to take her hand. She whipped it away but only then did she realize she was shaking. Anger, bubbling up as she fought off thoughts of her own demons, her own destructive behavior.

'There must have been a trigger for you to come here,' she said. 'A life-changing trigger. So what was it?'

'This is a lot.' He stood up from the bed. 'Angel, last night... This morning, it was great. We can do it again. But... maybe it doesn't need to get so heavy.'

He looked down at her, as though he expected a response, but she said nothing. He made his way to the door. Paused there. Sighed. What was he doing?

She could just let him go... or...

She bent forward, reached under the bed. Grabbed the knife. Not one of the shitty little ones they provided in the rooms, which were about good enough for buttering bread but not for actually cutting anything. Not one of those knives, but her own. The one she'd brought with her. A companion, of sorts. An ultra-sharp, ultra-sturdy hunting knife.

She jumped to her feet and, knife at the ready, rushed toward him.

11

He had his fingers wrapped around the door handle as she raced forward. He took a half step back to give himself space to open it as she quickly – almost silently – closed the distance. The handle turned. She was two steps away. She pulled the knife back, close to her side, ready to unleash with an upward jab toward his back. The knife would puncture through skin, flesh, bone, through his lung. A nasty blow. Fatal? Possibly. If not that one, then the second certainly would be.

But the first indication that her plan was awry was when she noticed his fingers slip from the handle. Her arm was already in motion at that point, the tip of the knife accelerating forward. She roared with determination, her intent the same as before, too late now to switch tactic...

He ducked and jumped aside as he spun around and she tried to adjust the knife's trajectory but couldn't do so enough and the blade glided through the air and sank into the door. Wedged deep. She went to yank it out but saw his counter move coming. He'd try to take hold of her outstretched arm, twist it, break it. So she let go of the knife's handle and stepped back into a defensive pose and blocked his flying fist then countered with a kick to his back as she circled around him and swiped his back leg. Then she grabbed him around the throat and pulled back to haul him to the floor.

She wrapped her legs around him, pulled the choke hold as tight as she could but he bucked and writhed and threw elbows at her and he was just too strong. He swiveled to pull himself – and her – onto his front. Angel dragged her body back, pulling his neck up, his face nearly pointed to the ceiling such was the crazy angle of his head to his body. She roared again with effort, envisaging tearing his damn head right off as he spluttered and clawed at her.

Then he found something. Desperation. A second level of fight. He dragged himself to his feet and charged forward with her still clinging to his back like a koala, still with her arms wrapped around his neck like a boa. Swiveling in the air, he propelled Angel hard against the wall. Her right shoulder took most of the force and she yelled out in pain and could do nothing about her arms coming free from him. He grabbed her wrist, twisted her arm around as he bent forward and sent her tumbling over him and into a heap on the floor. She screamed in pain as fire erupted in her shoulder – was it dislocated?

But it wouldn't stop her. She leaped up as he came for her again. She blocked a fist, a kick. She returned with a punch to his kidney, another to his chest which had him momentarily fighting for breath. He went to take hold of her again but she spun away from him, back for the door.

She grabbed the knife, pulled it free, swung it, saw his block coming. So she tossed the knife to her other hand, sent a knee up into his groin, then a push kick to his chest to send him up against the wall. She pinned him there with her left forearm as she pulled the serrated edge of the blade up against his neck.

Pause.

Sweat covered both of their faces. Both of them breathed heavily, chests rising and falling nearly in unison.

'You're gonna kill me?' Andre asked.

Angel didn't answer. Andre moved his weight forward, pushing his neck onto the blade as though testing her. She didn't budge and blood trickled out onto the blade and wormed toward the far edge.

'When did you know?' he asked.

'From the moment you first looked at me.'

He scoffed. Doing so caused the knife to dig a little deeper and this time she did pull it back, ever so slightly, and inwardly chastised herself for doing so.

No weakness, she told herself.

'What gave me away?'

'Everything about you, Andre. You're not an alcoholic. Probably never even had one too many at a party.'

He actually laughed at that, as though he found the situation amusing.

'Was it my six-pack that gave it away?'

Shit, was he really that vain?

'No. It was every one of your cringey answers. Like you'd learned about the disease from a kid's textbook. And you'd tried to cook up as many similarities to me as you could. You're not even married, are you?'

'No.'

'I can tell the ring's a prop,' she said. 'Too clean for a man who's been married for... What was it? Fourteen years? And there's no mark on your finger underneath. I checked while you were doing you know what to me last night.'

He kind of shrugged.

'You still let me fuck you?' he said.

'You thought that was for your benefit? How about, I got what I wanted from you? You were desperate for me. I saw it.'

'You're crazier than I was told.'

She dug her forearm further into his chest, pinning him closer to the wall, renewed the knife's position, the original small gash zig-zagging underneath the blade.

'Who are you?' she asked.

'Take the knife away and I'll tell you.'

Instead, she pushed the blade closer to him and a second line opened up along his skin and he squirmed as though only now doubting she had it in her.

'Five seconds, Andre. Fuck. Is that even your name?'

'No.'

'What is your name?'

'Mason. Mason Black.'

'That true?'

'Yes.'

'Who do you work for?'

'I told you. Take the knife—'

'And I said five seconds. And this time I'm counting. Five... Four... Three... Two...'

'OK, OK. I'm here because—'

She had no clue how he even did it. The move was impossible. The knife was so tight up against his throat. Still, he managed to find, not strike, just find a spot on her side where a cluster of nerves was located. As sudden as turning on a light, a surge of agony swept into her lower back, down her legs. It unbalanced her, sent her torso back only a few inches even though her feet remained planted. He turned his head and ducked under the knife and took hold of her wrist and turned it inside out. He hammered a fist down onto her already raw shoulder and swiveled her around as he took the knife from her grip. He swiped her feet from the floor and followed her down to the carpet where she smacked onto her back with a painful thud before he dropped down onto her chest, pinning her arms.

She cried out, eyes bulging as the knife flew toward her face...

Then just like that it stopped. Absolute precision. She dared not move but the tip of the blade was so close it felt like it had already moved beyond the edge of her pupil. Maybe it had, just a millimeter or two literally inside her eyeball.

'So what now?' Andre— No, Mason asked, sounding as calm as anything.

'Would you believe me if I said I'm sorry?' Angel said, not sounding anywhere near as cocky or confident as she'd wanted.

'Do we have a problem?' he asked.

'So many fucking problems, Mason.'

'I didn't come here to kill you,' he said. 'That should be obvious.'

'Then why?'

'To assess you. To see if you have it in you still.'

'*It?*'

'Ability. Fire. Hatred.'

Damn, she had so much fire and hatred. Ability? That depended.

'Who do you work for?' she asked.

'I'm asking the questions,' he said. 'I'll say it again. I didn't come here to kill you. So if I pull this knife away and toss it... This fight is over. Got it?'

She hesitated but then said, 'Got it.'

He did what he said he'd do but remained in place on top of her and even though she really, really wanted to throw him off and have another go at slitting his throat open... she didn't.

'Come on, then,' she said, sounding more sure of herself now that she didn't have a knife about to slice into her brain. 'Tell me why you're here.'

He didn't answer.

'I passed your damn test, didn't I? Why are you here?'

'To offer you a chance at redemption.'

'I'm too far gone for redemption.'

'OK, so I'll put it more bluntly. I'm offering you a chance for revenge.'

'Against who?'

'The man who destroyed your life.'

'You want me to kill my ex-husband? Shit, Mason, he's really not that important that some spook needs to come all this way—'

'No, Angel, not Paul,' he said, sounding a little frustrated. 'Think more big picture.'

She thought she knew what that meant, but she wouldn't say it even if she couldn't figure out why.

'Who?' she asked.

'I already said, the man who destroyed your life.' Mason broke into a wide smile. 'Ismail Karaman.'

12

UNKNOWN LOCATION, OMAN

He'd been held in rooms like this before. A hefty metal door, no windows, four walls of pockmarked concrete. The same aging material for the floor and the ceiling above which had a single old-fashioned light bulb that produced next to no light. And which was only turned on at sporadic intervals anyway – when Ryker was brought food or the guards came to let him relieve himself in a bashed-up metal pot.

The rest of the time he spent tied to the bolted-down chair. Hours and hours. More than a day. Perhaps two or three, he thought, although it was hard to tell with the monotony.

Plenty of time to think, to contemplate.

After his 'arrest,' the police had driven him for nearly two hours – blindfolded – until they'd arrived here. He'd remained blind-folded on the walk to this room. Down. They'd headed down, a couple of stories, the temperature of the desert outside dropping as they descended. The air down here was cool and stale. He didn't think they were by the coast anymore. Were they even still in Oman? He thought so, but couldn't know for sure.

He did wonder, a little cynically, whether this place was in fact the same location that he'd intended to take Karaman to. An old World War II bunker built and used by the British army as part of its defense of trade routes around the Gulf. Since that war, since Oman had been granted its independence, since the British army had formally left the area, the site had seen further use on a more clandestine level. A black site, as such places had become known. Most of those sites had been 'officially' closed down not long after their widespread use had first come to the attention of the international press. Yet this site remained intact, though unoccupied.

Or it *had* been unoccupied. The surroundings here certainly suggested it could be the same place. Certainly, a slap in the face for Ryker if it was.

He heard movement outside the door. The locks of the door releasing. Too soon for more food, too soon for the bedpan. Either he was being moved, or he had a visitor.

The door opened and Ryker spotted the two guards first. Not faces he'd seen before, but much like the other men he'd seen here, dressed in fatigues bearing the emblem of the Royal Army of Oman. Not police uniforms like the people who'd ambushed Ryker at the port.

The two grunts came into the room, assault rifles hanging lazily in their grips. They stood on either side of the open door where Ryker stared, sensing the men weren't alone.

The woman who appeared next didn't look like the grunts at all. No uniform for her. Just casual khaki trousers, a woolen sweater, and a tightly tied headscarf that framed her serious face.

Fatma Yaman.

'The Middle East expert,' Ryker said. 'Fancy seeing you here.'

She remained hovering in the doorway as a third guard rushed in with a foldout metal chair which he placed a few feet in front of Ryker before rushing out again. Yaman turned to the two guards and muttered something to them and they disappeared too, closing and locking the door behind them.

'Well, isn't this cozy,' Ryker said as Yaman took the seat in front of him.

'You can try and be cute with me, but I hope you realize just how much shit you're in.' It was the first time he'd heard her speak and her voice sounded exactly as he'd expected, Queen's English and all. Obviously, given her privileged upbringing and her prestigious education at Eton and then Cambridge.

'Perhaps you could tell me,' Ryker said.

'I do know what you did.'

'OK?'

She stared at him, her lips pursed, as though she thought he'd get the sudden need to explain himself that way.

'You broke into my home,' she said, her voice quavering as though the break-in had taken a toll on her. Ryker said nothing. 'You invaded my private life, the life of my family.'

Ryker still held his tongue.

'What gives you the right to do that?' she said with real disdain in her voice, her eyes pinched. 'To think you're above laws and rules of common decency.'

'Decency? You live in a world of lies and you're trying to tell me about decency?'

'You have no idea about me, my life.'

'I thought we established I probably do. Given I broke into your home and stole all of your secrets.'

'Secrets?' she said, shaking her head. 'Ryker, you are so off the mark. Your head, widened by your macho ego, somehow still rammed right up your ass.'

He smiled at that, at the matter-of-fact way she delivered the insult. She didn't seem to appreciate the reaction much.

'Tell me the truth, then,' he said. 'You knew exactly where

Ismail Karaman was. One of the most wanted terrorists in the world. You've been tracking his movements for years without ever making any attempt to capture him, kill him, bring him to justice, anything.'

Yaman didn't respond to that although Ryker hadn't exactly asked a question.

'And I've been in this game—'

'Game?' Yaman interjected, leaning forward in her chair, her look of disdain now even more scathing. 'That's your problem, Ryker. You really see this all as a game, don't you?'

'You have no idea.'

'I really think I do. You're an unhinged agitator. One who thinks because he was once a government asset, doing dirty work that saw him circumvent laws, kill people, in the name of his country, that he can still do whatever the hell he wants, when he wants, regardless of consequences, regardless of the destruction he leaves in his wake.'

'Come on, then,' Ryker said. 'Tell me. Tell me the logical, sound explanation for why you've been tracking Karaman but have done absolutely nothing with that intel.'

'I don't have to justify myself to you.'

'Why not? Because you can't, you mean? Not without exposing who you really are.'

'And who is that?'

Ryker chewed on that thought for a few moments. 'There aren't many reasons why you'd sit on that information. Why you'd let a monstrous terrorist not just live a free life, but one of privilege too.'

'Enlighten me.'

'Karaman works for the Syndicate. You're protecting him. Perhaps you work for them too. Or perhaps you were simply given a kickback to turn a blind eye. Plenty of people are easily corruptible for a bit of money. Or perhaps it's the people above you who are corrupt, and you're just toeing the line because you like your job.'

'You really think the only explanation is the "Syndicate"? An organization for which you don't even have any tangible evidence of its existence?'

'I see plenty of evidence.'

'You see a set of circumstances that fit your narrative. It's not the same thing. It's a conspiracy theory.'

'You're telling me the Syndicate isn't real?'

'I'm telling you you've waded into something that has nothing to do with you. And you've potentially caused a big problem in doing so, and I don't just mean a big problem for me. Ryker, taking your horribly inflated opinion of yourself out of the picture, can't you see the tightrope that is cross-border relations across this part of the world? Not just the countries here, with each other, but their relationships with the West?'

'So *that's* your explanation?' Ryker said. 'You were protecting Karaman so the UK government didn't fall out with the royal families over here who provide our good isle with all of that lovely black gold?'

Yaman tutted like a fed-up adult would with a headstrong kid. 'This isn't about oil. Please, just... I'm done talking about the whys. The fact is, you messed up. And now, your freedom, your life, is... in my hands.'

Ryker really didn't like how she said that last part but he didn't bite back.

'Does Peter Winter know I'm here?' Ryker said.

'Ah, yes, of course. Peter Winter. So you're confirming to me that he helped you set up this bloody rampage.'

'No. That's not what I said at all. What I asked was whether he knows I'm here.'

'You think he can rescue you?'

'I know he holds more political sway than you.'

'Sorry to disappoint you, Ryker, but—'

'I want to speak to him.'

'You don't get to make demands here.'

'If you care about your career at all, you'll let me speak to him.'

Yaman sighed and sat back in her chair. 'I'm feeling like you're really not understanding the gravity of your situation here.'

'I understand it just fine. You're a bogus intelligence agent who thinks she has more power than she really does. I don't know how you found out about my plans, but you've so far involved the Omani police force, the Omani army. If you really operated anywhere near my world, you'd realize that doing that has taken away so much of your upper hand already. Your hands are tied even more so than mine right now.'

'You think? There are six dead bodies floating in the Persian Gulf that suggest you might be a little more screwed than I am.'

'I didn't kill anyone.'

'Very convincing. Tell me about Brock Van Der Vehn, then. How did you meet him?'

Ryker thought about that for a moment. She knew Brock's identity. Did that mean she'd known the South African was helping Ryker even before the mission, or had they only identified him after filling him with bullets at the harbor?

'Me and Brock went way back,' Ryker said.

'Is that so?'

'It is. Given you seem to know so much about me, you probably realize I've met plenty of mercenaries like him.'

'So Peter Winter didn't introduce you to him?'

'No. He didn't.'

'Because that would be a really bad career move for your good friend, wouldn't you say? Putting together an ex-spy with a roughneck, bloodthirsty mercenary for an unsanctioned kidnapping plot on foreign soil that led to six civilians being shot dead.'

When she said it like that... Yeah, Winter was in the shit. If this woman had anything like the power that she obviously thought she had, she could ruin Winter.

'I need to speak to Winter,' Ryker said.

Yaman's face brightened, the first time he'd seen anything like a smile on her and it really didn't suit her at all. At least her sullenness carried a certain sincerity to it.

'Yeah, you *need* to speak to him. But you can't.'

Ryker humphed, trying to think of where to go next. He hated the satisfied look Yaman now had plastered on her face.

'So what's your plan?' he said. 'I have no useful information to give you, so you're not going to torture me.'

She shook her head. 'You're so basic, aren't you? Torture? Why would you even go there?'

'Tell me what then? Why am I here?'

She didn't answer. Which kind of made Ryker think she didn't know. She was waiting. On confirmation from her higher-ups as to which bus they wanted to throw Ryker under.

'Where's Karaman now?' Ryker asked. 'Have you set him free?'

She didn't answer again, though looked more satisfied by the minute.

'Look, I'll give you one last chance. Let me speak to Winter. You do that and I might forgive you for locking me up in here.'

Another head shake. 'Wow,' was all she said.

'Pretty please?' Ryker asked.

She stood up from her chair.

'I'll be back soon.'

'Once your boss has told you what to do with me? Do you get to make any decisions yourself or are you just a puppet? An empty vessel.'

She really didn't like that and glared down at him.

'You've still got a chance to do the decent thing here,' Ryker said. 'Let me speak to Winter.'

'No,' she said. Then she turned away from him.

Then Ryker sprang up from his chair. Yaman spun to face him, her mouth wide open in shock. Clearly, she'd had no clue Ryker had been steadily working on the handcuff lock with a splinter of wood he'd stashed in his underwear at the dock. She really should have paid more attention. Had someone else in the room with him. Or just realized who – and what – he was, given she claimed to know so much.

'No!' she shouted as she cowered back. The door swung open with force. Two guards there, rifles at the ready, but Yaman stood between the men and their target.

To start with, anyway. Ryker grabbed Yaman around the shoulder and hauled her back and she crashed to the floor with a thud. He rushed the closest guard and took hold of the gun barrel to push it away and kicked down against the side of the man's lower leg. *Snap.* He went down screeching, though not before Ryker had pulled the knife from the belt around the guard's waist. He tossed the knife and it spun and sank home into the thigh of the second guard whose rifle barrel swept upward as he pulled the trigger and he roared in surprise and pain.

Ryker flung himself toward him, easily took the gun from his grip, and tossed it. Swiped the guy's legs. Knocked him out with a kick to the head. He took the knife and turned to where the first guard was caught in two minds: Stay down and nurse his snapped leg or try and fight on. A spinning kick to his arm caused his rifle to fly free. Ryker hovered over him at the ready with the knife...

The guard held his hands up in surrender.

Ryker turned and pulled Yaman up from the floor and she

squirmed and moaned only a little before Ryker had her around the neck with one arm, the tip of the knife by her ear.

'You want me to insert this into your head?' he whispered to her.

'N-no!'

Rushing feet outside.

'Then call them off.'

Three more guards skidded into view outside the room, weapons trained but they all paused when they saw the predicament.

'Call them off!' Ryker boomed in Yaman's ear.

'It's OK!' she shouted to them. 'It's OK. Please, lower your weapons.'

The men hesitated but then slowly the barrels swung downward.

'I don't need to hurt anyone else here,' Ryker said, momentarily glancing at the two injured guards. 'So don't make me.'

No one said anything.

'Do you understand?' Ryker shouted, pushing the point of the knife against Yaman's skin. She squealed in terror and the men shuffled on their feet not knowing what to do.

'Yes!' Yaman screamed as if answering for all of them. 'I understand. *We* understand.'

'Good,' Ryker said before relaxing a little and smiling. 'So how about that phone call now?'

13

Yaman recovered remarkably well from her ordeal. Little more than an hour later she looked unfazed, confident, in control as she stood across the room from Ryker, arms folded, glaring in his direction as he hit redial on the desk phone.

A desk phone in a room that kind of looked like an office of sorts, with a few basic chairs and a bookshelf on one wall filled with messy files. The room even had the luxury of an overhead fan to move around the stuffy and stale air, but otherwise, this space wasn't much different from the cell Ryker had left. Bare concrete walls, no windows. At least the wooden door here had a small glass pane although it only looked out onto a dank, gray corridor.

'Ryker, if he's not answering—'

'He'll answer.'

He ended the call. None of the many attempts had gone through to voicemail; they just rang out endlessly. For more than half an hour. After holding Yaman at knifepoint it'd been a slow journey through the warren of corridors to this room. Yaman had remained amazingly calm with the knife at the ready to slice through her. She'd led them to this room as armed soldiers hovered. The whole time Ryker had wondered whether Yaman would simply lead him into a trap, but no. Perhaps she trusted that Ryker wasn't bluffing with his threat of violence, and it was clear however embroiled she was in the clandestine world of spies and dodgy individuals, she wasn't a fighter.

The guards remained on the outside of this room. Ryker could see two of their faces through the small window. Yaman had given them a very clear instruction to wait outside, to not do anything stupid. To not call for backup or try to storm the room.

And so far they'd stayed true to that. At least, as far as Ryker was aware.

But something about Yaman's calm demeanor unsettled him still.

'You don't really have much of a plan, do you?' she said, looking a little too pleased with herself.

'My plan? You and me stay in this room until I speak to Peter Winter.'

'And what if he doesn't answer?'

'I've got nothing better to do. Have you?'

'Actually, I've got *so* many better things to be doing.'

Ryker shrugged. 'There is another option.'

'And that would be? Wait... I let you walk out of here. Is that it?'

'No,' Ryker said. 'That's not what I want.'

Yaman looked a little surprised by that.

'What I want is to speak to Ismail Karaman. Alone. Just me and him.'

Her face screwed up with distaste as though he'd suggested something lurid. 'That's not happening.'

'I don't think you realize the trouble I had to go through in getting him here,' Ryker said. 'I—'

'Trouble? You think *you* suffered? Is that how you're characterizing the murder of six people?'

'You know that's not—'

'All I know is you came here on an entirely unsanctioned mission, to kidnap and most likely torture a man. Even putting aside the dead, you've broken who knows how many laws.'

'Laws? That's almost funny, coming from you.'

'Excuse me?' From the incredulous look on her face, he could tell she didn't like that insinuation one bit.

'You knew I was coming here, didn't you?' he said.

No answer.

'You had the Omani police ready to take me in. Karaman too. You didn't only find out what I was doing in the time it took us to travel from Dubai to here on that boat. You knew all along. But you didn't try to stop us. You could have done. But you didn't. Which raises a lot of additional questions in my mind. Most likely I'm just going to be a scapegoat for something. Collateral damage, potentially, although if that were the case I'm surprised I haven't already had a bullet in my head.'

He waited to see if Yaman had anything to say in response. Apparently not.

'So you asked what my plan is from here? First off, I speak to Winter. Then I get to speak to Karaman. When I'm satisfied I have what I need from him, you can have him and do whatever you want. Put him back on his ridiculously expensive yacht if you like, carry on enabling and protecting him and his cronies.'

'I—'

'Save it. I'm not interested.'

The addition of the hand held up to halt her really got her blood boiling. He smiled as he turned away from her and hit redial once more.

Finally, the call was answered.

'Winter, it's me.'

A slight pause before he answered. 'Are you OK?'

He didn't sound particularly concerned. Which suggested he hadn't heard anything yet about what had happened. So Ryker briefly explained. The snatch. Brock and his trigger-happy approach. The ambush by Yaman and the Omanis. Ryker's current predicament.

'Whoa, Ryker, back up. What are you... Six dead? In Dubai?'

'You sent me a madman,' Ryker said through gritted teeth, trying to contain his anger as much as he could.

'You gave me next to no notice for a wild mission. What did you expect? The nation's finest assets? But Ryker, slow down. Who is dead?'

'Karaman's guards. You're telling me you've heard nothing about this.'

'Nothing at all. And I've been keeping an eye out for news from the Gulf because I didn't know exactly when you were moving.'

'There's been nothing about Karaman?'

'Nothing about any of it. But... Karaman's alive, isn't he?'

'Last time I saw him he was.'

'And you're where now?'

'In a bunker with your good friend from SIS, Fatma Yaman.' Ryker turned to look over at her. Damn, she looked so pleased with herself.

'That scheming little bi—'

'She's in the room with me now, if you want to speak to her?' Ryker suggested.

'Pass me over,' Winter said.

Ryker pulled the receiver from his ear and held it out toward Yaman. 'It's for you,' he said.

She took her time coming over, Ryker unsure if her hesitation was due to wariness or if she was just trying to piss Winter off. When she took the receiver, she indicated for Ryker to step back then she turned from him and pushed her head down toward her chest and cupped her hand over the receiver.

Ryker tried his best to listen in but he could hear nothing that Winter said, and Yaman's short responses were just muffled mumbles.

As he waited, Ryker switched his gaze intermittently between Yaman and the guards outside the room. He could wait and see if Winter really did have the authority and sway over Yaman – and whoever she was working for – to get Ryker out of this mess, or he could just do it himself. Storm out there and tackle everyone who got in his way.

That would get him free from this bunker, but it wouldn't achieve his aim. He'd come here for Karaman. And he wasn't leaving without him, or at least not until he'd had time with the guy.

Ryker was caught in his thoughts, staring at the guards outside when he heard the clunk as Yaman replaced the handset.

'So?' Ryker prompted her.

'He really thinks a lot about you,' she said to Ryker in such a way as to confirm that she really didn't understand it. 'In this world, it's rare to see a person put their neck so far on the line for another.'

'He trusts me,' Ryker said. 'I see you're not familiar with the concept.'

'The phone call really didn't make much difference,' Yaman said. 'My plan was never to hold you here endlessly. I'm not stupid, Ryker. As you said, I involved the Omani police and army. There was already too much officialness to do anything... underhand.'

'Lucky me. So you're saying you're letting me go free because you have to, not because you want to.'

'Well put.'

'Except I'm not going anywhere until I've spoken to Karaman.'

Yaman shook her head. 'You can't.'

Ryker took a step toward her, an attempt at intimidation because he knew that despite her bullishness she definitely was still scared of him.

'I'm speaking to Karaman before I leave here,' he said.

'No, you aren't.' Her face broke out into an unlikely smile. 'Why do you think we kept you in that room, Ryker? Three days you've been there. Why do you think the delay in me coming to see you?'

Ryker processed that. She'd already made clear that she hadn't intended on keeping Ryker captive, torturing him, killing him, or anything as nefarious as that. No, this woman wasn't outwardly brutal, but she was conniving in the extreme, every action deliberate and most actions with a hidden objective.

'You get it now?' she said.

'Karaman's not here, is he?' Ryker said.

'He never was here. We took him away immediately.'

'Took him where?'

She looked at her watch. 'It's been a long journey for him, but... in about half an hour, he'll be landing. And that's when the real fun will start.'

'Where?' Ryker said.

'He's our country's most wanted criminal, Ryker. And justice will prevail.'

She said that as though she actually believed her own words. As though this was what she'd intended with the intel on Karaman all along.

'England?'

Yaman nodded. 'You can make your own way there.'

She turned and Ryker didn't stop her as she unlocked the door and stepped out.

14

BIRMINGHAM, ENGLAND

Mason pulled the car over on the cramped street of terraced houses. Not in a parking spot. There were none available. Other cars were already packed tightly on both sides of the road, so Mason could only stop alongside the parked cars, blocking the street to any other passing traffic until he moved on.

'I'll keep going, look for a space,' he said, craning his neck to look at number two fifty-two. She couldn't read his face; she didn't really know him well enough to understand what he was thinking in that moment anyway, though she was sure she sensed a certain mocking in what he saw outside, as though this place, the modest lives of the people here were beneath him.

Angel got out without saying a word and stood on the footpath for a few moments. She looked along the street as her warm breath swirled around her and up into the cold, dark sky.

No one around, even though it was only seven thirty.

She moved to the warped metal front gate that sat within a pretty shoddy-looking three-foot wall at the front of the house. She pushed down on the gate latch and opened the creaky fixture.

Damn. Paul had said he would fix that crappy thing years ago.

Lights were on in the house, the glow visible around the edges of the drawn curtains in the cramped lounge at the front. Angel stepped up to the door and pressed the doorbell. A couple of seconds later the hall light flicked on and through the frosted glass, she saw the figure emerge from the lounge. Paul, judging by the size and shape.

Angel sucked in air through her nostrils until her lungs were full, prepping herself, readying herself.

Paul opened the door and for a brief moment, they both stared at each other, no words. The smell of cooked chicken and boiled vegetables wafted out with the warmth of the house. Paul looked... like he always had. Tall. Clean shaven. Hardly any gray, no receding in his hairline even though he was pushing forty. Lean figure. Bright blue eyes that sucked her in even though she wanted to hate everything about him.

No, she *did* hate everything about him. Apart from their daughter.

'Paul, I—'

'You shouldn't be here.'

Now his face twisted in disgust like he saw her as the scum of the earth. The shit on the bottom of his best pair of shoes, rather than the woman who'd loved him for years and had brought their daughter into the world.

'I just... I'd really like to see her. I—'

'You should go.'

'Please, Paul.'

'I thought you were on that retreat again? What? You couldn't hack it? Same as always. Are you drunk?'

'No. Paul, please. Just let me say hi to her. There's...' She paused and sighed and tried to find the words. She'd practiced this so many times on the trip over. Rehearsed in her head and out loud with Mason.

'Who is it?' came a ratty female voice from further inside.

That was all Angel needed. Bella poked her head out of the lounge, then stepped into the hall, the contempt on her face even greater than on Paul's.

The audacity of that? Bella was the bloody imposter, not the other way around!

'Paul, why is *she* here?' Bella said.

'*She* has a damn name, bitch,' Angel responded.

'Angel? Yeah, good luck trying to convince anyone of that one.'

'Look, honey,' Paul said, turning around. 'Just give me a minute. I can handle this.'

That put Bella back in her place and she skulked off.

'Angel, seriously_'

'Just listen, will you. You can think what you like about me. Hate me, pity me, whatever, but she's still my daughter. And... I need this. *Help* me.'

'What's happened?' Paul asked, for the first time speaking to her with something approaching genuine concern.

'I... can't talk about it. I have something I need to do. I could be gone a while.'

'They pulled you back in?'

As ever, skirting around the subject of her other life, her job – old job – by only ever referring to it in cloaked, vague terms. But then she'd never divulged actual details of her work. But he knew enough, knew how dangerous it was, the risks she took. She had no way to explain that this wasn't *that* job, but something that had come about because of it.

Would he even know the name if she told him? Ismail Karaman. A name that meant so much to her, so little to him, even though both their lives – their daughter's too – had been so tarnished by him.

'Yeah,' Angel said. 'And... it's big. It might... get messy.'

She squeezed her eyes closed and tried to stay strong. 'Can I just see her? Two minutes. A goodnight hug.'

'She's not here. She's with my parents.'

Angel's heart sank.

But then she saw the bare feet appearing at the top of the stairs and Angel ducked down and locked eyes with her daughter. The most perfect being she'd ever seen in her life. Not so little now. She'd grown so much, but then it'd been six years already. Six years wasted. Angel flicked her eyes to Paul ever so quickly, a flash of anger, before beaming at Sasha.

'Hey, sweetie,' Angel said.

'Sash, go back to your room, now!' Paul blasted up the stairs and Angel had to hold herself back from grabbing him and sending him to the floor. When he turned back to Angel she saw nothing but hatred in his eyes.

'You need to go.'

'So, you're still a lying piece of shit, I see,' Angel responded.

'Go. Or you'll be sorry.' He pushed his face close to hers. She didn't budge. 'I'm not scared of you.'

'You know? You really fucking should be.'

Paul edged back and at first, Angel thought it was because of the genuine threat in her words, but then she realized he wasn't even paying her attention anymore, but looking beyond her to the road.

She turned to see the idling car, window down, Mason glaring over.

'What's this? Your new screw-around?' Paul said. 'Is he going to beat me up?'

Angel shook her head. 'You're pathetic,' she said to him. 'You always were. You always will be.'

'Says the alcoholic ex-con whose life is in pieces.'

'Thanks to you.'

'You good, Angel?' Mason shouted over.

She really wished he'd stayed out of sight.

'Time for you to go,' Paul said.

'I won't forget this. One day... you'll wish you'd treated me better.'

'Not likely.'

He slammed the door shut and she watched his figure darting up the stairs through the glass – was he going to admonish Sasha? It took everything for her to not break the door down and charge up after him.

But she had to stay strong. Sasha was the only innocent person in the whole situation. If Angel ran up there to confront Paul, and to... what? Smack him about? That did nothing to help her daughter. Paul wasn't violent. He was manipulative and scheming but he loved Sasha and she was sure her daughter was only about to get an angry earful about what a dangerous fuck-up Angel was.

She turned around and walked quickly to the waiting car, her legs shaking as adrenaline and anger surged.

She sank down into the passenger seat and put her hands to her face and screamed. A huge, long holler until her lungs were empty and nothing came out of her mouth but a weird rasp.

'You done now?' Mason asked, sounding as relaxed as anything. He looked almost amused by the whole thing, which didn't exactly help to calm her.

'You didn't have to show your face.'

'Why? What difference did it make? He wasn't going to let you see her, was he?' he said, as though he had a perfect read of her, Paul, the situation.

'Just get me out of here.'

'Where to?'

'A bar. A really fancy, expensive fucking cocktail bar. And you're paying.'

He didn't move the car and she glared at him and didn't like the questioning look on his stupid face.

'What?'

Mason shrugged.

'I didn't say I was going to get drunk.'

He shrugged again.

'Drive. Or I'll drag you out the car and reverse over you a couple of times on my way outta here.'

He smiled then laughed. She tried hard not to do the same.

'Let's go watch other people get wasted, then,' he said before thumping his foot down onto the accelerator.

* * *

The bar was good enough. A converted old bank not far from New Street Station in Birmingham. The large, airy interior had high vaulted ceilings and a huge bar cluttered with hundreds and hundreds of bottles of spirits – an exhaustive cocktail list to go along with it. The place wasn't super high-end – people weren't dressed to the nines, and there was no security to keep the riffraff out – but it was... good enough. And in reality, Angel wouldn't have gotten into anywhere more swanky tonight as it wasn't as though she'd packed some Jimmy Choos and her best little black dress or anything. Just leggings and a sparkly little crop top that gave her a lot more cleavage than she really had and that she knew would grab her some much-needed attention. Like from Mason. Although he hadn't exactly made an effort in his jeans, dirtied white trainers, and plain Nike T-shirt.

Whatever. Still, it was nice to see his muscles rippling through the top.

'You know, they still have the vault in place downstairs,' Mason said before taking a sip from the little straw of his cocktail. He looked at her, confused by her reaction. 'What?'

'You. With that drink. You look a bit...'

'Not manly enough for me?'

'Not what I expected you to have.'

He shrugged. 'I don't really give a crap about fitting into molds, making impressions.'

Which didn't fully make sense given his obvious liking for T-shirts that were a size too small. Regardless, the way he had to kind of crouch down to the table and grasp the tiny little straw between his thick fingers tickled her. She laughed when he did it again and for all of his confidence and bravado, she knew he was embarrassed from the way he nervously looked around as though hoping no one else was watching.

'I'll get a huge beer in a giant tankard next time, OK?'

He took the straw out and put it on the table and picked up the highball glass and took a bigger swig of the whisky-based drink – the orange slice tumbling over the ice toward his face as he did so, though he managed to pull the glass away just in time before the fruit smacked him.

Angel laughed again.

'Glad you're enjoying yourself,' he said.

'Anyway, you were saying?'

'I was saying about the vault, downstairs.'

'I'm intrigued why you thought I'd be intrigued by that?'

He shrugged. 'It's a cool feature.'

'No. Something else. What, you thought it'd play to my destructive side? A bank vault. Maybe some hidden treasures inside it still. Do you think I'd make a good bank robber?'

'What are you talking about?'

'Have you ever done anything like that before? A heist?'

He paused before answering, and she didn't know if he was only contemplating the question or if she'd somehow offended him with it.

'What do you think?' he asked.

'Yeah,' she said. 'I think you probably have. Because it's not too dissimilar to what we're planning now, is it? And we wouldn't be even thinking about what we're planning if we weren't confident of pulling it off.'

He slowly nodded in response.

'I wouldn't know where to start with cracking a safe, though,' he said with a wink.

'Shame. I thought maybe that's why you'd brought up the idea of the vault downstairs in the first place.'

'No. It's definitely empty. The door's wide open. I think the only reason they left it down there at all was because of how hard it'd be to dismantle and remove it.'

Angel sipped her drink until it was gone.

'Why don't you get me another?' she asked.

'Same?'

'Yeah. I'm going to go take a look.'

He headed off to the bar, and she headed off to the stairs down to the restrooms. But not without first lingering as she walked past the group of three men at the bar. Late twenties, early thirties, they were all smartly dressed in office gear. Professionals, full of themselves, enjoying a few drinks after work. The one on the left – the youngest and cutest of the three – had been giving Angel the eye in the mirror of the bar.

So as she passed she waited for him to lock eyes with her. She gave him a cheeky smile and he half swiveled on his bar stool.

'Hey,' she said to him, then carried on past and to the stairs without waiting for a response.

Just an opener. Just in case.

She kept her eyes on the other side of the bar from where he was sitting when she came back to the table. Mason was already seated again, two new drinks waiting. The same again for her, but a pint of beer for him. So her mocking had had an effect on him after all.

'Cheers,' she said to him and clinked his much bigger glass, and he reciprocated but looked a little sullen now. Perhaps because of the drink, or perhaps because he'd noticed the little exchange between her and the guy at the bar. Jealous? She liked Mason, and they'd had a lot of fun together the last time, but he'd lied to her. And now they had business together. And she knew not to mix business and pleasure.

If everything went smoothly tomorrow, then maybe down the line...

'H is late,' Mason said, looking at his watch then checking his phone. H being the third person joining them for their 'job'.

'He's not been in touch?'

'Not for the last hour or so.'

'We're in no rush,' she said.

Mason humphed.

'So you and H know each other?' she asked.

'Not really.'

'Not really?'

'I've heard of him before. Know about some of the things he's done. I've never worked with him before.'

Which was both a good and a bad thing. If they were best buddies that would put her in an awkward position, but having three people who barely knew each other work together on something so dangerous also carried obvious risks.

'Is he going to be just as mysterious as you?'

'Mysterious?'

'A closed book.'

'I'm not a closed book, I just haven't told you anything about me that you don't need to know.'

'You haven't told me *anything* about you.'

'Because you don't need to know it.' He laughed as though he'd just made a really good joke.

'You expect me to put my life on the line, but you won't even tell me about yourself. And it doesn't need to be about your professional life. Just about you.'

Because she already knew *something* about his professional life. That he'd worked for MI5 but had been kicked out because he'd been caught making money on the side out of some of his assets – money from drug deals, mostly. But she knew all that because it was in the public domain, not because he'd told her. He'd been hung out to dry by his employers, spent two years in prison even though from what she read he claimed he'd been set up. That his superiors had not only known about the deals but had wanted him to make them in order to gain the trust of the gangs he was working with.

'Go on, then,' he said.

'What?'

'Fire away.'

She thought for a moment. 'Where do you come from?'

'Not far from here. Lichfield. Born there, lived there until I left home at eighteen.'

She hadn't detected anything in his accent, and it felt a little odd to know he'd grown up only a few miles from her own hometown of Tamworth.

'You went to university?' she asked.

'No. I joined the army. Same as you.'

She squirmed a little at that. Hated that he knew so much more about her even though she'd told him little.

'But I knew it wasn't for me. I never saw active duty. I was more interested in... people. If that makes any sense.'

'Kind of.'

'But don't think I don't know *how* to fight.'

She already knew first-hand he had skills in close combat.

'I wasn't going to suggest that at all,' she said. 'So MI5 approached you?'

'Organizations like MI5 and MI6 have a way of knowing who's a good fit. You probably know that from experience. I'm guessing you didn't apply for your job either.'

True. Though she didn't bother to confirm or deny. 'You ever get married?' she asked.

'My job didn't provide much room for settling down.'

She couldn't hide her amusement at that answer. 'No, you just like playing the field too much.'

He rolled his eyes at that but in a playful way. She had him pegged.

'Maybe one day,' he said. 'But you...'

'Me, what?'

'You did get married, had a kid even, despite your job.'

'There's nothing unusual about people in the military having families. Even in the special forces—' which wasn't *exactly* what she did, but it was close enough '—it's a world away from the life of a spook.'

'I'm not talking about the military,' Mason said. 'I'm talking about your life after the military. When you *were* a spook. More or less.'

'A freelance security consultant. That's what they actually called it.' She said that with obvious disdain. 'And you want the truth?'

'Obviously.'

'I didn't do it for ideals or any of that bullshit. I did it for the money. I did it for me, Paul, Sasha. I thought I was creating a better life for the three of us. The money I was getting... It was good. Really good. And I knew I wouldn't have to do it much longer.

Maybe only one of two more assignments and I'd take a break after. I wouldn't need to work again for years.'

'Except you didn't get paid for that last job, did you?'

'No, I didn't.'

She downed a good portion of her drink, trying to push aside her rising distaste for how she'd been treated. Not just by her 'employer' but Paul too in the aftermath. And that evil bastard Karaman. But the truth was that not one person had stood up for her.

'Did they really screw you over too?' she asked.

He held her eye, his face hard as though he were reliving the betrayal in that moment and he didn't even need to answer the question. She got it.

'The same question to you,' he said. 'I know how everything fell apart after. But that day. On the rooftop in Beirut?'

'Yeah. I was screwed over after, but I pulled the trigger. I missed my target. I'd never missed before. I was a good sniper in the army and I was a better sniper freelance where there wasn't the pressure of war. But that day... I forever changed the life of a little girl, her family. So I got what I deserved, you could say. But...'

'But what?'

'I did my job out there. The mistake wasn't even out of error or anything like that but because someone figured out the plan, or someone betrayed us, and I was attacked. I was lucky to survive. Karaman lived, I was arrested by the Lebanese police, thrown under the bus, and no one on our side made any attempt to help me for nearly four years. The people I worked for... They had enough power to make it all go away, to bring me back home immediately rather than four years later as part of some crooked deal. A deal which only saw me spend more time behind bars here as I served out my minimum sentence.'

'But you do *know* why, don't you?'

'Yeah. I do. Karaman. You know, he actually visited me in prison?'

Mason shook his head. Of course, he didn't know that. How could he?

'He turned up one day, a few months after. To taunt me. To tell me my life was in his hands. They'd tortured me daily. Stress positions, white noise, sleep deprivation, waterboarding. But never for information or anything like that. Just because. Because of him. His wife wanted me dead because of what I did, but he wanted me to suffer. I was sentenced to ten years but he told me I'd never get out of that prison alive.'

'But you did.'

'I did. But... only because the landscape changed. I don't even know exactly what happened but finally, it made political sense for our government to care. I was traded. Nothing more, nothing less. But the damage was already long done by then.'

Mason nodded, as though he understood.

'So this is personal for you too?' she asked. 'With Karaman?'

'No,' he said. 'Like you said, the money for these ops is good. This is purely business for me.' He picked up his beer and took a drawn-out swig as if indicating he was done with the conversation.

And his cold answer was certainly delivered with clarity and surety.

There was just one big problem.

Angel was certain he was lying.

15

They had a third drink each, although Mason nursed his, disappearing from the table a couple of times to take calls on his phone. He claimed to have no wife or girlfriend, but he sure spent a lot of time communicating with someone.

'Who's chasing you this time?' Angel said when he returned to the table on the latest occasion. The phone was still in his hand and he initially glanced at the screen as though the answer was there.

'H,' he said and then hovered at the table looking uneasy. 'His train didn't make it to Birmingham. A track problem or something. He's stuck in Stoke, no more trains tonight.'

Just like earlier, his tone was off, meaning at least part of the story was fabricated. But which part and why?

'So we'll go pick him up, right? It's not that far.'

He contemplated that.

'Why don't you hang around here?' he said. 'I'll be back in a couple of hours. Then we'll head out together.'

So he didn't want her going out to meet H. Fine. Fine. She could entertain herself here. 'Sounds good to me.'

'Just don't go doing anything stupid,' he said, then looked

uncomfortable. As he should, because he had no right to say something like that to her.

'You got it, boss,' she said with a salute.

He didn't bother to finish his beer before he left.

She only took a couple more minutes to finish her drink before she got up from her stool to head to the restroom.

Except she didn't make it past the bar before the guy who'd given her the eye earlier spun around.

'You two have a fight or something?'

'Something,' she said and went to move past until he took hold of her arm. Not hard, but with purpose still.

'Is he your boyfriend?'

'Brother, actually.'

The guy's confidence, his stature, rose a little. But as she looked at him more closely now, he wasn't half as cute as she'd earlier thought. His eyes were dull, his hair thin and wispy, and his accent... Grating. Somewhere from the northwest, she thought.

'We're staying for a conference,' he said. 'Up from London, so we're only in town a couple of days. You live here?'

'Just visiting too.'

'Shame. You could have showed us some places.'

'Shame.'

'Still, you can join us if you like?'

'Join you for what?'

One of his two friends – who had been pretending not to be taking notice until now – guffawed at that.

'A drink. I'm buying.' He flashed his gold corporate card and Angel feigned that she was impressed. 'Actually, my company's paying.' He winked at her.

'I like champagne,' she suggested.

He chewed on that a moment, obviously debating if she was really worth it. 'Whatever you want.'

'Good answer. Because I'm picking. And it won't be the cheapest.'

He grabbed the menu from the bar and flicked to the extensive champagne list before pushing it out to her.

'That one,' she said, pointing to the second-most expensive: £500 rather than £800. No point in pushing things.

'Whatever the lady wants,' he said.

'I'll be right back.'

She brushed his shoulder with her fingers before sauntering off, hips swaying.

Mason had abandoned her, so why not at least try and have a little fun?

* * *

Evan. Thirty-three years old, although he looked younger than that if she ignored his crappy, straggly hair. He was from Cheshire, had gone to some private school there before studying at the London School of Economics. Now he – and his two buddies – worked in investment banking. He drove a Porsche. One of his friends had just used his bonus to buy a Ferrari, but Evan was saving his because he wanted to buy his own place next year. An apartment in the city. Budget of two million. Only him. No girlfriend because he'd tried going steady with someone a couple of years ago but she couldn't handle the high pressure and long hours of his job. But he'd devote himself to the right woman. But he absolutely wasn't looking for a stay-at-home partner. Someone who wanted him for his money. He wanted a career-driven woman who could challenge him profes-sionally, intellectually.

He told her all this without her barely asking a question. In fact, she probably could have guessed most of it without him even opening his mouth.

His friends left him for another bar when Evan and Angel were each on their second glass of champagne. The expensive drink wasn't for those two, it was for Evan to continue to try to win over Angel. And as far as he was concerned, he was doing a great job even if in all honesty he'd bored her within the first five minutes of the one-sided conversation.

'What about you?' he asked, and it seemed like a real discomfort for him to have to switch the conversation around.

'Me?'

'What do you do?'

'I used to be in the army.'

She let that hang there although he showed no particular reaction.

'Now I'm a security consultant.'

'Security?'

She nodded. He really didn't know where to go next, judging by his lack of follow-up. Or maybe he just really didn't care what she did. She pushed her cleavage up a little and he practically drooled. He only wanted one thing from her.

Well, same.

'I really need to pee,' she said, fixing him with a smile as she patted his leg.

She got up, her legs a little wobbly and he laughed at her as she regained her balance before she teetered toward the restrooms. He hadn't moved when she arrived back, though he had once again refilled her glass.

He took a sip from his own and then just kind of stared at her as though waiting for her to say or do something, but she left the drink there and within a few minutes he'd had most of his.

'You're not having any more of your champagne?' he asked.

'I'm just taking my time. Didn't you see my Bambi on ice impression before?'

He laughed. 'But if you don't drink that glass, you don't get another bottle.'

She picked up her glass and took a big swig and he looked really pleased with himself.

'I told you I was in the army,' she said. 'You think you can out-drink me?'

He laughed. 'Actually, probably not.'

He downed most of his drink and then did that gasp thing that people do when they've had too much too quickly.

He checked his watch. She did the same.

'Actually, Evan, honestly, I've got an early start tomorrow.' She finished off her drink.

'Where are you staying?' he asked.

'Nearby.'

'I can walk you.'

She thought about that. 'But no funny business.'

He put his hand to his heart. 'I'm a gentleman.'

She smiled but then the smile slipped away, and she put a hand to her head and groaned.

'You OK?'

'Actually, I think that last glass really went to my head.'

'Come on, I'll get you back to your hotel.'

She stood up from her chair but initially struggled to take her weight before Evan took hold of her arm and pulled her toward him and then toward the exit.

'Which hotel is it?' he asked once they were out in the cold of the night.

'It's...' she said and then pulled out of his grip. 'Are you sure *you're* OK?'

'Yeah, I'm... fine. Are we...'

'Shit, Evan, you look really out of it.'

'Your hotel. Which... way?'

He went to take her arm again but she shuffled away and he went staggering past and it took everything not to laugh out loud at him.

'Evan, oh my God. Let me help you.'

She pulled his arm around her shoulders, put hers underneath, holding his side to guide him.

'That champagne must have been stronger than we thought.'

They made it around the next corner but Evan was becoming more and more out of it by the second, Angel taking more and more of his weight.

'Let's go down here,' she said, glancing along the street to make sure it was clear before she took him down into the darkened alley.

She moved on past where the arc of light from the streetlights reached, beyond some industrial dumpsters. She let go and gave Evan a gentle prod to send him stumbling to the floor where he rolled into a heap.

She kneeled down to him.

'I saw what you did, you dumbass,' she said with little feeling.

He said nothing. No real words anyway. Just a mumbling slur.

'How many women have you done this too?'

Nothing.

'I really hope, for the sake of other women, I'm the first.'

She felt in his pockets and found the little plastic bag with a few tablets in it.

'Unfortunately, I'm thinking this is just... you.'

She crushed the tablets up and tossed them into one of the dumpsters.

'But I'm also thinking this will probably be the last time for you.'

She paused a moment as she looked down at him, a little unsure if he was even still conscious or not. Yeah, he was. He just couldn't move.

She had a choice. She could just leave him, or she could call the police. But would they even do anything?

In her experience, swift justice was better than no justice.

'You wanna know the truth?' she asked.

No answer.

'I really don't like to drink anymore. I've got a bit of a problem.' She took off his shoes and took out her pocketknife and with a bit of effort cut the shoes in half before tossing the pieces into the nearest dumpster.

'Those cocktails I had with my brother? Friend, actually. But they were mocktails. You probably thought I was getting drunk already but when I sat down with you I was stone-cold sober.'

She pulled off his jacket, slashed it into pieces then cut through his shirt to remove that. He wasn't even that hot underneath. Scrawny and pudgy at the same time. Too much time drinking and drugging girls in bars.

'And the champagne? I was swapping our glasses over and over every time yours was looking a little too empty. You just didn't notice 'cause you were too busy staring at my tits.'

She emptied his pockets onto the ground next to him then took hold of his belt buckle and he squirmed, almost as though he still thought this was going well for him given where her hands now were. She unclasped his belt, pulled down his trousers.

'And it was only when I noticed the taste change that I realized what you'd done. I mean, after that I only swapped one more time, obviously.'

She cut his trousers up, tossed those too. She picked up his wallet. His lighter. Took his cash and set the rest on fire, dropping the burning pieces of leather and plastic by his face. He barely moved away, just kind of turned and shuffled his face to save it from the heat.

Next, she took his phone, removed the SIM, and snapped it in two. She stomped on the handset until the glass was obliterated.

She kneeled back down to him and used the tip of the knife to lift up the elastic of his boxers a little.

'To leave, or not to leave,' she said.

No response. So she slapped him on the cheek and his body twitched and he mumbled and grumbled something but he was so far out of it now.

'You actually wanted to have sex with me like *this*? That's just... fucked up, Evan. And just to be clear? I might actually have screwed you otherwise.'

She shivered. Not because of the nasty thoughts but because it really was damn cold out.

Should she leave him with at least a little dignity?

No. Screw it. He didn't deserve any better.

She cut off his boxers and held her nose, scrunched up her face as she pincered them, as little skin as possible touching the fabric as she tossed them into the dumpster.

'Good luck,' she said, putting the knife away.

She walked to the edge of the alley, feeling no real satisfaction for what she'd just done even though she really wanted to. Actually, if anything, she worried she'd gone too far and she hated that. The guy was a sicko. He needed to be punished. But... How long could he stay out there before he died from the cold?

'Shit,' she said under her breath as she emerged from the alley, in two minds. She stared up to the dark sky, busy thinking, then spun around when she spotted movement. A couple walking down the street toward her.

OK. Leave him. He didn't deserve any better.

Without hesitation, she walked quickly the other way. She called Mason as she went.

'All good?' he asked when he answered.

'Yeah. How far away are you?'

'I'll be back in ten minutes. Meet you by the station.'

Eleven minutes later she stepped into the back seat of his car. She got a quick intro to the burly, bearded man in front – H – before Mason got them moving.

'You sure you're OK?' Mason asked.

'Yeah, one hundred percent, but... Do you think we could make one stop before we head on?'

Mason sighed. 'For what?'

'For me.'

He caught her eye in the mirror and something about the dismay in her voice or on her face must have swayed him.

'Sure. Where to?'

* * *

'Sweet dreams, Princess,' Angel said.

She kissed Sasha lightly on the forehead, but her daughter didn't move under the covers, didn't stir at all. In the darkened room Angel could barely make out her daughter's features but knew her eyelids remained closed.

A good thing, really, but a small part of her wanted her daughter to see her. She wanted the acknowledgment, wanted to have a real embrace.

Still, just seeing her was the tonic she needed after tonight. All thoughts of Evan and whether he'd been rescued or was now a frozen corpse were erased.

Angel straightened up, wondering what Sasha was dreaming of.

Did she ever dream of her?

'I'll see you soon,' Angel said, even though it felt like a lie.

She reluctantly pulled herself away and moved for the door, creeping out onto the landing. An orange glow swept up from down below, casting thick shadows across the wall. She could hear the TV down there but saw and heard no signs of anyone moving about.

Satisfied – as far as she could be, at least – she edged silently toward the master bedroom at the back of the modest two up, two down. The window in the bedroom remained partially open. She paused for a beat as she stared into the darkness outside. All clear. She grabbed the windowsill and pushed her body through the gap.

As before, the street outside the house was quiet. On the opposite side of the road, the endless row of parked cars abruptly stopped where the double-yellow lines outside the school began. Angel moved to the last of the parked cars whose front end fell across the yellow markings. Not a problem at this time of night. She eased into the seat and sighed. The engine was off, had been since she'd left – no rumbling engine, no lights to not draw attention – but because of it the inside of the car was cold, though the air was thick and stale.

Mason didn't start the engine. He was too busy staring at her. In the darkness, she couldn't be sure what the look on his face meant.

'You're done now?' he asked.

'Done,' she said.

He said nothing more as he continued to stare and then H turned around too, a much less friendly look from him.

'What's your fucking problem?' Angel growled.

He shook his head – disgust, or just disgruntlement, she wasn't sure – before both men looked forward again. Mason turned the key and the aging engine rumbled to life, the noise cutting uneasily through the otherwise quiet street.

'Then let's get this show on the road,' Mason said before putting his foot down.

16

LONDON, ENGLAND

The skyscrapers of Canary Wharf rose toward the dull gray sky in the distance. Not far beyond them, further west, sat the heart of the capital, the plethora of tourist traps, many of the most prominent revolving around the country's royal families – past, present, good, bad, and ugly. Of those tourist spots, one of the most famous remained the Tower of London, a castle originally built by William the Conqueror at the end of his conquests in 1066, although many people knew of the castle mainly for its use as a prison. It had been first used as such in 1100, and all the way through from then to the mid-twentieth century, surviving war after war, sieges, and an ever-changing social and political landscape all around it. Stones and mortar nearly a thousand years old that would tell so many stories – often violent, always morbid – if they could. Yet the Tower of London still retained a renowned public image, seen as a national treasure to many, and a prime destination for visitors from the world over.

So very different to the reputation and image of the building just a few miles down the river, and now across the street from Ryker. An altogether more plain-looking prison, most of it hidden behind a formidable concrete wall. No tourists here, even if some of the most infamous people in the country had lived here. Some still did.

Belmarsh Prison. Once known as Britain's Guantanamo Bay due to its prominent use in housing suspected terrorists in the early twenty-first century, sometimes for years on end without charge until courts had intervened to rule such treatment as going against human rights and unlawful. On UK soil, at least.

Still, even two decades on, Belmarsh remained notorious, both for its often-cited harsh treatment of inmates, and their high-profile status.

Murderers, rapists, terrorists.

Ismail Karaman.

'Good morning,' came a familiar voice.

Ryker looked from where he stood by the side of the road to see Winter approaching, long, thick coat over his nice suit, reusable coffee cup in his hand. As ever Winter looked fresh, clean, well groomed. Ever true to his desk jockey position. Although perhaps desk jockey was by now an unkind way to continue to think of Winter. He'd never been a field operative, but he'd certainly seen his fair share of close shaves with death. Mostly with Ryker not far away.

'You didn't get me one?' Ryker said, nodding to the drink.

'You normally just get what you want, when you want it,' Winter said, but he looked a little unsure of his words, as though he'd intended them to be a joke even though the delivery held a bitter edge.

'You ever been in there before?' Ryker indicated over the road.

'I have. It has a deserved reputation, let's just put it that way. But I'm sure it's a beach holiday compared to some of the places where you've been locked up.'

Ryker huffed. Again, Winter's joke fell a little flat.

'I'm surprised not to see a wall of paparazzi here.'

'For you, you mean?' Winter said, laughing this time at his own weak joke.

Ryker didn't follow suit. Strike three. Winter shrank a little, but Ryker wasn't going to hide the fact that he was still seriously annoyed with Winter for setting him up with Brock Van Der Vehn.

'There'll be plenty of reporters when Karaman gets his day in court,' Winter said. 'But for now... He's locked up tight.'

'He should be locked up tight four thousand miles away.'

'You think he's evaded justice by being here? Why, because you didn't get a chance to torture him?'

'Because I didn't get a chance to get the truth from him. And now I'm not sure I ever will.'

Winter held Ryker's eye but didn't have any response.

'You really fucked me over,' Ryker said.

Winter's face soured, his eyes pinched. 'Are you serious? You're here in London, a free man, because of me and only me. And how many times is that now that I've had to bail you out of a mess of your own making?'

'A mess of my making? You teamed me up with a damn trigger-happy psychotic.'

'Van Der Vehn?'

'Yeah, Brock Van Der Bloody Vehn. Seriously, Winter, what the hell were you thinking?'

'I was thinking I had forty-eight hours to find you a suitable team member for an entirely illegal and off-the-books capture and extraction mission. Who did you expect? James Bond?'

Ryker said nothing.

'I didn't know him,' Winter said before sighing. 'I got his background, I saw his experience. I felt he was a risk worth taking as I didn't exactly have many options. I... realize he probably wasn't ideal.'

'Not ideal? He killed six people. Six people who didn't have to die to get our man.'

'And he lost his life because of it,' Winter said in an almost accusatory way. As though he believed Ryker had somehow set Brock up. Which he hadn't, really. He'd just known how Brock would react in that situation and had decided not to go along with it. Ryker certainly didn't feel bad about the guy's death.

'The bigger question is how did Yaman and MI6 know about our plan?' Ryker said.

'Our plan? Ryker, this was all your plan. I was just a helping hand.'

'That's not how Yaman sees it.'

'I don't care how she sees it.'

'But you should care about the fact that she was there, in Oman, waiting for me. Who else knew about what we were doing?'

'No one. Me, you, Brock, that was it.'

'What about the person who recommended Brock?'

'It wasn't as simple as a recommendation. No one knew any details, Ryker. Not through me, if that's what you're insinuating.'

'Except she *did* know. And she played us for fools.'

'She played *you* for a fool. The fact is, Ryker, this outcome isn't as bad as you think it is. Karaman is where he belongs. Behind bars.'

'If we can even get him to trial before his mega-millions lawyers derail everything. And even then his charges are all based on years-old crimes. None of this will help crack open the Syndicate if he simply keeps his mouth shut.'

'You don't know that.'

Ryker shrugged.

'But *you* could have made him spill everything he knew?' Winter said, sounding dubious.

'Maybe I could have.'

'And you've still got a shot. Just... You need to do it the official way.'

'With zero leverage.'

'Not zero leverage. How do you think regular police forces, lawyers, get convictions? The process works.'

'Not for people like Karaman. Not in my experience.'

Winter sighed and looked at his watch. 'Come on, it's time.'

* * *

A windowless room, though quite different to the one back in Oman. This one was brightly lit with off-white painted walls and a linoleum floor. A radiator across one wall spewed out heat, making the room almost stiflingly hot. Not a great way to spend taxpayer money. A Formica-topped table sat in the middle of the room. Ryker occupied one of the two chairs nearest to the locked door. Ismail Karaman sat on the opposite side of the table, his hands cuffed to a metal loop on the tabletop.

No Winter or prison guards or lawyers in here. Just Ryker and Karaman. Still not quite as 'personal' as Ryker would have wanted, though. Not here, in the UK, in the official prison system. And not with that little camera up in the corner of the room recording everything. Winter would be watching live, others too.

Ryker and Karaman had already sat through nearly ten minutes of silence. Not because Ryker had nothing to say but because he wanted to see if Karaman's inquisitiveness would eventually get him to open his mouth first. Ryker had nowhere better to be, so he was more than happy to wait it out.

Back in the Gulf, Ryker hadn't paid much attention to Karaman's appearance. But now... Even in his light blue prison garb, he looked confident, self-important. The way all rich businesspeople did. Even those who doubled as terrorists.

'I do know who you are,' Karaman said and Ryker showed no reaction at all to the words, even though inside he felt more than a little smug that Karaman had broken first.

So Ryker kept his mouth shut a little longer.

'It was dark out there on the water, but I'd recognize your ugly face anywhere.'

He was talking about Dubai. The attack on his yacht. He didn't really know who Ryker was, just that Ryker was the one who'd snatched him.

'They were good people,' Karaman said, anger coming through in his voice now. 'Friends. Men with wives, sons, daughters. All of their lives ruined because of you. Why?'

Ryker still held his tongue.

'Your friend... I only wish he hadn't died so quickly. He didn't deserve the easy way out. As for you...'

Ryker still didn't respond. At least not straight away. But, truthfully, he was intrigued as to exactly what threat Karaman was about to deliver.

'As for me, what?' Ryker asked.

Karaman's gaze flicked from Ryker to the camera and back again.

'You know what?' Ryker said when it was clear Karaman had decided not to follow through. 'I couldn't give a crap about your friends. Or their families. Those men were scumbags, just like you. Otherwise, they wouldn't work with a scumbag like you. And their families? Better off now, believe me. We did them a favor. The whole world, in fact.'

Karaman was trying his hardest to hide his anger. Ryker could tell by his tightly clenched knuckles, his clenched jaw.

'You want to know why those men are dead?' Ryker asked.

No answer.

'Because of *you*.'

A slight shake of Karaman's head.

'Because of the Syndicate,' Ryker added.

Karaman gave no reaction to that. Not a twitch, flinch, or anything. Not unexpected, really.

'You know about the Syndicate,' Ryker said. A statement rather than a question. 'Tell me about it.'

No answer. He really wanted to grab the guy's head and smash his face off the table a couple of times to see if that would warm him up.

'I actually know quite a lot about the Syndicate,' Ryker continued. 'A lot more than you probably realize.'

Nothing.

'Tell me about your relationship with Andrew Lebedev,' Ryker said.

'Who?' Karaman answered, doing his best impression of a dumbass.

'Lebedev. You know, the mega-rich son of an oligarch. Had each of his dirty fingers in dodgy politics and business deals across Europe, the Middle East. I think you've been on his yacht before. Vice versa. Whose is biggest? That's what counts to people like you, isn't it?'

Karaman smiled, nodded, as though having a eureka moment.

'Ah, yes, I remember reading about Lebedev. He got arrested here, didn't he? But then he ended up in Russia. I read something about a car accident in Moscow?'

'Oh, yeah. Very accidental, I'm sure. Lebedev was a rich guy. Horribly wealthy, really. But to the Syndicate? Probably just one of many. Someone useful in brokering business deals, in getting easy-to-reach politicians on side. But look what happened to him when he came unstuck. The Syndicate didn't think twice about killing him. His family? Collateral damage. They meant even less than he did to those in power.'

Karaman said nothing.

'Tell me how you first met Lebedev.'

'I never did.'

'Liar. I've seen the paper trails. Offshore entities, money laundering on a scale most people wouldn't believe was possible without someone raising a red flag, without some sort of investigation. But when everyone with any sway is part of the process... I'm talking about billions swirling in a merry-go-round, financing political campaigns, terrorists, rebel groups. Lebedev benefitted personally from these schemes. I've seen money going to *you* from those same entities too.'

Ryker spotted a chink in Karaman's steely facade, but it had gone again in a flash.

'And just look at what happened to Lebedev when someone – me, mainly – came too close to the truth and tried to expose him. The same people who had him killed would sacrifice you the first chance they get too.'

'If that were true, then there really wouldn't be any point in me talking to you anyway, would there? You, nor anyone else, would be able to protect me.'

This time it was Ryker's turn to stay silent and Karaman seemed to grow in confidence as a result.

'Do you know who betrayed you?' he asked.

Ryker wouldn't have answered even if he knew the answer.

Karaman smiled. 'Because it's very obvious to me that you were betrayed. I don't know much about you, but I already know, I see the *type* of man you are.'

'I really doubt that.'

'Oh, believe me, I do. And I think I can guess what you had planned for me. It certainly wasn't a nice cushy cell in England and an interview room like this, was it?'

Karaman's smile grew further.

'The situation tells me two things.'

He paused, as though hoping Ryker would ask what he meant by that.

'Firstly, it tells me that you have some friends in what you believe are high places. Otherwise, you'd be in a cell too for what you pulled in Dubai. But secondly, it tells me you and your friends have enemies much closer to home than me.'

Ryker tried his hardest to hide his increasing agitation. Karaman was right. He had been betrayed, to Yaman. He still couldn't figure out her role in the bigger scheme, whether she was corrupt or not. If Karaman was her ally, why had she brought him to England as a prisoner rather than just setting him free?

'Perhaps it's you who needs to watch your back,' Karaman said, before sitting back in his chair – as much as he could with his wrists cuffed to the table. A signal that he thought he'd delivered a knockout blow. But it wasn't really.

One name continued to swirl in Ryker's mind as he toyed with where to take the conversation next. Fatma Yaman. For all Karaman's worth in uncovering truths about the Syndicate, Ryker couldn't stray from the fact that Yaman had played him. And he hated that, and he especially hated that he didn't yet know who she answered to.

He was about to pursue that with Karaman when a knock at the door halted his intended question. Karaman looked even more amused now by the interruption.

Ryker hesitated a moment before he got up from his chair.

'I asked not to be disturbed,' Ryker said to the closed door.

'Yeah, well, things change.' Winter.

'Open up,' Ryker said and the next moment the locks released and the door inched open. A prison guard stepped out of the way as Winter came forward. Ryker glanced over his shoulder, double-checking Karaman remained seated and cuffed and that this wasn't some sort of unlikely escape plan.

Not this time. He moved closer to Winter, so the conversation they were about to have wouldn't be overheard. 'Please don't tell me you think I've crossed a line already, because you've no idea how hard it is to just sit there and talk—'

Winter held a hand up to stop Ryker. 'I just had a call from... a colleague.'

'And?'

'And Fatma Yaman was killed this morning. In her apartment.'

'Yaman's dead?'

'She's dead.'

Ryker turned his head to Karaman who stared over, a knowing look on his face. But how could he possibly know?

'How?' Ryker asked Winter.

'The facts are still coming out, but... Coincidence isn't the word I'm thinking right now.'

'Me neither.'

'We can go over there.'

'OK.'

He didn't bother to say anything more to Karaman as he pulled open the door fully to step out, but the prisoner's parting words caused Ryker to stop momentarily.

'See you soon, James Ryker.'

Ryker winced at the unexpected use of his name and only heard the start of the hearty laugh that followed before he grabbed the door handle and yanked the door shut.

'I'm not finished with him,' Ryker said to Winter. 'In fact, I'm not even started yet.'

He stormed off down the corridor, trying his best to erase Karaman's taunting words from his mind.

17

The high-rise apartment building in Kensington looked out of place in its surroundings. Nestled quite obtrusively among rows of handsome Georgian terraces and larger brick office blocks from the early twentieth century, the towering glass-fronted structure had a prime position commanding views over Hyde Park a block away. It was a wealthy area, with high-end shops dotted around and luxury cars crammed along the roadsides, but like many things, wealth came in varying degrees.

Fatma Yaman lived in an apartment that was likely worth three or four million pounds, but that wasn't unusual in this part of the capital. Many of the most prestigious homes, on the most sought-after roads, like those only a hundred or so yards away that sat directly across from the park, cost multiples of what Yaman's apartment was worth. Those were reserved for the mega-rich. Household name businesspeople, movie stars, sports people, but also those who went more under the radar with their vast wealth. Bankers, hedge fund managers, real estate entrepreneurs. Also, increasingly, rich foreign nationals, most commonly Russian oligarchs and those connected to them, and those belonging to or connected to the ruling families of the oil-rich Arab countries.

It wasn't a surprise to Ryker that Yaman – an intelligence agent specializing in Middle Eastern affairs – had chosen this part of London to live in, though it did leave something of a sour taste, especially when put together with the standard of living she'd become used to on a government salary.

'You know who paid for this place,' Ryker said when Winter came off the phone.

'And that's important because?'

'I don't see you living it up in a multi-million apartment in Kensington.'

'Her husband is a businessman.'

'Yeah, and her dad was too. Now he's a big donor for the Conservatives. But, back to hubby. He's a tech investor, originally from Jordan. Has a controlling stake of an AI business, another in a parts supplier embedded in the manufacturing process of every major phone maker outside of the US.'

Winter looked a little surprised at Ryker's knowledge. 'Your point being?'

'Conflict of interest mean anything to you?'

'I think the people who deal with those matters are considerably higher on the MI6 payroll than either me or you.'

'I was never on the MI6 payroll.'

'Beside the point. Fatma's role in MI6 didn't prevent her from being married to a guy just because he's from the Middle East.'

'Obviously not. And where is Mr Yaman today?'

'On a business trip. Qatar, I believe.'

'Hmm.'

'You're actually suggesting that he had something to do with this?'

'No. Not yet. But I'm suggesting there's plenty we don't really know about Fatma Yaman and her husband.'

Winter stared at Ryker as though expecting him to elaborate further.

'Are we going inside or not?' Ryker said.

'Yes,' Winter said, sounding as agitated as he now looked. 'But you need to be on your best behavior in there. This is a murder investigation being run by the book.'

'As opposed to what? A global conspiracy being unpicked singlehandedly by a rampaging madman?'

Winter didn't do a very good job of hiding his smirk. 'You said it, not me. But we're the guests of the Metropolitan Police here. So please... Best behavior.'

'You said that already.'

'I'm glad you were listening.'

Winter turned and Ryker followed to the twelve-foot glass double doors, outside of which stood a uniformed police officer. Winter did the talking. Ryker caught the name DI Dalton, who Ryker presumed was the guy Winter had been on the phone to earlier. They were given the green light from the PC and carried on into the airy atrium, to the elevator bank. Up to the fifteenth floor. Two more police officers stood on the outside of Yaman's apartment and as Ryker and Winter stepped in through the door a young woman decked out in white CSI gear rushed up to them.

'Hi, I'm Kelly,' she said, a little jovially under the circumstances. 'Please put these on.'

She pointed to the shoe covers and masks and gloves. No full suit required for them, apparently. Once Winter and Ryker were ready she ushered them along the corridor, Winter walking a little tentatively, Ryker thought, as though he wasn't quite ready for whatever they were about to see.

'In there, to the left,' Kelly said, coming to a stop at the end of the corridor at the entrance to the grand, open-plan space. Even on a cloudy winter's day, light streamed in through the tall windows across the far side. Ryker's eyes briefly fell to the balcony door which he noticed was ajar, the lock obliterated.

Surely not because of him, though. He'd broken in through that door almost two weeks ago. No way the owners had left it like that since then. The first thing they would have done after noticing the break-in was to secure the place.

'Gentlemen, this way,' came a gruff voice from around the corner.

Ryker followed Winter that way to where a squat man stood by a marble-topped kitchen island. He wore a suit but had on the same shoe covers and gloves as Winter and Ryker, and glasses perched above his face mask.

'I'm DI Dalton,' he said, his voice a little muffled by the mask.

'Peter Winter.'

'James Ryker.'

The guy seemed to pause on Ryker for a moment.

'Right, right. So... She's over here.'

Ryker had already figured that because of the long smudges of deep red that were streaked across the glossy white kitchen tiles, arcing around to the far side of the island.

They hadn't made it all the way around there before Yaman's body came into view. Barefooted, wearing nothing but a nightgown, she was splayed out on the floor, her skin covered in blood, most but not all of it dark and dried.

Winter could barely look at her and Ryker could understand why. He hadn't gotten along with Yaman, still didn't know her true allegiances, her intentions, but seeing her like that, in her own home, so vulnerable and... dead... Not pleasant.

'What do you know?' Winter asked.

'Early days,' Dalton said. 'We're still waiting on full forensics clearance before we move the body but the pathologist has been and the initial verdict was that she likely died from blunt force trauma. There's a nasty mess at the back of her head. Looks like the ornament there.'

He pointed to the metal object on the floor a couple of feet away from the body. Some sort of sculpture of a person, limbs all twisted. Modern art. The bottom edge of the plinth had hairy, bloody gristle hanging off it.

'It looks like a frenzied attack. Her right forearm is broken. Her collarbone too. She has bruises on her torso, face, and lacerations. It looks like she was bludgeoned, hit multiple times with that thing as she fought off her attacker.'

'And she crawled over this way,' Ryker said, looking around to where the blood trail started.

'There's blood spatters around the doorway, but nothing we've spotted further afield than that. So my working theory is that she came from the bedroom – given her clothing – and surprised the intruder in here. They fought. She... lost.'

'Why was she crawling that way?' Winter said. 'Further away from the exit.'

'Most likely she just... panicked,' Dalton said.

Maybe. Or maybe something else.

'We're thinking this was a robbery gone wrong. The balcony door has been forced. In the bedroom, the walk-in closet has been ransacked. I haven't been able to confirm as the husband is still away but I'm thinking jewelry and cash were probably taken. There's a safe but it's still locked, but if the intruder killed her before they got to the loot, most likely they then did a quick smash and grab before running.'

'The balcony door?' Winter said, looking that way. 'We're on the fifteenth floor.'

Dalton shrugged. 'There's signs of forced entry there. Nothing at the front door. But... Yeah, looks like we've got a daredevil burglar.'

Ryker said nothing.

'I've already checked and the neighboring apartments are all occupied. No one heard anything or saw anything.'

'So if the attacker did come in through the balcony... We've no idea where they started off?' Winter said.

'Not yet.'

'Any CCTV?' Winter asked, looking around.

'Nothing recorded in here, we don't think. The alarm wasn't set. There are cameras in the communal areas. We've got it all locked down but haven't started looking yet.'

Winter glanced at Ryker and Ryker nodded as though answering an unspoken question.

'We've dusted for prints and there's plenty around the doors, as you'd expect,' Dalton continued. 'But we'll need to do analysis back in the labs to eliminate the family, housekeeper, and so on, so it's too early to say whether we have our perp or not.'

'Have you spoken to the husband?' Winter asked.

'He's flying back as we speak. Their daughter is with grandparents in Surrey.'

The three of them went silent, Ryker turning conflicting thoughts over in his mind as he focused on Yaman's body.

'I know you guys are... you know... with the intelligence services. And she was too. But... is there anything I need to know here?'

Both men looked at Ryker as though he held the answers, but Winter then took the lead and answered. 'No,' Winter said. 'You carry on your investigation as normal. Unless you're told otherwise, this has nothing to do with her job. Keep me informed of any developments at all.'

Nothing to do with her job? Winter surely didn't believe that.

'The CCTV,' Ryker said. 'No one's reviewed it yet?'

'No. Like I said, we have it locked down. There's a security guard on-site who has access.'

'And he can give *us* access?' Winter asked.

Dalton didn't look too happy about the proposition. 'As long as you record everything you do down there. I don't want any... mishaps.'

Neither Winter nor Ryker questioned what he meant by that before they headed on out. Ryker waited until they were in the elevator before he opened up the conversation.

'Obviously, the break-in is a hoax.'

'Fifteenth floor Spider-Man? Yeah. Obviously. Why would anyone even think to go in like that?'

Ryker huffed. 'I didn't mean that. The thing is... That's how I got in.'

'Jesus, Ryker—'

'But that was two weeks ago. I used an empty apartment one floor down for access. Climbed up, across the outside...'

'You really are insane.'

'Not really. But I don't believe anyone else came in that way.'

'Because no one else is as crazy as you?'

'Maybe. But like I said, I don't think they came in that way. I think it's a message. To me. Whoever killed her... They probably walked right in the front door. The balcony door, the robbery, that's all faked.'

'To frame you?'

'To frame me, or just to stick two fingers up at me. Them telling me they know what I did.'

'*Who*?'

'Exactly.'

The elevator doors opened and they both stepped out but then Winter paused before they carried on to the security office.

'But none of that even starts to explain why Yaman became a target.'

'Of course it does. She knew too much.'

'About what?'

'About Karaman. And she was the one who brought him back here, to England.'

'I thought you were trying to tell me she was in bed with the Syndicate.'

'She was, or she wasn't, but they still made the decision to kill her.'

'But which is it, Ryker?' Winter said, and he sounded angry again. As though he didn't like that Ryker didn't have all the answers. 'Was she killed to keep her quiet, or simply for revenge for having Karaman brought here under arrest?'

The problem was, Ryker didn't know the answer to that.

'Let's go see what we can find on the cameras,' he said.

* * *

Ten minutes later the security guard, who'd introduced himself as Adil, clicked away on his mouse, opening and spacing out several windows on his two large computer monitors. The boxy room was cramped with him and Winter and Ryker all squeezed in. The police officer who'd been standing guard over the lobby area remained outside; not enough space for him in here even if he'd wanted to be involved.

'Take it from after it went dark last night,' Ryker said. 'Say, 5 p.m.'

There was no definitive time for when Yaman had been attacked but the last known contact with her had been a call with her husband around 9 p.m. After that nothing until the maid had found the body not long after eight in the morning.

'There you go,' Adil said and the six screens played in unison.

'I don't even know where to look,' Winter said.

'Concentrate on the fifteenth-floor feed,' Ryker said. 'However the attacker got in, I'm sure they left through the front door.'

Adil sped up the feeds, only slowing whenever a figure appeared on the fifteenth.

'That's her,' Ryker said. Adil slowed the speed to real-time and sure enough Fatma Yaman strolled casually along the corridor – away from the camera – toward her front door at around 6 p.m. Nothing untoward. No obvious nervousness or fear in her movements. She opened the door and disappeared inside.

'Keep playing,' Ryker said.

Five minutes passed. No one else appeared.

'No one followed her in,' Winter said.

'Speed it up again,' Ryker suggested.

The footage sped up. 8 p.m., 9, 10, 11... Midnight. 1 a.m.

'Stop,' Ryker said, although Adil had done so before Ryker had finished the word.

It landed on 1:13 a.m. No one had been seen in the corridor for several hours. Until a dark-clothed figure stepped out of the front door of Yaman's apartment. Black trousers, hooded top, the hood pulled up over a baseball cap. Gloves. The person looked along the corridor then walked purposefully – but didn't run – for the elevators, head down the whole way.

'He's not carrying anything,' Ryker said. By which he meant there was no obvious loot.

He switched his gaze to the feed for the elevator as the man stepped inside, head still down, not even a glimpse of his face.

The man stepped out on the ground floor and, hands in pockets, strode for the front entrance. Out through the doors.

'Wait!' Ryker shouted and both Winter and Adil jumped. 'Top-right feed.'

Which was of a camera perched high on the outside, looking back toward the building entrance. Ryker hadn't spotted that before, on the outside. From the angle, it must have been on a streetlight or even in a tree.

'Go back a couple of seconds, slowly.'

Adil did so and hit pause before Ryker asked him to.

For just the briefest of moments, the man had lifted his head. Not a full-on view of his face, but...

'You know him?' Winter asked.

'No,' Ryker said. 'But it's something to work with.'

Winter huffed as though he didn't agree. 'We saw him leaving, but not arriving,' he said. 'So she didn't let him in to start with.'

'No,' Ryker said. 'So let's go back in time, see if we can find him entering. Concentrate on the corridors for the adjacent floors this time.'

Which took a whole lot longer than the previous search, a more hit-and-miss approach, but finally they found him.

'That's definitely him,' Ryker said, looking at the moving figure on the sixteenth floor.

'It's not even 11 p.m.,' Winter said as the dark-clothed man stopped outside an apartment – one floor up, three along from Yaman's.

The figure disappeared inside.

'What happened over the next two hours before he left Yaman's?' Winter said. 'Did he stay on the sixteenth floor? Or was he in Yaman's home the whole time?'

The latter potentially added a whole new complexity to the situation. It meant the attack was anything but rushed, frenzied, as it had been made to look. Had she actually been held, questioned, tortured?

'Come on,' Ryker said, turning around. 'Adil, thank you.' He carried on out.

'Ryker, hold up!' Winter said, scurrying across the glossy tiles of the atrium to catch up. 'You're done here?'

Ryker stopped and turned to him. 'Yeah.'

'But... there's more we can do on the CCTV. Don't you want to speak to Dalton again too, to discuss what we've found with him?'

'You can. Or we can follow up with him later.'

'But—'

'The fact is, Winter, I know everything I need to know for now.'

'Which is?'

'Fatma Yaman was assassinated.'

'Yeah, and—'

'And we don't know by who, but we know *because* of who.'

'Karaman?'

'Exactly. So we go back to Belmarsh.'

'And you think he's just going to spill everything he knows to you now?'

'Yes. Because this time we do it my way.'

18

'You again?' Karaman said when the guard opened the door and Ryker stepped inside.

He glanced over Ryker's shoulder, as though surprised to see Ryker entering alone.

The guard closed and locked the door, leaving Ryker standing there, staring down at Karaman.

'I already told the detective, I'm not doing any more interviews without my lawyer.'

'Yeah,' Ryker said. 'That's right. Your lawyer. Who I understand you had in here with you while I was gone earlier. Except, he's not here now, is he?'

'You can't—'

'What?'

Karaman glared but said nothing more.

Ryker remained standing a few moments longer, then looked up behind him to the camera in the corner. He kept his gaze there until the little red light flicked off, then he faced back to Karaman whose confidence had ebbed away a little.

'Looks like you're not in charge of the rules here,' Ryker said.

He moved forward and took a seat.

As with the first time he'd been in this room with Karaman, Ryker initially opted for the silent treatment. And once again his guest broke first.

'So what is this?' Karaman asked. 'Your attempt to intimidate me?'

'No. I haven't started on the intimidation yet. You'll know when I have.'

A further silence.

'Did you manage to sort out your emergency?' Karaman asked, barely containing his smile.

'Not yet. But I'm presuming you know by now that Fatma Yaman is dead.'

'Who?'

'You know who she is.'

Karaman shrugged.

'So did your lawyer tell you about her murder? Or have you got someone else on the inside here giving you information?'

Karaman didn't answer.

'Did *you* order the hit?' Ryker asked.

'I don't even know who you're talking about.'

'You should have been thanking her. You're only here, in England, because of her. If it'd been down to me you'd still be in Oman with several pieces of you missing by now.'

Karaman snorted, looked disgusted. 'You really think a lot of yourself, don't you? All your macho talk.'

'My first question is this,' Ryker said. 'Did you have her killed?'

'You asked me that already. I'm locked up in prison. How could I do that?'

'Answer the question.'

'No. I didn't.'

'Do you know *who* ordered the hit?'

A pause this time before, 'No.'

Ryker sat back in his chair and sighed.

'What do you know about her?'

'Nothing.'

'I'll tell you about her, then. She worked for MI6. Middle East expert. She had a lot of files on you. Intel on places you lived, visited. Intel on associates, businesses, money trails.'

Karaman looked entirely unperturbed.

'She had so much information that could have buried you. But she never did. To protect you? That's what I thought before. Now I'm not so sure.'

Ryker paused. Karaman said nothing in response, so Ryker decided to carry on.

'Her intel was how I found you. I stole it from her. My plan was to interrogate you. But somehow she caught wind. Took you back. Brought you here. Now she's dead.'

'It's a terrible thing,' Karaman said.

'Yeah, it is.'

'But it had nothing to do with me. I'm in prison. You may have noticed.'

'Tell me what you know about the Syndicate,' Ryker said, deciding to go for the meat.

'I don't know what that is.'

'Who do you answer to?'

'Allah, of course,' Karaman said with a smile.

'How do you know my name?' Ryker asked.

'Someone told me.'

'Who?'

'It's not important.'

'It is. Otherwise, I wouldn't ask.'

'Does it worry you?'

'It intrigues me, more than anything.'

There was a momentary standoff, but Karaman remained confident and smug. He wouldn't be pretty soon.

'Why don't we back up a little,' Ryker said. 'All these questions but we don't even know each other. So, tell me about your life. How you went from Islamist terrorist organizer to living on that hundred-million-dollar yacht in Dubai.'

'It cost a lot more than that, actually.'

'Yeah? Tell someone who gives a shit about stuff like that. But come on, seriously. Twenty years ago you were some dumbass religious nut who thought you'd get a few virgins in the afterlife if you spilled the blood of some infidels. Or, to put it another way, you decided to set up terror campaigns, suicide bombings, shootings, which saw innocent men, women, children murdered.'

Ryker paused. Karaman didn't say anything.

'You're not denying any of that.'

Nothing from Karaman.

'Seriously, though, what kind of god would be impressed with such barbaric behavior? Only a shithead of a god would reward anyone for such cowardly, vindictive acts. And that's all you were then and all you are now. A coward.'

Karaman still said nothing but he was clearly riled up. Knuckles clenched. A vein throbbing at the side of his head. Was it the talk of his god that offended him or the personal insults?

'But still,' Ryker carried on. 'You went from that coward, twenty years ago, to this corrupt mega millionaire today. So, did you get rewarded by your god for those terrible acts? Or did you just come to the realization that he doesn't actually exist? And in this life, you get what you take. Because there's nothing noble about how you got your money. Stealing, fraud, corruption. Drugs? Trafficking? Are those things not haram? Or does your religion, your dedication to Allah, only count in certain circumstances?'

'You know nothing about me. My life. My religion,' Karaman said through gritted teeth.

'So, tell me. How'd you make your money? How'd you go from that bottom-feeder terrorist to living on that yacht?'

No answer.

'You knew Yousef Selim,' Ryker said.

No answer and no tell on Karaman's face.

'Was he a close friend of yours?' Ryker asked.

Karaman didn't say a word.

'Is that how you knew my name? Because of... our history?'

Karaman still gave nothing away.

'Did you know I'm the man who killed Selim? I gave him what he deserved. Actually... No, he probably deserved a lot more pain than I gave him. But he's dead because of my hand.'

Karaman mumbled something under his breath now. His first language. Ryker didn't catch all of the words but got the gist. A pledge to his god to make Ryker pay.

Ryker smiled. 'Rarely have I felt the satisfaction I did the day I watched his life ebb away in front of me.'

Karaman clenched his jaw but didn't respond, although Ryker knew he was seething.

'Knowing that you and he were friends... You wouldn't believe the added motivation I now have in bringing your cushy life crashing down around you.'

Karaman shook his head but didn't say a word.

'Tell me about the Syndicate,' Ryker said.

No answer once more.

'Would you prefer me to try this a different way?'

No response at all.

'Very well,' Ryker said. 'It's time for the intimidation.'

But he didn't move.

Karaman looked confused as if he'd expected something more sudden, severe.

After a few moments of rising tension, Ryker stood up from his chair and took out the gum he'd earlier stuffed into the corner of his mouth. He reached up to the camera and stretched the gum out across the lens. Just a little extra precaution in case someone outside the room decided to betray his trust and turn it back on to have a quick peek.

Ryker turned back to Karaman who seemed a little amused by the charade. Probably not the correct response, really – perhaps he still doubted Ryker.

Ryker burst forward, grabbed the table, and lifted it from the ground, tipping it toward him and causing Karaman, with his cuffs attached, to be dragged forward, off his seat. He groaned in shock or pain or something else.

Ryker didn't give Karaman a chance to recover. He lifted his foot and Karaman squirmed and cowered as Ryker smashed his heel down onto the metal ring on the tabletop. Well, he aimed for the metal ring, but it was impossible to hit that without also hitting the cuffs and Karaman's hands and wrists too and the prisoner yelled – definitely pain this time – and then roared when Ryker smacked his foot down a second time and the ring snapped free from the table.

As Karaman writhed Ryker took hold of the Formica top and dragged it to the door and wedged it under the door handle.

'My hands!' Karaman yelled, clutching his stricken body parts to his chest. Ryker strode over and Karaman cowered, perhaps finally realizing the predicament he was in. 'What are you—'

Ryker crouched down and grabbed Karaman's lower right arm, squeezing hard as he turned the guy's wrist over and pulled up the sleeve of his prison garb.

'Tell me about this,' Ryker said, prodding the lumpy, shriveled patch of flesh a few inches up from Karaman's hand.

'You can't... do this!' Karaman shouted. He looked from Ryker to the door, opened his mouth to yell. 'Hel—'

He didn't manage to finish the word before Ryker threw a full-blooded punch into the prisoner's stomach, knocking the air from his lungs. He followed up by taking hold of Karaman's right palm and pushing the hand back toward the wrist.

'Shout out again and I snap it,' Ryker said.

He glanced at the door. The table was wedged firmly. Not unbreakable but it'd take some effort to get through. But there was no indication yet that anyone on the outside even knew of the ruckus, so Ryker had time.

'You've... My fingers!'

Which Ryker took to mean Karaman thought Ryker had already broken them, and at least a couple of digits did look to be hanging at pretty awkward angles.

'There's a lot more bones to break yet,' Ryker said, pushing the hand further back and feeling the resistance as the wrist bones were strained.

'You'll burn in hell!' Karaman shouted.

'Hell? I've been living in hell most of my life. The things I've seen, done. Chasing down vermin like you. When I go? The vast nothingness I receive will be peace. A peace you'll be craving for pretty soon.'

Ryker briefly let go of Karaman's hand, then took hold of the pinky on his left hand and bent it back until he heard and felt a snap.

He stifled Karaman's shout of pain by shoving his hand over the guy's mouth while he retook hold of his right wrist, turning it over to reveal the scarred flesh once more.

'Tell me about this,' Ryker said. 'Or, more specifically, tell me about the tattoo you used to have here. The one you burned off. Why? Because it's haram, isn't it? To ink your body like that, to alter what God gave you. But the Syndicate aren't believers. And neither are you, deep down.'

Karaman shook his head. He was shaking. Fear, pain, anger. Sweat globules were popping up on his forehead, his confidence shot.

'Tell me about the tattoo. The double-headed eagle.'

'There was no tattoo!' Karaman shouted out. 'You want to know about this? I was burned. By a fire caused by a bomb dropped on my apartment block by my own government! I was twenty years old. Friends of mine were killed! Because we didn't believe in our corrupt leaders. This is my reminder.'

'Liar!' Ryker shouted and he pushed Karaman's wrist again and the captive quivered with fright. Ryker sent a fist into his side. Onto the now-treated gunshot wound from the extraction. Still pretty damn raw around there given the bulging of Karaman's eyes. 'You're lying. I've seen the tattoo. On the dead body of Davis Bracey. Others too. I'm pretty sure I would have seen it on the dead body of Andrew Lebedev, except his corpse was so badly charred once they pulled it from his burned-out car that there was no way to tell.'

Karaman shook his head, opened his mouth to say something then stopped, either because he had second thoughts or maybe because he was already delirious with pain.

'I'll tell you who I didn't see the double-headed eagle on. Fatma Yaman. I'd had my doubts, but she wasn't one of you after all, was she?'

Karaman didn't answer.

'A double-headed eagle,' Ryker said. 'You had it etched on you, just like all your cronies on the Syndicate. But what? When they sent you off on assignment you had to get rid of it to try and prove you're a good Muslim? When was that? When you were that eager Islamist setting bombs and brainwashing young men into carrying out suicide attacks? Or was it only later in life, when you were trying to prove your faith to the oil sheiks?'

'You have no idea what you're talking about!'

'You think? OK, so how about this? Do you even know what the double-headed eagle represents? Because I've been paying attention.'

Karaman huffed rather than answer.

'Well, keep up, because I'm going to breeze over several thousand years of history because I really don't have all day here.'

Karaman shuffled and squirmed as though trying to get Ryker to release him but a further push against his wrist and a further fist to his side – which was now leaking blood – got him to settle down pretty quickly.

'The double-headed eagle as a symbol is believed to go back to the bronze age,' Ryker started, talking like he was delivering a lecture, 'but its now widespread use is most usually directly or indirectly linked to the Byzantine Empire. You know, the guys who ruled over southern Europe, north Africa, the Middle East, your own country, Türkiye, for hundreds of years after the fall of the Roman Empire, before the emergence of the Ottoman Empire. So the double-headed eagle is a pretty ancient symbol, the two heads representing the physical and the spiritual, or something like that. But a lot of people think the outward-looking heads were simply a nod to the Byzantine's claims to power stretching across Western Europe and to the Middle East. You with me so far?'

Karaman gave no response, but he continued to hold Ryker's gaze.

'Strangely, though, this symbol consistently crops up not just across millennia, but across all manner of clashing cultures. The Byzantines, Anatolian Muslims, the Ottomans, the Holy Roman Empire, the coat of arms of Ivan the Terrible, the Kingdom of Mysore in India. It's on the modern-day Albanian flag. It's used as an emblem for several Orthodox Christian churches, the Scottish Rite of Freemasonry, the Hellenic Army. It's on flags and municipal coats of arms in Austria, Hungary, Spain, Italy, Serbia, Croatia, Germany, England.'

Karaman slowly shook his head, looked disgusted as though he found Ryker's words deeply offensive.

'So, tell me,' Ryker continued. 'Why is this one emblem so pervasive through so many varying societies?'

No answer.

'Because it represents something more than people realize. Something in common between all those peoples, places, cultures.'

'You're insane.'

'No. I'm not. It's a representation, sometimes deliberate but probably often accidental, of power and control. And I really don't know how it all started, whether different people in different places over the centuries even knew what it meant or where it all came from, but it's no surprise to me that a shadow group of powerful and corrupt shitheads like you, like the Syndicate, would use such a symbol to show your affiliation. So tell me about *your* tattoo.'

'I told you. I burned my arm in a fire in Türkiye.'

'You're a liar.' Ryker let go of Karaman's wrist and took another finger. He didn't snap it straight away but got ready to and Karaman tensed up, waiting. 'You're part of the Syndicate.'

Karaman said nothing, but then, it hadn't really been a question. A thud on the door behind Ryker echoed around the room.

'Ryker! What the hell are you doing?'

Winter. He sounded angry.

'We're fine!' Ryker responded. 'Just talking.'

He ignored Winter's complaints as he – or maybe one of the prison guards – unsuccessfully tried to open the door.

'You better be quick,' Ryker said to Karaman, pulling on the finger a little more. 'Tell me about the Syndicate. Who do you take orders from?'

Karaman shook his head.

So Ryker snapped another finger and this time didn't bother to muffle the man's cries.

'Winter, we're good in here!' Ryker shouted out. 'We said we'd do it my way. *This* is my way. So back off until I'm ready.'

He got no response but the activity beyond the door died down momentarily.

Karaman's head rolled as though he was battling to stay awake. Ryker slapped him to bring him around.

'You want me to stop?' Ryker said before delivering another heavier slap. 'Then give me something! A name. Who's in charge?'

He got ready with another finger and Karaman stared wide-eyed. 'I don't know anything! I'm just... I do what I'm asked! I get communications. In person. I set up a deal here, move some money there. That's it!'

Which wasn't dissimilar to what Bracey had claimed too. Except he'd ultimately given up Karaman's name. Karaman would give him something if Ryker was only given the time here.

'Who gives you the instructions!' Ryker bellowed, once again taking the finger to the limit.

'I don't know them!'

'No, you must know more. Who's in charge? One person? A group?'

'I don't know! They're nameless! Faceless! How else is everyone protected?'

'I don't believe you.'

Snap.

Karaman yelled even more loudly this time, maybe not because the pain was any worse but because of the increasingly frenzied nature of the conversation. The ruckus at the door grew louder again, the table scraping, creaking, as Winter and the others outside reinvigorated their attempts to break in.

'I'm only going to ask one more time. Next up is your leg. I'll smash your knee to pieces. You'll never walk again. Give me names.'

Ryker stood up off him and raised his foot and brought it crashing down... onto the floor.

Karaman flinched and cried out and then nearly laughed when he realized what had happened.

'Oops, missed,' Ryker said. 'I won't a second time.'

He lifted his foot again.

'You want a name!' Karaman shouted. 'I'll give you a damn name. One of those from the top. Andrew Lebedev.'

'No. Give me the name of someone who isn't already dead.'

Karaman somehow managed to find a smile in response to that.

'What?' Ryker said, deciphering the response. 'Lebedev's...'

'You said yourself how badly charred that body was.'

Ryker didn't get a chance to say anything more. The next moment the tabletop cracked in two and Ryker spun around as the door burst open. Two prison guards rushed in, Winter a step behind them. All three men paused as they circled around Ryker, looking somewhere between bewildered and mad as hell.

'I warned you,' Winter said to Ryker. 'Jesus, Ryker, I warned you not to do anything stupid!'

Ryker said nothing.

'What are we supposed to do now?' one of the guards asked as his hands hovered by his side, ready to grab a baton or his cuffs or pepper spray or perhaps a first aid kit for Karaman.

'Lock him up,' Winter said. 'You need to lock him up.'

Not Karaman. Ryker. And he didn't resist at all as the guards came for him, cuffs at the ready to take him away.

19

Angel finished filling her backpack then zipped the top closed. She pushed back against the wall and pulled the cap over her face then rested her head against the wooden wall of the barn.

'You're looking pretty relaxed there,' H, who was still messing with one of his weapons next to her, said.

'I've always liked the countryside,' Angel said. 'Nothing but fields and trees and fluttering butterflies and...' She could tell by the look on H's face that he wasn't buying it. Actually, she hated the countryside. Hated it for many different reasons, but not least because out here the stench of manure wafted in through the airy gaps in the single-glazed windows of the unfinished barn conversion. 'Why wouldn't I be relaxed?'

'You don't think this is a big deal?'

'Did I say that?'

'So you're just hard as nails. Nothing fazes you.'

'I didn't say that either.'

H scoffed. 'I've worked with women like you before.'

Angel took the bait. She sat up straighter, lifted the brim of the cap so she could see him. He looked pretty damned pleased with himself as he caressed the barrel of his AK-47 like it was a cherished possession.

'Women like me?'

'Army. Police. Whatever. Women who have just a little bit too much testosterone and it really goes to their heads. Think they can mix it with the big boys just because they have more edge than the rest of the fairer sex. But... when it comes down to it, you're basically just a teenage boy with a bad attitude.'

'Bad attitude? And you're basing that on what?'

H laughed. 'So you're not denying the rest of what I said, then?'

'Every word that came out of your mouth was utter bullshit. So yeah, I'm denying all of it.'

H put the weapon down on his lap.

'It's simple physics, love. What do you weigh?'

She didn't answer.

'Go on, what do you weigh?'

'Sixty-three kilograms, pretty much dead on.'

H laughed again. 'Like I said, teenage boy territory.'

'Brawn isn't all that counts in my world, in the jobs I've done. And if you think muscle is all it takes... then you're as dumb as you look, you moronic ape.'

'Ooh, I touched a nerve. Now you're resorting to insults about my looks. Very classy, Angel.'

'Why don't you just drop it.'

He held his hands up in defense. 'I'm just playing with you. Banter, that's all.'

Which was a lie, but she didn't bite back this time.

'We're going to be putting our lives on the line together tomorrow morning,' H said. 'I want to make sure I know who you are and that you've got my back.'

'I do what I need to do to get the job done,' Angel said. 'That's all you need to know. Where the hell is Mason, anyway?'

She turned, stood up, stretched out, and looked at the grimy window next to her. He was still out there, by the cars, phone to his ear.

'Who do you reckon he's talking to?' she asked.

'Probably whoever's paying us. Or whoever's really running this thing.'

'And who is that?'

'Don't know.'

'Honestly?'

'Honestly,' he said. 'I'm just a hired gun. Same as you. But you know his past, don't you?'

'Not much of it.'

'MI5. Spies. They're all the same. Once a spook, always a spook. *You* should know.'

'I was never a spy,' Angel said, sounding genuinely offended. Because she was. She hated the term. It sounded so... grimy.

'No? Not what I read,' H said.

'And what did you read?'

'You know. About you, that shot from a rooftop in Beirut. Karaman, the little girl. You spending a few years in prison because of it all.'

She didn't respond.

'Sounds to me like they did you over.'

'Yeah, they did.' They? Her employer. Because they could have done more to rescue her. Done *something*. But mostly she blamed Karaman.

'You have nothing to say about any of that?'

'You said all that needs to be said. What about you? What's in your past? Other than the obvious.'

'The obvious?'

'You were army. Infantry to start with. You probably started at sixteen because you were too dumb or just too into the idea of shooting people to go to college or anything.'

He nodded and smiled as though he found the truth amusing.

'But... I see something in your eyes,' she added. 'A hardness. A coldness. But also chinks in what you think is your indestructibility. You were special forces of some kind, same as me. You've been hurt, and you've hurt others, and you've seen some bad shit and it affects you in ways you can't describe. Actually, in ways you just don't like describing because you think it makes you weak to even think about it.'

He looked far less amused after that. She'd hit a nerve.

'Am I wrong?' she asked.

'Mostly right. But that's not all I am. And unlike you and Mason, there's nothing about me on the internet, believe me. I'm not dumb enough to get caught out like that.'

Just like that, his bravado was back. The guy was so full of himself. Angel really wanted to bring him down a few notches but... what was the point?

'I don't even know your name,' she said. 'It feels a bit unfair that you know so much about me and Mason.'

H shrugged. 'And that's the way it's going to stay.'

Angel returned her focus to the outside.

'How long have you known him?' H asked.

'A few days.'

'You trust him?'

'Enough.'

'Same. But I'll be watching my back until I get my money.'

The conversation paused and Angel kept her focus on Mason. He looked over toward her but then quickly away again, then he walked around the other side of the nearest vehicle as though he needed more privacy.

'Have you slept with him?' H said.

'Why would you even ask that?'

'That's a yes, then,' he said with a self-satisfied chuckle. 'But you only met him a few days ago?'

'Yeah. Up in Cumbria.'

'And you've been with him every night since then?'

'What is your damn problem?' Angel said, pulling her attention away from the window and sending H a death glare.

He once again held up his hands in defense. 'Hey, I'm sorry. Didn't mean to push your buttons.' Which was the biggest lie he'd told so far. 'I wasn't trying to get at you for screwing him. But seriously, were you with him two nights ago?'

'Actually, no,' Angel said definitively and feeling quite satisfied about being able to do so.

'Interesting,' H said, reaching into his pocket and pulling out his phone. He stared at the screen as he typed away.

'What is?' Angel said after a while.

H shrugged, carried on doing what he was doing.

'What's interesting?'

He smirked and she really hated that he'd reeled her in so much.

'Does this face look familiar to you?'

He held the phone out and Angel moved closer. She took the phone from him and pulled it closer still. On a small screen, with a grainy image, it was hard to tell for sure, but...

'So?' H said.

'You think that's Mason?'

'You said it, not me.'

It *could* have been Mason, but it could have been hundreds of thousands of people. The picture – possibly a still from CCTV – showed a poor-quality glimpse of a man's face. Caucasian. Not too old, not too young. A thin face, no particularly distinguishing features.

'What's the point?' Angel said.

H reached out for his phone and she handed it back to him.

'This picture was released by the Met a few hours ago. This guy is wanted for murder.'

'Murder of who?'

'Fatma Yaman.'

'And she is?'

'Apparently an intelligence analyst. Which, given what we both know about these things, most likely means she was MI5 or MI6. I also have it on good authority that she was responsible for bringing Ismail Karaman to England.'

'Shit,' Angel said.

'Karaman comes back to England after years on the run. Two days later the person responsible is found murdered in her home in London.'

'You honestly think it's Mason?'

'Ask yourself, what does it mean if it is?'

She really didn't know. Did it even make sense?

'I think it means—'

'How are you two getting along?' Mason asked. Angel jumped at his voice and H looked amused by her reaction. Obviously, he'd seen Mason before she had and had chosen not to warn her.

'We're just peachy, aren't we, Angel?' H said.

'Yeah,' she said.

'So, we're all set?' Mason asked.

'Packed up and ready to go,' H said. 'We were talking though, and Angel did just have one question for you?'

Mason looked from her to H and back again, it was clear from the suspicion on his face that he didn't like something.

'Yeah? And?' he said.

'Who were you speaking to?' Angel asked.

'You don't need to know.'

'Maybe we do,' she said. 'If you want us to be in this with you, we need to know you're not screwing us.'

'Hey,' H said, trying to look and sound all innocent. 'This is her talking, not me. I tried to calm her on this already.'

Bastard.

'I've already explained this situation to you,' Mason said. 'Your part in this is to help me get to Karaman. You get paid for that. What happens after you're paid has nothing to do with you.'

'I'm good with that,' H said.

'Angel?' Mason prompted when she didn't respond.

'Run me through the plan again,' she said.

Mason raised an eyebrow, looking at her as though fed up with her awkwardness.

'Which part?' he asked.

'Top level.'

'We go to London. We take Karaman. We bring him back here. We wait for the money to arrive. Three offshore bank accounts, one for each of us. Three point three million, and a bit, each. When we're happy, we pack up and go to the drop-off and leave Karaman there. No exchange. No chance for us to be screwed.'

'But who are we leaving him for?' Angel asked.

Mason sighed. 'Angel, I know what you're thinking—'

'Do you?'

'Yes. If it was down to you, you'd put a bullet in his head and be done.'

She clenched her teeth, ground them hard.

'But this is better. The money you're getting for this will set you up for life.'

'But where is Karaman going?'

'We're not setting him free. Just trust me on that.'

'How can I trust you when you're not giving me any real answers?'

'If you want out, then get the fuck out. Now is the time.' He pointed toward the door.

Angel said nothing.

'Remember who I was, Angel. The type of people I know. You know as well as I do that if we leave Karaman in the British legal system he'll never face justice. His lawyers will have him back in the Middle East in no time one way or another. And there's little value to any of us if all we do is kill him.'

'I'm not so sure about that,' Angel said.

'Well, I am. The people I'm working with… Karaman has value to them. Great value. Not in monetary terms but because of who Karaman is and what he knows. He's not getting off lightly. Where he's going… It's going to be a damn sight harder for him than Belmarsh.'

The room fell silent. Angel chewed over Mason's assurances. The simple fact was that he wasn't going to give her any more information than he already had. No names, no real specifics about who he answered to or Karaman's fate.

'This time tomorrow you'll have your money,' Mason added. 'And a new life.'

But maybe it was her old life that she wanted more than anything, even if she knew she could never have it.

'So, are we good?' H asked.

He'd really loved the whole thing. Setting Angel up like that when he had no intention of challenging Mason.

'We're good,' Angel said.

'I really hope so,' Mason responded. 'Get the cars ready, we're heading out in ten.'

He disappeared off again. H looked so smug.

'Happy now?' she asked.

'Hey, all I did was raise some legitimate doubts. Don't you feel better for getting it all out?'

Strangely, the fact H was apparently cool with it all... It did make her feel that little bit better, even if she hadn't gotten to the point of questioning Mason about Fatma Yaman. Did it really change things if he *had* killed the agent who'd brought Karaman here? She really didn't know, because she knew from experience that nothing was ever black or white in the clandestine world of secret agents.

'The point is,' H said, 'putting aside the sex, none of us knows the other that well. And I know you don't like me. That's fair. I'm an acquired taste. But ask yourself this, Angel. If things don't go to plan, if it turns out this threesome isn't quite as cohesive as it needs to be, and you haven't been told everything you needed to know... Whose back have you got? Me, the guy who you know is in this for the money, and nothing else, and who'll do whatever to make sure *we* get paid. Or the guy who you know isn't being straight with you because he's still got at least one foot in the world of spooks.'

He didn't wait for a response. Just picked up his backpack and strode on out.

* * *

The sun wasn't yet up and outside the car it was dark and freezing cold. Angel was tired, hours on the road, hours of prep. The last twenty-four – or was it forty-eight? – hours were a blur and she was exhausted, but sleep could wait. She was wired on adrenaline and caffeine. She was ready to go.

'That's it?' H asked, looking out across the road to the closed gates.

'That's it,' Mason said. He looked at his watch. 'We don't have an exact time. Between 7 and 7:30 a.m. is the expectation.'

'Reporters are gathering already,' Angel said, indicating the cluster of people huddled together in the dark. It wasn't even 6 a.m.

'Which is good for you,' Mason said. 'The more cover we have, the more bystanders we have to cause a panic, the easier this will be.'

'Yep,' H said. 'We're really gonna fuck their shit up out there.'

'Let's go over the basics one last time,' Mason said. 'Rule number one?'

'Non-lethal only,' H said.

'The police, the guards, bystanders are innocents as far as we're concerned, and none of us needs the extra heat of murder charges if we're ever identified.'

'Which we won't be,' H said, sounding confident of that.

'Use the rifles and your blanks for effect,' Mason added. 'To get people running. If you need to put anyone down, use close combat or the tranquilizers.' Which were loaded into their modified pistols.

'Got it,' Angel said.

'Rule number two?' Mason asked.

'No hostages,' Angel said. 'Only Karaman.'

'Rule number three?'

'No comms unless we have a problem.'

'Good,' Mason said. 'You break any of those and you're risking everything, for all of us. Logistics?'

'Three vehicles. Three exit routes,' H said.

'Except if we hit a snag and one of us needs assistance,' Angel added.

'Because we don't leave anyone behind.'

'Because we don't want any of us identified.'

'Seems like we're all on the same page, then,' Mason said. He fired up the engine. 'Let's go get a drink. In thirty minutes, we'll be in position.'

20

Two nights. Two long, dull nights he'd spent in this cell. Meals had been dropped through the hatch, but he'd had no visitors. No opportunity for a phone call. No one to take him out to be interviewed by detectives or anyone else. He'd not been charged with a crime yet either, and they couldn't hold him much longer without doing so.

Ryker threw the tennis ball against the ceiling again as he lay on his back on the hard bunk. It bounced off and onto the wall and back into his hand. He had no idea who'd left the ball in there in the first place, but he was grateful; it'd provided some distraction from monotony at least. Perhaps Winter had left it, almost like an apology. Or like a master would leave a toy for a dog when they left their pet in a crate when out of the house.

He tossed it again, with pinpoint accuracy, and the ball fell into his palm with him barely moving.

He sat up in the bed. Repeated the same, but this time off the floor and wall. Over and over. Over and over.

Until he heard a noise outside.

He missed the catch and the ball bounced off the bunk and

rolled along the floor toward the door, which swung open. Winter took a step in. He looked confused as he glanced down. He picked up the ball, turning it over as though unsure of what it was. Then he tossed it outside and Ryker heard it pinging away along the corridor floor. He clenched his fists.

'Good morning,' Winter said. The door remained open behind him. A prison guard was standing in the doorway, arms folded, glaring.

Ryker was quite tempted to jump up and make a run for it.

'Good?' he said.

'How've you been?'

'Is that a serious question?'

'Yes.'

'I've been treated well,' Ryker said. 'By the guards. Not by you.'

'You really think that?'

'What is this? A couple of days in prison is supposed to make me think twice? Supposed to make me feel regretful?'

'Clearly you don't.'

'Not even a little bit. Is he still here?'

'He's still here. Broken bones and all.'

Ryker said nothing to that.

'What you should probably stop to think about isn't whether or not your tactics would lead to where you want them to lead. And it's not whether you think Karaman deserves to be hurt like that. The point is... by completely disregarding laws, and everything I'd said and throwing it back in my face and doing what you did right under my nose...'

He seemed to lose his train of thought.

'You think I disrespected you,' Ryker said. 'Is basically what you're saying. Because we both know damn well, in our world, that we get things done however they need to get done.'

'Maybe. But you still have to play by certain rules.'

'Your say so, you mean.'

'Yes, my damn say so!' Winter shouted and stamped his foot at the same time and even if Ryker didn't find the guy in any way intimidating there was no doubting his level of anger right then. 'Because someone still has to hold people like you to account!'

'So what do we do now?'

'You're not being charged. There's nothing to charge you with. There are no witnesses, no evidence of a crime. Karaman hurt himself in a fall.'

'It took you two days to come up with that?'

'You can stay here longer if you want.'

Ryker stood up from the bunk.

'But let me make this really damn clear for you, Ryker.'

'I'm listening.'

'You're done here. Whatever mission you were on, personal or otherwise, is over as far as I'm concerned. You won't get to see Karaman again. You're leaving this prison today and if you want my advice, I think you should probably just take off. Get out of the country for a while. Carry on your quest somewhere away from me. Or better still, just go and lie on a beach somewhere.'

Ryker did his best to hold his tongue. He really didn't like Winter's tone with him, nor his demand, but he also had to be realistic. Without this man's help, Ryker almost certainly wouldn't have the opportunity to walk out of Belmarsh a free man.

'You're telling me to stop investigating Karaman? The Syndicate?'

'I'm *asking* you, in very strong terms, to think very carefully about what you're trying to achieve, and how you're going to achieve it from here.'

'Because you won't be helping me anymore?'

'If you cared for me or my career at all, you'd decide to look elsewhere for help, for a while at least.'

Which was an odd way to put things. But Ryker got the point. Winter had had enough of him. Wanted him to clear off so that he couldn't cause any more trouble. But Ryker hadn't set out to cause trouble for Winter, that had never been his aim. His aim was to take down a corrupt network of influential criminals. Did that not count for anything?

Yeah, actually it did. Which again was why Ryker was being allowed to walk out a free man today.

He didn't like the situation but he had seen it for what it was.

He hovered a moment longer, a lingering thought at the forefront of his mind. Karaman's parting words about Andrew Lebedev. Ryker had wanted to discuss that with his 'friend' for coming on for two days but he'd been given no chance to.

Given how this conversation had just played out, he'd keep the lead for himself.

'Thank you,' Ryker said, and Winter looked more than a little surprised by the response. 'Shall we go?'

'Follow me.'

They headed out along the corridor of cells, along another couple of corridors to a reception area about as bland as one would expect for a prison.

'You're doing this the proper way,' Winter said. 'The record of your arrest stays. You need to go and sign whatever they're asking you to sign and collect your things.'

By 'things' Ryker guessed Winter meant the few belongings Ryker had taken into the interview room with Karaman, which consisted only of half a pack of gum and a burner phone. He didn't even need those items, but he'd get them. Yet... Something about the indignity of the whole thing wasn't lost on him and he was sure Winter really enjoyed the moment even if he still looked and sounded aggravated merely by Ryker's presence.

Ryker headed over to the duty sergeant at the desk, Winter hovering behind. He spotted the gaggle of reporters outside.

He turned around to Winter and raised an eyebrow and knew that Winter would understand the question.

'Yes, it's for Karaman. He's going to court today.'

'Are you?' Ryker asked.

'Irrelevant to you.'

'Because I'm not.'

'You definitely are not. If you need help getting a flight or a ferry out of England, let me know.'

'I think I'll manage just fine.'

'Are we all good here?' Winter asked. Not to Ryker but to the desk sergeant.

'All good.'

'See you around, Ryker.'

And with that Winter headed on out.

21

The morning was cold, but dry at least. No sign of any sunlight yet, the area outside the prison lit up only by the sporadic street lighting and the orange glow that encircled London like a forcefield.

Angel kept her head down, the cap pulled low so her face was shielded from the CCTV cameras. She knew exactly where each one was positioned and hadn't moved from this exact spot – where she knew she'd remain most concealed – in the twenty minutes since she'd arrived.

The number of reporters and photographers had steadily grown in that time. As Angel stood with the backpack over her shoulders and the camera in her hand, she was just one of them as far as everyone else was concerned. She counted twenty-four people in total now. Not a complete circus, although she expected perhaps more would be present outside Woolwich Crown Court to welcome Karaman there – not that he'd make it...

Despite the huge furor that had blanketed the UK's press over the last few days, after news that Ismail Karaman had finally been captured and brought back to the UK to face historic terror charges, Angel knew the world was a different place now. In the early part of the twenty-first century, especially immediately after 9/11, the war on terror in the Middle East had been all-consuming for the West, and Ismail Karaman had made his name as one of the main instigators of a swathe of attacks against the US and the UK in the years that followed. Back then Karaman had been vilified by nearly everyone, called out for his heinous crimes by all who mattered. Yet even as Angel had scoured social media that morning, she'd seen post after post not just from nutjobs but from sometimes prominent left-wing journalists who now called into question the narrative. Claiming Karaman was misunderstood. That his actions years ago were not those of a terrorist but of a rebel, striving for justice for an oppressed people. That the US government in particular was the real aggressor and the responsible party for the deaths of the terror attacks. And those views weren't confined to Karaman's actions, but to other prominent terrorists too, Bin Laden among them.

It made Angel hate Karaman even more. From what she could see, many of the followers of such rhetoric were the younger generation. People who hadn't been born or were only tiny children at the time of 9/11. She had been young then too. She'd signed up for the army still a teenager and had been heavily involved in the still waging conflicts in the Middle East in the many years that followed. Most of the younger generation had grown up in a safe haven for the very reason that people like Angel had put their lives on the line to prevent such atrocities as 9/11 from reoccurring.

Now people were calling for this man, this monster, to be freed and returned to his homeland. Claiming that the powers that had brought him back to the UK were the evil ones, circumventing laws like political bulldozers in the process of extraditing him to face what they claimed couldn't possibly be a fair trial.

Angel let go of the camera. She'd been crunching it under her grip, channeling her distaste and anger that way. An ache shot down from her shoulder and into her arm – pain from the fight with Mason a few days ago. But it dissipated, or she at least blocked it out as she looked across the group of people and to Mason on the other side. He gave her a look. A look that said... She didn't know what.

A murmur spread across the gaggle of people. Angel heard noise from beyond the huge metal gates. Four police officers came out of a side entrance, bright yellow hi-vis jackets on, G36C Heckler and Koch carbines in their grips. Two stood on either side of the gates as sentries, their faces hard and their stances purposeful.

They'd expected the armed officers. They'd deal with it. Angel glanced over at Mason again, but he was paying her no attention now.

That was fine. It meant he was ready, that there were no problems.

The gates rolled open, the flashing blue from behind them becoming more and more engulfing the wider the opening became. Two police motorbikes crawled out first. An armored van next. Then the prisoner transport van. Another two motorbikes at the rear.

Cameras clicked and flashed. Everyone in the group jostled for position knowing that within seconds the motorcade would be gone.

Angel heard a rumbling noise from further afield. No one else paid attention initially, too busy focusing on the vehicles in front. But she braced herself because she knew.

As the gates slowly rolled closed, the motorbikes at the front looked like they were about to take off to lead the vehicles – with Karaman on board – away, but then one of the officers put his foot down onto the tarmac and looked to his left. To where H in his van was steaming toward them. Then the crowd finally realized too. People started murmuring, questioning, then pushing and shoving.

Finally shouting when they realized that the speeding van was headed straight for them.

Angel pulled the balaclava over her head. Mason had done the same. No one had noticed at all. She took hold of the camera. Unscrewed the large lens...

She looked over at Mason and he nodded.

She didn't even see him draw the weapon, he was so fast. The next moment the barrel of his AK-47 pointed in the air and he let rip.

The booming gunfire had the desired effect. Within a couple of beats, the group of civilians were in pure panic. Some dove for the ground. Others ran in all directions, into each other even, shoving others to the ground.

H's van blasted onto the scene and swiped right into one of the police motorbikes sending the driver flying. Tires screeched as he slammed the brakes but the van didn't stop in time before it smacked into a traffic bollard. Exactly where he'd intended to be because with the gates almost closed again, the motorcade was now blocked in. They had at least thirty seconds before the gates opened again to give the transporter the chance to retreat. Hopefully more. Easily enough to immobilize Karaman's van.

Angel charged forward, hunched down, tossed the lens – the explosive – under the transport van. She raced around to the back and pulled the sticky bomb from her backpack and slammed it onto the locked door.

She turned and darted away, heading for H's van for cover.

Boom.

The first explosive detonated, and as she skidded to a stop and turned. The transport van was in midair, fire billowing from underneath. It had only just crashed back down when the second bomb exploded and Angel ducked and covered herself as the blast wave and grit and small shrapnel burst toward her.

A momentary lull followed. Literally a moment, because as she was still recovering her senses H jumped out of his van and let rip with his AK-47.

'Go get him!' he shouted out to Angel.

She raced for the mangled van...

* * *

Ryker knew something was wrong when he heard the engine in the near distance, the vehicle approaching from the far side of the emerging motorcade and at speed. Winter had gone, leaving Ryker standing outside, by the entrance still, his belongings in his pocket as he decided whether to walk into the city or call for a taxi. And then, he needed to decide what he'd even do when he got to the city. Find a hotel? Get the first plane out of the country? That was clearly what Winter wanted.

Those thoughts still rumbling, Ryker looked from the transporter that he knew Karaman was in and over to the fast-approaching van. The photographers and reporters hadn't noticed, too busy trying to get a glimpse of Karaman as though doing so would be some mega scoop.

Ryker looked from the van to the policemen on foot, to the motorcade, back to the van.

No. That thing wasn't stopping.

And Ryker was still debating what it meant, what he'd do, when booming gunfire burst through the air. Not the police, as he at first thought, but a shooter, dark clothes, head covered with a balaclava. People raced about like headless chickens. The four armed officers on foot... They hunkered down, likely trying to hurriedly work out a plan of action that wouldn't involve shooting through a group of scared pedestrians.

The onrushing van sped past and Ryker winced as it only

narrowly missed pulverizing one of the officers on the bikes before it smashed into a traffic bollard.

Then Ryker saw them. Another balaclava-clad attacker. But this one looked to be a woman. She raced for Karaman's transporter, chucked something underneath...

Not something. He knew what it was.

Ryker raced forward and ducked down and held an arm to his face at the first explosion. He had to drop flat to the floor for the second, the force of which would have smacked him off his feet otherwise.

He jumped back up. Smoke, fire, chaos all around. A second shooter jumped out of the now smashed-up van. He let rip with an AK-47. But... Blanks. They were firing blanks. Otherwise, there would have been bloodied bodies lining the tarmac already.

Ryker spotted the woman who'd laid the two bombs. She rushed for the back of the transporter. Ryker raced that way too. Shots from the police officers were ringing out now – and it was live fire from them. Blood burst out of the leg of a photographer who was hit in the crossfire and he collapsed to the ground screaming. The shooter from the van pulled a pistol. Two quick shots at the policeman. Two hits. But the shots were muffled. Not from a silencer. There was no explosive. She was firing darts.

The woman dragged Karaman from the transporter. Ryker was about to dive forward and tackle her until a bullet whizzed by his ear and he ducked and the next moment a figure bundled into him from behind, knocking him to the ground.

A big bulky figure wearing hi-vis.

The police officer barked at him as they wrestled. Tried to cuff him. Perhaps he even recognized him from the prison and thought the attack was down to him.

'I'm not one of them!' Ryker roared.

The officer took no notice so Ryker had little choice. He took hold of the guy's wrist, turned it inside out, and bounced to his feet and thumped his heel down onto the man's knee. Ryker twisted further on his arm, pulling the officer onto his back, his hand up above him, bones pushed to bursting.

'I'm not one of them,' Ryker said again a moment before a dart whizzed into the officer's stomach. Ryker wrestled the policeman's gun free and raced for cover on the other side of the transporter. He quickly glanced around. More police officers were swarming now from inside the prison, but not many were armed. Several were on the floor already, not moving.

Ryker spotted one of the attackers, edging away, along the road, as he fired his rifle indiscriminately toward the crowds. Blanks again, he was sure.

The others?

There. Two of them. Running across the grass, toward the trees. A road lay the other side, a hundred yards away. One of them was the woman, her frame much slighter. She was pulling Karaman who couldn't take the weight on one of his legs. Her accomplice provided covering fire.

Ryker set off after them. He checked the weapon he was holding as he moved. A carbine. A good weapon. Compact, light. Accurate at distance. He lifted it, not breaking stride. Heard shouts behind him. He didn't turn, didn't pay the shouts any attention until bullets pinged into the ground by him.

The police were shooting at him!

He darted to the side, turned, and fired off, deliberately missing the chasing figures but causing the two police officers to cower back at least. He ran for the trees. Ryker heard an engine again. But it was not the same van as before. The revs were more high-pitched. He looked to see a car speeding from the other side of the prison, from where he'd seen the shooter heading moments before. The vehicle was gunning toward his friends.

Ryker lifted his weapon again to the threesome ahead of him. He fired a single shot to gauge his aim. The bullet smacked into the ground a few inches from Karaman's trailing leg. Ryker slowed a little to take a more accurate aim.

Bang.

He hit the woman in the ankle.

Bang.

He hit her accomplice in the back of the thigh.

He would have gone for center mass, but he was sure they'd both be wearing Kevlar and he wanted them down.

The woman stumbled and went to the floor. The man collapsed forward, rolling along the grass.

The car...

Was heading right for Ryker now.

He sank down to his knee, and let rip. Bullets pinged into the metalwork, into the windscreen. Hard to tell in the dark but he must have hit the driver...

Definitely hit, because just as Ryker was about to dive out of the way, the car suddenly swung right as though the driver had involuntarily tugged on the wheel. It careened over the grass, jolting over a hump before it smashed into a tree.

A police motorbike raced toward Ryker from the prison. He fired one more shot. Missed. But the rider pulled on his handlebars and the bike skidded and the rider toppled and bounced along the ground.

The officer would be fine. Most likely.

Ryker went to move but again had to cower, this time behind a tree, as more bullets came his way from the police. He sent covering fire back toward them, spun back the other way...

Where'd the other two attackers gone? Where was Karaman? Ryker couldn't see them at all.

He made a dash toward the smashed car. He looked through the broken driver's window.

'Damn it!'

He noted the empty but bloodied seat, the passenger door wide open.

He looked up to see the man hobbling away toward a parked van on the road ahead. The other two were even closer to it, only a few yards from the door.

The woman, still dragging Karaman, looked behind. Spotted her friend. He beckoned her. She shouted out in warning as Ryker lifted his weapon and fired.

Four shots. Leg first, then torso and the man twisted as he fell and at least one of the bullets sank into his side. Under his Kevlar? Maybe, because he didn't move as he lay on the ground.

Ryker renewed his focus on the woman. Pushed on. Her other friend was nearly at the van but she was lagging behind with the extra weight of pulling Karaman with her.

'Stop!' Ryker shouted out, but, if anything, his instruction caused her to find extra strength and move faster. Ryker took aim once more and pulled the trigger but received nothing but an empty *click* in return this time.

He was out. He had no more magazines. He tossed the weapon and sprinted and the woman only realized he was on her at the last second and yelled in panic – was she yelling at Ryker or her friend? Ryker wasn't sure. But she let go of Karaman and turned and ducked and...

Ryker ran straight through her. He took her around the thighs and lifted her off the ground and thumped her down onto the soggy ground.

She tried to hit him, to claw at him as Ryker wrestled for control of her arms to pin her down. He managed it for a mere couple of seconds, ripped off her balaclava.

Ryker stared down at her face. A momentary pause in the chaos before he heard the engine revs and looked up to see the van's brake lights flick off before it shot away.

'Looks like you're on your own.'

But she wasn't finished fighting. She writhed and bucked and hauled up a knee which dug into the small of Ryker's back. She twisted her shoulder and pulled one of her arms free and flailed at him. She hit him in the face and then in the kidney as Ryker fought for control once more.

Then a gunshot from the side. The police. Ryker hunkered instinctively, defensively, and the woman took her opportunity. Her free hand grasped at her side and Ryker only saw the pistol at the last moment as she pushed the barrel up toward his chest.

He grabbed her wrist and twisted off her to create a moving target and as they tumbled he fought to take the weapon. She fired and Ryker sucked in air at the jabbing impact...

Not a bullet. If it'd been a bullet, right there by his heart, he'd have been dead in seconds. But the shock was enough to give the woman the advantage, and with the dart sticking out of his chest, she wrestled free from Ryker's grip and rushed for the road.

Ryker went to stand. Noise all around him. Police officers closing in. He glanced at the ground where moments ago the shooter from the car had laid. Gone now too.

Ryker tried to speak but couldn't. Tried to move forward but he fell down onto one knee.

Feet thudded around him. Warnings were shouted. *Hands in the air.* Ryker couldn't even if he tried.

He face-planted the floor and seconds later was out cold.

22

'What the actual fuck!' Angel screamed as she thumped the gas pedal of the car. As she did so a cacophony of pain erupted in her leg, shooting up from where the bullet had torn across her ankle.

She wasn't sure who she was shouting at. Mason and H for leaving her, or that would-be hero for shooting her, tackling her and fighting her and causing her to be left behind.

Three vehicles. Three exit routes. Except if we hit a snag and one of us needs assistance. Because we don't leave anyone behind.

Except they had. They'd left *her* behind. Alone.

How had H even got up again? She'd seen him gunned down.

Wired on adrenaline she pushed past the pain in her leg and raced through the streets, still relatively clear in the early morning, dawn only just approaching. South was the immediate aim. South, to make it look like they were heading for the coast and the quickest way out of the country, but then loop back to the east and north to the safe house. But that'd be in a different vehicle. This one was simply for the getaway.

Three vehicles. Three exit routes. Except she'd already decided not to take her planned route. She was taking Mason's. Whatever had happened to H there was no way he was capable of driving. Mason was driving that van.

She'd find him. Figure this out.

And it took a lot less time than she thought. Less than three miles, in fact.

She took a right. A busy crossroads lay fifty yards ahead that even in the early morning was likely to be a sticking point, but it was a necessary point to traverse to get clear of the most congested part of the city.

Except it looked like Mason hadn't been patient enough. He'd tried to run a red or had just got unlucky or something because at the other side of the junction, the van was impaled on the traffic light. Smoke billowed from its crumpled hood as bystanders stepped from their cars, looking bewildered and unsure whether to approach the crash or not.

It had only happened seconds before. Otherwise, some good Samaritan would have put aside any doubts and gone up to the van already.

Angel sped up. Pedestrians became wary of the approaching fast car as though sensing another smash, or just that some bigger event was about to take place that they couldn't yet comprehend.

She skidded to a stop, tires screeching, people cowering away. She pulled on her balaclava, grabbed the AK-47 and – doing her best to ignore the pain in her leg from the gunshot – rushed out to the van.

'Stay back!' she screamed and waved the gun around, and everyone took notice. No heroes here.

She reached the driver's side and yanked open the door.

'What the hell?'

Not Mason. Not H. Who the fuck was that behind the wheel?

The guy was bleeding badly, his head hanging forward. She went to lift it to see his face, to check his pulse but his eyes sprang open and he yelled, and she saw the glint of the knife coming toward her.

'Bastard!' she roared back and had that little bit more strength and focus than he did to first defect the blow and to help the knife on its way up into the guy's neck.

His hand fell from the grip and Angel yanked the knife out, and blood poured as she stepped away. She swooshed the rifle around again as she moved for the back of the van. She opened the doors.

'Shit!'

An absolute mess. H's body lay twisted and lifeless. She jumped in and took only a few seconds, checking his pulse, to know he was gone.

'What happened?' she asked Mason, but he was groggy too. He had a nasty-looking cut above his eye to go with the gunshot wound in his leg and he cradled his hands to his side. Another bullet or what? 'Can you talk?'

'Get us... out of here,' he groggily replied.

The handcuffed Karaman was the most awake out of all of them but said nothing as Angel grabbed him and pushed him out of the van to the ground. She was a little bit more gentle with Mason, but only a little bit.

She jumped down onto the road and waved the AK-47 around again.

'I said stay back!'

She let off a few rounds for effect and anyone who hadn't already taken cover jumped for safety. No one stepped in to try to stop her as she bundled the two men into the car.

Sirens closed in nearby. No doubt the police had received countless calls from the bystanders. But she was done.

Seconds later they were heading away.

We don't leave anyone behind.

Yeah. Except they'd left *her*. And she'd just left H. Because he was dead and she didn't have the time to drag a dead body with her.

And she'd left that other man too. The driver.

Whoever the fuck he was.

* * *

Nearly two hours later Angel pulled the car off the single-track road and onto the winding gravel driveway, the safe house a quarter of a mile further ahead, still out of sight beyond the undulating terrain.

She tensed up. As though the entire day hadn't already been tense, starting with the initial attack going wrong and that damn hero nearly screwing everything up. Then finding Mason and the others in the smashed van. Then the changeover to the current car around the back of the abandoned roadside restaurant next to a grimy petrol station.

Actually, that part was probably the least stressful as it had just felt good to be out of the getaway car and into this much nicer vehicle that hopefully wasn't yet on any kind of police watch list.

Yet despite everything that had come before, she tensed up again as though a last-minute hitch was imminent. As though she was about to ride over the crest of the hill and see the safe house in the distance with a swarm of blue lights around it, armed police, snapping dogs, snipers, helicopters...

Absolutely nothing.

She sighed in relief and slowed the car, crawling the last part of the journey, her eyes busy scoping out in case of a sudden ambush. But there really was no one else there at all. No vehicles or houses even in sight of this isolated place.

She took the car around the back of the converted barn and parked up, shutting down the engine. She turned to look at the two men in the back. The sack over Karaman's head meant she couldn't tell if he was staring at her or not, but she thought from his upright pose that he was definitely awake. Mason, on the other hand, was slumped up against his window.

'You good?' she asked, reaching out and nudging his leg. He shuffled and murmured but couldn't find the strength or the focus to give a coherent response.

'Doesn't sound like it to me,' Karaman said, his voice calm and confident and a juxtaposition to the fact he was handcuffed and bloodied. Her eyes rested on the bandages covering his hands. She had no clue what that was about. 'I think he's losing a lot of blood.'

And Mason definitely was. Which really wasn't a good thing at all. Not just because of the obvious ramifications for his well-being, but because of the amount of red stuff which had leaked all over the car. DNA everywhere. But worse – for her – was the blood left at the two scenes in London. The bodies too. The blood in the abandoned car.

Nothing she could do about any of that now.

She stepped out and opened Karaman's door first and pushed the barrel of her AK-47 against his temple.

'Stay there, or I won't just shoot you, I'll put a bullet in your balls first and watch you writhe in agony while I decide my next move.'

Karaman didn't offer any response so she slammed the door and he jumped in shock. She went to the other side and pulled Mason out and had to take most of his weight to keep him on two feet.

'I'll get you inside,' she said.

He said nothing and she practically dragged him into the cold and damp safe house – the same place they'd been last night as they prepped. A simple barn conversion that consisted of a single-story dwelling with two bedrooms and a large open-plan space, although it'd never been fully finished. Walls remained plain plasterboard, light switches hung off walls – where there'd been one fitted at all – loose wires dangled here and there. Floors were plain poured concrete. No heating, but the plumbing worked at least and someone – perhaps the builder for his own use during the work – had installed a cheap toilet and basin in the cloakroom.

She propped Mason against the wall in the bigger of the two bedrooms. She pulled his head straight but it just lolled back onto his shoulders.

She slapped his cheek and that seemed to wake him up a little.

'Mason?' she said.

'I'm... good,' he said.

'What happened?' she asked.

He shook his head. Kind of. Before his eyes slid closed again and his head rolled.

She lifted his shirt. He had another gunshot wound on his side. In and out. It was bleeding pretty badly, his clothes sodden, but she thought the bullet had at least missed his organs. And the exit hole was a bonus as it meant no bullet to extract.

'I'll get you stitched up,' she said.

She got no response before she got back to her feet and limped out to retrieve Karaman. She needed to tend to her own wound too although she knew it was only a nasty gash, the bullet tearing across her skin and muscle. Painful, but not as bad or as debilitating as it could have been.

She opened the car door then stepped back with the rifle pointed at him. A rifle filled with blanks, but hopefully Karaman hadn't twigged to that yet.

'Are you injured?' she asked him.

He turned his head to her but said nothing.

'Are you hurt?' she asked again.

'Well, what do you think these bandages are for?' he said, showing his hands.

'I mean, did you get hurt in the escape. Shot?'

'No.'

'Then you can walk. So get out of the car.'

He didn't move straight away but then slowly, clumsily, he pulled himself out and onto his feet and he stood there facing her, cuffed hands hanging in front of him.

'Why do I feel like this isn't the rescue I'd hoped for,' he said.

'Because it isn't. You're not in prison anymore but you're not free. And I won't hesitate to—'

'Shoot me? Be careful, lady.'

She tightened her grip on the gun. The way he said that last word... So demeaning.

'You can't kill me, can you? So before you go threatening to shoot me, just let us get that straight.'

'I'll kill you if I have to.'

'No. If you wanted me dead, I would be already. And whoever you are you're not on my side otherwise I wouldn't have these cuffs on and my face covered like this. So whatever is happening – ransom, I don't know – you need me alive.'

She let go of the rifle and it slapped her thigh as it dangled on its strap. She strode up to Karaman and either he didn't hear her coming or didn't care, because he didn't move as she grabbed his hand and crushed one of his bandaged fingers in her grip. He jolted and shook.

'I *will* hurt you,' she said. 'Now move.'

She retook a firm grip over his hand and pulled to encourage him forward and whether through pain or whatever else he acquiesced and moved with her. She took him through to the second bedroom and eased him down onto the floorboards. She left him there for a few moments and went back to empty the car before returning to the bedroom with the rope in her hands. She bound Karaman's ankles first then used the rest of the rope to tie him to the ice-cold radiator.

'Looks like I'm not going anywhere,' he said with an unnecessary chuckle. 'Why don't you take this sack off my head now?'

She paused in the doorway, thinking over his words.

'You don't want me to see your face, fine. But—'

'Yeah, I don't want you to see my face,' Angel said. 'But to be honest, I *really* don't want to see yours.'

She headed back to Mason with the medical supplies. Far from a full kit, but hopefully enough to help him in the short term.

'Hey,' she said, nudging him and trying to rouse him but he was even more groggy than before, his body slumped toward the floor now.

'I'm going to undo your belt. Pull your pants down. Don't go getting any funny ideas.'

She smiled as she spoke, trying to grasp some sort of positivity, but the complete lack of response from him soon saw an end to that.

With a bit of tugging and heaving she finally managed to pull his pants toward his knees, by which point he was laid out on the floor. The gunshot wound on the back of his leg didn't look too bad, although she had to dig around for the bullet. Mason squirmed and shouted out as she did that – was that a good sign? She put on a basic dressing before going to the wound on his side which was undoubtedly worse and still oozing blood. The angle of the hit had torn a deep line through the flesh on his side and she did her best to clean it all and stitch it up.

'Mason, wake up,' she said, pulling his body up again, back against the wall. 'You need some fluids.'

She took the bottle of water and tipped it toward his lips, but the liquid simply sloshed down his front.

'Mason, seriously, come on.'

She paused and stared at him, trying to find inspiration for something.

'We did it,' she said. 'We got Karaman.'

But H is dead and who the hell was the fourth guy you didn't tell me about?

She checked her phone. No calls or texts or anything but she hadn't expected any. She spent a couple of minutes scanning the news. Every site was awash with stories. Some called it a daring escape. Others an abduction. Some had rightly connected the crash not far from the prison and even referred to the two dead bodies found in the van, although she could find nothing yet that identified the dead men, or Mason.

Or her.

Definitely a relief, but she wouldn't allow herself to properly relax until this was over and she had the money in the bank and Karaman was out of her sight forever.

'Tell me what we do next,' she said to Mason. 'How do we get the money? Who do I need to call? Where do I need to take Karaman?'

Mason didn't give any response at all. Not until Angel reached into his jeans pocket for his phone. As she drew it out, he put his hand onto hers and she wasn't sure if it was to help her or stop her, but the next moment his fingers slipped away and back to the floor as she turned the phone over and looked at the screen.

Locked. And it needed a PIN, rather than just his thumbprint or face ID which would have been much simpler for her.

'What's the code?' she said.

Nothing.

So she slapped him again, harder this time and she had to really hold herself back from just hitting him again and again until he properly woke up and gave her a full explanation for how everything had gone so damn wrong.

'Mason! Wake the fuck up! What's your code? Who do I need to call?'

He slowly shook his head. His eyelids flickered. He opened his mouth to speak...

'What?' she said, moving closer. 'Say it again.'

'I'm... s... sss...'

'You seem to be confused!' came a shout from the next room. Karaman. She ground her teeth together.

'I'll be back,' she said to Mason before leaving him and she stood in the doorway to the other bedroom glaring down at her prisoner. 'Excuse me?'

'You seem to be confused. You think he's still on your side.'

She said nothing.

'I know you're there,' he said.

'Where else would I be?' she replied.

'So what was the deal?' Karaman said. 'How did he rope you in? He pretended you would get paid to take me, hand me over to my enemies?'

Again she didn't respond.

'How much?' he asked.

She didn't say a word, she was too busy trying to contain the anger and frustration that threatened to explode out of her. At Karaman and at Mason.

'He screwed you,' Karaman said. 'And you want to know how I know that?'

'How?'

'Because I was in the van. You weren't. I heard the conversation.'

She had to push her heels down into the ground to stop her legs

shaking from surging adrenaline, even though doing so only aggravated her gunshot wound.

'What conversation?'

Karaman laughed. 'The guy you brought here. He's in charge?'

'Maybe I am.'

'No. You're not. So it's him. The thing is, your other buddy, the
dead guy, wasn't too happy. He couldn't understand why they left
you behind. Not part of your rules or something. And he couldn't
understand who the guy driving the van was.'

She pushed the heels of her hands against her temples, trying
to think.

'Do *you* know?' Karaman asked. 'The guy driving the van? Did
you know him?'

'Of course I did.'

'Then why'd you kill him?'

She didn't answer that. How did Karaman even know?

'And your friend next door? Ask me how he got that gunshot on
his side. And why the other guy in the back of the van with me
didn't make it.'

'Tell me.'

'They were arguing. Then fighting. The driver tried to get them
to see sense but couldn't. It started off with angry words, then they
tussled. The van was swerving all over the place. It was only a
matter of time. Then two gunshots. Then the crash. Next thing I
know you arrive. Now here we are.'

Angel had no words and she hated that, because it meant
Karaman knew she was listening, and he knew she was in turmoil.

'The way I see it... Maybe the guy you left behind was the one
still on your side,' he said. 'Because the man in that room next
door? He screwed you. You were supposed to die. Either out there,
or maybe in here. But whatever deal you had with him... It was
never real.'

She turned around to walk away but his voice stopped her.

'You don't like what I'm telling you, but you know it's true. Otherwise, you wouldn't have stood and listened to me. You can sit and wait now, but for what? He'll recover and kill you. Or whoever he's working for will arrive and kill you. So maybe you need a different plan from here.'

She carried on out but his words were eating away at her.

23

Ryker didn't recognize the room he woke up in, but at least it wasn't a prison cell, nor an off-the-grid torture chamber. Not a hospital either, he didn't think, although the small room did have the same kind of plainness and sterile cleanliness to it. Ryker was spread out on a single bed with a hard mattress, still clothed, although his coat and shoes had been removed. Other than the bed the room only had a single, basic plastic chair, a shoddy-looking bedside table, a door and a window that was covered by a venetian blind.

He went to straighten up but a wave of dizziness spread and he had to clutch at his forehead and squeeze his eyes shut as he waited for it to pass. Once clear he stepped off the bed and took a couple of seconds to steady himself on his feet. He checked himself over. No injuries. Nothing major, anyway. His grogginess was purely down to the aftereffects of the tranquilizer dart.

Damn lucky for him it'd been a tranquilizer dart and not a bullet.

He walked, pretty clumsily, to the window and used two fingers to part the slats of the dusty blind.

Not what he'd hoped to see. Iron bars lay other side of the

window. He recognized the grass verge across the road. The trees beyond. The old red brick building off to his left.

Someone had gone to town with police tape, lines of it pulled all over, wrapped around trees, traffic bollards, streetlights. Uniformed police in bright yellow jackets roamed.

He was still at Belmarsh prison.

In the prison.

He spun around when he heard someone at the door. Someone *unlocking* the door.

'Winter?' Ryker said, looking from his old boss and to the two uniformed police officers beyond him. They stayed outside as Winter stepped in and closed the door. He didn't lock it.

'I saw you were awake,' Winter said and without indication, Ryker's eyes soon found the small camera up in the corner of the room.

'Why am I here?' Ryker asked.

Winter looked a little confused then his face mellowed as though understanding the aggravation in Ryker's question. 'You're not in the prison. This isn't the prison infirmary. It's the... I don't know what it is really. We're in the staff quarters.'

Good news at least.

'Though there was a point, early on, before anyone had made sense of the chaos, when I didn't know if...'

'What?'

'If you were part of it.'

Ryker shook his head in disgust. For everything they'd been through together, sometimes Winter revealed exactly how little faith he had in Ryker.

Possibly due to previous form – as he saw it – but still.

'Karaman?' Ryker asked.

'Gone.'

'How long was I out?'

'Nearly three hours.'

'You didn't think to try and rouse me? Adrenaline would have worked.'

'Honestly? No. I didn't consider it at all. I needed the time to figure things out for myself.'

'Figure things out? You mean figure out what happened to Karaman? Or figure out what to do with me?'

'Both, Ryker. And I won't apologize for that. Remember the conversation we had this morning?'

'Yeah. I was hit by a tranquilizer, not some memory eraser.'

'Good. Then you'll appreciate that I needed to consider whether what happened with Karaman changes any of that.'

'And does it?'

'First I have a few questions for you.'

'I have a lot more for you, but shoot.'

'Do you—'

'Wait,' Ryker said, holding a hand up to stop Winter. 'You don't want to invite your police buddies in? Get a tape recorder going? Should I call a lawyer?'

Winter sighed. 'Ryker, no lawyer would ever take you on. You'd be the end of their career, all of the shit you've done. Sorry.'

Winter said that entirely deadpan, but Ryker sensed just a little bit of humor still.

'OK. Fire away,' he said.

'Do you know who took Karaman?' Winter asked.

'Do you?'

Winter sighed again, showing his growing irritation. 'Please, let's do this properly, get our facts, opinions, everything aligned.'

'That's a great idea. Except the way you set it up was more for you to question me. Not to get our thinking straight.'

'I'm not in the mood for your petulance. Do you know who took Karaman?'

'So I'm guessing you didn't catch any of them.'

'I didn't say that. I'll ask a third time. Do you know who took Karaman?'

'No. But I saw the face of the woman.'

Winter said nothing.

'You know one of them was a woman, don't you?'

'Actually, yes, we do. After you ripped off her balaclava there's CCTV of her face, although she did her best to hide it still, and there's nothing clear enough that has enabled an immediate ID.'

'What about the others?'

'No IDs yet. But... We're hoping we will soon. We found two of the assailants dead less than three miles from here. Their getaway van crashed, although it wasn't the crash that killed them.'

'Explain.'

A third sigh from Winter. Not irritation this time, more building up to something. A sigh for every occasion. 'Why don't you take a seat.'

'I'm fine.'

'Well, I'm not. I'm exhausted.' He slumped onto the bed and took a moment as though he needed to compose himself. 'There were four assailants—'

'Sorry, but that's twice you've said assailants. Perhaps it's just semantics, but it's not clear to me what you think happened here. Are you saying you think those people were working *for* or *against* Karaman?'

'The working theory is that they helped break Karaman out of prison.'

'Unless you have some clear evidence of that, it's a big assumption.'

'As opposed to what?'

'Maybe they were kidnappers.'

'You think he was kidnapped? For ransom? By who?'

'I didn't say I think he was kidnapped, but it is a possibility. Unless you're telling me otherwise. The one thing I do know for sure is the woman was white. English. I think they all were. I heard them shouting, talking to each other. No foreign words or anything like that.'

'You said yourself that you think Karaman is connected to this worldwide group of super-rich people in power. So why wouldn't his rescuers be white, British?'

'Again, I didn't say they wouldn't be. I'm just explaining what we *do* know. You said two were found dead. Caucasian like the woman?'

'Yes.'

'But they weren't killed by the crash?'

'The driver of the van was stabbed through the throat. Another guy was found in the back of the van with multiple wounds but one of two gunshot wounds he had likely killed him. The police are still piecing things together, but it looks like the woman caught up with her accomplices. After... after she shot you.'

Ryker balled his fists as he took himself back to the moment. He'd so very nearly got her.

'She chased after them in another getaway car. She arrived at the crash seconds after it happened. She threatened bystanders with an assault rifle as she bundled her friend and Karaman into a car.'

'So who killed the van driver?'

'It's a good question. But... it might have been her.'

'It could only have been her or one of the other two.'

'Probably not the dead guy.'

'*Probably* not. Either way, it doesn't make a lot of sense.'

'Not yet.'

'But nothing's been heard from the... attackers?'

'You mean like a ransom? No. Nothing. Which does tend to

suggest that Karaman was broken out of prison rather than a kidnapping, like you suggested.'

Ryker did agree, but he was reluctant to tell Winter that even if he didn't know why.

'Did anyone get hurt?' Ryker asked. 'Police, civilians, I mean.'

Winter scrunched up his face in such a way as to suggest he was about to break some bad news.

'Eight police officers are in hospital. Several of them were shot, and we think it was mainly with their own weapons as we believe the attackers were initially only using blanks.' Which Ryker had figured too during the melee. 'But... For once, Ryker, I'm glad to say no one – no one innocent, at least – was killed. And... This I hate to say, but word going around is that a lot of people are thanking *you* for that. You won't be named publicly, but you are getting a lot of mentions across social media already. And I mean a *lot*. Off-duty special ops. MI5 agent. Rumors are flying as to who you are. *What* you are. I even saw a meme of you running across the grass, shooting away, with Tom Cruise's head superimposed.'

Ryker smiled and Winter tried really hard to keep a straight face but eventually failed.

'Go on, say it,' Ryker said.

'Say what?'

'Begins with an s, ends in y, has some gold in the middle.'

'I'm not sure what I've got to apologize for.'

'No? Four hours ago you basically told me I was done here. To get lost. Just as well I didn't do that, don't you think.'

'Maybe. Except they still got Karaman, didn't they? So your intervention wasn't exactly a major success either.'

'Way to bring me down again.'

'Someone has to.'

They both went silent and Ryker spent the time in his thoughts. He really didn't care for any plaudits from the press, on social media, whatever. Not even from Winter. The fact was, he didn't like how things had ended because Karaman had still gotten away.

'They used blanks,' Ryker said. 'Why do you think that was?'

'We'll know when we catch up with them. For now, let's just be thankful about it.'

Ryker humphed. Winter apparently didn't think it was a big question. To Ryker, it was potentially huge in terms of figuring out who had attacked that motorcade and why.

'No sign of the getaway car since?' Ryker asked.

'The Met is working on tracking it through ANPR. I haven't checked over the last couple of hours where they've got to with that.'

'So, are you part of this or not?'

Winter looked a little put out by the question. 'Officially?'

'However you look at it.'

'The Met is in charge and are the ones making public statements, although MI5 is already looking to step in and I think it won't be long before they take over fully in the background.'

'That didn't answer my question.'

'But was your question really about me, or about you?'

'It's about both.'

'You know I don't have any official role on UK soil.'

'And yet here you are.'

'Here I am because I was helping you.'

'Was, or are?'

Winter sighed for about the tenth time in the conversation. 'Why don't you just ask the question you really want to ask me?'

'Fine. Do I still have my marching orders?'

'If I say no... that you're good to stay, to help, will you play by *my* rules?'

'You mean I have to ask you every time I want to do something? How about every time I take a leak?'

'I mean, when I say stop, you stop. When I say no, you don't do whatever it is I'm asking you not to do.'

'Like a well-trained dog.'

'Well-trained dogs are huge assets in many situations.'

'I'm sure.'

'Just promise me one thing, Ryker. If you're staying, if you're helping, the goal here is to get Karaman back. That's it. You find who did this, and you get him back. And then, and only then, will we consider what happens next.'

'Deal.'

Both men went silent a moment.

'So where do you want to start?' Winter asked as Ryker's mind rummaged with that exact question.

'With everything the Met already knows. If we can find the identities of the dead attackers, and the two who got away, that'll help hugely. In the meantime, we track that getaway car. We need to find Karaman before it's too late.'

'Too late for what?'

'Let's not wait and find out.'

Winter got up from the bed. 'Better get your shoes and coat on, then.'

24

'And there's no sign of the car after that point?' Ryker asked, turning from the screen and to the Met cyber specialist standing behind him. Davis, he'd said his name was, although it wasn't made clear if that was his first or last name.

'Not that I've had access to,' he said, sounding as grumpy as he looked.

Ryker wasn't yet sure whether the grumpiness was because he was standing while Ryker took over his equipment or because it was already clear the guy was being asked to operate with one hand behind his back and so had little of use to tell.

'You have to understand that that last camera isn't even our jurisdiction,' Davis added. 'We have no direct access and only have that crappy data because Kent police sent it over.'

'And what exactly is your remit, right now?' Ryker asked him.

'I don't have a remit now. I've reviewed everything available to me. License plate recognition cameras, CCTV towers. I've plotted the trail of what I can find from the attack at Belmarsh all the way through to this last sighting on the M20. That's all I've been asked to do, and I don't have any more data to review anyway.'

Ryker got up from his chair.

'OK, thank you,' he said, offering his hand to the guy who looked at it a little suspiciously before he took the offer of a handshake.

'You're... done?' Davis asked.

'Like you said, you don't have anything else for us to look at.'

He shrugged and Ryker left it there. He and Winter walked out of the room and along the corridor and didn't speak until they bypassed the elevator and started down the stairs. A little used stairwell with bare, echoey concrete.

'I know that look,' Winter said.

'You do?'

'It's your caught-between-two-minds look. It means you saw something there that piqued your interest, but also something that's pissed you off.'

Ryker humphed in response. He hated that Winter saw him so transparently. No one else did or ever had.

'MI5 are already pulling the shutters down,' Ryker said.

'Maybe. Maybe not.'

'No. They are. The Met is perfectly capable of making this a national investigation, jurisdiction isn't the issue. They could pull data from every police force in the country if they wanted. If they had the authority. Davis would be swimming in data for weeks, like a pig in shit.'

'We don't know for sure that they aren't trying to make that happen. The data part, not the shit.'

'Don't we? Davis just said he's not going to get any more data to review. Only what the Met themselves have direct access to, and the data he's had from Kent, which isn't much.'

'Enough to conclude the car went that way.'

'But only up to the first point it disappears?'

'You're taking what he said at face value? You're right, the Met could request access to camera records from every single force in the country, but they won't get an instantaneous response. The attack was only this morning and I'm sorry to say, Ryker, that these things can take time.'

'Or not happen at all,' Ryker added. 'Or be deliberately stalled. Like the identification of the attackers.'

'Excuse me?'

'The woman? The two dead men? DCI Anwah said they haven't made any progress in identifying them.'

DCI Anwah being the lead detective in charge of the investigation for the Met, who had been gracious enough to greet Ryker and Winter at Scotland Yard, but in the twenty minutes he'd spoken to them before he'd given excuses and hurried off for something or other had given them very little useful information and a lot of obfuscation. Since then they'd spent nearly an hour with Davis but it looked like that was about all the insight they were going to get from the Met.

'Maybe they really haven't made any progress,' Winter said.

'I was part of the attack. I fought those guys off. So did a dozen armed police officers. The attackers weren't perfect, and I made it a right mess for them, but they weren't amateurs. They were well-trained, well-equipped, well-planned. Army, ex-army, police, whatever, but I'm betting they are in the system one way or another and wouldn't be hard to ID given the two bodies in the morgue.'

Winter kind of huffed at that but didn't refute it.

'And the one that got away?' Ryker countered. 'The one the woman dragged from the van? I shot them both. They'd have been bleeding all over the scene, never mind the van. So we can add their DNA to the mix to be identified, yet Anwah said nothing at all about that.'

'Police forces never appreciate the likes of us poking our noses in,' Winter said. 'You might be reading too much into this. Maybe they're just not telling us everything they know.'

Ryker stopped and Winter followed suit. He looked a little wary, as though he was worried he'd awakened a beast and Ryker was about to toss him down the stairs.

A little dramatic perhaps, but Ryker definitely was feeling a lot more on edge now than when they'd arrived at Scotland Yard not even two hours ago.

'Stop being an apologist,' Ryker said. 'I get that the police have constraints, but this is something else. MI5 have their claws in here and they're shutting things down.'

'Why do you think they would do that?'

'To protect themselves. They know more than everyone else does and don't want the police or anyone else stepping on their toes from here. Maybe they're even protecting one of their own assets.'

Winter seemed to contemplate that a few moments and Ryker got them moving again.

'The problem is,' Ryker added, 'I don't know which answer it is, but I do know we won't find out any more here.'

Ryker pushed open the door on the ground floor and they stepped out into another corridor, the main entrance at the other end, although right the other side of them was a quieter fire exit. Which was why Ryker stopped again.

'So, we're done here?' Winter asked.

'*I'm* done here,' Ryker said. 'You're welcome to stay and see if you can break down some barriers.'

'So now you should probably tell me what lead you're about to follow.'

Ryker raised an eyebrow in question.

'I saw the look on your face when you left Davis to it. You saw something on those cameras, didn't you?'

'I saw a *lack* of something.'

'And that would be?'

'The car, obviously, after they lost it on the M20.'

'As Anwah said to us both, the main theory the police are working on is that the attackers took Karaman south toward the coast. That most likely they'd have a boat waiting somewhere in Kent to take them across the channel to France.'

'Not my theory.'

'No?'

'No. It's a bluff. We have the car heading south through Kent. It was picked up on camera after camera, then... poof. Disappears just off the motorway.'

'It came off the M20 onto a black spot. The whole country isn't covered by cameras. Yet.'

'Of course, they took it into a black spot. It's the best way to switch vehicles. That's why the car wasn't seen again.'

'OK? So they switched vehicles and carried on toward the south coast.'

'If they were intent on switching vehicles only, they would have done it much sooner, not after traveling out of London, into Kent, along the M20.'

Winter seemed to consider that for a moment. 'So you're saying... what?'

'That them heading south was a bluff. When they switched vehicles they doubled back the other way. And the fact the police aren't following that line tells me one thing.'

'Which is?'

'MI5 definitely is. In fact, they'll probably have the Kent police scouring the coastline to keep everyone else looking that way.'

'Actually, they really do.'

'Good. Because that helps if I'm wrong.'

'But I sense you don't think you are.'

'Of course I don't.'

'So, we're going to Kent?'

'We? Since when have you gone out into the field with me? Anyone?'

'Only since the last time I got you out of prison, actually. I'm going to see if a more direct presence might help keep you more... under control.'

Ryker didn't like the sound of that at all. 'Why am I thinking about dogs again?'

'I have absolutely no idea. But back to the point, we're going to Kent?'

'We're going to follow their route. We're going to find that car. And with any luck, we'll then figure out where they really went before MI5 does.'

'Then let's get to it,' Winter said with a nervous grin, like a kid who was about to go on a white-knuckle rollercoaster for the very first – and possibly last – time.

'Follow me,' Ryker said, leading the way.

25

'How's your wife?' Ryker asked as he drove.

Winter didn't respond. Just stared at Ryker like he'd asked something terrible of him.

'What?' Ryker prompted.

'You don't need to do that.'

'Do what?'

'Make this something that it isn't.'

'You're reading too much into the question,' Ryker said. 'And I'm sorry if I haven't asked about her, your personal life, for... probably years.'

'Definitely years.'

'It's not like we hang out.'

'This isn't hanging out.'

'Still... I was just asking.'

'OK. And the answer is she's doing great. I think her new man is really into her. Treats her well, is always there for her. Probably buys her flowers just for the hell of it. At least that's what she makes everyone believe.'

'Shit. Sorry.'

'Ryker, she left me three years ago.'

'Like you said, we don't exactly hang out.'

'And yet you remain one of the constants in my life.'

He didn't say that in a particularly happy way.

They both fell silent, Ryker concentrating on the road as a BMW came blasting up to them in the outside lane. Ever wary, Ryker got himself ready – mentally – as though an ambush was imminent. But the car flew on past. A hundred and ten miles an hour, hundred and twenty probably.

'I did wonder,' Ryker said.

'Wonder what?'

'Last year when we... reconnected again. It'd been a while and you were working in Israel, not London. I thought it was just a transfer but...'

'Now you think I ran away?'

Ryker shrugged.

'I guess it was an opportune move, sure. Honestly, if that move had come up when we'd still been together, I would have taken it still. And I know she wouldn't have come with me. She got out at the right time. For her.'

Ryker didn't know what to say to that. He felt bad for him, even if Winter didn't exactly sound heartbroken.

'You might think of me as just a guy who sits behind a desk. A normal guy, with normal relationships. But that isn't me. I might not be the tough guy you are, running amok across the world, but I've dedicated my whole life to my job, and I do it because I truly believe it makes a positive difference to the world.'

'And because you get to spend time with me.'

Winter laughed. 'Actually, when I hear your voice on the other end of the phone, or see your name crop up in my internal news feeds, I sometimes wish I was that other guy. An accountant or something.'

'Liar. I tell you what. When this is done? We go out. Just me and you. A pub. Beers, food. What do you say?'

Winter looked at him like Ryker had just suggested they start a satanic cult or something.

'Seriously,' Ryker said. 'Why not?'

'I'll do you a deal. If we get this done, without you crossing the line – *my* line – then yeah. Let's do it.'

They shook on it. Then silence took over for a while. A silence that became increasingly uncomfortable as Ryker sensed Winter had something on his mind.

'You haven't told me what happened at Belmarsh yet,' Winter said, sounding a little sour now.

'Which part of what happened?'

'You and Karaman. When you broke his fingers. What did he tell you?'

Ryker thought long and hard about the question.

'Not as much as I'd hoped.'

Silence again. Although Ryker felt Winter staring.

'What?' Ryker eventually said.

'I thought we were turning over a new leaf here. How about a bit more honesty.'

'I haven't lied—'

'But you haven't told me everything either.'

Ryker thought and sighed. 'He has a mark on his wrist. Looks like a bad burn scar. Well, it is.'

'And?'

'I think he used to have a tattoo there. A double-headed eagle. Davis Bracey had the same tattoo. I've found it on... others too.'

'Others? What others?'

'The point is, Winter, it really does mean something. It's the Syndicate.'

Ryker glanced over and noted the dubious look.

'It's a bit... in your face, isn't it? A tattoo showing membership of a secret society?'

'Whatever you think of it, it's there.'

'Except you said Karaman only has a scar.'

'He claims from a bomb attack he survived.'

'You don't believe him.'

'No. I don't. But... Karaman didn't deny being involved in the Syndicate. He told me he was a courier. A doer. Someone who took orders.'

'From who?'

'Andrew Lebedev, for one.'

Winter huffed. 'Which fits with what you knew already. It was the link to Bracey and Lebedev which took you to Karaman.'

'He also told me that Lebedev isn't really dead.'

'But... You really believe that?'

'I don't know.'

'If Lebedev is still alive... then...'

'The body from the car was cremated. I don't know how we even go about getting proof one way or another.'

'No. Neither do I.'

'But Karaman knows more than he told me. I know it. He's the one who can take us further into the Syndicate.'

'Perhaps. But remember our deal, Ryker. Your aim here is to get Karaman back into custody. Nothing more than that.'

Ryker didn't say anything.

'Ryker, do you—'

'I hear you. Loud and clear.'

The next moment Ryker took his foot off the gas and switched on his turn signal for the approaching exit.

'This is it,' he said.

He took them off the motorway, slowing almost to a stop on the exit ramp as he craned his neck to look up out of the car.

'That's the camera,' he said. 'Where the getaway car was last picked up.'

'And now we go on a needle-in-a-haystack search through Kent from here?'

'So cynical. No. Actually, we go on a search of a less than one-mile radius. Because I did my homework while you were getting this car.'

'OK, explain,' Winter said.

'There's a blackspot immediately after this camera, but it doesn't go on forever. There are two roads at the top of this ramp. To the right takes us to the nearest large town. It's two miles away. CCTV towers cover the main in and out routes there and the car wasn't spotted going that way.'

'There are no turn-offs before the town?'

'There are. But only for residential streets. I don't think that's where they're hiding, and if they abandoned the car there I think it would have been reported by now given the furor in the news.'

'Possibly, but not absolutely.'

'No. But we're looking for most likely here. Most likely they took that car and dumped it somewhere quiet, where they already had a new vehicle waiting. They wouldn't have wanted themselves seen out in the open on a residential street. Too many risks.'

'Plausible. So in the other direction?'

'In the other direction, we have two busy A-roads, a smaller town, and a village. The A-roads and the town have cameras, and the only roads in and out of the village lead from the A-roads. So there's only a small area, about a mile radius, between this exit and the crossroads for the first A-road that's not covered. We search every street between here and there.'

'Then let's get to it. We have about thirty minutes of daylight left.'

But they didn't complete the task within that timeframe, and eventually, they'd scoured every street with no luck.

'It was a big assumption that they switched cars,' Winter said.

An assumption Ryker wasn't yet ready to give up on.

'So now what?' Winter asked.

'We keep looking.'

Winter looked far from convinced but then they'd already done a once-over of the area Ryker had earmarked. He knew Winter had already doubted his approach before they'd started, but now he had to face his own doubts too.

'We'll go back to the start,' Ryker said.

Winter didn't have to say anything for Ryker to know that the guy wasn't impressed by the idea. But he set off again anyway, taking them back onto the main road, the junction for the M20 less than a mile away.

'There!' Ryker said, flooring the brake pedal. Winter shot forward in his seat as the car slammed to a stop outside a shabby-looking gas station.

'Jesus, Ryker! If you need to fill up—'

'It's not the gas station I'm looking at.'

He continued into the parking lot for the gas station, straight through and over to the closed-down restaurant on the other side. No cars there, but the tarmac carried on around the back of the brick building, into darkness.

Ryker took them that way, slowed the car down to a crawl. He checked his mirrors as he moved. The petrol station was out of sight behind them. When he looked forward again he hit the brake and stared beyond the corner of a huge dumpster. A flash of light had caught his eye, his headlights catching on... The corner bumper of a car, its back end poking only a few inches beyond the dumpster.

Ryker shut down the engine and had his fingers on the door handle when Winter grabbed his arm.

'We could get some backup here,' he said. 'Seriously. If that's the car, how do we know they're not inside that building?'

'If they are? All the better,' Ryker said. 'If you want, stay here. I'll go check the car.'

'I'll come,' Winter said after a moment of hesitation.

The early evening was blisteringly cold with a clear sky above. Ryker's breath swirled up into the moonlight as he walked slowly, silently, toward the car, Winter a half-step behind him. He heard no sounds from inside the building, no indication anyone was in there or had been at any recent point. They reached a side door.

'Padlocked,' Ryker whispered to Winter who nodded in response. 'And the front was locked tight too.'

A few more steps and they'd reached the back of the car.

'Yeah?' Ryker said, smiling as he looked from the license plate to Winter.

'Yeah,' Winter responded before looking all around him, even more apprehensive now than before.

'They're not here,' Ryker said.

'You don't know for sure—'

'Yeah. I do. They're not here.'

Winter jumped in surprise when his phone vibrated in his pocket. Ryker held back a laugh as Winter fished the device out and stared at the screen.

'I need to get this,' he said, moving purposefully back for the car. For safety, or perhaps just for privacy.

Ryker followed him, intrigued, though the hushed way in which Winter took the call suggested he didn't want Ryker to overhear. He glanced over to the gas station. Lights were on there even if it did look more than a little dilapidated. Lights on. A camera on the roof.

Ryker strode that way.

* * *

Fifteen minutes later he returned from the gas station with the image on his phone. Winter had finished his conversation and was leaning up against the bodywork of the car. He didn't look happy.

'Sorry,' Ryker said. 'I should have unlocked the car.'

He pressed the button on the key fob but Winter didn't move inside.

'Actually,' Ryker said, 'we hit gold here.' He turned the phone around to show Winter the picture. He expected a more enthusiastic response, but Winter stared, deadpan, arms folded.

'The guy let me see his CCTV recordings for fifty pounds. It didn't take long to find this. He doesn't get many customers, apparently. But his cameras are good because he's been robbed twice in three years.'

Winter humphed.

'His camera caught the car coming in. It's not a great view of the license plate but the timeline, color, everything else matches. We never see Karaman or the attackers, but what we do see is this second car leaving not even two minutes later. And this time we get a clear shot of the license plate.'

'Good work,' Winter said, though he still didn't sound happy.

'And the problem is?'

'The problem is the phone call I had just now.'

'Because?'

'Three of the attackers have now been identified.'

Which was a surprise, because as Ryker had suggested earlier, he thought MI5 was deliberately trying to keep quiet the identities. Was he wrong or had something changed?

'And that's bad?' Ryker said.

'When you find out who they are... Yeah, I think it might be.'

* * *

'I know her,' Ryker said, pulling his phone down, looking away from the screen.

Winter drove this time. Ryker wanted to do as much research as he could as they traveled.

'You know her?'

'The name. I've never met her. But don't forget I've done a lot of investigation into Karaman and his past. Angela Everett. Also known as Angel. The Angel of Death, the press called her. She was a sniper for the British army, later special ops, apparently. You told me before that MI6 had tried to take out Karaman? There's never been any official confirmation of their involvement, but the story goes she was part of an assassination attempt against Karaman in Lebanon. But she made a mistake and missed her shot. She hit Karaman's daughter instead. It didn't kill her, but still... There was a fallout, political as much as anything else. MI6, the British government left Everett out on her own in Lebanon to face justice. She was imprisoned in Beirut for attempted murder and spent four years there before she was finally repatriated to serve out her sentence here.'

'You said "story". So you think some or all of that isn't true?'

Ryker paused before answering because actually, he wondered how much of this Winter already knew himself.

'I don't know. But whether she was ever working with MI6, she's someone who potentially has beef with Karaman. Highly unlikely that she'd be his rescuer.'

Winter huffed and then sighed. 'What about the other two?'

'I don't recognize their names. I'm still searching but there's not a lot I'm seeing about them online. What were you told?'

'Nothing has been released publicly. What I know came from a very good source I have. *I* shouldn't even know. But the other two, the dead guys from the van, are Harvey Harman and Sean Doyle. Harman is ex-army too, although he spent more time working as a mercenary in Africa. A gun for hire. Some of the ops he was on... I *know* they were linked to MI6.'

'Surprise, surprise.' The description bore a striking similarity to Brock Van Der Vehn. Ryker didn't dwell on it. 'And Doyle?'

'He was the driver of the van. Irish republican. A former foot soldier for the IRA, apparently. He's never been convicted of anything, but...'

'But maybe that was because he was a protected asset?'

'It's possible, isn't it?'

'So, let's lay this out,' Ryker said. 'We know the identities of three of four of the attackers. Which in itself tells us something.'

'In what way?'

'Doyle was the driver, you said. So Harman was the dead guy in the back of the van. Everett is the woman I fought with. The fourth, as yet unidentified guy, is the one who was bleeding all over the place who Everett took away with Karaman. I don't believe they couldn't ID him too.'

'Someone's covering for him?'

'Most likely because he's the one in charge. The others... Perhaps they were always meant to be expendable. Scapegoats. Everett had a past with Karaman. Perhaps look into the other two more and you'll find the same. One thing is for sure, though.'

'And that is?'

'The attack has the hallmarks of being an inside job. MI5, MI6. Whether it's rogue operatives or the whole damn organization collectively behind it.'

'You believe our own intelligence services broke Karaman out of prison? Even though it was Fatma Yaman of MI6 who brought him here?'

'You mean Fatma Yaman who was killed in her apartment in a robbery gone wrong? Fatma Yaman, who had years of intel on Karaman but had never done anything with it?'

'I agree this looks bad. Really bad,' Winter said. 'But I assure you there is no officiality to what's happening here. If this has any links back to MI6 or MI5 then it's rogue operatives who've put together this crew. The question is, who are they and why?'

'No. We already know the why. The Syndicate. This is what they do.'

Winter sighed, as though he thought the mention of the Syndicate was unnecessary, or that he still didn't believe its power and reach was as extensive as Ryker did.

'Then why break Karaman out rather than just have him killed like Bracey, Lebedev?'

'Because for whatever reason, Karaman still has worth to them.'

'OK. So we're left with only the who,' Winter said.

'And that's what I'm going to find out.'

26

The plan had never been to stay at the safe house long. A few hours, Mason had said. They had brought no food at all. At least they had water from the taps, but by the following morning Angel's stomach was cramping like crazy and she was seriously tempted to jump in the car and head to the nearest town to buy some snacks.

Not yet.

She'd slept on the floor of the unfinished kitchen, using her backpack as a pillow. Everything ached as she stood up and refilled her plastic water bottle from the only tap in the house in the downstairs bathroom. She downed nearly the whole bottle and filled it again then moved to Mason's room, hobbling on her injured foot which throbbed with pain. The door was already open and she paused in the doorway a moment. He looked... brighter. If that was possible for someone who was curled up on the floor, eyes closed. Some color had returned to his skin, at least.

'Mason,' she said. He stirred. Opened his eyes. Groaned.

She crouched by him and pulled on his shoulders to help him upright. He locked onto her gaze and then groaned again.

'You OK?' she asked.

He shook his head.

'You want more water?'

'Yeah.'

She'd managed to get him to drink two full bottles last night, the fluid at least enough to start replacing the volume of blood he'd lost, if not yet the blood cells necessary for life. A blood transfusion would be a more direct treatment, but she wasn't about to stick a needle in her arm and drain her own out, so unless she went to a hospital to get them to do it the right way, transfusion wasn't an option. His body would replenish its lost supply over time. If she could keep him alive.

She spent several minutes with the water at his lips, a few splashes at a time until the bottle was empty.

She looked at his phone on the floor next to him.

'Have you heard anything?' she asked him.

He shook his head.

'Who do we call? We need to get this done. The longer we keep him here—'

He had the audacity to put a finger up to her lips to stop her talking.

'I need... I'll call them,' he said, his voice strained, a grimace with each elongated word.

'When?'

He closed his eyes.

'Mason, what the hell happened? Who was that other guy?'

He only shook his head in response.

'How did *that* happen?' she asked, pointing to the bandaged wound on his side.

He opened his eyes a little more widely. A threat of some kind, perhaps. Accusatory.

'Tell me what happened in the van,' Angel said, unfazed. 'With H?'

'I... I'll get this... sorted,' Mason said. 'Just need... time.'

'Or you could tell me who to call and I'll do it,' she said.

He looked away, then closed his eyes.

'Mason... If you try to screw me... Just don't.'

He kept his eyes closed, didn't move or otherwise respond as she got up and left the room.

'Has he admitted it yet?' Karaman called out.

Angel sighed and went to his room.

'Of course, he hasn't,' Karaman added when she reached the doorway. 'Because he knows he's in no position to fight you right now. Waiting only benefits him. Not you.'

'What would you have me do?' she asked. 'You want me to call 999 and get you sent back to prison?'

He slumped a little, perhaps at the mention of the police.

'Do you even know who I am?' he asked.

She didn't answer.

'Let's say, even if you're just some dumb mercenary with no soul or conscience, taking on jobs for big paydays, you still probably know *something* about me. Because why would you take on such a risky job in the first place without knowing. So you're aware I have money.'

'Why are you so sure this is all about money?'

'Because I heard your friends arguing. Remember? And it's the only explanation that makes sense to me given the position we find ourselves in. My point is that I can get you money, more money than you were promised by your *friend*. You just need to help me get back to my people.'

'That's not happening.'

She turned to walk away.

'You want to know the code for his phone?'

Her heart thudded a little harder in her chest, then ramped up even further at his taunting laugh.

'Yeah. I get it. You're thinking, how could I possibly know?'

'You couldn't.'

'Just like I couldn't know what you look like with this sack over my head. Or what your friends look like. And I couldn't have seen you push that knife into the driver's neck. I couldn't have seen your friends wrestling and then pull guns on each other and…'

'And what?'

'And maybe you should have got a better sack.'

She turned and moved a little more cautiously toward him.

'You have hair the color of hay,' he said. 'Dark brown eyes. I think… you're quite pretty, actually. In a plain kind of way.'

She only half paid attention to his words, instead staring closely at the sack as she neared.

'And the code for his phone is nine–two–four–nine–one–seven. You can trust me, or you can just go into the room next door and find out for yourself.'

She crouched down by his side. Her face only inches from his. Now she saw it. She really should have done before. And so should Mason and H. The sack had a tiny hole in it. She had no clue how. Maybe it'd been there all along. Maybe Karaman had bitten through it. Maybe the hole had opened up in the melee. It was small, really small. But so close to his eye, it was easily big enough to give him at least glimpses of what was happening around him. Big enough to see everything he claimed? She didn't know.

She whipped the sack off and tossed it and had to work hard to show no reaction when she noticed his wide grin.

'That's better,' he said taking in a huge inhale of air. 'I can breathe properly now. And I can see your face properly too. Actually, you're prettier than I thought.'

'That means nothing coming from you.'

He didn't look in the least put off even despite her harsh tone. 'I know you,' he said.

He looked so damned pleased with himself. Kind of like how he'd looked when he'd visited her in prison.

'Yes,' she said.

'It's been a while.'

'A lifetime for me.'

'But you must be pleased at least that you're free now. That wasn't my choice for you.'

Although he really didn't sound too bothered. As though he already knew of the pain and torment she'd suffered because of him, not just in prison but after too.

'You really hate me, don't you?' he said.

'The question is irrelevant here.'

'Maybe. So you're going to go get his phone now?'

She didn't move. How the hell had she got to this position where it felt like Karaman – *her* prisoner – was the one calling the shots?

So she reached out and grabbed his bandaged hand and squeezed as hard as she could until the smile had dropped away from Karaman's face, which twisted into a grimace. He eventually let out a harrowing scream.

'Yeah. I'm going to go check his phone,' Angel said. 'But not because you said so. And if you continue to try to play me—' she stood up and drilled her heel into his gut and he doubled over in pain '—this will only get much, much worse for you.'

She walked out tall, confident, but it was all a show because despite her bravado, inside the turmoil continued.

Mason's eyes were closed. She tiptoed to him, unsure if he was asleep or dead.

Definitely not dead, as she noticed a small rise and fall to his chest, his breaths slow and shallow. But he *was* breathing, at least.

Only she didn't know if that was a good thing or not anymore.

She crouched down by his side and inhaled slowly, a strange

odor tickling her nose. She took a few moments, not making any noise as she breathed in and out, her brain processing the scent. Not a good scent. Pungent. Acidic. Infection. Most likely the big cut on his side. She had no medical training, but she knew that smell. So soon after the event it perhaps wasn't too late to turn things around, but she'd need medical supplies, antibiotics. Which meant she'd need to leave the safe house. Leave Mason and Karaman alone there.

She closed her eyes and thought.

No. She couldn't do it. Not yet. And how would she get antibiotics anyway? She'd have to steal them and that would only create more problems.

She reached forward, hand outstretched. She pushed the tips of her fingers into his pocket, being careful not to disturb him, the maneuver of taking his phone feeling more dishonest this time compared to earlier.

She grasped the cold device and slid it out then let out a long and almost silent sigh. Mason hadn't even flinched. A coma? No. She really didn't think so. He'd been lucid – relatively, at least – not long before.

She thumbed in the passcode Karaman had given her... The screen remained locked. She typed it in again. Still locked. A third time. Nothing.

'What the hell?' she whispered. Karaman was playing her. Again. How did he still wield so much sway over her even in his current predicament? She jumped in shock when she realized Mason's eyes were open and he was staring at her.

'What are you... doing?'

'It fell out of your pocket,' she said, holding the phone out to him.

She knew he didn't believe her, but didn't question her answer as he took the phone back and clutched it close to his belly.

'What are we doing, Mason?' she asked.

He didn't answer.

'You know you're only here because of me,' she said. 'If I hadn't got to the van… What do you think would have happened to you? You certainly wouldn't have come away with Karaman, if you'd come away alive at all.'

He still didn't say a word and she once again struggled to contain her growing anger at the thought of being duped.

'H shot you,' she said. 'Because he realized you were trying to screw us.'

'No,' Mason said, shaking his head.

'It explains the fourth guy, too. You used me and H to get to Karaman, but you'd never intended on us reaching here with you. Either you hoped the police would kill us or *you* would have, right?'

'It's not… true. H… He's the one.'

'You want me to believe you?'

'You have to.'

'Then put the call in. Or let me do it. Why are we waiting?'

'We wait for them. That's the deal.'

'You're telling me you don't even *know* who to call.'

He nodded. She was fifty-fifty on whether she believed him.

'We wait for them,' he said again. 'It's taking… more time. Probably… because we messed up. Too much heat.'

He winced and writhed in pain and his phone dropped to the floor as he clutched at the bandage on his side.

'I think it's infected,' Angel said. 'Let me see.'

He reluctantly held his hand in place but didn't have the strength to stop her from pulling it away. She lifted the corner of the dressing for the long entry wound and the pungent smell ramped up. The flesh beneath was a mix of red, yellow, and white pulpy mess.

'Shit,' she said before she could catch herself.

The expression on Mason's face said it all. He knew it was bad too even if he hadn't looked.

'You want to wait?' she said. 'Honestly? I don't know how long you've got.'

'Help... me,' Mason said. 'Please.'

'You want me to go get some supplies? Leave you here with Karaman? Do you really think I'm that stupid?' However, the reality was that she really didn't think he had the physical strength to make a sudden play on her, run away with Karaman, or anything like that.

'Please,' he said again.

'No,' she said. 'You already told me, we need to wait. So waiting is what we'll do. Even though it might kill you.' She stood up. 'Unless, of course, you do know who to call after all.'

She walked out without waiting for a response.

27

Nearly twenty-four hours had passed since Ryker and Winter had found the abandoned getaway car in Kent. A busy twenty-four hours that as yet had no payoff, and Ryker's frustrations were beginning to build as nighttime once again approached. He'd traveled north out of London alone. Winter hadn't been with him since the night before when they'd arrived back in the capital from their sojourn in Kent. Their short-lived partnership had come to a necessary end as it'd become clear that Winter was more useful on the inside at the Secret Intelligence Service than out in the field where he got to chaperone Ryker, but didn't really provide much other use. The identities of the three attackers remained a closely kept secret, no mention of it, or even whispers, among the press or across social media channels. Winter really shouldn't have known about it either, hence why he wanted to be back in London, among his own circle of clandestine people, to see if he could figure out where the bottleneck of intel was occurring, and why.

But he hadn't left Ryker entirely on his own, unaided. First thing that morning Ryker had been back inside Scotland Yard with Davis, with a new ream of data to review from London, and latterly from Essex Police and Suffolk Constabulary as Ryker – and Davis – tracked the movements of the second car northward, past London.

Which had culminated in Ryker traveling northward too, into rural Suffolk. The last two hours had been spent much like the previous evening, with Ryker painstakingly searching across the area of land where the car had eventually 'disappeared' into a blackspot free of the network of road and license plate recognition cameras that increasingly covered swathes of the UK.

But Suffolk was known for its rurality, and with the lack of big urban centers came a lack of Big Brother monitoring, and the blackspot that Ryker had to search over here covered an area of some twenty square miles – much larger than in Kent. Only a tiny part of the county really, which consisted of 1,500 square miles with a population of less than a million people.

Ryker took a right turn down a narrow road wide enough for only one vehicle. A winding road with six-foot tall hedgerows on either side, rare glimpses of what lay beyond only when passing gates for the many farmers' fields, or when coming upon isolated homes.

As he rounded a corner he spotted a car parked up a hundred yards ahead. A big black SUV, tucked into the side by a turning for a gravel drive. Ryker slowed his car down, partly to get a good look at what lay past the turning, and partly because the way the car had stopped provided so little room for him to pass on the narrow road.

He crawled by. No sign of where the gravel drive led because of the crest of a small hill, but what he did see was two men, on their feet, standing on the near side of the hill. Regular-looking guys, in casual clothes. One looked off to something in the distance that Ryker couldn't see, a phone pressed to his ear. The other stood by his side, although the low rumble of Ryker's engine – or maybe the sound of his tires on the tarmac – caught his attention and he turned, arms folded to look over in Ryker's direction.

Ryker had no clue who he was, had never seen his face. But a certain type of person had a certain type of look. A seriousness in their eyes, their facial features. A relaxed rigidity in their stance that showed they were ever-ready. Ryker knew the look well because it would be what others saw in him.

The men hadn't moved from their spot before Ryker carried on past. And he kept going fifty yards, a hundred, until the next gated entrance where he pulled the car over to the side of the road. He took a quick look at the GPS screen. He hadn't seen the house or barn or whatever it was down the drive, but a building was plotted on the digital map, a couple of hundred yards from where the men had stood.

Ryker looked at the dark field by him. No buildings in sight that way. No cattle or other animals in the field that he could see. The metal gate was closed but not locked. Ryker stepped out of his car and opened the gate then got back in and reversed his car back, fully off the road and behind the hedge. Not entirely hidden from anyone passing from the far side, but if that car went past him, the people inside would get nothing but a fleeting glimpse in their mirrors, if they saw anything of him at all.

Engine and lights off, he sat and waited. Not for long. Less than ten minutes. He heard it before he saw it. The headlights flashed across the road in front a moment later and then the hulking SUV headed on past, didn't slow up. They hadn't spotted him.

Ryker turned the engine back on but left his lights off for now. He waited several seconds before edging back onto the road, two options fighting for control in his mind. Follow the car, or go and see what those men were looking at. Maybe Karaman was in the vicinity, in a building down that track. But maybe those men were searching still, like Ryker. If he lost them now, he wouldn't find them again. He wanted to know who they were, and where they were going next. He could always retrace his steps back to here to look at that property if it turned out that's where he needed to be.

Follow.

Out here, where there was so little traffic, it would be obvious if he got too close, so he held back a few more seconds. In a little over a mile they'd come to a T-junction. Going left would eventually take them to the nearest town; going right would wind through more farmland. He traveled slowly initially, the car not in his sights at all, which at least meant he wasn't in their sights either. He reached the T-junction and paused, looking carefully left and right. There. In the far distance to the left.

He took the turn and sped up. Traffic built up as he approached the outskirts of Bury St Edmunds, a small but historic and picturesque town. One which, in classically English style, had a layout of twisty, crisscrossing roads that pre-dated motor cars by hundreds of years. Which ultimately made it completely inadequate for cars to easily traverse, with a network of slow junctions to overcome.

Which was good news for Ryker because it meant he could close the distance on the SUV slowly, methodically, and without drawing too much attention. Soon only three other cars separated him and them. They carried on through the town. Other cars came and went, but Ryker always kept a safe enough distance. At least until they neared the far end of the town, and the road opened out and Ryker found himself directly behind the SUV.

As they sped up Ryker let the target drift away a little but kept it in his sights now. A mile. Two miles. Brake lights. Turn signal. Ryker slowed too and once the SUV had gone off the road he hung back a little more before eventually following them into the parking lot of a large out-of-town hotel. The SUV had carried on around to the side of the two-story building. Ryker parked up on the nearside and got out, deciding it was easier to stay unseen on foot.

He crept toward the far side of the building, the dusk gloom providing him some cover in the unlit parking lot. He stopped behind a parked van and peeked out. The SUV, parked now, lights off, sat right by two other parked vehicles. A dark sedan, another slightly smaller SUV.

One man stood by the cars. The same guy who'd looked in Ryker's direction earlier.

Ryker dialed Winter.

'Still searching?' Winter asked.

'Maybe not.'

'You found it?'

'It? The car? No. I found something else. How quickly can you get me something on a license plate?'

Winter sighed. 'Do you want to explain why first?'

'Because I think I'm not the only one out here looking for Karaman, and I want to know what I'm up against.'

'I've heard no news at my end,' Winter said, sounding dubious.

Still, Ryker read the license plate and Winter was in the midst of caveating what he could provide and how long it would take when the side door to the hotel opened and a man stepped out. The other man he'd seen earlier, on the phone. Except now he'd changed. All black. Not full-on combat gear but not exactly casual attire either, with black boots, cargo pants, and a thick jacket. He was also definitely more bulky than he looked before. Kevlar.

And he carried a big black holdall. Not a huge bag, but the way his hand strained and the way he pulled his shoulder up showed it was heavy.

'Ryker, are you still there?'

'Wait,' Ryker whispered when he realized the man wasn't alone.

Two more came out of the hotel, in the same clothes, with the same bags. Then another. Then another. Finally came a man who was more casually dressed. He didn't look much like the others. He was older. Out of shape in comparison.

'We have a... situation,' Ryker said.

Winter didn't answer straight away. Apparently, the seriousness of Ryker's tone had caused him to pause for thought.

'Go on,' Winter said.

Ryker pulled back behind the van. He'd seen enough.

'It's a raid,' Ryker said.

'What are you talking about?'

'They've found Karaman. SIS. And they're going to take him back. By force.'

'That makes no sense. Ryker, there is no raid. Not by SIS. I've heard nothing.'

'Then why is Frank Podence of MI6 standing fifty yards from me with a tactical crew?'

Podence. The MI6 pencil pusher who'd tried to close down Ryker's work on the Syndicate.

'Podence is there? MI6 doesn't have any jurisdiction on UK soil.' Technically correct. MI6's remit, in theory, was foreign intelligence gathering, and they only had authority to carry out operations outside the British isles. Yet spies be spies. Or something like that.

'And yet here he is,' Ryker said.

'That's...'

'What? Impossible? Do I really need to explain it all to you?'

'Ryker, if you—'

'This is the Syndicate. And Podence is with them.'

'Ryker, please—'

'I'm going to stop them.'

'If you—'

Ryker ended the call then turned the phone off as he rushed back for his car.

28

———————

Darkness was approaching. Nearly the whole day had come and gone with nothing happening. Angel had checked on both Mason and Karaman frequently. Mason slept most of the time. Karaman remained bright and alert and ever eager to accost Angel and lure her into conversation.

Which explained why she was sitting against the wall across the room from him.

'It wasn't the right number,' she said. 'The PIN code you told me.'

'I figured, given we're all still sitting here doing nothing.'

'So you lied to me about that.'

'I didn't lie. I was unsure of the last two digits. I saw the first four clearly. For the last two, he turned the phone so I had to guess based on what I thought he pressed. If I was wrong, there aren't many combinations for what it could be, though.'

'One hundred.'

'Sorry?'

'It'd be a hundred. You know the first four digits but not the last two. A hundred combinations for those two. Zero–zero through to nine–nine.'

'No. Because I saw where he typed. You can narrow it down further. The question is, why haven't you tried again?'

A good question really, and one she didn't have an answer to. Other than that Mason had asked for them to wait, so she'd waited.

She was hellishly hungry now, the cramps in her empty stomach like nothing she'd ever had before. But she'd survive. The question was, would Mason? Or would he eventually break and realize something needed to give?

But then she was surprised he'd held out this long, as each time she'd gone to check on him through the day he'd only seemed more groggy – when he was awake at all – and the smell from his wound worse.

'Who did that to you?' Angel asked a few moments later after watching Karaman mess a little with the bandages on his hands.

He sent a curious look her way as though she'd asked for his darkest secrets.

'To tell you that would be to tell you my life story.'

'Excuse me?'

He scoffed. 'By which, I mean I'd have to explain how I've been mistreated not just in recent days, but for decades. Used and abused.'

This time Angel scoffed and Karaman twitched and looked a little offended by her reaction.

'Why do you hate me so much?' he asked.

'You really have to ask?'

'*You* shot *my* daughter.'

'Shot, yes. But she survived.'

'She can't walk without a crutch. The bullet obliterated the nerves in her leg.'

Angel worked hard to hold back her emotions at the thought of a young girl irrevocably damaged because of her.

'*You* were my target,' she said. 'You should be dead.'

'You should be a better shot.'

'I'm a better shot than anyone you've ever met in your life.'

'And yet you shot my daughter, not me.'

Angel said nothing.

'So let me get this right,' Karaman said. 'You worked for... who? Some offshoot of the UK government carrying out dirty operations.'

Still, she kept her mouth shut.

'Oh, Angel, believe me, I know how that world works. You were tasked with assassinating me. But you missed. You hit *my* daughter. You changed her life, mine too. And now, all these years later, you come back to get your revenge on *me*?'

'You think *your* life changed that day? You have no idea.'

'So, tell me. You think I ruined your life?'

'I didn't miss you because of a bad shot. I missed because someone attacked me. Someone tried to stop me from shooting you. But that part wasn't spoken about in the press, or at my trial. Like it didn't happen at all. A whole new reality. You said yourself you know how the clandestine world operates. Well, so do I. They make shit up and they can make it stick, or if things go wrong they can just pretend they were never involved at all. I only ever did my job, but I spent years in prison because of that day. I've done my penance for hitting your girl.'

'They screwed you over,' Karaman said, sounding almost sympathetic. Or, at least, not as angry as before.

'No. *You* screwed me over. I remember you coming to visit me. I remember what they did to me in that prison because of you.'

Karaman slowly shook his head. 'You're giving me way more credit than I deserve. Yes, I came to visit you. My wife begged me not to. But... I was so angry. With you. With a lot of people. I said some bad things to you that day. Things I shouldn't have said. But whatever happened to you before or after that day was nothing to do with intervention from me. In fact, after seeing you in that place, I moved on. For the sake of my wife and daughter.'

She really didn't want to believe him. So why was it so hard to think of a comeback?

'The only question to ask,' Karaman said, 'is why did it take the people you were working for so long to come to your aid?'

She said nothing to that.

'If you want your revenge, why haven't you just put a bullet in my head?' Karaman asked.

'Because I'd get five minutes of satisfaction for killing you. What I want is my life back. *A* life back.'

'But you don't even know where the money is coming from. Or who you're giving me to.'

'According to you, I'm getting no money anyway. I've been set up. Right?'

Karaman didn't say anything to that, though definitely looked a little smug.

'But this does bring us right back to your original question,' Karaman said.

'What does?'

'You asked who did this to me?' He held his hands up.

'To tell me that would be to tell me your life story,' she said. 'Used and abused. Something like that.'

He sneered at her, apparently not liking her dismissive tone.

'What do you know of me?' he asked.

She didn't answer the question straight away. Something about the way he asked it suggested whatever she said, he'd pull it apart and tell her something different.

'You're from Türkiye,' she said. 'Born into a wealthy family. Your father was into real estate and made a fortune in the seventies and eighties as cities across the Arab world looked to spend the billions from their oil revenues on new property developments.'

He nodded and kind of smiled as though impressed with her knowledge. Not what she'd expected.

'You were brought up in a Westernized home, had everything a kid could want or need most likely, but for some reason – probably because you're a megalomaniac who wanted to put his own stamp on the world but didn't have the drive, determination or whatever that his father did – you turned to religious extremism instead. You stuck two fingers up to the Western world, to the capitalism that had brought riches to your family, and you instead went out of your way to spread hatred. You used your millions to fund terror cells. You personally oversaw attacks on US and UK soil, on embassies around the world which resulted in tens, hundreds of deaths. You—'

'OK,' he said, holding his hand up to stop her. 'Before you go too far in—'

'Go too far? I'm only just getting started. You became one of the most wanted terrorists in the world. At the very least you deserve to spend the rest of your life in some shithole prison cell for your crimes. But quite frankly, what you really deserved was a bullet in your head all those years ago and I only wish I could have achieved that back in Beirut.'

'Except you've missed a fundamental part of my story,' Karaman said, apparently unfazed by her angry exchange.

'Yeah?'

'I've been played, just like you have.'

She tried to respond to that but found herself caught in two minds. Karaman took pleasure in her confusion – a glimmer of a smile had appeared for a flash before his face returned to something a lot more somber.

'I'm not the terrorist you think I am.'

He let that hang. Did he expect a response from her? Sympathy?

'I never was that man. You think I rejected my upbringing? The world of riches I was born into? Yes. I did. Because I saw how much it stank. Greed, corruption. Not just the leaders in the Arab states, but the Western governments, businesspeople, eager to make money at any cost. Men who had no real values whether religious or otherwise, just a desire to take, take, take, and screw everyone else. *That's* what I tried to rebel against.'

Angel worked that over. She didn't believe it. Or, more to the point, she didn't want to believe it.

'All those attacks that were supposedly in my name? Lies. And you should know how easy it is for those in power to concoct lies, even outrageous ones, and make them stick.'

'If that were true...'

'It *is* true. You said yourself I grew up in a Westernized home, my family wasn't that religious. And neither was I. Not then, not now. I'm no Islamist. I only ever wanted peace for my people, not outside influences causing us more pain for their own gains.'

'And yet, as a wanted terrorist, you weren't hiding somewhere off the grid in a gloomy cave. Instead, you've spent years a free man, ever richer. You were brought to the UK from Dubai, right? Where they found you living on a yacht worth hundreds of millions.'

Karaman had the audacity to laugh at that.

'*Found.* But that's my point, Angel. I was never on the run. You think the British government, the Americans, have been hunting me all this time? You think the British government suddenly *found* me? Like I'd been lost to them and not simply living the life that it was agreed I could live?'

Angel shook her head as she tried to make sense of his explanation. 'You're lying.'

'I'm not lying to you. Yes, I have money – a lot of it – and I have power in the right circles because of it. I got to live this life because

I got the agreement of the right people and appeased others because of my wealth and political reach. Publicly I remain terrorist number one. A noose around my neck should I ever try to expose the truth, the lies. In reality? I've been a pawn in a much bigger game for decades. A go-between. A source of intelligence. An *asset*.'

'Except you *were* brought back here to face the truth. So how does that reality play into your little story?'

'Story? Angel, you haven't been listening. This isn't a story. Why did I get brought back here? That's a very good question. Someone, somewhere, has turned on me, despite me playing by their rules this whole time.'

'Who?'

He held his hands up again. 'I don't know. But if you find the man who broke my fingers to interrogate me, perhaps he'd have some answers for you. For us both. What you should really be asking yourself is—'

'Stop talking.'

'Why—'

'*I said stop talking*,' Angel hissed.

The realization that spread across Karaman's face moments later suggested he knew why. A soft, muffled voice. From the room next door. Mason. On the phone and trying to be discreet about it.

'Bastard,' Angel said as she shot up and for the door.

She concentrated on the voice as she marched forward, trying to make out the words but they were muffled by the walls, drowned out by her own roaring inner beast. She flung open the bedroom door and Mason, still crumpled on the floor, gazed up at her, the phone grasped pathetically in his grip, up to his ear.

'Angel...'

She strode forward and he cowered and pulled his hands up in front of him in defense. Angel went to swipe the phone from him, but he whipped it away and she ended up instead smacking the side of his face.

He tried to hit her, but she blocked with her forearm and the phone fell from his grasp and clattered along the cold, hard floor. She sank to her knees and balled her fist and smashed it into his side. Onto his bandaged wound. He squealed like an animal and collapsed down, writhing.

She moved over and retrieved the phone. The call had ended. She tried to unlock the screen. No. The PIN she tried was still incorrect.

'Who were you speaking to?'

He stared at her, trying to compose himself, perhaps trying to overcome the pain in his side, but more likely trying to concoct a lie.

'Who do you think?' he said, no hint of remorse.

'And? What did they say?'

'I don't know. I didn't get... to finish... did I?'

'Even when caught you still won't admit it, will you?'

'Admit what!'

'Whispering like that. Did you hope I wouldn't hear?'

'Angel! Please... I don't know what *he's* said to you—'

'This isn't about Karaman.'

'Of course, it's about Karaman!' Mason shouted with force and for a moment it was like he'd forgotten all about the state he was in. 'I'm on your side.'

'Then tell me your code. I'll call them back. I'll speak to them. *I'll* get this sorted.'

He glared but didn't say anything.

'Mason, tell me the code or—'

'Four–four–eight–five–nine–one.'

'What?'

'I said—'

'You changed it.'

'Changed it?'

She scoffed. 'You heard Karaman talking to me. You realized he saw you, didn't you? You changed it so I couldn't—'

'Angel! Please! I don't understand.'

She typed in the number and the screen unlocked. She took only a few seconds to scan over the phone. It was almost entirely blank. Nothing but pre-installed apps. No browsing history, no contacts, no text messages. No outgoing calls and just a single incoming call that had lasted for thirty-eight seconds.

They'd called him, not the other way around. Had he been telling the truth after all?

'What happened?' came the voice on the other end when she dialed the number back. A man. English accent. A gritty voice that she didn't recognize.

She said nothing.

'Mason, are you there?'

She still didn't say a word.

'Mason?'

'Angel, please?' Mason said. She ignored him but sank down next to him.

'Who is this?' the man asked.

'This is Angel.'

Silence for a few moments. She was about to check if the call was still running.

'Is Mason dead?'

She looked at her accomplice. 'No.'

'But he's in a bad way.'

'He is. He won't last long out here.'

'And Karaman?'

'He's fine.'

'What do you want?'

'The money I was promised.'

'But I haven't been given what *I* was promised.'

'Which is what?'

'Karaman. And... all loose ends... removed.'

'You can still get that.' She refused to look toward Mason as she said those words.

'You know where the meeting point is?'

She read off the pre-agreed coordinates for the drop site. She received a mocking laugh in response.

'So, he didn't tell you the actual rendezvous, then.'

She did now look at Mason whose face had gone white, his eyes glazed.

'You're about a hundred miles short. But I'll ask you again. What do you want?'

'I told you already. The money that was agreed. Ten million. Although it looks like my cut's a bit bigger now.'

'No deal.'

'Excuse me?'

'Ten million? Except look at the mess already caused. This isn't how it was supposed to be. The risks are greater now.'

'Then I'll kill Karaman right now and you'll never see or hear from me again.'

She pulled the phone away from her ear and her finger hovered over the red button. She so wanted to press it and just follow through with the threat.

Instead, she slowly pulled the phone closer to her ear again.

'Two million,' the man said. 'And that's me being generous, and because I want a swift resolution here. I *need* a swift resolution.'

It was still a life-changing amount...

'Angel? Is that a deal?'

'Deal.'

'Like I said, the money is yours when I get Karaman. All loose ends eliminated. You understand?'

'OK.'

'I'll call back in two hours with a new rendezvous. Be ready.'

The call ended.

She glanced at Mason. He looked so defeated.

'Anything to say?' she asked.

Apparently not.

'Did you hear?'

Still nothing.

'Sounded to me like he really doesn't care who delivers Karaman. As long as there are no... loose ends.'

Mason shook his head as if in defeat.

'I was a loose end?' she suggested for him but still he didn't say a word. 'Now you are.'

But, to her surprise, he reacted first. He reached to his side and pulled out a handgun. A handgun that hadn't been on him before. She would have known because she'd checked him over. She'd had his shirt up, his jeans around his knees. He hadn't been armed then. He'd retrieved it since she'd last left the room.

He twisted the gun toward her but she grabbed his arm and pushed the barrel off course. He pulled the trigger and the gun boomed but the bullet sailed away toward the far wall. She snapped the gun from his grip and thudded the butt into his side. Did the same a second time and Mason yelled then quickly tried to regain his composure. But he was struggling.

Mason reached out and grabbed her around the neck. Just one hand, because his left hung uselessly as though he had no use of that side of his body, the infection or the pain too great. He tried to choke her but he had so little strength it was like a small child was holding on to her.

She didn't even bother to move his hand away.

'You piece of shit,' she said to him.

She pulled her body back and his hand fell free and to the floor. She grabbed his empty backpack and shuffled back toward him.

'Please,' he said.

'One way or another, you're dead,' she said to him. 'It's kinder this way. Quicker.'

He barely moved as she pushed the backpack against his face. His hand flailed, one last desperate attempt at survival, but he didn't even make contact with her as she pushed the gun barrel into the fabric.

She pulled the trigger. Her body jolted from the recoil and his quivered from the deadly blow, and then seconds later flopped. She let go of the backpack and his body slumped to the ground.

Smoke rose up from the hole in the fabric. The smell of gunpowder caught in her nose, mixed quite grotesquely with the acrid smell of his badly infected wound, fully exposed now with the bandage twisted off.

She stood off him and left the room without looking back.

She intended to go out and get some air, but Karaman's voice lured her to him.

She stood in the doorway.

'He's dead?' he asked.

She nodded.

'It was him or you. Like I told you.'

'Except you didn't know the code for the phone really, did you?' she asked. 'So why the lie?'

He held her eye but didn't say a word about it. Had he spoken a word of the truth to her?

'So, the deal's done?' he asked when she turned around.

'No,' she said. 'It's not. Not yet.'

She left before he could respond.

29

Ryker didn't hold back on his way out of the town and into rural Suffolk. Darkness had arrived, and with it the unlit, narrow country roads became all the more perilous, but Ryker traveled at speed. He wanted as much time, as much advantage as he could get when he arrived at his destination. A destination which the traveling armed crew had already had the benefit of scoping out.

Even so, Ryker decided not to approach the building from the front. The GPS showed that another road lay behind the property, across fields and through a small area of woodland. No direct access by car that way, but Ryker didn't mind making the final approach on foot. Plus, having an alternative escape route to the soon-to-arrive ambush had to outweigh the negatives of the need to traverse unknown territory on foot.

He parked the car off to the side of the road. He hadn't seen another vehicle for more than two miles. No signs of any houses out here. The night was cold and quiet, pitch black, barely even any moonlight given the thick cloud cover.

Ryker opened the creaky metal gate and stepped into an expansive field. He could make out little so used the GPS on his phone to help guide him. He quickly read the messages from Winter as he walked. They did nothing to deter him. Winter flitted from outright ultimatums to urging caution, but the conclusion was that he had no idea what Podence was doing out there and there was no sanctioned operation to recover Karaman tonight by MI5, MI6, anyone.

That was enough for Ryker. He didn't need to understand the whys and wherefores. There were only three options. Podence was there to either kill Karaman, take him back into custody, or free him. Ryker saw the first of those as the least likely and the third the most likely as it explained the unsanctioned operation, even if it didn't explain everything else.

Ryker didn't need a full explanation right now. He just needed to make sure he got to Karaman first because none of those three options helped his objective of breaking open the Syndicate. He'd figure out the rest after when Karaman was back under his control.

Ryker put his phone away as he emerged from a thicket of oak and beech trees, and the building came into view a hundred yards away. A converted barn, he thought, the outline of a vehicle visible by it, although too indistinct in the darkness to figure out the make and the model. Ryker wasn't able to do that until he'd crept right up to it.

He felt no real satisfaction on confirming it was the car he was looking for. Only a renewed sense of urgency. Even standing a few yards from the building, he saw and heard no signs of life. At least he didn't yet hear anything amounting to an attack. But he didn't have time to dwell. He knew he'd at least face Karaman and two armed assailants in the building, but possibly more. And he wasn't armed.

Nothing he could do about that now.

He edged toward a back door, every step delicate but deliberate. He picked a fist-sized rock from the ground as he moved, held it tight in his right hand. Better than nothing.

He reached the door and stopped. Still no sounds from inside, no lights on that he could see, although the door was solid wood and at least half of the windows at the back of the barn were boarded up.

Ryker tried the door handle. Locked.

Given time was of the essence, he had little other choice. He lifted his foot and crashed it into the hinges side of the door. The door creaked and strained. Ryker hit it again and punched the door inward. The hinges wrenched free, taking a hefty amount of the frame with them.

Ryker burst into the room. A kitchen?

He stopped dead when he sensed the presence. Even before she spoke. Even before the pressure against the side of his skull.

'Don't—'

Move, he presumed she was going to say, but she didn't get the second word out before Ryker burst up, swatting at her arm with the rock, pushing the handgun away from him. She fired and the room lit up in a burst of light as Ryker dropped the rock and grabbed and twisted on her arm. She tried to move with him, spinning her body around to avoid him pulling her into a hammerlock. So Ryker changed tactic and let go and snapped the gun from her grip and lifted his heel to push her away from him.

He pointed the gun her way as she reeled back. He didn't need to give the same instruction she'd intended moments before. As she righted herself it was clear she got the message.

'How many of you are there?' Ryker said, risking a look to his left, toward the corridor, making sure no one else was about to rush him from there.

She didn't answer. So he lowered the gun and fired and she flinched as the bullet sank into the wood floor, throwing up splinters onto her legs.

'I said, how many?'

'It's *you*. Again.'

Her eyes pinched as she spoke, and the words came out with pure hatred as though she thought he was seriously out of line for spoiling her party a second time.

'How. Many.'

'Me. Just me.'

'You sure about that?'

'Actually, there's me too,' came a shout from another room. Karaman?

Everett laughed. 'He does that.'

'What about—'

'I shot him in the face,' Everett said, not sounding bothered by that at all. 'You wanna see the body?'

Actually, he kind of did, as he really didn't believe her.

'Once I'm happy, I'm taking Karaman,' Ryker said.

'Like hell you are.'

She took a half step forward, as though egging Ryker on. But then both of them looked to the smashed in back door. Both of them had heard the noise outside. The ever so light movement of feet. Indistinct really, if they hadn't both been so alert, so on edge.

'They're not with me,' Ryker said, speaking more quietly.

'No?'

'Although I have seen them already. Five men, maybe more. Tactical gear. Plenty of big guns judging by the bags they were lugging.'

He could see the confusion, the dilemma on her face, which only cemented that she wasn't expecting this crew's arrival. That they weren't on her side. Did that mean she was on his?

Yes, at least for now.

'You're lying,' she said.

'Wait around to get shot up by them if you like.'

The sounds outside had died down again. Which likely meant

everyone was in position and they were simply waiting for the green light from whoever was in charge. Podence? Or was he too important to be out on-site?

'He's in the second room on the left,' Everett said.

He guessed she meant Karaman, rather than her dead friend.

'Show me,' Ryker responded.

She dashed off, Ryker right behind her, ready and waiting should she try to attack or should her 'friend' not have a bullet in his head and jump out on him.

No need. He spotted the body as they rushed past the first room, sprawled on the floor, a bag draped over the head.

Everett headed on into the next room. Ryker slowed as his eyes fell on Karaman. His hands were cuffed, he was roped to the radiator, but he looked surprisingly upbeat as though this whole thing was a game for him.

'James Ryker? You keep... appearing.'

'Tell me about it,' Everett said sounding sullen as she crouched down and began to work on the ropes.

'No time,' Ryker said. He moved over and enjoyed seeing Karaman squirm back as he lifted his heel. He hammered it against the side of the radiator, pushing the fixture away, parallel to the wall. The fittings cracked although the radiator remained suspended. At least until Ryker grabbed the cold metal and yanked it and the whole thing snapped free, chunks of plaster coming with it. Water gushed from where the valve had snapped off.

'Not... subtle,' Karaman said.

Ryker said nothing. He didn't get a chance to retort even if he wanted to because his attention was drawn to the sound of an object bouncing across the floor of the corridor. Then the window behind smashed and the same sound was replicated, but closer by this time as the small metal projectile clanked toward him.

'Get down!' Ryker yelled as he threw himself to the floor and buried his face in his arm.

The explosion from the flash-bang grenade made it feel like his whole body had momentarily been crushed in a vice. The intense flash of light was at least mainly blocked out by squeezing his eyes closed and covering his face.

The second grenade exploded a moment later. Ryker battled through the turmoil in his insides and the smoke in the room as he rose up and reached out and grabbed Karaman and pulled the man to his feet.

'Move!' Ryker shouted at him and Karaman only resisted for a moment before Ryker dragged him for the doorway.

A volley of gunfire greeted him, coming from the front of the property, the bullets whizzing down the corridor, blasting into the floor and walls.

Ryker edged back to safety, turned to Everett.

'What weapons have you got?'

She searched a bag in the corner of the room. 'Only this,' she said, clutching at an AK-47. *Only* that, as though the heavy-duty rifle was a water pistol.

'Blanks still?'

'Not this time,' she said.

'Cover us,' Ryker responded. She didn't move immediately, as though she didn't agree they were on the same team, but then Ryker spotted movement beyond the now-smashed window behind her and he raised the gun he'd earlier taken from her and let off two warning shots and it seemed to convince her.

She moved to the door, pressed herself up against the frame, then nodded to Ryker. He rushed out into the corridor with Karaman, hoping the attackers would at least be careful with their fire with the asset so close. Everett jumped out a beat later, fired toward the front of the house as she backtracked.

The next explosion caught Ryker completely off guard. Not a flash-bang this time. The real deal. An RPG? The force of the explosion, which hit the front corner of the barn, sent Ryker flying. Fire and superheated air and shrapnel blasted over him.

He was dazed. He heard voices. Shouting. Thudding footsteps. Was vaguely aware of sweeping lights. Gunfire. Not aimed at him. Then...

'We need to go!' Everett shouted as she surged toward him. 'Now!'

He took a couple of seconds to get back to his feet. A couple more to look around, through the smoke.

'Karaman?' he asked her.

'Gone!'

More gunfire arrived from the front, beyond the flames, and convinced Ryker to race for the back door after Everett. She headed out and Ryker followed. He saw the man there before she did. Up against the wall, a few yards on the other side of the door. He'd gone around to block them off, no doubt. He pointed his weapon at Everett's back.

'Down!' Ryker shouted at her and his voice caused the attacker to think twice. He should have just pulled his trigger. Instead, Ryker got his shot off first. A narrow miss. But he hit home with the second and third. Two chest shots. Into the man's Kevlar, but at short range enough of an impact to send him onto his back. A third shot hit him in the leg as he lay on the ground. No chance of him chasing them now.

Ryker continued to race forward, up alongside Everett. Another explosion boomed behind them. Not as powerful as the last, now they were outside, but as Ryker looked behind him... The barn was unrecognizable, an inferno. Beyond the flames, to the far side of the barn, he spotted headlights twisting through the darkness, moving away.

Ryker stopped running.

'What are you doing?' Everett shouted at him.

'They got him.'

And with the prize in their possession, there was no sign that the attackers were bothered about chasing after Ryker and Everett. Or perhaps they thought them dead.

Ryker spun and pointed his gun at her head.

She snorted. 'Wow. Thanks.'

'Toss the rifle.'

'You serious? What if they—'

'Whether they come after us or not, toss the rifle.'

She slowly took the strap off her shoulder and dropped the weapon.

'That wasn't part of your plan?' Ryker asked although the answer was pretty obvious.

'You think I wanted to be blown up? I've been screwed. More than once.'

'Do you know them?'

'Haven't got a damn clue. You?'

'Maybe.'

They both went silent.

'So what? You're gonna put a bullet in my head out here? Or turn me in?'

'There's only one thing I want here.'

She said nothing. He thought she might have understood.

'Karaman,' Ryker said.

The look on her face changed. From sullen, defeated, to intrigue.

'Don't think I'm bluffing when I say I won't hesitate to kill you.'

She still said nothing.

'But I can get us out of here. Away from them. No police.'

'And the catch is?'

'No catch. Just an understanding. We get out of here. You tell me everything you know. After that... You're not my problem.'

She flinched when another boom came from the barn. But it was only a secondary explosion, or part of the structure caving in on itself.

'Let's get out of here,' she said.

30

They'd stayed on the road less than an hour. Enough to get clear of the burning barn, enough to conclude they weren't being followed by a chasing pack from Podence's team. Not long enough for Ryker to figure out what the hell was happening. Which was why they'd opted to stop the car at a motorway service station – somewhere public but also private enough – where they remained in the car to go over everything again and again.

'So, you were in this for money,' Ryker said, sounding as bitter as he felt.

Angel shot him a glare. She'd asked to be called Angel, not Angela or Everett, though it was certainly not a moniker that he immediately felt suited her much.

'No,' she said. 'I already explained why. Karaman—'

'Ruined your life. Except he didn't, did he? You messed up on that rooftop. You paid a price.'

'No! That's not how it was. Even Karaman agreed I'd been screwed over.'

'You *talked* to him about it?'

'I mean... Yeah. We talked.'

She looked away as though ashamed about that now. Like she'd had some sort of reverse Stockholm syndrome. Was that even a thing?

'Exactly what did you two share with each other?'

'You want it verbatim?'

Ryker didn't answer, knowing that she was being sarcastic, but actually verbatim would have been ideal for him.

'You have no idea what the last few years have been like for me. Did I mess up in Beirut? Maybe. I honestly did everything I could that day, and if it hadn't been for that man attacking me... I would never have missed. Karaman would be dead. My life would be... normal. Instead, I spent years in prison, my husband left me, took my daughter from me.'

The way she choked up on those last words revealed that the destruction of the relationship with her daughter was the most painful part of the story.

'OK. I get it,' Ryker said, trying but failing to sound sympathetic in that moment. 'But back to the kidnapping. How did you—'

'I told you already. I was at rehab.' She closed her eyes and growled, admonishing herself. 'Not rehab, exactly. A wellness retreat. I—'

'Alcohol?'

She sent him that glare again. 'Alcohol, pills, whatever I could get my hands on to escape mentally. I'm a fucking mess, haven't you figured that out yet?'

'The fact you were drawn into a kidnapping plot kind of reveals that, yeah.'

She obviously didn't detect the intended lightheartedness of his comment as her facial expression only further soured.

'I've been *trying* to get myself straight.' She shot him a look. 'You know, so far I've heard absolutely nothing about you. About how you came to be at that barn. About how you were at Belmarsh. Why we're here now. You're not police. You're obviously not part of any official investigation or operation, right?'

Ryker hesitated before answering. 'Correct.'

'So my guess is we're not that dissimilar, really. Our backgrounds, at least. The things we've had to do in the past for our jobs. You don't have to tell me who you work for, or worked for, but are you telling me you're A-OK up here?' She tapped her temple. 'That your whole life has been all singing and dancing and martinis shaken not stirred and—'

'No. I'm not. Not at all. But let's get back to why we're here.'

'Because Mason Black came to me. He offered me the job. Told me I'd get paid a third share of a ten million haul if we broke Karaman out of prison and got him to Black's contact.'

'And this was when?'

'Like... ten days ago.'

'You didn't know Black previously?'

'Not at all.'

Ryker hadn't come across the name before. He was the 'other' guy. The one who'd gotten away from Belmarsh with Angel and Karaman. But the timing also didn't make sense to him. Black had gone to her before Karaman had even been back in England. Before Ryker had even taken him from that yacht in Dubai. So the initial intention hadn't been to free Karaman from Belmarsh. But what? Maybe Ryker would never know now with Black dead. Most likely the plans were simply fluid and once Karaman came to Belmarsh his extraction from there quickly became the new aim for the hastily put together crew.

'And you shot Black?'

'Yeah. Because he lied to me. He would have killed me if he could have.'

'OK. Let's back up a bit. The other two men—'

'Harvey Harman and Sean Doyle. As you said. I didn't know

that. I knew Harman only as H. I didn't know Doyle at all. Never met him. When I saw him driving that van... That's when I first suspected I'd been lied to because it wasn't part of the plan.'

'You killed Doyle too?'

She held his eye for a moment as though having a momentary doubt that answering would incriminate her. That this was all just a sting to get evidence for a murder charge.

'Yes.'

'So, you killed Doyle. Harman was dead in the van—'

'And I took Mason and Karaman back to our planned safe house. The agreement was that we went there to wait for contact and then we would make the exchange.'

'You never questioned who you were handing Karaman over to?'

'Of course, I did. I was only told we weren't letting Karaman go free. That wasn't ideal as I want Karaman to suffer, but ultimately it was enough for me. As I told Karaman, killing him wouldn't give me a life back. The money... might have.'

Ryker huffed. It didn't sound like she believed that last part much now.

'Mason played us all,' she said. 'You know what I think?'

'No. That's why we're talking.'

'I don't think we were ever supposed to go back to that safe house. It was a decoy Mason had set up to throw me and H. The plan was always for us to be killed and for Mason and Doyle to escape with Karaman. Take him somewhere else. Probably straight to those people who attacked us earlier.'

'What makes you say that?'

'Just... how it played out with Mason. And I spoke to his guy about the exchange.'

'Yeah?'

'On the phone. Even as Mason lay there dying, he was actually trying to communicate with his guy behind my back. Probably explaining how the plan had gone to shit and deciding what they'd do about me. But I took the phone from Mason and I spoke to the guy. You know what I figured out in just a few seconds?'

'Go on.'

'Whoever it was, getting Karaman was all he cared about. Mason wasn't one of them. He was only another pawn. But the guy on the phone played me a second time. Told me to sit tight and he'd let me know about another exchange site. Offered me two mill.'

'A bit of a decrease.'

'Because of the fallout from the snatch. Because of *you*, basically.'

Ryker shrugged. 'Yeah. Really sorry. But you still took the bait. Killed Mason while you waited for their next move.'

'I didn't have much choice but to wait.'

'Except all you did was give them time to get that crew together. Most likely they'd been in the area a while already. Even when you spoke on the phone they were probably only a few miles away, getting themselves set up.'

Which also explained why the police investigation was so narrow from the start. Podence didn't need the police to help trace Karaman; he'd already known where Karaman was.

'And that's everything I know,' Angel said. 'So... What do we do from here?'

She sounded hesitant, as though unsure if Ryker would now dispense of her, or at least go back on his word and have her arrested.

'I said to you before. I only have one aim here. Getting to Karaman.'

'But... why?'

'You said you were part of a team sent to assassinate him. You never asked the question why?'

'I know about Karaman's past,' she said. 'His terrorism links—'

'Links? They're not links. Karaman personally orchestrated attacks which led to hundreds of deaths.'

He didn't like the way she stared at him.

'What?'

'That's what I used to think too.'

'Used to?'

'Everyone's heard that narrative. Number one most wanted, et cetera, et cetera. But... He told me it's not true. That he was set up. He's been an asset, an unwilling asset, for years, a noose around his neck because of the lies about him from his past.'

'*He* told you that,' Ryker said, trying not to sound so insincere. 'A world-renowned terrorist told you that he wasn't really a bad guy and you believed him?'

'No,' she snapped, clearly not liking his tone. 'He didn't say he wasn't really a bad guy. He didn't tell me he did those things for a good cause or something, as a rebel. What he said was that he hadn't done those things at all. He'd been set up, years ago. It was all about leverage. A way to get him – a rich and influential man from the Middle East – to play along.'

Ryker really struggled to believe it. He'd seen the videos. The calls to arms from Karaman, instructing others to spill blood. But... Was it possible he'd been forced into that position?

Possible. Highly unlikely, but possible.

'The Syndicate,' Ryker said.

Angel raised an eyebrow in response. A thought struck Ryker.

'Show me your wrists,' he said.

'Excuse me?'

'Just roll up your sleeves and show me.'

She looked confused, reluctant, but did so.

'Checking if I ever tried to slit my wrists?' she asked.

Her wrists were clear.

'Actually, no.'

She looked even more confused now. 'Then what?'

'Did you notice any tattoos on the other guys? Mason Black in particular?'

'No,' she said. 'I didn't. And I would have seen.'

He thought he knew what she meant by that but didn't bother to ask.

'You mentioned the Syndicate?' she said. 'What is that?'

'It's what they call themselves. A network of powerful criminals. A collection of some of the richest people in the world, acting in cahoots, circumventing laws to maintain power, sometimes over entire countries, all for monetary gain. They've started wars, they've rigged elections through blackmail and extortion. I *know* they exist because I've already scratched the surface—'

'You're telling me you thought Karaman was one of them?'

'Yes. But...'

'But maybe he's not as powerful as you thought he was. Maybe, if what he told me is true, he's just involved through coercion?'

He really wasn't sure if he'd go *that* far... yet.

'Perhaps I've been looking in the wrong place,' he said. 'Or at least, putting too much on getting to Karaman, getting him to break. Perhaps the answers were closer to home the whole time.'

'This Podence guy, you mean? You think he's... What? In charge?'

'In charge? Maybe not. But he's at least one hundred percent on the inside. Controlling assets like Karaman from a privileged position within MI6. A secret society being controlled by someone within an officially sanctioned secret society.'

'So we don't need to find Karaman. We need to find Podence.'

He didn't say anything to that suggestion, mainly because he was working over the use of the word *we*, but also because his phone had started to ring.

'Give me a minute.'

He climbed out of the car, his skin prickling from the cold as he did so.

'Congratulations,' Winter said. 'You've made the news for the two millionth time in your life.'

'Excuse me?'

'You're a wanted man, Ryker. For being part of a plot to help Ismail Karaman escape from prison.'

'What the fuck? You told me—'

'I know what I told you. But the position has changed and I'm—'

'Frank Podence,' Ryker said. 'He's got Karaman. He's the one behind everything.'

Winter paused a moment, suggesting that was news to him.

'Tell me what's going on,' Ryker said.

'You'll see for yourself on the news shortly. MI5 carried out a raid at a farm in Suffolk, trying to capture Karaman and the people who'd snatched him. Except the criminals had rigged boobytraps. Karaman is believed dead. Two people from the crew got away. Angela Everett. James Ryker.'

'You know that's not true.'

'I didn't say I thought it was true. I'm telling you what the press and the world will soon be told.'

'Karaman isn't dead!'

'Are you sure about that? Because I have it that a body was found in the barn. Yet to be identified, but—'

'A barn that's still ablaze?'

'Is it? Are you still there?'

'Of course, I'm not still there. But the body is Mason Black. One of the kidnappers.'

'And Angela Everett?'

Ryker didn't answer.

'Is she with you, Ryker?'

Was there any point in lying?

'Yes.'

Winter tried to get his angry words out but initially struggled. 'What... the hell are you doing!'

'What I've always done. I'm trying to do the right thing. Podence is the one. He's with—'

'Don't even think about mentioning the goddamn Syndicate right now! This has gone beyond a joke.'

'I never said any of it was a joke.'

Silence. Except for the sound of Winter breathing as he likely thought of what further rebuke he could throw Ryker's way.

'You know I had nothing to do with breaking Karaman out of Belmarsh,' Ryker said. 'Podence is playing everyone for fools. Karaman, dead? Most likely he's halfway back to the Middle East already where Podence can continue to use him as a puppet.'

Winter said nothing to that.

'I'm not asking for anything from you,' Ryker added. 'If your hands are tied or you've just had enough of looking out for me, then fine. But I'm not done. Especially not now that my name is out there, being dragged through the mud. Again. I'm going after them both and I *will* make this right.'

The silence on the other end continued, and Ryker checked to make sure the call was still connected. Then he heard Winter sigh.

'Good luck, Ryker,' he said before the line went dead.

31

The morning was cold, crisp, but the sun was out at least and gently warmed Ryker's back as he worked away. He held the bundle of wires in his left hand, using the fingers on his right to count through them...

'These four,' he said, isolating the chosen ones.

'You're sure about this?' Angel said from behind him. He glanced at her. The sun behind her cast a strange glow around her face, shoulders. Almost angelic...

He shook his head at his own thought.

'Only one way to find out,' he said.

He snipped through the wires in one go then looked over his shoulder at Angel again and both of them held their breaths as though awaiting an obvious response.

'Is it... done?' Angel asked, sounding dubious.

'It's done,' Ryker said. He closed the metal door to the electrical box and rose back up. He looked along the street. A few cars were moving by, a few pedestrians, but no one paid him or Angel any real attention.

'Come on,' he said. 'We don't have long.'

Angel checked her watch as they marched back the other way, along the row of handsome, redbrick Edwardian terraces.

'How long, exactly?'

'Depending on traffic? Thirty minutes after she leaves the house. Which should be in... about one or two minutes. If she sticks to her usual schedule.'

Angel shook her head and Ryker wasn't sure if it was in horror or amazement.

'And you figured this all out... because...'

'I told you already. Podence was already on my radar as someone who was blocking intel on the Syndicate. But I prioritized someone else over him.'

'Fatma Yaman.'

'Yes. Because I thought her role meant she had more direct access to intel on Karaman. Which... I guess was right. In a way.'

'But Yaman's now dead?'

'She is. And it wouldn't surprise me if Podence were behind it.'

She stopped walking and Ryker followed suit. 'What?'

'I think... H showed me a picture of the suspect who killed her. A CCTV image.'

Ryker knew the image. It was the one he'd helped find.

'And?'

'I think it was Mason Black.'

'Did he tell you that?'

'No. I never got the chance to ask. But it makes sense. That Mason was working with this Podence guy.'

'I guess it does.'

He was angry with himself for going after Yaman to start with rather than Podence. How much of the mess could have been avoided if he'd made a different choice?

They started walking again.

'So you'd already scoped out Podence's home,' Angel said. 'Figured out the security. Watched him and his family to determine their regular schedules so you could eventually break in.'

'Exactly.'

Angel snorted. 'You don't do half measures, do you? Remind me never to get on your wrong side.'

'I'd strongly advise you to remember that,' he said with a wink.

They were four houses away when Ryker slowed up in his step. 'There they are,' he said, referring to the uniformed child and smartly dressed woman who emerged from the front door. The woman ushered the kid down the steps to a waiting black car.

'In a rush,' Angel said.

'Always. Normally shouting at the poor kid for not doing something or other quickly enough.'

Moments later the black car blasted past, engine revving.

'She didn't notice the electricity went down?'

'Doesn't look like it. And if she did she'd probably assume it's a blown fuse or whatever. Would it stop you getting out the house if it happened when you were already late for the school run?'

Angel didn't answer and looked upset by the question. Ryker realized it had probably made her think about her daughter and that other missed life. A source of undoubted mental torture for her.

'And the alarm system?' Angel asked.

'It's a hybrid system. The base unit and individual sensors are all wired and mains powered. But if the electricity cuts off—'

'Which it has—'

'Then battery units switch everything to a wireless mode. Which connects the base to the individual sensors through radio signals.'

'So cutting the mains hasn't disabled the alarm, just turned it wireless.'

'So we can use this to block the signals,' Ryker said, taking out the jammer. 'Tricking the base unit into thinking everything is in good order.'

'Something makes me think this isn't particularly new for you.'

They reached the front steps and Ryker did one more check along the street. All clear.

'You could say that. You ready?'

'Yeah,' Angel said, not hesitating before she headed up the steps, reaching into her pocket as she did so.

The tools were Ryker's but she'd asked to do her part, and clearly it wasn't the first time she'd picked a lock because less than thirty seconds later she turned the handle and opened the door. They paused for a second, awaiting the sound of the alarm which didn't arrive, before she pushed the door open fully and they both stepped inside.

Ryker closed the door behind him. He checked the alarm box on the wall. It hadn't been set anyway, Podence's wife apparently in too much of a rush.

'We need to be quick,' he said, checking his watch.

'But you want us to stick together.'

'Sorry. But... yeah.'

'Whatever. Lead the way.'

So Ryker did. Ground floor first. The house was spread over four floors. Each was long and narrow with rooms of a mixture of sizes coming off the landing, but all with tall ceilings and classy, no doubt expensive furniture.

Nothing of interest on the ground floor. The basement next, but that only contained a guest suite and a home gym.

Ryker heard the noise as he moved from the basement stairs into the hall.

'Someone's coming!' he whispered to Angel as she came out into the hall behind him. The front door handle turned.

'There!'

Ryker pulled her into the downstairs bathroom, through another door and into a cloakroom. He pulled the door to. There was no handle on the inside. He heard footsteps and then voices echoing from out in the hall.

'I asked you three times already if you had everything you needed!' Podence's wife shouted. 'Where is it?'

'I don't know!' the kid shouted back. '*You* must have put it somewhere!'

'I didn't put it anywhere. Think, Ryan, think!'

'It might be... with the coats.'

Angel shuffled on her feet as if trying to alert Ryker but it wasn't as if he hadn't already heard.

The door to the bathroom opened. Footsteps close by outside. He heard the breaths of Podence's wife right on the other side of the door, could smell her floral perfume. She took hold of the handle, the door moved a couple of inches and light streamed in, right onto Angel's wide-eyed face.

'Mom! I got it. Come on!'

'Jesus, Ryan!'

She stomped away and only moments later, when the front door banged closed again, did Ryker let out a long sigh. Angel burst out laughing as she pushed open the door but then abruptly stopped and turned to face Ryker.

'What would you have done? If she'd seen us?'

'We don't need to worry about that now.'

And he didn't want to think about what Angel would have done either.

'Let's get this finished.'

Ten minutes later they'd scoured the next two floors, but found nothing of interest, much to Ryker's dismay. At Yaman's home, she'd had a desktop computer. The contents of that hard drive had led him to Karaman. But it appeared Podence was more careful than his colleagues, leaving no electronic equipment lying around at all, even in his plushly finished office.

'Wait a second,' Angel said, feeling around inside a tallboy cabinet in the corner of that room. She pulled her head back out. 'Come take a look.'

She looked really pleased with herself and as Ryker peered inside he saw why. But then his optimism faded as quickly as it'd arrived.

'A safe,' he said, looking at the metal door behind a false panel at the back of the tallboy.

'Tell me you don't want to get in there,' she said.

'We have about ten minutes left before mom returns home.'

'You know how to crack a basic safe like this, though, don't you?'

'Do you?'

'Yeah. This one...' She looked back inside. 'It's a pretty simple electronic lock. I'd be inside in less than an hour.'

'Like I said – mom will be home in a few minutes.'

'So tie her up and go to town on this thing.'

She was deadly serious too. 'I'm all for doing what it takes, but she's innocent.'

'As far as *you* know. Except she's married to enemy number one. And you've already broken into her house.'

'She doesn't know that. And she won't if we leave quietly.'

'Fine. We could probably even just take the whole thing. A safe this size would only weigh seventy, eighty kilos.'

'Great, let's lug it down the street and onto the tube. We can toss it to each other like a basketball as we go.'

Angel hesitated, looked unsure. 'You're being sarcastic.'

'Yeah, I'm being sarcastic. Sorry, but we leave it. This time, at least.'

He really did hate that idea, but it was the best option. He walked out of the room without waiting for a comeback and headed down the stairs to the hall. He took one last look in the kitchen. Were they really about to leave here entirely empty-handed?

He turned to head for the exit. Angel stood in the kitchen doorway, a wide grin on her face. She held up the handbag.

'You're kidding me?' he said.

'What? This is off limits too?' She sounded really despondent about that.

'No. I meant, she seriously left it?'

'Must have brought it in when she returned, then left it on the sofa in the lounge when they rushed back out.'

She put her hand in, drew out the phone. 'Yeah?' she asked.

'Yeah,' he responded.

But then Angel's momentary triumph dropped away again. 'What the...'

She put the handbag on the kitchen island as she walked over to the bookshelves in the corner where an array of picture frames were on display.

Ryker went over to her side. She stared at one picture in particular. Podence, his wife, another couple who Ryker didn't recognize. The men were dressed in black tie, the women in classy-looking ball gowns. They stood inside a huge marble-covered atrium.

'You know them?' Ryker asked.

'The woman with the Podences. Not the man.'

'And?'

'And the last time I saw her was through the scope of a sniper rifle as I lay on a rooftop in Beirut.'

'You're kidding me?'

'I'm not kidding you. I remember every damn detail of that day and those memories will never fade. She traveled with Karaman that day. With him and his family.'

'But do you know who she is?'

'Yeah. I do. Her name is Melike Arhan. She's Ismail Karaman's sister-in-law.'

32

Ryker and Angel took the first opportunity to leave the UK. The Eurostar terminal at St Pancras was as busy as ever, which at least helped them to blend in with the crowds. The moments waiting for their passports to be checked were nervy as hell, but they weren't stopped by any police, or by the border guards, and were soon on their way into Europe. Not that either of them were traveling on passports with their real names.

'I told you we're probably more alike than you realize,' Angel said as they settled down into their seats.

'Because we both kept some souvenirs from our past lives?'

'Not souvenirs, actually. My IDs are my own. Sourced and paid for.'

'You must have some good contacts, because that's a legit passport you were waving around back there.'

'I know,' she said with a wry smile. 'Same to you.'

She rested her head back, looking up, and sighed. 'Do you think we'll get all the way without hitches?'

'I honestly don't know. Just because we'll soon be out of the UK doesn't mean we're home free.'

'In my experience it takes time to connect police forces across the continent whether or not you're involving Interpol. The fact we've acted quickly should help.'

She spoke calmly about the predicament, as though cross-border travel as a wanted criminal was entirely normal for her. *He'd* had to do it many times in the past, but he rarely came across other people who had, and who had come out the other side still free.

'I'm pretty confident we'll be good now at least until we get out of the Schengen zone,' Ryker said. 'After that we have a border check in Romania. Bulgaria. Finally Türkiye.'

'If we go through the official border crossings.'

'We will unless we feel a need not to.'

'Three nights before we get to Istanbul?'

Which was where the Arhans lived. Melike Arhan being the sister of Ismail Karaman's wife. Ryker so far knew little about the Arhans but he had three days now to do as much research into the couple as he could. Perhaps it was a stretch to think they were involved in the Syndicate, or that Karaman was with them, but even if he wasn't the Arhans were now people of interest, and the fact was that Ryker was sure Karaman would have left the UK by now. The Middle East was an obvious destination, so traveling in that direction – away from the UK where he and Angel were wanted by the police – was the best course regardless.

'Three nights, six trains,' Ryker said as he settled back in his seat.

'Time to catch up on some sleep then,' Angel said, then she shut her eyes. And stayed that way.

So Ryker took out his laptop and Podence's wife's phone. He connected the two and took only a few minutes to break through the phone's security. He'd do this part quickly. If Podence's wife had already realized her phone was missing – stolen – it wouldn't take long and it'd be easy to track it through GPS, especially if she alerted her husband who had access to MI6 resources. So Ryker would copy everything he could then dump this phone in Paris at their first changeover. Before that point he needed to sift through as much data as he could.

He'd managed five minutes before the train arrived at Paris Gare du Nord.

Angel awoke as the train slowed.

'Damn, I forgot how quick it was to get here.'

'There'll be plenty more time for sleep yet,' Ryker said.

'You find anything?' she said, indicating the phone.

'Nothing that leaps out. But a whole host of new contact info that could prove useful. I'll filter it all and match it against the data I have from Yaman's computer, plus from the SIS databases I can still access if her accounts haven't been locked down already, and see if anything comes out of it.'

And he still needed to do the same with Melike Arhan and her husband, Hakan – a partner in an accounting firm, according to his LinkedIn profile – to see what mentions he could find of them in records Yaman had access to.

'Come on, let's go,' Ryker said.

They left the station for the short walk to Gare de l'Est, where they'd take a TGV to Stuttgart. Ryker dumped the phone in a trash can as planned. Angel seemed more edgy than before as they walked, the bustling city surrounding them. Traffic, pedestrians, sirens.

'You OK?' Ryker said.

'I'm fine.'

There really wasn't any time to dwell as they were soon on their next train. A super-fast blast across France and into Germany, arriving in Stuttgart a little over three hours later. Next up after that was the sleeper train to Budapest.

That train finally gave Ryker and Angel more time to settle, for them to openly talk, for Ryker to work without fear of someone seeing his screen. They bought a ticket for a two-bed cabin on the *Kalman Imre,* although the reality was that the cabin was smaller than a lot of the prison cells Ryker had been unfortunate enough to stay in. Two tiny bunk beds lined one wall with just enough space the other side for Ryker to stand up and stretch in. A little sink sat in the corner; bathrooms were shared between the whole carriage.

'It's not exactly the Orient Express,' Angel had remarked as she'd jumped up onto the top bunk when they'd first walked in.

No. Nothing like the luxury of old. Although it didn't seem to bother her much as he'd heard barely a peep from her since, keeping true to her previous comment about wanting to sleep. Perhaps because she needed rest, or perhaps as a way of avoiding conversation with Ryker.

And he left her that way for nearly three hours before waking her.

'Angel,' Ryker said, knocking the underside of the top bunk with his fist.

'What?' she said without hesitation, sounding entirely alert. Had she actually been awake the whole time?

'You need to see this.'

She jumped off the bunk, landing on the coarse carpet with barely a sound. She looked dubious as she sat back on the mattress next to him. He indicated the screen and she stared for a few moments and he waited to see if she'd understand without his need for explanation. She reached out and scrolled, taking in the full document.

'Is this real?' she asked.

'It's real.'

'And this is, what? Just sitting there in an MI6 database?'

'It is. A database that not many people have access to, and even fewer people have probably looked at this file since it was put there. But still, it's there.'

She buried her head in her hands, breathing more heavily.

'This is… This is too much.'

'But you were right,' he said. 'They lied. About everything.'

'I didn't even shoot that girl!' Angel said, her infuriation muffled because of her hands.

'Not unless you shot her with a 9mm, from that rooftop several hundred yards away.'

Ryker looked again at the screen. To the hospital report that was filed within a heavily redacted dossier covering the attempted assassination of Ismail Karaman in Beirut. Except the hospital report was very clear that the bullet taken from the little girl's leg was a 9mm projectile. And looking at the photographs it was obvious she'd been hit with something small rather than the much larger and more powerful bullet from Angel's sniper rifle which would have caused significantly more damage.

'Why?' Angel asked, lifting her face which had gone red and blotchy, her eyes too.

'Which part?'

'Why me? They could have just gotten me out of the country, but they let me go to prison for something I didn't even do. Why did they do this to me if I did nothing wrong out there?'

It was a good question. And Ryker really didn't know the answer.

'My take?' he said. 'The assassination of Karaman was sanctioned by MI6, but Podence or whoever else who was protecting Karaman found out. But they only found out last minute. Which was why you were attacked on that rooftop as they tried to stop you, just in time.'

'But I did shoot my rifle. A single shot.'

'But you didn't hit that girl.'

'Then who did?'

'Were you the only one out there that day?'

'No. There were three of us. But... only one close enough to shoot her like that.'

'Do you know their name?'

'No. I knew nothing about him.'

Blue. Kind of like H, she'd only met him right before the job. Red she knew, but not Blue.

'Maybe he fired the shot, trying to get Karaman.'

'Or maybe it was just a wayward bullet as he fought off an attacker, just like I had to.'

'The fact he wasn't captured and put on trial like you were suggests most likely he's dead. Probably died out there that day. But Karaman, Podence, they got their revenge on you. Even though they knew you didn't fire that bullet.'

'I wish they'd just killed me too.'

'No. You get to live so you can bring these people down. We'll make them pay, not just for this but for all their corruption, their crimes.'

She scoffed and sent daggers his way.

'I wish I was like you,' she said.

'Like what?'

'No real cares. No real life.'

'Excuse me?' She sounded really bitter and he didn't like it at all.

'You still haven't told me about your past but I see it in everything you do. This is all like a game for you. Blasting from one melee to another, kicking ass, taking down the baddies, shooting, stabbing, whatever, because you just like the damn drama.' He cringed at her words. The way she described him made him think of Brock Van Der Vehn. He buried the comparison as best he could. 'But what's it for, really? What does it all even mean to you?'

'It means I get to make a difference.'

'Yeah, well, I never wanted to make a difference. I just wanted to do my job and be with my family. The Beirut op? It would have been one of my last.'

'Do you know how many times I've said something similar? Yet here I am still.'

'But I'm not you. I'd already made the decision. I wanted out. I'd done my time, sold my soul, I just wanted my husband and my daughter. *I was in love.* Everything good in my life was stripped away because of that one damn bullet. It doesn't even matter that I didn't fire it—'

'Yes, it does. It means everything.'

'To you, apparently. And that's your problem. You've not lost like I have.'

'Which just shows you know nothing about me.'

'Yeah? So come on, then, tough guy. Tell me. Sure, you've probably been wronged and you go out and get your revenge. But what have you actually lost in your life? You probably never had anything to lose.'

'I lost my wife,' Ryker said and the simple response seemed to knock Angel, who had no immediate comeback. 'And I loved her more than anything.'

'I...'

'And you want to know her name?'

Apparently not because she didn't answer.

'Angela. How about that for coincidence? Angela Grainger. She was an FBI agent. We met... in an unusual way. We were both lost souls, I guess. But the love was real. And it's the only time I've ever experienced it. And it's the only time I ever will because the pain of losing her was too much. I'm never going through that again.'

'She died?'

'She was murdered. Because of me. Buried in the garden of our home while I was globetrotting, trying to dish out justice on deserving scumbags. You know, kind of like the guy you just described before.'

'I'm... sorry.'

'If I'd just stayed with her, which was what she begged me to do... she'd still be alive. Just like if you'd stopped one job before... you'd still be with your daughter. But you didn't stop, did you? And neither did I.'

Angel didn't say anything.

'I can see your pain,' Ryker added. 'And I've never had a kid so I can't fully imagine what it's like not being a part of your daughter's life when you love her so much. But at least be grateful she's alive, and well, and don't ever think I don't know pain too. The person I am today is only because of the torment I've been through.'

He waited to see if she had anything in response. Apparently not.

'I do what I do after all these years not because I'm some bloodthirsty mercenary,' he said, 'but because there are still bad guys out there who won't be taken down otherwise. But I also do it because it keeps me moving forward, away from that pain in my past. I'll never forget, but if I stop and do nothing...'

He trailed off, losing his train of thought.

'I misjudged you,' Angel said, holding her hands up. 'Sorry.'

Ryker's phone lit up with an incoming call. No ringtone or vibration but both of them looked at the screen and Ryker knew Angel was wondering who was calling as he answered. He turned away from her but didn't feel the need to leave the cabin.

'Yeah?' he said.

'I'm guessing you've already left the UK,' Winter said.

'Yeah.'

'Want to tell me where to?'

'No. Any news your end?'

'Nothing's changed here. Your names are still out there, so you did right to leave. But I do have some intel for you.'

'You do?'

Winter sighed and then said nothing as though having second thoughts.

'I played to Podence's ego,' he eventually said.

'Sorry?'

'I called him. Emailed him. He ignored me the first few times, but the simple fact is that I'm still one of them. Still on the inside. So he couldn't just cut me off cold without sending the wrong signals. As far as he knows, I know nothing about his treachery. And... we spoke.'

Ryker gripped the phone a little tighter. 'What did he say about me?'

'Not a lot. Mostly he talked about me, actually. About ensuring I knew where my loyalties lay so that when the authorities caught up with you, I didn't go down too.'

Even tighter. Ryker imagined the device shattering in his hand.

'It didn't end particularly friendly,' Winter added. 'So I'm afraid he told me absolutely nothing – no confessions about Karaman, other than confirming the news reports that he's now dead.'

'Which he isn't. So what's the intel?'

'I know where he's going.'

'He *told* you?'

That didn't seem likely, given what Winter had just said about the conversation.

'No. But don't forget the circles I hang around in, Ryker. I know a thing or two about cloak and dagger.'

'OK?'

'I had a... friend on side with me. Tracking Podence's phone in real time. Podence is in Istanbul. Looks like Karaman's gone home.'

'Got it,' Ryker said, betraying no emotion even though he was beaming inside that his hunch had been right.

'Oh, but Ryker, that's not all. I know exactly where he is in Istanbul. Although I can't guarantee for how long.'

'I'm listening.'

Winter told him the location, and Ryker thanked him before ending the call.

Angel gave him an imploring look, but he held his tongue a few seconds more as he processed the conversation.

'It looks like we just hit the jackpot,' he finally said, unable to stop a wide smile from spreading across his face.

33

The hardest parts of the journey were over, every cross-border security check completed without any hiccups. The final leg of the expedition saw another sleeper train take them from Bucharest to Istanbul. A long haul, and one that didn't provide a full, undisturbed night's sleep because of the middle of the night security check at the Turkish border at Kapikule. A check that hadn't caused any problems for Ryker and Angel, but still, coming out the other side, with their sleep interrupted, and their final destination finally in sight, both were restless.

'Three nights,' Angel said. 'Three nights sitting in tin cans and we didn't get wasted once.'

'I thought you were clean.'

'I'm trying not to be an addict. And I haven't mixed pills and alcohol for nearly a year. I still want to enjoy a drink. Sometimes you just really need it.'

'Isn't that how you spiraled before? Drinking to self-soothe.'

'You're saying I lack self-control?'

'No.'

'Well, you'd be right. Of course, I do. Don't all addicts? Anyone can stop themselves from doing something if they try hard enough. Sometimes I just don't want to try.'

'There's no catering car on this thing, anyway. Nowhere to get a drink.'

She sighed. 'I wasn't suggesting now. I meant we should have before.'

She jumped off the top bunk, landing with aplomb like she always did.

'I'm going to take a shower.'

She headed out to the communal bathroom at the end of the carriage with her things.

Ryker lay back and stared up at the top of the bunk. He just wanted the journey to be over now. He'd rarely spent so much time in such a confined space with another person out of choice. It wasn't that there was tension between the two of them. As Angel had pointed out, and as Ryker had come to realize, they really did share a lot of similarities, both in terms of their past lives and perhaps even their current lives. The way they'd been mistreated by others stuck out most.

Despite all that, neither of them were on the train for any sort of bonding. And so they hadn't really, instead spending long periods of the journey in silence.

But it was nearly over now.

Ryker checked his watch. She'd been gone ten minutes already. Not that long for a shower, he supposed, but he'd been in the shower room earlier and it wasn't exactly a heavenly experience. The quicker the better had been his aim.

Fifteen minutes.

Nearly twenty.

Ryker got up from the bunk and unlocked the cabin door and peered along the corridor. Dark and quiet. Quiet in the sense that he saw no one, at least, because the racket of the rattling train was always present.

Ryker stepped out and closed the door behind him. He walked slowly toward the end of the carriage where the crappy little toilet and crappy little bathroom sat. He hadn't quite reached there when he realized both were empty. The door to the toilet swung back and forth with every jolt of the train. The bathroom door had a little green symbol by the handle. He tried it anyway, pushed it open. Stepped in. Steam still sat around the edges of the mirror from recent use of the shower, but no one was inside. No belongings either.

Had she bolted?

Unlikely. Why would she have bothered with a shower beforehand? There wasn't a scheduled stop coming up, either. Most importantly, why the hell would she have waited all this time if her only objective of traveling with Ryker wasn't to get to Karaman but to escape, and with it evade any crimes she'd committed back in the UK?

No. She hadn't run.

A banging noise behind him. Ryker spun, sank a little, knees bent, hands at the ready. But there was no one there. He moved out to the corridor. No one there either.

He was sure he heard the sound again. More muffled this time.

'Angel?' Ryker shouted out, not particularly caring about disrupting anyone's rest at that moment. He took a couple of steps back toward their cabin.

'Angel!'

A more distinct thud this time. Ryker moved along the corridor with more purpose, past the first cabin, the next too.

'Angel?'

'Ryk—'

Third door. He tried the handle. Locked. He pounded it with his fist.

'Open the fucking door!'

He yanked on the handle, tugging it back and forth. Another thud from inside.

Movement to his right. From their cabin. A man stepped out. Ryker didn't even need to see who he was, whether he was armed or not. He was an imposter. A target. Ryker rushed him. He only saw the suppressed handgun whip up at the last moment.

Too late to stop his own movement. Too late for the guy to properly take aim.

Ryker dove forward, taking the man by the waist, clean off his feet, and thumped him down onto the floor. Ryker's weight pressed down on him to add to the hefty impact, pushing the air from the guy's lungs. Perhaps breaking a couple of ribs too, to go along with the broken jaw after Ryker smashed his fist into it.

He took the gun and hit the man's skull twice with the butt until his head lolled.

Ryker jumped up, dragged him back into the cabin. He quickly checked his pockets and took his phone. No other weapons.

Ryker didn't have time to restrain him.

He pulled the door closed as he dashed back out to the corridor. He raced along to where he'd heard Angel. There was no hesitation as he slammed into the door with his shoulder. The door simply wasn't made to withstand that kind of force and it crashed open, knocking into the back of a woman standing there. Ryker took in the scene in a split second.

A woman by the door, gun in hand, facing away from him. Two other figures at the far end. Angel on her knees, face bloodied, hands bound. A man behind her, with a knife to Angel's throat.

Ryker lifted his foot and used it to propel the woman further forward. She stumbled toward Angel and her companion. Angel squirmed and fell to her side to avoid the woman collapsing on top of her. Ryker lifted the suppressed gun. He fired a single shot which hit the hand of the man in front of him and the knife came free. Ryker charged him. Grabbed him by the back of the head and slammed his face into the metal upright for the top bunk. He collapsed to the floor.

'Ryker!' Angel shouted, her eyes on the wide open door.

He sensed the movement behind him. Spun that way as he crouched down. It was the guy he'd just fought outside – clearly not as out of it as Ryker had thought. He fired another shot, straight into the man's gut. He fell forward, onto Ryker and they both dropped down onto the bottom bunk.

The man's arms flailed as he tried to wrestle for the gun, tried to hit out at Ryker's side, his face. Ryker pulled the trigger again, but the bullet missed this time and sank into the mattress above him. A cloud of white cotton filling burst free.

Ryker heard a sickening squelch and the man's strength evaporated. His body quivered a moment, glassy eyes staring down at Ryker before Angel pulled the knife free from his skull.

Ryker tossed the dead guy off him as blood gushed. He jumped back to his feet.

'Angel, no!'

But she paid him no attention as she whirled around, sank low and drove the knife into the back of the neck of the man on the floor. She tugged the knife free as she twisted the other way, toward the woman who was only just pulling herself up, her back against the far wall as she tried in vain to reach for her weapon.

She realized at the last second she wouldn't get it and instead tried to turn her head away, whipping a hand up to protect her face. But it was too little too late with the knife already thrust toward her.

The blade went right through her hand, and then through her eye...

Angel let go of the handle and the woman remained in position, her body twitching as her life rapidly ebbed away. Her hand and arm remained suspended awkwardly, grotesquely, with the knife handle protruding.

Angel slumped down next to the dead woman, panting.

'Thanks,' she said to Ryker through her heavy breaths.

'Same to you.' Although he recognized that he didn't really sound very thankful.

He stood up and moved to the door and pushed it closed. As best he could, anyway, with the lock broken. He looked over the carnage in front of him. Three dead bodies. A hell of a lot of blood.

'What?' Angel said, obviously sensing his mood.

Although he couldn't quite explain right then, with adrenaline still diminishing from the high of the fight, what he was thinking. Surprise, at seeing how capable Angel was in the heat of the moment, or shock at how ruthless she was? Ruthlessly efficient. Brutal, savage. Three lives taken in a matter of moments.

'What?' she said again, more challenging this time.

'You didn't have to kill them,' he said.

'Fuck you. You weren't the one on your knees with a knife to your throat.'

She lifted her head to show the nick to her skin. Her left eye was badly swollen too. Her lip and nose were bleeding.

'They jumped me when I left the bathroom,' Angel said. 'A gun to my face, a knife to my throat. They pulled me in here. Tied my hands.' Which were now untied, Ryker noticed, though he hadn't spotted the moment when she'd overcome the knots. 'They were asking about you. Where you were. What weapons you had.'

'What language?'

'English. But not English accents.'

Each of them had pale features, though, and could have been

from anywhere on the European continent. Plenty of places further afield, too.

'The bastard felt me up too,' Angel said, looking at the man who'd been standing behind her. 'Slipped his hand down my pants and told me exactly what he'd do to me if I didn't cooperate. If I didn't tell him everything he asked for. That bitch stood there grinning like it was a fucking game.'

Ryker checked over each of their pockets. No IDs. A phone each. Two guns between them. A spare magazine for each.

'Given the lack of ID, they must have got on in Türkiye,' Ryker said. 'Unless they have another cabin somewhere with more belongings.'

'Whether they got on in Türkiye or wherever else isn't really the point,' Angel said. 'How the hell did they track us?'

Ryker thought about the question.

'You dumped that phone in Paris,' Angel suggested.

'It's *possible* they followed us because of that,' Ryker said. 'But why wait all this time to confront us?'

'You've been on your computer for hours a day,' Angel said, more than a little accusatory in her tone now. 'Maybe they've been tracking it. Either the device itself or because of all the databases you've been in and out of.'

'I've got some damn hefty software to stop that.'

'Then what's your explanation? The only other contact we've had with the outside world was that phone call you had with your buddy, Peter Winter. Are you sure you trust him?'

'I trust him,' Ryker said. 'There's no way he sent these three after us.'

And he spoke without hesitation, with confidence, but was he one hundred percent on that? No, he couldn't be. A very sad fact.

'Yeah, well, I never even met him, so I'm not as sure as you are,' Angel said. 'And it'd make some sense. He works alongside

Podence. How do you know Winter's not been part of it the whole time?'

'I just do.'

'That's a pretty poor way to try and convince me.'

'I don't need to convince you of anything. The simple fact is that we would have had a much better chance of figuring out who they were if you hadn't killed all three of them in the blink of an eye.'

'Oh, so you have a problem killing people now? You think you're so damn morally superior to me, to everyone else, don't you?'

Ryker didn't bite back, only shook his head.

'Somehow they tracked us,' he said. 'And judging by what they did to you, they weren't playing around. Now we're stuck with three dead bodies and for all we know more people still keeping tabs on us from... somewhere.'

'Yeah? So what are you suggesting?'

'We get off at the next stop. We dump everything we've brought here. Clothes, bags, electronic devices. Everything.'

Angel paused a moment, holding his eye. Clearly, she didn't like something about the proposal, but it really was the best idea.

'Fine,' she said.

'The fact everything's so quiet still at least suggests no one heard the suppressed gunfire over the din of the train. Let's get this mess tidied up as best we can. We've got about an hour before we stop.'

They dumped all of the bodies on the bottom bunk and put the sheets from both bunks over the top so they at least didn't have to see the corpses anymore. There was little they could do with the resources they had in the cabin to tidy up the bloodstains. Ryker really didn't envy the poor soul who first walked in once he and Angel had alighted.

When they finished, their own things packed and ready and waiting, they both jumped up onto the top bunk, their legs dangling, Ryker hunched down awkwardly so his taller frame fit under the ceiling – still a better option than perching below next to the dead bodies.

'You can hate me, whatever. I'm not in this to make friends,' Angel said. 'Never have been, never will be.'

'I never said I hated you.'

'Then why the attitude?'

'For all we know they were just carrying out orders. They were told we were the bad guys. On the run for murder. I won't hesitate to kill someone if I know they—'

'Oh, so you *are* the moral arbiter?' Angel said. 'It's OK to kill someone if James Ryker says so, but not until that point?'

'That's not what I was saying.'

'Sounded like it to me.'

'I don't think we're going to resolve this. The real problem here is that... I don't come across people like you very often. Reflections of myself.'

'You don't like what you see?'

'I'm not sure I do. Not if others see me as some unhinged killer.'

'Wow, so now I'm unhinged?'

'That wasn't a direct reference to you.'

'Just indirect?'

'No. It's... It's hard. Seeing someone like myself. Seeing the vulnerability, the mental toll. We've both been let down by so many people.'

She edged a little closer to him and nestled her head onto his shoulder. It surprised him, given the conversation they were having. But maybe what he'd just said explained it all. Yeah, Angela Everett was tough in many ways. She could handle herself physically and had no qualms in dishing out violence to keep herself safe. But she was also vulnerable.

'You want to know the truth?' she said.

'About what?'

'About how I felt when I was in here with them.'

'Yeah?'

'I was terrified. Genuinely terrified. Not just of being killed, but of what they would do to me. Did I flip out? Yes. Because I knew I had to do everything I could to stop them. And it really is as basic as that. I had to hurt them so they couldn't hurt me.'

'Then you succeeded,' Ryker said. 'Because they certainly can't hurt you now.'

'No. They can't. But the story of my life is that there's always someone else who will. That's why I have to be ready. Always. Ready and willing.'

Willing? Did she mean willing to kill? Because Ryker now had absolutely no doubt about what she was capable of.

Yet two words turned over in his mind. Self-control.

Anyone can stop themselves from doing something if they try hard enough. Sometimes I just don't want to try.

Even as she lay resting on him, calm yet somber, her closeness comforting to him in a way he hadn't felt enough recently, those words from her felt all the more dark and deadly.

34

Changing trains only delayed Ryker and Angel getting to Istanbul by a few hours. They still arrived before noon on a cold, crisp but sunny day. And they arrived without further incident.

They'd dumped all their previous belongings, including phones, laptops, even clothes on the stop off, and arrived in Istanbul with full new outfits from an early opening outlet store. They also had weapons now too. A handgun each, taken from the attackers on the train, although they had limited bullets and no time to source more.

'I'm surprised we didn't have a welcome party at the station,' Angel said as they walked away into the city.

Ryker didn't say anything in return, his mind too busy trying to figure if that was a good thing or a bad thing.

'I mean, even if it wasn't another hit squad sent after us,' Angel continued, 'someone must have found those bodies by now? So where was the police cordon? The swarms of officers trying to figure out what happened on that train?'

Good questions.

'Ryker, are you even—'

'I'm listening, but I really don't know.'

She stopped walking and huffed. 'Yeah? So what's your plan now? Just rock up to this place and attack?'

'Yes.'

'You and me versus whatever, whoever we find there.'

'Exactly. What else are you suggesting?'

'Time and patience, perhaps.'

'We have neither, though, do we?'

She laughed at that. He hadn't meant to be funny.

'I'm serious,' Ryker said. 'We already know someone was tracking us. It's only a matter of time before another crew comes after us, or the police catch up with us. And we have no idea how long Karaman and Podence are even staying here before moving on.'

'Maybe they have already. Especially if they know we're coming.'

'Maybe. Or maybe the two of them are so damn self-assured that they're waiting for us.'

'Oh, great. So now you're suggesting we're walking directly into a trap?'

Ryker shrugged. 'What's your alternative? Sit and wait for... what?'

She didn't answer this time.

'We hit now, we hit hard.'

'Go hard or go home, as they say.'

'Damn right.'

* * *

As dusk approached, they were on the choppy waters of the Bosphorus, Ryker steering the rented bow rider steadily toward their destination. The rental company wanted the boat back before dark. Ryker was about to disappoint them. They'd at least get to keep his hefty cash deposit.

During the intervening time in the city, they'd further equipped themselves as best they could for what lay ahead. Ryker ignored the gnawing doubts at the back of his mind about whether they were ready.

They had to be. No other way to do this.

The low winter sun headed down on their west side, the European side of the water, while the waterfront properties across on the Asian side basked in the orange glow of the last of the day's rays. The water they were on sat as the boundary of two continents, the city that surrounded it a strange mix of history and culture from both places. Although from his current viewpoint, there was really no difference between east and west, and both sides had luxury waterfront properties crammed along the shore.

'There it is,' Ryker said, slowing the boat further. He indicated the white colonial-style building built almost directly on the water, with only a small, enclosed grass garden in between. In the Yenikoy district of Istanbul, they were a few miles removed now from the main hub of the city, but the properties here remained tightly packed. Big and very expensive villas on small plots, all clamoring for a piece of the waterfront.

'And you don't know who owns this place?' Angel said.

'No.'

'But it's not the Arhans?'

'I don't know for sure if it is or it isn't,' Ryker said. 'But I do know their main residence, the one I showed you a few minutes ago, is on the Asian side.'

And now behind them. They'd stopped outside there for a few minutes but had seen no signs of life.

'But originally you'd planned on going to that one,' Angel said, sounding more doubtful all the time.

'Yeah,' Ryker said. 'Because that's why we were heading here at all. The Arhans were a lead. But Winter's given us this place.'

'You really do trust him, don't you?'

Ryker didn't answer.

'And how accurate do you think his information was? The Arhans' place is, what? A mile down the water? And it's on the Asian side. Part of me can't help but think that Karaman would have taken the first opportunity he could to get off European soil.'

A fair point.

'As far as we know, the Arhans aren't part of this,' Ryker said.

'Do you even know anything about them?'

'Not much. But I know there's no mention of them in any of the SIS files I've scoured. At least, nothing except for basic profiles because of their closeness to Karaman. They aren't our targets.'

'Yet,' Angel said.

'Yet. At least not until we find or see something that changes our minds.'

'Everyone's a good guy until they put a gun in your face.'

'Something like that.'

Ryker took his hand from the throttle and the engine quietened down. He picked up his binoculars and studied the moving shapes for a few seconds. He turned to Angel and passed her the binoculars.

'Take a look.'

She did, spending a little more time than Ryker had.

'I don't see Podence or Karaman,' she said, sounding disappointed.

'No. But what *do* you see?'

'Four men so far. Two on the outside. Two moving about inside. In the downstairs.'

Where lights had just come on with darkness approaching.

'Just four guys? Doing... guy things?'

She sighed again. 'OK. I'll be specific. The two inside I'm not so sure about from this distance with these shitty binoculars. Dark clothing but I really can't tell much more than that. The ones on the outside... Black suits, white shirts. They're security guards.'

'Security guards tend to guard something.'

'We're looking at a row of waterfront properties that each cost north of ten million euros, or hundreds of millions of lira to the locals. Plenty to guard around here. But...'

'But what?'

She pulled the binoculars down. 'Most likely they know we're coming.'

'Maybe they do. Maybe they don't. But given everything else we know—'

'It looks like we probably found what we came here for.'

Ryker smiled. 'Yeah. It does.' He pulled on the throttle and the boat chugged forward, heading away. 'So let's get ourselves prepared. We hit at nightfall.'

They split up for their approach to the property. Ryker stayed on the boat. Angel would go in from the roadside. Ryker turned the engine on the bow rider off when he was a hundred yards from the property and the craft slowly drifted further toward the houses. As focused as he was now, thoughts rumbled deep at the back of his mind about the last time he'd been on a boat. On the much warmer waters of the Persian Gulf, en route with Brock Van Der Vehn to capture Karaman from his mammoth yacht.

So much shit since that night.

But unlike that night, Ryker wasn't getting into the water here. Thankfully. He'd go straight up onto the private dock.

He took hold of the oar and slowly directed the boat, making a beeline for the neighboring property.

'Where are you?' Ryker said quietly.

'By the wall,' Angel said, her voice coming through the tiny bud in Ryker's ear. 'Waiting for a couple of cars to pass then I'll be up and over.'

'I'll be onshore in a couple of minutes,' Ryker responded, his eyes busy on the villa in front of him, and the two men patrolling the outside. Much harder to see them now in the dark, no lights on in the garden. Much harder for them to see him too.

He came up alongside the neighbor's jetty and used his hands to guide the boat slowly, almost silently, along the wood. The jetty came to an end, but he had enough momentum to send him onward to the next one, the boat hopefully less notable from this sideward angle of approach.

The bow gently nudged up against the next jetty. Neither of the guards were visible to him from this spot because of the elevated position of the garden from the water, and their stationing close to the back edge of the house.

Ryker jumped from the boat, staying crouched. He quickly tied the boat, an escape if he needed it. Then he scuttled along the wood, staying low and hopefully out of sight.

'I'm inside the front garden,' Angel said. 'Another two guys out here. They haven't seen me.'

'Try and keep it that way,' Ryker said.

He reached a set of three stairs that led up to the grass and paused there.

'Let me know when you're ready to go in,' he said.

He could hear her breaths but she didn't respond straight away and Ryker risked a peek, momentarily stretching up.

He spotted the two guys, casually guarding still.

'OK. I'm by a side door,' Angel said. 'Ready to breach.'

'You'll know when to go.'

Ryker jumped up. The nearest guard – the taller of the two – spotted him right away but other than looking over and stiffening he didn't otherwise react.

Ryker started talking. Loudly. Quickly. He spoke in Russian, a language they perhaps wouldn't understand. He waved his arms about, saying how he was lost, needed help. Boat had run out of gas.

The other guard had taken notice and closed the distance to his friend as he spoke into a radio attached to the lapel of his jacket.

The taller one held a hand out to halt Ryker, shouting in Turkish. Telling him to stop moving. Private property. Trespassing. And so on.

Ryker took no notice. He kept moving forward, arms aloft to show he wasn't a threat.

Well...

Lights burst on in a couple of the downstairs rooms, the upper level of the villa still in darkness. Ryker spotted movement beyond the glass – more guards readying themselves? But no one came out.

'Time to make a scene,' Ryker said.

Angel didn't respond but he heard breaking glass a moment later. The guards heard it too. Both of them reached for their holstered guns, drawing their weapons.

But they weren't quite quick enough.

Ryker already had his gun out and at the ready. Four quick shots. All hits. Two into the thighs of each guard, causing them to stumble back and to the ground, fighting through surprise and pain as Ryker rushed them. He tossed his gun at the taller guard who still seemed determined to fight back. The guy had to duck to avoid the flying object and Ryker launched his boot under the guard's chin and even winced himself at the horrific crunch. That man was out of the fight.

Ryker prized the gun free then sank down and turned. The

other guard was on his backside, battling through pain. When he saw the gun pointed at him he did the sensible thing and lowered his weapon.

'Toss it,' Ryker said, switching to English.

The guard understood just fine and a couple of seconds later tossed the gun away into the garden, toward the water.

'Hands in the air,' Ryker said.

The guard did as asked, and Ryker moved over, patting him down to make sure he had no other weapons. He took the radio and launched it into the water.

'Please, I'll—'

Ryker didn't know what, because he smacked him around the head with the gun and the guard slumped down.

'Angel?' he said.

'I'm good,' she said in a whisper.

She'd caused the initial diversion for the guards inside, but the plan now was for her to hide. Keep the remaining guards guessing and looking in different directions.

'I'm going in,' Ryker said.

He moved for a set of patio doors. No signs of anyone beyond on the inside. He pulled up against the wall and peeked beyond the glass of the doors to a luxurious kitchen. Spotless. No one there.

Ryker reached out and tried the handle of the door. Unlocked. He opened the door and stepped inside, keeping low as he dashed as quietly as he could across the dining space and toward the two open doorways. He pressed himself up against the wall between them, managing a glimpse beyond each on his way. One led to a big, open hallway, the other to a plushly decorated lounge.

No one in sight in either.

He stopped, waited, and listened.

The house was quiet. Too quiet.

'You good?' he whispered.

No response, although he could just make out her breathing. Most likely she couldn't respond without giving herself away.

He heard a noise from out in the hallway. Someone moving stealthily. But then he heard a sound coming from the lounge area too.

The next moment rapid-burst gunfire blasted, holes punched into the wall right by Ryker and he flung himself forward, away from the wall, closer to the ground, and scurried for the kitchen island for cover.

He didn't get there before two metal objects clanked alongside him. Much like back in Suffolk. Ryker rolled along the ground, curled up, pushed his head down...

There was no explosion this time, though. Instead thick, noxious gas poured out of the canisters, rapidly engulfing Ryker who coughed and choked, his eyes burning within seconds even with them squeezed tightly shut.

His gun was kicked from his grip. He took a blow to his back, to the side of his head. He flailed desperately before hands grabbed him, roughly. They yanked him up, dragged him away, his feet bobbing and sliding across the tiled floor as he tried to hold his breath, tried to keep his eyes squeezed closed. He lost his sense of orientation as he battled to stay in control, but the air eventually cleared and he managed to open his eyes and keep them open just as he was tossed forward and he rolled ungainly on the floor.

Even before he'd pulled himself up, taken in his new surroundings, he heard the voice.

'You can stay right there,' said a man. A voice he didn't recognize. Staying on the floor, he looked across the wide-open space of a marble-covered room to see a big, burly suited man standing there, gun in his grip, down by his side. Another guard. Although Ryker sensed perhaps this one was more important than the others. Older. Sterner. In charge.

Two other figures came into view behind him and Ryker blinked a few times, his eyes still stinging like hell, tears blurring his vision and he wasn't sure at first if he knew the newcomers or not.

But with a bit of effort and focus... He knew them. Podence. Karaman.

Ryker got ready to bounce back to his feet, but halted when he heard the cocking of a gun to his left, just behind him. Another to his right side. He glanced both ways, noting the barrels a few feet from him, both pointed at his head.

'Yeah,' the big man in front said, a grin on his face that looked twisted through Ryker's still clearing vision. 'Like I said, you can stay right there.'

35

'Where is she?' the big man demanded.

'Who?' Ryker said.

'Don't give us that crap,' Podence said, sounding as riled as he looked, but not in the least bit worried. As though this whole thing was nothing more than an annoyance. Karaman, on the other hand, looked entirely cool and calm. 'We know she's with you.'

'Who's with me?' Ryker said, perfectly happy to play dumb for two reasons: Firstly, it gave Angel more time. Secondly, he already sensed Podence would only get more agitated.

'Angel,' Podence said. 'Where is she?'

'Angel?' Ryker said. 'You mean... Angela Everett? Why would she be with me? Wasn't she working with you? Didn't she help you break that bastard out of prison?'

He nodded to Karaman who exchanged a glance with Podence.

'I hear you,' Angel said. *'I'm guessing they got you.'*

'Ryker, enough of the crap,' Podence said. 'Where is she?'

'Clearly not in this room,' Ryker said. 'What is this room, anyway? Some grand ballroom or something? Who the fuck even has a room like this in a *home?*'

'*Ballroom, got it,*' Angel said.

Podence opened his mouth to speak but Ryker cut him off.

'Wait,' he said. 'I've seen this room before.' Marble floors. Marble columns. Big chandeliers, a huge bay with sash windows fifteen feet high. 'In that picture in your townhouse in London. You're with your wife. The Arhans, too.'

Podence looked really mad now. Had he not known about the break-in?

'Are you not going to introduce me to everyone else?' Ryker said. 'Obviously I know my bestie, Ismail, pretty well. But not the big man there who looks like his mom screwed a bulldog. Or bullfrog, maybe. Nor the two chumps behind me pointing guns at my head.'

'*OK. So, five in there with you?*' Angel said. And he was about to respond to confirm when, '*Shit, Ryker!*'

He tried to show no reaction as he heard banging, muffled breathing, gasps, groans coming through the earbud. Someone was attacking her. Or she was attacking someone.

'Hey, idiot, I'm talking to you!' Podence shouted, and Ryker tried his best to focus there and not on the sounds in his ear that no one else in the room could hear.

'Yeah?' Ryker said. 'Except I'm not really interested in what you've got to say. Not unless you're about to tell me all about how you're the one I've been looking for all this time. The one behind the Syndicate, coordinating everything.'

Podence scoffed. 'Excuse me?'

'Come on, Frank. Be frank.' Ryker chuckled at his pun, hoping to further annoy Podence. 'I've seen the files.'

A thudding sound from somewhere behind Ryker got everyone's attention. Frogface lifted a radio up and then turned and muttered something to Podence and Karaman.

'Looks like we have her,' Podence said to Ryker.

'Angel,' he said in return, hoping to prompt a response from her, but got nothing. Not even the sound of her breathing now. Either she was dead, or the earbud had been compromised.

'Great,' Ryker said. 'So when she comes in this room you can explain to her exactly how you set her up. The lies that saw her lose all those years in prison. Saw her lose her daughter.'

'Me?' Podence said, putting a hand to his chest, his face screwed up to show his incredulity. 'You really think I'm the one who—'

He stopped again when Frogface turned to him once more. He muttered something into his radio and then he, Podence and Karaman all turned to the look past Ryker, over his left shoulder. He twisted his head that way too. To where there was a closed door, the handle moving down. Frogface now had his gun up, pointing to the wood of the door. The other two goons kept their weapons trained on Ryker.

The door slowly creaked open. Ryker glanced to the foot that poked through. Angel, he knew straight away. So she was alive, at least. She shuffled on in, an arm around her neck, a gun...

It looked pretty good at first glance. It looked like the man behind her was choking her, forcing her forward with the gun pressed against her temple. But Ryker knew within a beat that it wasn't the true story. That the man behind her was already dead. That she was dragging him, the man's head and shoulders hunched forward, her arm twisted behind her to hold the gun up – in his limp hand – against her head.

The ruse didn't catch Frogface off guard for long. Ryker could tell by the anger spreading across his mangy features as he readied to pull his trigger. But she only needed that initial distraction. Just enough to get her into the room without a spray of gunfire greeting her.

'Angel!' Ryker shouted as though the warning would help her.

Maybe it did. Maybe it didn't. Sudden moves, noises, always elicited *some* reaction. But before a single gunshot was fired from anywhere, a huge explosion from somewhere beyond Angel rocked the room. The whole house shook, the floor shuddered. Windows blew out and dust and grit-filled air blasted and swirled.

Ryker didn't try to make any sense of it before he moved.

Angel shot first, straight at Frogface. Ryker twisted to his left and grabbed at the guard there who was busy trying to decide whether Angel or Ryker was his target, or if the threat of the explosion trumped everything.

Ryker grabbed the guard's arm, yanked down and the man pulled the trigger and hit the guy to Ryker's right in the face. Ryker twisted the arm further around, sending him to the ground, then squeezed his finger over the man's on the trigger and the second shot caught him in the neck. Blood sprayed as Ryker prized the gun free.

He went to jump up but a second explosion, even more powerful than before, sent him flying. One of the marble columns fell toward him and he rolled out of the way just in time before it smashed to the floor and clumps of stone and plaster clattered everywhere.

Bullets pinged across Ryker and he again had to roll for safety as a third explosion sent flames and heated air blasting across him.

He heard Angel calling out, although her voice felt distant in his ringing ears. *Don't move.* It gave him some focus and he rose back up, gun held firmly in his grip, the barrel aimed at the corner of the room. At Karaman.

'And you don't fucking move either,' Ryker said.

Podence was armed. Karaman was not.

'Drop it, now,' Angel said. She stood five yards from Ryker, double-grip on the handgun. The wall behind her, the door she'd come from was ablaze, flames leaping up, crawling across the ceiling. 'Drop it or I shoot your dick off first.'

She fired and Podence flinched as the bullet hit the desk to his left at groin height. He dropped the gun.

'What the hell did you do?' Podence said.

Ryker didn't quite know what he meant, though he did momentarily glance at the now-dead Frogface on the floor in front of him. To go along with the two Ryker had dispatched. The other dead man in the doorway. How many more had Angel fought and killed to get in here?

'Gas explosion,' Karaman said. 'Probably in the kitchen. Ever resourceful, Angel.'

He spoke almost with affection and with it she seemed to lose a little of her hard edge.

'But the real question is what did *you* do,' Angel said to Podence. He only shook his head in response. 'I've seen it,' she added. 'The hospital files from Beirut. I never fired the bullet that hit his daughter. I went to prison for nothing. Because of *you*.'

'You two!' Podence shouted in despair, glancing from Angel to Ryker. 'I... I...'

'And Karaman told me everything,' Angel said. 'How you framed him for being a terrorist. How you've played him ever since. And he's not the only one, is he? That's what you do. You and the Syndicate. From the shadows, you play this twisted game with other people's lives. You *ruined* my life. For what?'

'You stupid woman,' Podence said before looking at Ryker. 'You actually think all this is because of that damn Syndicate or whatever you want to call it? That there's some group of people who meet up in secret to plot against the world? What, do we wear big robes and walk around muttering like loons?'

'The Syndicate is real,' Ryker said.

'Whether it is or isn't, I'm not part of it!'

Everyone in the room flinched as a part of the ceiling above them gave way and a burning wooden joist swung down, crashing between Ryker and Angel.

Flames had taken hold around three walls of the room now, only the bay window behind Podence and Karaman, the garden beyond, still untouched.

'You have about two minutes before you burn to death in here,' Angel said. 'And I'm not moving until you admit what you did to me.'

Another crash from somewhere outside the room. Another ceiling or wall caving in. The heat in the room was almost unbearable now, smoke building up all the time too.

'Show me your wrists,' Angel said to Podence.

Podence looked really confused.

'Show me your fucking wrists!' she screamed.

Podence shook his head, lifted his left sleeve. Nothing. He more slowly lifted his right sleeve. Hesitating. Delaying. He looked from Angel to the ever-increasing flames all around him.

'Do it!' she shouted out.

He lifted his sleeve ever so slightly more, revealing a swirl of black ink.

But then a wayward flame from the wall by him licked at Podence's shirt sleeve and he batted at it in panic.

'OK!' Podence shouted, pulling his sleeve back down. 'I knew about that day in Beirut. It's true. I tried to stop the assassination. I guess... I did. And yes! I gave the order to give you no help out there. To let them make an example of you. But only because *he* told me too.'

He pointed to Karaman.

'Angel,' Karaman said, still sounding horribly calm. 'Remember what I told you. How they've lied to me, *used* me for years.'

'It's him who's lying to you!' Podence shouted, looking more and more edgy with flames encircling him. 'Everything I've done has been because of *that* man! For fifteen years I've been living under threat, knowing that if I don't do what I'm told then it's my family they'll hurt first. Ryker, you came to me, you told me you thought Karaman was a messenger for the Syndicate. No, he *is* the Syndicate!'

Ryker held his eye on Karaman as Podence spoke. Podence's words were tinged with distress, anguish, and Ryker didn't think it was just because of the threat from the gun pointed at him, or the prospect of getting caught up in the fire. The evil glint in Karaman's eye told Ryker everything he needed to know.

'Angel. You know the truth,' Karaman said to her.

From super-composed, she now looked ready to crumble. As though the weight of everything that had gone wrong in her life weighed down on her all at once.

'Liar!' she shouted at Podence and she pulled the trigger and the bullet smacked into his forehead. His body remained suspended for what seemed like way too long, with a stunned look plastered on his face, before he caved to the floor.

She twisted to the right, as though to turn her gun to Karaman, but then carried going until the barrel was pointed at Ryker.

'Angel?'

'Kill him,' Karaman said. 'Angel, you must kill him. You know he'll never let you live after what you've done.'

'Angel?' Ryker said.

But then he realized she wasn't actually looking at him, but behind him.

'Ryker, down!'

Ryker ducked as bullets sprayed and two men burst through the flames. He tried to turn his gun on them but before he could another smoldering beam swung down from above. Ryker threw himself to the right. The wood grazed his arm as it fell and knocked the weapon free.

As he jumped back up, he spotted Karaman across the room, dashing for the windows.

'Ryker!'

Angel. He spun to her. The two men who'd run in were down already. One had a neat bullet hole in his forehead. The body of the other was on fire, next to the wood that had narrowly missed Ryker. The beam extended right across the room.

To Angel who was crushed underneath.

'Ryker!' she yelled again, sheer panic in her voice.

He rushed over to her. The beam lay across her gut. There were no flames at this end yet but the wood smoked and hissed. Ryker put his hands underneath but it was charred and hot as hell and he winced as he whipped his burned hands back.

'Ryker, help me!' Angel pleaded as she grabbed hold of his arm.

'I will.' He took off his jacket and wrapped it around his throbbing hands for protection. He tried with everything he had to heave the wood off her.

It didn't move even an inch.

The far end was wedged into a crevice in the wall. No way to push it, he had to lift.

He looked across the room. Grabbed a fallen piece of wood which he used to try to lever the beam up. But the wood snapped in two and he fell back and to the floor. Flames jumped up his leg and he had to beat them back down with his jacket to stop them from spreading.

He coughed and spluttered. Smoke rapidly filled the room now, the fire eating up the remaining oxygen. The remaining air was so hot it felt like his lungs were burning from the inside.

'Ryker!' Angel shrieked, even more desperate than before.

Her legs were ablaze.

He smacked at the flames. Tried to smother them with his

jacket. It made little difference and they were rapidly taking hold of the rest of her.

She grabbed his arm and pulled him close.

'Tell me I did the right thing,' she said through gritted teeth, her agony clear. 'Tell me I made a difference.'

'You did. You really did.'

She held her other hand out and slapped something into his palm. Something small. He didn't look before she spoke again.

'Shoot me!' she yelled before she screeched even more loudly and the wood on top of her reignited all the way to the very end, the flames leaping toward her face.

Ryker stood up, stepped back, the heat overwhelming. The smoke in the air choking.

He lifted his gun and fired a single shot then turned and, head down, rushed for the windows.

There was no sign of Karaman there now. But Ryker recognized the whoop-whoop sound outside.

'No!'

He jumped through the blown-out window frame, rolling into the fall on the slabs outside. He adjusted his aim with the gun.

The helicopter hovered outside. Karaman was there, another goon by his side who helped him clamber up the rope, a man on the inside ready to pull him the rest of the way.

Ryker squeezed the trigger...

Click.

No bullets left.

He roared and tossed the gun but it just bounced lazily along the grass. Karaman and the others hadn't even seen him. Ryker rushed forward, fully intent on a desperate leap to grab hold of the departing craft.

But he stopped himself a few yards short, realizing his last-ditch attempt would be futile.

As the helicopter rose above him, Karaman finally looked down at Ryker. He smiled. Saluted.

Then the helicopter turned and flew away over the water.

Ryker stared back at the inferno. He dropped to his knees, trying to get his breathing back under control now he had air to breathe. Trying to ignore the pain from his heavily blistered skin. He opened his charred palm to look at the object Angel had given him.

A locket in the shape of a heart. He didn't need to open it to see who'd be on the tiny picture inside.

He squeezed his hand shut, pain and anguish shooting through him. Then he rose up and rushed toward the water for the boat.

36

Ryker didn't leave Istanbul after the fight. He laid low while the carnage played out in the media, while his wounds healed, while he awaited Winter's presence.

Winter appeared on the third day and he and Ryker agreed to meet out in the open, by the water on the European side in the Besiktas area, a few miles south of the burned-out mansion.

Ryker arrived early and took up a place on a bench in the sunshine, overlooking the water, the ornate Dolmabahçe Palace directly behind him. Which also meant the area was pleasantly busy with tourists.

He spotted Winter approaching, still a slight hobble to his walk, several years after a bomb blast had taken many lives, but not his.

Winter sat by him and the two of them looked at the water in silence for a few moments.

'Your burns are OK?' Winter eventually asked.

'They will be,' Ryker said, looking at the white fabric wrapped around his left hand. He had similar bandages from his right wrist up to his shoulder. On the back of his neck. His lower left leg. 'Nothing that the bandages and time won't heal.'

'You were lucky.'

'Yeah.'

'I'm... sorry. About Everett.'

'Angel.'

Winter didn't say anything to the correction.

'She was a good person,' Ryker said.

Still, Winter said nothing.

'If she hadn't been wronged like that... Who knows how her life would have turned out. She should have been a big asset to the likes of MI6. Instead Podence, the Syndicate, created a monster.'

He squirmed at that last word. He hadn't meant it. Angel hadn't been a monster, not in the sense of being evil, at least. The real her had certainly been pushed aside by something much darker. But in her last throes, she'd shown herself to be noble, courageous, even if she remained deadly to the end.

'She'll get a posthumous pardon,' Winter said. 'It's not been officially announced yet, but I'm going to make it happen as soon as possible. Her family deserve to know the truth.'

'Thank you,' Ryker said. 'And Podence?'

'There's a hell of a lot more investigation to come yet,' Winter said. 'To unpick all the deceit that's rippled through his career, but... I think he was telling you the truth.'

'Which part?'

'The threats. Podence wasn't leading the Syndicate. He was carrying out acts at the behest of people far more influential and more powerful than him.'

'And do you know who those people are now?'

Winter sighed. Which usually meant he was about to say something that Ryker didn't want to hear.

'The thing with the Syndicate... I'm not saying it doesn't exist, but, Ryker, it's not like it's this secret society with handshakes and a group of men walking around in the candlelight with big robes on.'

Ryker scoffed. 'You know that's pretty much what Podence said, right before he died. So the official MI6 line hasn't changed, even now?'

'There is no official line. But that's my take based off everything I know.'

Ryker glared at his long-time ally. Winter shrank a little as though he understood exactly what Ryker was saying, accusing him of.

'And Lebedev? Did you look into whether he faked his death?'

Winter took his time answering. 'There's no evidence he's alive. I think Karaman was messing with you. Like he messed with Angel, with Podence, *everyone*.'

'No evidence he's alive? Is there concrete evidence he's dead?'

'There's DNA confirmation. From the crash scene. Very convincing dental records. All signed off by a certified pathologist.'

'But no body or remains to re-perform that DNA test on.'

'No. But even if he hadn't been cremated, I don't think anyone would have the appetite to do that, anyway. Certainly not the Russians.'

Ryker humphed. He didn't really have anything else to say about it. The evidence that Lebedev was really dead wasn't irrefutable, as records could have been doctored or falsified, but in reality it was as strong as he could expect.

'Ryker, you need to trust me,' Winter said. 'The Syndicate, if it exists like you think it does, isn't something we can break open in one go. But we'll go after each and every person connected to Karaman, Lebedev, Podence, where we see evidence of crimes. I promise you that. And if there's any rot left in MI6, MI5, I'll see it's cut right out so it can never return. I honestly will, whatever the politics involved.'

'And what about me? Do I get to help cut that rot out? To find the other corrupt billionaires running amok.'

'You? But you're dead, aren't you?' Winter said with a smile just a bit too bright and cheery.

Ryker humphed. But yeah, technically Winter was right. James Ryker was dead. Every major news site that had carried the story of the carnage in Istanbul had him down as one of the fatalities. At his own request. He'd get a state-paid burial along with Angela Everett, both of them heroes, killed in the line of duty as they attempted to bring down a terror cell being run by the escaped terrorist, Ismail Karaman.

Ryker's life was simply safer that way. Whatever the Syndicate was in practice, whoever was still left who cared, if they believed Ryker to be alive he'd be a target.

'And what about Karaman?' Ryker asked.

'I honestly haven't any intel on where he is now. But you know as well as I do there aren't that many countries that would welcome him.'

'You think he's back in the Middle East?' Ryker said, looking directly across the water as he spoke, Asia almost within touching distance.

'I said I don't know. But it'd be a good place to start.'

'Have you?'

'There is no official investigation under way to find him and recapture him.'

'Why not?'

Winter sighed. 'Because SIS can't police the entire world. And right now there is no tangible threat from Karaman to the UK, Syndicate or no Syndicate. But like I said, the Middle East would be a good place to start looking for him. If someone was to look for him.'

A pretty big hint.

'And if that someone is me?' Ryker suggested.

'I'm not going to warn you off. I'm not so naive to think it'd make a difference. But I do ask only one thing from you.'

'And that is?'

'Try to do it as quietly as you can. For your own sake as much as anything else, but also to reduce the chances of any fallout in a region that you know damn well is only ever a single bullet away from a new wave of terror attacks.'

Ryker didn't say anything and they both sat there in silence a few moments. Ryker focused on the Bosphorus once more. Thoughts of two very different fateful nights that started on rippling water burned in his mind. Both left a horribly sour taste still.

He'd remove that taste for good.

'So you're good?' Winter said.

'Not yet,' Ryker said. 'But I will be.'

Two months later

Some would call it hiding in plain sight. Ryker would call it being a narcissistic megalomaniac who thought he was bigger and more important than the world around him. A man who literally thought he was untouchable.

Which was the only explanation for why Ismail Karaman had so quickly returned to his life of wealth and privilege on board a super yacht. Not in the Middle East though, as Winter had suggested. That other yacht remained in Dubai, but Karaman wasn't exactly short of cash, or other 'friends' who had such big beasts, and Ryker had tracked his man thousands of miles from his home to the waters of the Pacific, and the shores of Malaysia.

Two weeks Ryker had been here. Two weeks the boat had been moored in the same spot, less than a mile from Telaga Harbour, a popular yachting destination on the island of Langkawi. Mountainous rainforests rose up behind the harbor. Occasionally Karaman made trips to the shore, perhaps to explore the beautiful island. Perhaps for some female 'company'. Perhaps to enjoy the local cuisine, although more frequently he took deliveries directly to his yacht. Of both ladies and food.

Like this morning. When, for the tenth straight day, he had the exact same order being delivered from the exact same restaurant – a little stall just off the beach that served traditional Malaysian fare. Nasi Goreng with satay beef skewers was Karaman's go-to dish. Every morning the same young man would drive the food on his moped from the restaurant to the harbor, where the same second young man would take the food on his little put-put boat out on the water and over to the yacht.

Karaman was a good tipper, apparently. Fifty ringgits for each of the young men, each day. The moped driver was called Isa Dahari. The boat guy was Sammy. Ryker didn't know his last name. He hadn't needed to, really, because he'd never spoken to him face to face.

He had spoken to Isa face to face. A few times over recent days. Which had culminated that morning in Ryker giving the young man two thousand ringgits to allow Ryker to take a quick look at the food order before he took it from the restaurant to the harbor.

That exchange had come all of ten minutes ago. Ryker watched now from his high perch in the hills behind the harbor, the binoculars up to his face. Isa had already made the handover and was heading back to the restaurant. Sammy was out on the water, steering his little craft toward the yacht.

He arrived. Karaman didn't have the decency to greet the young man at the stern for the handover, although did stand up from his sunbed on the top deck to wave down.

Minutes later, as Sammy made his way back to shore, Karaman was tucking into his food. It didn't take long for him to finish it. He went back to his sunbed after that to soak up some more of the early morning rays.

After twenty minutes Ryker wondered if he'd fallen asleep up there...

No. He came back down. Minutes later he was on one of two Jet Skis that bombed away from the yacht. His daughter was on the other. She'd joined him on the boat only two days ago. A nice little jaunt away from boarding school in Dubai which, technically, was still in full swing. Coincidentally her arrival had coincided with a temporary pause to Karaman's female companions. What a good dad.

The two of them swirled around on the water for a few minutes, never venturing too far from the yacht and the men watching on from there.

Until Karaman did.

At first, it didn't look like anything untoward. Rather than twisting left and right, staying close to the yacht, his Jet Ski simply carried on away in a straight line, further and further from the boat. His daughter took notice but didn't follow. Perhaps she'd been told not to go too far.

After a while, Karaman's Jet Ski slowed and the white churn from behind it died down.

Then Karaman slumped onto the handlebars. The next moment his body slid off and into the water.

His daughter raced over but didn't climb off her Jet Ski to get into the water after him. The goons from the yacht managed to get a boat into the water to chase after their boss but by the point they reached the abandoned Jet Ski, Karaman had already been in the water... No, *under* the water for more than six minutes. No sign of him at all in that time. No bobbing head. No flailing arms. He'd simply gone straight down.

And Ryker knew, given the concoction the man's breakfast had been laced with, that he never would return to the surface alive.

He pulled the binoculars down, stood up straight, and began the walk down the narrow rainforest trail for his motorbike.

37

TWO DAYS LATER

The weather in London was quite different to Malaysia. Cold, gray, and very wet. Not a pleasant welcome 'home' for Ryker. He probably wouldn't stay long.

Winter was waiting for him in Covent Garden, a huge golf umbrella keeping him dry in the rain.

'Enough room for me under there?' Ryker asked.

Winter looked him up and down as though it was a hard question to answer.

'Not really,' he said, but Ryker shuffled closer to him anyway and Winter moved the canopy across a little to mostly cover them both.

'So?' Ryker asked.

'I presume you're going straight for the meat. Karaman?'

'Why not.'

'Official cause of death is heart attack, although his lungs were filled with water so drowning is listed as a secondary cause.'

'But natural causes.'

'He was a fifty-eight-year-old man who'd enjoyed an exuberant lifestyle. Apparently, he was at high risk. His own very expensive private doctors had told him so. High cholesterol, high blood pressure, et cetera, et cetera. All you did was speed up the process a bit.'

Ryker didn't like the way Winter said that. As though his intervention had been unnecessary. As if it had not really made much difference.

Except it had to Ryker. And it would have done to Angel too.

'I am actually impressed,' Winter said. 'That you managed to achieve it so cleanly. Although I'm not going to ask how.'

'I'm not sure I'd tell you.'

'But I will always be second-guessing whenever I'm eating or drinking near you in the future.'

Which suggested he did know how Ryker had done it really – the method of delivery, at least. But Ryker didn't bother to say anything more about it.

'The main thing is, there's not even a whisper of outside involvement,' Winter said. 'Which means there are no brewing problems or high alerts as we await retaliation.'

'Good to hear.'

'You know what else is good?'

'The weather?'

'I got a new job.'

'Yeah?'

'Official title is Head of Ethics.'

Ryker stifled a laugh, although apparently not quite well enough and Winter looked a little offended.

'You should be happy for me. It means I get to be in prime position to make sure SIS is cleaned from the inside out and we never have the likes of Podence playing us for fools again.'

'Ha, yeah. Good luck with that. Spies always be spying.'

'I get it, you're a cynic. You've been burned by SIS and the like more times than me.'

He looked at Ryker's hand – the scars from the recent burns still plainly evident – and his cheeks reddened. 'You know what I mean.'

'I do. And I'm pleased for you. It's a good career move. And I'm also pleased it's you in that position. I think you'll make a difference.'

'I'm genuinely flattered. And from your standpoint... Head of Ethics... might underplay my role just a little.'

'In what way?'

'In the way that I'm only one step below the Chief of the Secret Intelligence Services now.'

Ryker whistled. That actually was a seriously senior role for his old friend.

'To think you were just some snot-nosed coffee maker and file sorter when I first met you,' Ryker said.

'Ha! I was a highly qualified intelligence analyst in my early thirties by that point actually, but it's interesting that's how you remember it. And I'm only two years younger than you, don't forget.'

Ryker shrugged.

'Back to my point though, I even have the Head of Clandestine operations reporting to me. To make sure everything's... above board.'

Ryker nodded. He thought he knew what Winter meant by that. Although the man was kind enough to spell it out a moment later.

'Which means I have a very close eye on *all* field operations. And also a say in how those operations are handled.'

'Are you offering me a job?'

'No. Because I know you wouldn't take it.'

'But you'll be in touch when you need my help.'

'I will be.'

'And is SIS officially looking into the Syndicate under your watch?'

Winter didn't answer straight away. Likely composing how he'd frame the bad news for Ryker.

'There's no official recognition of the Syndicate as an entity,' Winter said. 'And maybe it never really existed in that form anyway. But it is recognized that Ismail Karaman was at the top of a group of rich, powerful individuals who—'

'You believe he was at the top?'

'From all the intel I've seen, it really does look that way.'

'So we cut off the head of the snake.'

'You could say that.'

'But what about everyone else who was playing to his tune?'

'I already explained my new role to you. I'll get the rot out of SIS. And I'll make sure anyone on the outside who was in cahoots with Karaman is identified and brought down, one way or another.'

'And I definitely want to know about that.'

'And I definitely want to know about whatever you find next. Because I'm not stupid enough to think that you're about to go and sit on a beach for the next few months.'

They both went silent. Ryker watched the thick raindrops bouncing on the ground as pedestrians scurried about trying to find shelter.

'Remember what we talked about last time we were together?' Ryker asked.

'My ex-wife?' Winter asked with a chuckle.

'Yeah. And we agreed that, when we got the job done, we'd go out. Just you and me. Beer, maybe some food. A bit of release for us both.'

'I think the deal was that you had to get the job done without you crossing the line.'

'*Your* line. And didn't I?'

Winter thought about the answer for a bit too long.

'Yeah. For once you probably did.'

'Then let's go. Oh, and you're paying, hotshot.'

Ryker winked and moved off before Winter could protest.

* * *

Ryker's hangover the next day stank almost as much as the weather.

They'd had a good night. Had drunk way too much. Had chatted like two old friends, which they kind of were after so many years working so closely, even if that had been the first time the two of them had done anything close to socializing together.

Why now? Ryker wondered as he traveled northward to the Midlands, a single stop to make there before he carried on to... somewhere.

He didn't find an answer to the question. Perhaps it didn't matter. One way or another, Peter Winter remained a constant in Ryker's life. And given his new role at SIS, and Ryker's ever-present appetite for righting wrongs, it looked like that would likely continue.

He found a parking spot several houses away and walked along the wet tarmac on a street of terraces to the home he was looking for. He opened the creaky gate, headed to the front door, and knocked. He heard the footsteps from beyond. Hefty footsteps. An adult rather than a child. A man opened the door. Ryker hadn't met him before but felt he knew a lot about him anyway, and something about the arrogance and coldness in his eyes only confirmed what he already thought about this person.

'Hi, I'm a friend of Angel's,' Ryker said, holding his hand out to the man who looked at it like it was dirt. Ryker left his hand there and eventually, the man did reach out to take it.

Ryker grabbed his hand and crushed it in his and pulled the man close.

'You piece of shit. You didn't even have the decency to turn up to the funeral.'

The man murmured and squirmed and tried to take back his hand, but Ryker only held on even more tightly.

'I'll break every bone if you don't stand still and listen to what I have to say.'

The man moaned pathetically and nodded.

'She was a good person,' Ryker said. 'She was let down by everyone around her.'

'She… was a dangerous alcoholic!'

'She was insane with guilt and regret. And she was framed. I'm sure you know all that by now because it was in the papers, on the news. And you got the invite to the funeral, didn't you?'

He muttered incoherently, his body trembling from the pain in his hand. Ryker felt a pop. He didn't care.

'Did you enjoy seeing her spiral?'

No answer now.

'All she ever wanted was to be loved. To be able to love her daughter, but all you ever wanted was your new life with your new woman. Who you'd probably been screwing even before Angel was set up. You must have thought all your dreams had come true the day she was put behind bars thousands of miles away.'

'P… Please!'

'Now this is what you're going to do. Call your daughter down.'

'M… My—'

'I'm not going to hurt her. You have my word.'

When the weasel said nothing, Ryker added, 'Do it now,' and he finally let go of the hand.

The guy looked on the verge of tears.

'Sweetie!' he shouted out, his voice cracking. 'Please come down.'

The young girl appeared at the top of the stairs and hesitantly made her way down.

'This man is...'

'A friend of your mom's. Your real mom.'

She stood by her dad, shielding herself behind him. Her protector.

Ryker crouched down so he was at her level.

'You didn't know her very well,' Ryker said. 'But I did. And I know she loved you more than anything in the world.'

She looked from Ryker and up to her dad as though seeking his opinion on what Ryker had said.

'I don't know what your dad's told you about her, but Angel... That was what people called her. Did you know that?'

She shook her head.

'She was a hero. But she was treated really badly. You know she had to go to prison?'

The girl nodded.

'But she was tricked. She only went to prison because some bad people made up some really bad lies about her. And people who should have helped her didn't.'

The girl looked completely lost with what he was saying.

'You've seen the news, haven't you?' he asked her.

She looked at her dad again and so did Ryker. Actually, Ryker sent him a death glare.

'Your dad'll show you when I've gone. But it's been in the news all around the world. Your mom is a true hero. She helped save many, many lives. You know James Bond?'

Another nod.

'Well, Angel was like him, but even more kick-ass. Believe me, she could take on anyone. But... She got killed.'

He hung his head, trying to erase from his mind the memory of the moment. Angel's body enveloped in flames. The shock, pain, despair on her face knowing it was over. Willing for death. Leaving him with no choice but to pull the trigger.

'I was there right before she died. She gave me this.'

He held out the locket, which dangled from his hand. For the first time in the conversation, the girl's face brightened. She took the locket off him and opened it up and looked at her dad, smiling.

'It's me,' she said.

'Your mom carried that everywhere with her,' Ryker said. 'It was the most important thing she had. *You* were the most important part of her life.'

Ryker stood straight, locking eyes with her dad one last time.

'You're gonna tell her the truth about Angel. Everything she needs to know. And if you don't, I'm turning up on your doorstep again. Got it?'

The guy didn't respond before Ryker turned and headed back for his car.

His next destination...?

He'd figure that out soon enough.

ACKNOWLEDGEMENTS

The most common question I get asked as an author is where do my ideas come from? It's the hardest question to answer as I really don't know. Sometimes entire stories can come to me seemingly from nowhere, and other times I'll need several days of contemplating, deliberating, just to get a half-written story out of a road-block and moving once more. Does it get easier? Yes and no.

I've written coming on for thirty books now and the process is certainly familiar, if not necessarily any more straightforward. *Angel of Death* is the twelfth James Ryker novel, and the first one I've written in nearly two years, and there were definitely times when I felt unsure about how this one would turn out. But, honestly, I have to say that having now come to the end of the process, and having read and reread the manuscript multiple times, I genuinely think this is one of my favourite James Ryker stories.

I'm really grateful to all of the assistance from everyone at team Boldwood for the input I've received in turning this one into the firecracker that the finished product is. I hope too that readers, both those loyal to James Ryker, and ones who are picking up the series at this stage, will agree. Thank you, team Boldwood, and thank you, readers, for all of your support.

ABOUT THE AUTHOR

Rob Sinclair is the million copy bestseller of over twenty thrillers, including the James Ryker series. Rob previously studied Biochemistry at Nottingham University. He also worked for a global accounting firm for 13 years, specialising in global fraud investigations.

Sign up to Rob Sinclair's mailing list for news, competitions and updates on future books.

Visit Rob's website: www.robsinclairauthor.com

Follow Rob on social media here:

- facebook.com/robsinclairauthor
- x.com/rsinclairauthor
- bookbub.com/authors/rob-sinclair
- goodreads.com/robsinclair

ALSO BY ROB SINCLAIR

The James Ryker Series

The Red Cobra

The Black Hornet

The Silver Wolf

The Green Viper

The White Scorpion

The Renegade

The Assassins

The Outsider

The Vigilante

The Protector

The Deception

Angel of Death

The Enemy Series

Dance with the Enemy

Rise of the Enemy

Hunt for the Enemy

Standalone Novels

Rogue Hero

THE
Murder
LIST

**THE MURDER LIST IS A NEWSLETTER
DEDICATED TO SPINE-CHILLING FICTION
AND GRIPPING PAGE-TURNERS!**

**SIGN UP TO MAKE SURE YOU'RE ON OUR
HIT LIST FOR EXCLUSIVE DEALS, AUTHOR
CONTENT, AND COMPETITIONS.**

SIGN UP TO OUR
NEWSLETTER

BIT.LY/THEMURDERLISTNEWS

Boldwood

Printed in Great Britain
by Amazon